By day, **Maggie Wells**
she pens tales of int
sheets. She has a we
endings. She is the p
shameless flirt, and yo
this mild-mannered married lady to find a naughty streak
a mile wide.

Dana Nussio began telling 'people stories' around the same
time she started talking. She's continued both activities,
nonstop, ever since. She left a career as an award-winning
newspaper reporter to raise three daughters, but the stories
followed her home as she discovered the joy of writing
fiction. Now an award-winning author and member of
Romance Writers of America's Honour Roll of bestselling
authors, she loves telling emotional stories filled with
honourable but flawed characters.

OZARKS DOUBLE HOMICIDE

MAGGIE WELLS

AGENT COLTON'S SECRET INVESTIGATION

DANA NUSSIO

MILLS & BOON

First Published in Great Britain 2023
by Mills & Boon, an imprint of HarperCollins*Publishers* Ltd
1 London Bridge Street, London, SE1 9GF

www.harpercollins.co.uk

HarperCollins*Publishers*
Macken House, 39/40 Mayor Street Upper,
Dublin 1, D01 C9W8, Ireland

Ozarks Double Homicide © 2023 Margaret Ethridge
Agent Colton's Secret Investigation © 2023 Harlequin Enterprises ULC

Special thanks and acknowledgement are given to Dana Nussio for her contribution to *The Coltons of New York* series.

ISBN: 978-0-263-30726-9

0523

This book is produced from independently certified FSC™ paper to ensure responsible forest management.

For more information visit: www.harpercollins.co.uk/green

Printed and Bound in the UK using 100% Renewable Electricity at CPI Group (UK) Ltd, Croydon, CR0 4YY

OZARKS DOUBLE HOMICIDE

MAGGIE WELLS

For Sara, whose boundless enthusiasm and bottomless faith are an inspiration to all who are lucky enough to have her on their side. I'm so proud to be a part of Team Megibow!

Chapter One

"Hey, Chief?"

Lieutenant Ethan Scott looked up to find one of his agents, Jim Thompson, hovering in the threshold of Ethan's office. It wasn't the greeting that made Ethan tear his gaze from the crime scene photos he was enlarging on his computer, but the hesitancy in the words. A big man, Thompson was usually full of bluff and bluster. But now, the blank expression on his face told Ethan his detective was shocked.

The guy had twenty years with the Arkansas State Police under his belt, and more than a dozen of them here with the Criminal Investigation Division. Shocking Agent Thompson wasn't an easy thing to do.

"What is it, Jim?"

"Powers." Thompson spoke the name softly. He stepped into the office, darting a glance over his shoulder as if checking to see if anyone in the office had heard him utter it.

Ethan nodded. He was too familiar with the name. The Powers family was all anyone around here had talked about for a month. Tyrone Powers Junior ran Powers, Powers & Walton, one of the most prestigious law firms in Northwest Arkansas. His brother, William, was a sitting US senator. And the son, Tyrone III—also known as Trey—was one of Company D's highest profile arrests in years.

"Grace is in Little Rock doing a depo on another case. Let Mr. Powers know she'll get back to them," Ethan responded tersely, then turned his attention back to the photo he'd been studying.

Special Agent Grace Reed had uncovered enough evidence to tie the Powers kid to the disappearance and subsequent death of a young woman named Mallory Murray, and since then, Grace, one of his best in the field, had been caught in the crossfire between prosecutors and the Powers family's formidable defense.

"No, that's what I'm trying to tell you, about Trey, uh…" Jim started again.

Ethan jerked his attention back to Thompson. "What about him? Please say he violated the terms of his bail."

Ethan was only half joking. He'd love to go snatch the smug jerk up and lock him away. With Powers behind bars, his legal team wouldn't be quite so keen on throwing every roadblock they could find in front of a trial date.

"He's dead," Thompson replied.

The bluntness of the answer left Ethan feeling as shell-shocked as Thompson appeared. "Crap." Swallowing hard, he raised a hand to rub his forehead. "Suicide?" he asked, eyes still downcast.

It was a logical assumption, considering the ever-growing list of charges pending against him, but Ethan had a hard time buying it. Guys like Trey Powers tended to be too egotistical to self-harm. They had all been operating under the assumption the arrogant young attorney had been raised to believe he was untouchable. Above the law. But you never knew what went on beneath the surface in any person's life.

"No, sir. He was shot," Thompson corrected, jolting Ethan from his musing. "Both he and his father, um, Tyrone, were found dead this morning. I just got off the phone with the Benton County Sheriff's office. They're requesting our help."

Ethan shot to his feet. "Did you say both Trey and Tyrone Powers are dead?"

"Yes." Thompson nodded. "Sheriff Stenton said the wife came home and found them. Right there in the house."

Ethan gave his head a sharp shake, hoping to jostle the information Jim was giving him into some semblance of sense. "Are they thinking murder-suicide?"

Agent Thompson's indication of the negative came slow and deliberate. "No, sir. They say it looks to be a double homicide. Both were a single GSW."

The pronouncement made him drop back into his seat. Hard. Double homicide. The murder of a suspected murderer. And his father. A wealthy, prominent, politically well-connected man. The brother and nephew of a US senator.

This case would be beyond big.

There'd be a megawatt spotlight on this case until the killer was caught and brought to justice. It was the sort of investigation that transformed careers—for better or worse.

He was startled from his thoughts by the bleat of his desk phone. A glance at the display showed the caller to be Captain Will Hopkins, Ethan's boss.

Picking up the receiver, he said only, "Scott," by way of greeting.

The man on the other end didn't bother identifying himself. "Have you heard?"

Ethan blinked, wondering how his boss had gotten the news. But he didn't ask. Arkansas was not a heavily populated state, but the connections between its residents were as intricate as a spiderweb. Now that he'd had a minute, he wouldn't be surprised to learn the news had already made it to the governor's office in Little Rock.

"About the Powerses? Yes, sir."

"I want you on this personally," Captain Hopkins said in his usual brusque manner. "It's going to be a jurisdictional circus with the Bentonville police, the Benton County Sheriff's department and Lord knows who else besides us involved. I want you to run point."

"Yes, sir," Ethan responded, his gaze meeting Jim Thompson's for the first time since he picked up the phone. "I'm on it."

"Now," his boss stated.

Ethan rose from his chair, and Thompson's jaw dropped as Ethan started gathering his things. "Packing up now, sir. I'll need to run home and grab a bag—"

"Make it quick. I've dispatched forensics already. I don't want the locals getting too deep in the questioning though." He exhaled loudly, and Ethan could almost picture the man removing his glasses and rubbing at the bridge of his nose. "You know from the case with Trey Powers this is going to be a tricky one. The wife found the bodies. If I understand correctly, she's a lawyer herself, and by now she probably has half the lawyers at PP&W sitting on top of her."

"No doubt."

"You're my ace in the hole on this one," the captain asserted.

Ethan nodded. "I'm on my way. Check in with you once I get the lay of the land."

"Ten-four," Hopkins responded, then promptly hung up.

Ethan replaced the receiver, his mouth pulled into a grim line. Not many people in the Criminal Investigation Division were aware Ethan had a law degree as well. He didn't talk much about the six months he'd spent as a public defender, and how it drove him to pursue a career in criminal investigation, rather than defense. Watching people he knew to be guilty as sin get off on technicalities because the police were overworked and undertrained had been too frustrating to witness.

"He's sending you?"

Thompson hung back in the doorway, watching Ethan gather his computer, phone and cables, a look of surprise mixed with indignation heightening the older man's color.

"He is."

"You haven't been out on a case since you've been here."

Ethan's lips quirked, but he kept his head down, running through a mental list of all he'd need.

"True."

"Have you ever, uh—"

Thompson had the diplomacy of a battering ram, but at least had the good sense not to finish his question. And since he wasn't wrong about Ethan's lack of field time after joining Company D, Ethan let it slide.

"Don't worry, I caught some nasty cases down in Little Rock. I know what to do," he reassured the other man.

In truth, he couldn't wait to get at it. He'd been desk jockeying ever since Captain Hopkins recruited him for the job. Hopkins didn't care that he'd promoted Ethan over every agent already working as an investigator out of the Fort Smith offices. And, frankly, Ethan hadn't either. At the time.

He hadn't imagined how lonely it could be commanding a somewhat resentful crew in a town where he knew absolutely no one. He liked to think that in the past few months he'd cultivated some respect from the agents under him, but Thompson's incredulity was mildly insulting.

"It was bound to happen sometime," he said as he shoved everything into his computer bag. "I am an investigator, after all."

He gave Thompson a solid clap on the arm when he squeezed past the older man's bulk. As the senior agent in the company, Thompson would be in charge with Ethan out of the office. That should appease him somewhat. "I know you'll keep things running smoothly. I'll check in with you later once I talk to the captain."

Thompson gaped after him, his eyes darting to the desks where two other agents sat working, then to the empty desk Grace Reed usually occupied. "Do you want me to call Grace and tell her?"

Ethan didn't look back, nor did he slow his stride toward the door. He couldn't help feeling Thompson would take a little pleasure in telling the only female agent in the company that her biggest collar to date would not be facing justice after all. Not in a courtroom anyway. No, he'd make the call himself.

"I'll call her on my way," he said over his shoulder.

At the door, he stopped to look back at the open-plan office. All eyes were on him. And for the first time since he took over as their section chief, he felt no waves of hostility emanating from them.

Since he had their undivided attention, he gave one last direct order. "We're going to start getting media inquiries. I don't want there to be any comments coming out of this office at all. Refer all questions to the media liaison." He looked from one agent to the next. "Got it? No comments."

"Got it, Chief," Thompson replied, then gave him a sharp salute.

Ethan waited until he turned away to roll his eyes at the older man. He felt a sharp pang of remorse for what the other agents would likely have to endure under Thompson's command, but the man had seniority.

Sliding into the state-owned SUV that came as one of the perks of the promotion, he headed to his apartment to pack. Since he'd never fully settled into his place in Fort Smith, he figured it would take him less than thirty minutes to gather what he needed and hit the road. Still, given how quickly the news had traveled through the various law enforcement agencies, he figured he'd better get his call in to Grace Reed before taking the time.

He knew he was already too late when she picked up right away with a resigned greeting of, "Morning, Lieutenant."

Lieutenant. The use of his rank did not bode well for the conversation. Usually, she called him Chief. And until now, he and Grace got along well enough. They shared the uneasy camaraderie of being the two outsiders in the section.

"I take it you've already heard."

"About Trey Powers? Yes, sir."

"And his father, too," he added.

"Tyrone is…was," she corrected herself, "an interesting man."

Ethan didn't need to see her face to know the compliment was loaded with subtext. "I have no doubt." He drew a deep breath, then hurried on. "Obviously, we'll have to go through the formalities of dropping the charges against the younger Powers."

He heard her sharp intake of breath and winced. If he'd been in her shoes, he'd have felt the sting of it, too. "Yes, sir."

When she added nothing more, he figured he ought to let her have all the bad news in one fell swoop.

"I don't know if you've heard, but Captain Hopkins has assigned me to the double homicide."

There was a pause that lasted a breath too long. "I had not heard. Congratulations. This will be a big case."

"It will." For better or worse, he thought grimly. As he turned into the parking lot of his apartment complex, he felt the full weight of what he was about to tackle settle on his shoulders.

"Listen, I know you're feeling conflicted right now. We all are. You've put in a lot of legwork on the case against Trey, and I want to assure you that your efforts were not wasted."

"No, sir."

Her brief responses made it clear she understood those same efforts were unlikely to be rewarded in any way she deemed satisfactory. He'd been there before. There was nothing worse for a cop than to have a suspected murderer slip the charges, no matter how it happened. There would be no closure for either Agent Reed or the victim's family. Worst of all, no justice for the victim, Mallory Murray.

Pulling into his usual parking space, he killed the engine. "Listen, I have to pack and get up to Bentonville, but I want you to know I'd appreciate any help you can give me as far as background on the family," he continued.

"Of course," she answered succinctly.

He sighed again. "I know this whole situation is a bitter pill to swallow, but I have a feeling I'm going to need every resource I have at my disposal for this case."

"I'll do everything I can to help."

Her tone was still brusque, but a couple degrees warmer than it had been. He'd take it. "I'll be in touch. Probably a lot. You and the knowledge you've amassed in bringing those charges against Trey Powers are the greatest assets we have at the moment."

There was another prolonged pause, then, to his relief, Grace said, "I'll send my notes before I leave Little Rock. You'll have everything I know about the Powers family and the players at Powers, Powers & Walton before you hit Bentonville, Chief."

Chapter Two

Michelle Fraser sat back in the plush sofa cushions and looked around the exquisitely decorated sitting room. The home Tyrone Powers had purchased for his second wife did not disappoint. It was decorated with the sort of subtle sumptuousness only the very wealthy could afford. Plump cushions, thick rugs and rich window treatments. All in white.

Or sort-of white.

Michelle was no interior design guru, but she was savvy enough to be fairly sure not one swatch in the color palette used to decorate this elegant room had been tagged as *white*.

She imagined the throw pillow beside her to be called *parchment*. There were swirls in the plush throw rug beneath her feet that strayed dangerously close to *oatmeal*. And the watered-silk draperies that hung from ceiling to floor? The pearlescent sheer almost begged to be called *oyster*.

"Right, Michelle?" a husky voice implored, derailing her train of thought.

"I'm sorry?" she responded, jolted from her ruminations. "I was strategizing. What were you saying?"

Beside her, Tyrone Powers's wife—now widow—sat in bloodstained workout gear, staring down at her hands. "I was only saying I submitted to them taking adhesives for gunshot residue first thing. I wouldn't do that if I had done it. My willingness to cooperate with the police has to count for something."

Michelle nodded and involuntarily looked down at the other woman's hands. She'd been allowed to wash them once she'd submitted to the field testing, but there were still streaks of dried blood in the creases of her knuckles. "Of course." Then she remembered the role she was supposed to be playing in this farce. "But you should have waited until I got here."

"I also let the sheriff know that I'm willing to hand over my clothing," the petite blonde seated on the sofa beside her said decisively.

Michelle gave herself a mental shake. She was supposed to be the one advising Kayla on these matters, not the other way around. But here she was, shell-shocked and wondering how the hell she ended up here, while the woman beside her sat preternaturally calm, cool and collected.

And covered in her husband's blood.

"Again, you should have waited until you had counsel present."

Kayla gave her a shadow of a smile. "Doesn't matter. I still would have submitted to the testing. Plus, I do know what I'm doing. I haven't forgotten everything I learned in How-to-Be-a-Lawyer School."

"Then we can assume you are aware no matter how cooperative you are, you're still their number one suspect until another candidate appears," Michelle said gravely.

"I didn't kill my husband," Kayla said without equivocation.

Kayla's singular focus on Tyrone was disturbing. "Your stepson was shot as well," Michelle reminded her tartly. "How about him?"

Kayla stiffened. "I'm not going to pretend Trey and I were best friends or anything, but no, I didn't kill him either. Which the forensics will prove."

Forensics were only going to work in her favor if evidence of someone else pulling the trigger became apparent. Presumably, traces of Kayla would be found all over the crime scene. After all, she did live here.

From the moment Harold Dennis, the family's attorney and one of the senior partners at PP&W, called from his vacation, Michelle had been trying to work out ways to keep the police from taking her client into custody.

"Tell me again where you were this weekend," Michelle prompted.

She wasn't exactly sure why she went with this particular question. Maybe it was because she was still wondering how the hell she'd gotten roped into defending this woman against possible double homicide charges. Plus, something about Kayla's answer sounded off to her.

Kayla gestured to the eggshell-pink yoga pants and matching hoodie she wore. "I told you, I was doing a wellness retreat."

Michelle's eyes narrowed as she studied her client minutely. She had no reason to believe Kayla was lying, but every fiber of her being was telling her she was. "At a spa? A resort? Was there anybody who can place you at this retreat?"

Kayla hesitated only a second before shaking her head. "I was only trying to have a sort of meditation-yoga-self-care weekend," Kayla informed her. "The past few weeks have been…hectic, and I needed to get away by myself for a little while."

"Where did you go? What was the name of the spa?"

"Well—" Kayla gnawed on her lip for a moment "—I didn't actually go to a spa. I had the spa come to me."

"The spa came to you," Michelle repeated, keeping her tone deliberately level.

If she'd been questioning this witness on the stand, she would have gone in for the kill at this point. Kayla's story was riddled with holes. She only hoped none of those were bullet holes.

"Listen, I need you to level with me," Michelle said in her most no-nonsense tone. "You know how this goes. You know that any inconsistency in your story is going to result in you booking a room at the kind of place you never want to visit." She exhaled her frustration. "Come on, Kayla, you were in this job before I was. You know the spa story isn't going to hold water. You have to tell me the truth now."

"I was at our lake house. Alone." Kayla looked down at the hands clasped in her lap, but she didn't say anything more.

"You were at your lake house alone and…" Michelle prompted.

"Drunk," Kayla answered in a whisper.

The younger woman lifted her chin and hit Michelle with the most direct gaze she'd managed since their conversation began. "I was at our lake house alone getting drunk and staying as drunk as I possibly could."

The tingling at her nape eased. This was the truth at last.

"Why?" she asked directly.

The sheriff would be coming back any minute, and they needed to move beyond couching questions in niceties and social deference.

"Why not?" Kayla retorted. "I wanted to escape for a weekend."

Michelle looked around the expensively furnished living room in what was undoubtedly the nicest house in one of the city's most exclusive gated communities. What in the world made a person like Kayla Powers want to get away so badly? But that wasn't the question at hand.

"Okay, so you were at the lake house alone. Did anybody see you there? Any staff? Grocery delivery? Food delivery?"

Kayla shook her head.

"Did anyone local see you stop to pick up provisions? A grocery store clerk? Package store?"

"I brought wine from Ty's cellar," Kayla said, gesturing to the door. "I didn't eat much. Grabbed some snacks and stuff from the pantry, figuring anything else I might need would already be at the lake house." She wet her lips and a wry smile tugged at the corner of her mouth. "Turns out the corkscrew was right where I left it."

"Why were you trying to get away? Had you and Tyrone had a fight?"

Kayla shook her head. "No. Ty is Ty. Same as always." She tossed off the last with a careless shrug. "I mean, I'm not sure he noticed whether I was here or not, but that wouldn't be unusual. At least not these days."

"You two were having trouble?" Michelle prodded.

"Not trouble," Kayla said, a shade defensive. "Just...marriage." She heaved a sigh, then rolled her eyes. "I guess the new had worn off, you know? For both of us, really, but mostly for him. But Ty has always run hot and cold. He gets focused on things and can't see anything else. With all the stuff with Trey..." She trailed off and stared pensively at the Carrara marble fireplace. "I thought I was okay with things cooling down. Mostly, I was. The more disinterested he was, the more freedom I had," she said, her voice hardening.

Harold Dennis was going to have a conniption when he found out how far she was letting this go, but at the moment, she didn't have time to worry about the family lawyer's wishes. He'd better be hightailing it back to Arkansas if he wanted this handled any differently.

As it was, Michelle had somehow managed to get her part in this whole mess upgraded from defending a spoiled young man against possible reckless homicide charges to defending his stepmother in an undisputed double homicide case. And though she operated under the guise of being a criminal defense expert, she was actually an attorney who specialized in forensic accounting. An undercover federal agent who'd spent the past two years gaining the trust of Harold Dennis and the other big shots at Powers, Powers & Walton.

Before Michelle could formulate her next question, a sharp rap came on the door. It turned out to be more a warning than a request. Sheriff Stenton stepped into the room without waiting for a reply. A tall man with dark hair and a sharply squared-off jaw entered behind him. Unlike the sheriff, he wore plainclothes, but the aura of cop practically oozed from his pores. His bearing was straight, his shoulders almost as angular as his jawline and his eyes were alert and watchful.

Fighting the urge to place herself between this sharp-eyed man and her client was strong, but Michelle resisted. Shielding Kayla would only make them look at her even harder. Since Kayla had voluntarily submitted to the residue tests and fingerprinting, they were taking the full cooperation route.

"Mrs. Powers, Ms. Fraser, this is Lieutenant Ethan Scott from the state police Criminal Investigation Division out of Fort Smith," the sheriff said by way of introduction.

The sheriff's manner was slightly less deferential than he'd been before the lieutenant arrived, and that made Michelle uneasy. She eyed them warily as the sheriff settled himself into one of the plush armchairs situated adjacent to the sofa, where she sat beside Kayla.

"I'm sorry for your loss...losses," Ethan Scott amended as he gave them each a nod.

She waited for him to settle himself like the sheriff had, but Lieutenant Scott opted to stand. A subtle but effective power play. Michelle wanted to surge to her feet as well, but she wasn't willing to give him the satisfaction of believing them to be anything but open to the additional resources assigned to the case.

The sheriff's attitude remained cautious. She could work

his hesitancy. With the lieutenant, however, she'd have to tread more carefully.

"Sheriff, as I'm sure you can understand, this has been very traumatic for my client." Michelle divided an even look between the two men before proceeding. "We are happy to cooperate with the investigation in any way, but I believe remaining here is causing Mrs. Powers distress."

As if on cue, Kayla began to wring her hands. "I never expected them to even be here when I came home today. They should be at the office," she said, turning and searching Michelle's face as if she might have any answers as to why the two dead men were not in their proper place.

"I understand, ma'am, and we do appreciate all of your help," the sheriff said with genuine sympathy. "But I'm hoping you won't mind answering a few more questions now that the lieutenant has arrived. We need to make sure we have a good grasp on the timeline."

Michelle sighed. They had already been over Kayla's departure from, and arrival back, at the house multiple times, but it wasn't like she could object to going over the basic information once again.

"Ask your questions, Sheriff," Michelle said quietly. "Then, can we agree this will be enough for today? Mrs. Powers is going to have her hands full as it is. She'll need to notify family and make arrangements."

They all knew the last part was pretense. By now the double murders had been all over the news, but still, one would be expected to place calls.

"Of course," Sheriff Stenton answered agreeably. "Now, you said that you left here early Saturday morning. About 7:00 a.m.?" he asked in a drawl as thick and slow as molasses.

"Yes, we've established that," Michelle responded for her client.

"Excuse me, but… Mrs. Powers?" The sheer command in

Lieutenant Scott's tone drew all eyes to him. "I am sorry for your loss, ma'am, but I really would prefer to hear your version of events rather than ask questions." He darted a glance at Michelle, then returned the full force of those storm-cloud-gray eyes on Kayla. "If you wouldn't mind walking me through everything you did since leaving here Saturday morning."

Kayla twisted her hands in her lap again, but this time her fidgeting worried Michelle. She saw the lieutenant's gaze drop, too, and knew she needed to deflect attention away from her client's nervousness. Reaching over, she placed her hand atop Kayla's and gave what she hoped would appear to be nothing more than a reassuring squeeze.

"Tell them everything you can," she said gently, not daring to peek at the lieutenant as she spoke. "Once you're done, we'll turn your clothes over to the forensics team and get you out of here."

She could feel Lieutenant Scott's stare, but Michelle pretended not to notice. If he thought she was going to let her client stay here and be grilled while they carted the bodies of her husband and stepson from the house, or worse, be taken into custody after the questioning, he was going to have to come at her with some hard evidence of Kayla's involvement beyond discovering the bodies.

"I left here Saturday morning at about 7:00 a.m.," Kayla began cautiously. "I drove straight to the lake house."

"You didn't stop for gas or any groceries?" Stenton asked.

She shook her head. "I had everything I needed here or already at the house, so there was no need to stop," Kayla responded.

"And this lake house is on… Beaver Lake?" the lieutenant asked.

"No." Kayla shook her head. "No, it's the Powers family's place over on Table Rock Lake."

"And it's in Carroll County?" the sheriff prompted.

"Yes, sir," Kayla responded automatically.

Lieutenant Scott nodded as if digesting this bit of information. "Thank you for the clarification. Please go on."

"I was at the lake house alone most of Saturday and Sunday. I wanted to get away for a weekend. We've had a lot of social activities lately and it's been a bit of a whirlwind." She shrugged. "I did some yoga, watched some movies on Cineflix. Cooked. Drank some wine," she added, her voice slightly wobbly on the last word. "I packed things up this morning and came back. I thought I'd be coming home to an empty house. Ty's usually at the office early every morning, and Trey doesn't live here with us. I wouldn't have even gone into the family room if I hadn't heard the television."

"So you entered the family room and…" the lieutenant asked leadingly.

"I saw Trey first." Kayla closed her eyes. "He was slumped over the arm of the sofa. Then I saw Ty at the other end." She stopped and swallowed hard. "I mean, I saw his shoes," she corrected. She opened her eyes then and looked directly at the lieutenant. "He'd fallen over onto the cushion, but his legs were sticking out." She made a gesture indicating a diagonal angle.

"And then?" Lieutenant Scott prompted.

"I remember thinking how weird it was that they were watching NewsNet," Kayla said quietly. "Ty never watched NewsNet. He preferred to get his information from multiple media outlets, preferably print." She smiled sadly at that. "Lawyers. We like things in writing."

Michelle gave her a soft, understanding smile, but didn't chuckle at the joke. The two officers simply stared at her blankly.

"His brother's in politics, so he's supersensitive to spin. Wouldn't trust anything that didn't come straight from a wire service and hadn't been vetted by one or two or more sources. He thought television news was trash."

"What did you do then?" the lieutenant persisted.

Michelle bristled. Her client was giving everything that she had as far as her impressions of the crime scene. She didn't appreciate his pushing her into recalling the gorier aspects of the morning's events.

"I ran to Ty," Kayla said, looking down at her knotted hands again. "I ran over and shook him. I guess I must have. I ended up with his head in my lap and tried to make him talk to me. I was calling his name, and…oh my God, there was so much blood," she said in a whisper. "So much blood."

"You hadn't noticed the blood until that moment?" Lieutenant Scott asked, his tone dubious.

Michelle was about to object but Kayla simply shook her head. "No, not really. At least, it didn't register. I didn't really realize that Trey was dead, too, until I couldn't get Tyrone to respond to me."

"But you didn't touch your stepson's body?" the lieutenant asked.

Kayla looked up at him, her brow furrowing as if the answer should have been obvious. "What? No. I wouldn't…no. Ty was my husband. I could see Trey was dead, and I…we didn't have a close relationship." She gave her head a shake. "Why would I go to him first?"

"What kind of relationship did you have with Trey Powers?" Lieutenant Scott asked abruptly.

Kayla glanced over at Michelle, who jumped in.

"What relevance does her relationship with her stepson have, Lieutenant?" she asked stiffly.

"Her stepson happens to be dead as well," Ethan Scott responded as if explaining the most rudimentary facts to her.

"True, but Trey Powers was also a grown man at the time

that Mr. and Mrs. Powers were married. She would not have had any kind of maternal connection with Trey."

Lieutenant Scott eyed Kayla speculatively, no doubt mentally calculating the age difference between Michelle's current client and the one that lay deceased in the other room.

"Trey Powers was almost three years older than my client," Michelle supplied. "She was closer in age to him than her husband."

"I see," Scott replied, making a note of the fact.

"If you've got all you need in terms of timeline," Michelle interjected, "I think it would be best if we get Mrs. Powers's clothing bagged and allow her to freshen up at this point."

"One more question," Lieutenant Scott cut in as they rose.

Michelle's chin went up and she answered for her client. "One more."

"Does your house have a security system that would monitor anyone coming or going either along the driveway or to the garage?"

Kayla blinked, then turned to Michelle, her face lighting with hope. "Yes. As a matter of fact, it does." She reached for her mobile phone and scrolled until she found the right application. "Here. This is the security system. You should be able to see me leaving here on Saturday morning and coming back this morning."

Michelle heard the note of triumph in her client's tone and hoped Kayla's confidence was born of the truth. If the security system corroborated her client's story, it would go a long way toward clearing her name.

She watched as Lieutenant Scott thumbed through the various camera angle views until he found one that satisfied him. "Okay, I see you leaving the garage Saturday morning. The time stamp says 7:09 a.m.," he told Sheriff Stenton.

"Sounds about right," Kayla said briskly. "And today I

wouldn't have been home more than ten or fifteen minutes prior to making the 911 call."

Ethan Scott's brows furrowed as he stared down at the phone. "Sheriff, what time did the 911 call come through?"

Stenton looked down at his notes. "I show it came through at 10:46 a.m."

The lieutenant hummed, then made to hand the phone over, but rather than giving it back to Kayla, he gestured for Michelle to take it. "Unfortunately, it appears the home security system cameras went off-line sometime Saturday afternoon."

Chapter Three

The moment the door closed behind Ms. Fraser and her client, Ethan turned to Sheriff Stenton and asked, "How do you like the widow for it?"

Stenton shook his head. "It would be the simplest answer, but my gut is telling me no. I can't imagine being the second wife there'd be a lot for her financially. The first Mrs. Powers took Tyrone to the cleaners. Got a chunk of everything that wasn't held in the family trust."

Ethan nodded, digesting this information. "There are other motivators. It isn't always money."

"True. Only most of the time." The older man shook his head and gave a rueful smile. "Either way, I don't see this sort of crime being this particular lady's style. You know what I'm saying?"

Ethan thought it over for a moment and had to agree. "I don't feel it in my gut, either."

"She's been nothing but cooperative since the moment we arrived on scene. She's truly shaken, you can see there. And she's no fool. If she did this, she'd know she'd be the prime suspect. Wouldn't she want somebody else to discover the bodies and make the call? It would be easier to play the shocked and grieving widow without being covered in blood."

Ethan sent the county sheriff a sharp look. The man

was far more astute than his good old boy demeanor let on. "Good point."

"Do you plan on taking her in for formal questioning?" Stenton asked, conceding the lead on this case without putting it in so many words. "I mean, you're welcome to use any of the offices available at the county building, if that's your inclination."

Ethan paced the immaculately appointed room, rolling the idea around in his mind. The sheriff was right. Mrs. Powers was cooperating, and with the help of her attorney, had offered them everything they could gain by taking her in, while at the same time blocking any opportunity they might have to question her further.

They would have her clothes, the residue tests and her fingerprints. Her lawyer would know that her client was a person of interest in this case and would hopefully keep her client from doing anything rash. There wasn't any reason to take her into custody for additional questioning other than for the optics, and Ethan couldn't see hauling a young and obviously shattered widow into the station coming across as a win on the nightly news.

He shook his head. "No, I don't think that will be necessary. As long as her attorney is open to her client being available to us as more questions arise, I think we'll be better off seeing what forensics can find here at the scene and looking into the security issue."

There was a tap on the door, and Michelle Fraser stuck her head into the small opening, almost like he'd conjured her.

"Gentlemen? May I?"

Ethan barely started to nod before she stepped into the sitting room and closed the door behind her once again.

"Mrs. Powers's clothing has been bagged by Deputy Herrera," she informed Sheriff Stenton. "I agreed to the deputy staying close by while she showers and changes into clean clothes." She then shifted her icy-blue gaze to Ethan. "Will you need us to come in to make a statement beyond anything we've discussed here today?"

"No," he said. But it came out a shade too sharply.

He wasn't sure exactly why Ms. Fraser got his hackles up. She was acting in a professional manner. Still, he couldn't help thinking of Grace Reed's astute impression when asked about the defense attorney.

"She acts like an attorney, but she watched us do everything like a cop," Agent Reed had told him.

Caught in the laser beam of Ms. Fraser's unflinching gaze, Ethan could understand what his agent had meant. He'd dealt with dozens of lawyers over the years and hundreds of law enforcement personnel. If he were going to slot Michelle Fraser into one of the two fields based on his initial impression alone, the only thing that would nudge her into the attorney grouping would be the cost of the expensive suit she wore.

But her stance, her guarded expression and the way she scanned and read a room like the sweep of radar looking for a blip said *cop* to him as well. Of course, it wasn't unusual for persons formerly in law enforcement to attend law school and become attorneys. However, in his experience, they tended to gravitate toward prosecution rather than defense. They also lost some of a cop's watchful edge after a few years seated safely behind a desk.

Ms. Fraser appeared to be as sharp as a tack.

He'd seen her in the news footage covering Trey Powers's arrest and subsequent arraignment, of course, but hadn't registered more than she was the attorney for the opposition. She was far more arresting in person than she appeared on camera. Almost charismatic. He could see how Grace Reed had said the woman baffled her.

Ms. Fraser was a mass of contradictions wrapped up in a neat designer suit. Her hair was cut into one of those no-

nonsense styles. A sleek cap that framed her heart-shaped face. Standard businesswoman hair. It shouldn't have been remarkable at all, but it was.

Most of it appeared to be colored a mahogany brown so deep it edged toward burgundy, but the bits surrounding her face—quarter-inch-wide sections pointing to her chin—were bleached nearly platinum blonde. He was no hairdresser, but he knew there was no way this color came from Mother Nature. Those streaks certainly were not put there by the sun. By all accounts, PP&W was a very conservative law firm. He couldn't help wondering if her hair color was a form of rebellion or misdirection.

"—the security firm."

Ethan shook himself from his observations in time to see her hand a slip of paper to the sheriff. "I'm sorry, what were you saying?"

She took a step back, then gave him a frank once-over as if trying to determine if he was up to going toe-to-toe with her. It was all Ethan could do to refrain from straightening his shoulders.

"I was saying, Lieutenant," she began in an exaggeratedly patient tone, "that my client has provided the name of the firm that handles the security for the Powers family lake house."

She cocked her head, and when she appeared to be satisfied that he'd heard her, she continued. "The lake house is held in the family's private trust, and as such only Tyrone and his brother William have access to request surveillance video from the property. Mrs. Powers has provided the contact information so that you may get in touch with someone at that company directly since neither her husband, his presumed heir or his brother are available at this time."

"Where is Senator Powers?" Ethan asked.

Ms. Fraser shrugged. "He's overseas. From what I'm told,

he left last Friday night to meet up with a congressional junket heading for eastern Europe."

He was impressed and more than a little annoyed she was able to rattle off the man's presumed whereabouts so readily. After all, the senator was not her client. And there was that condescending tone again. If she and her client were being so transparent, why did she sound like she had a secret?

Her confidence nettled him. Maybe that was why he couldn't resist jabbing back.

"Impressive. Did he clear it with you personally before leaving?"

The attorney glared at him for a moment, then gave him a slow blink that told him he'd set himself up to be knocked back again.

"No, but his departure was well documented on the evening news. The Powers Family Foundation hosted their annual gala that night. The senator was only able to come for the cocktail hour before he had to catch his flight back to Washington, DC."

"Were you at this gala?"

The question popped out before he could vet it, but in the moment she hesitated before answering, he decided it was legit. After all, both deceased persons and his prime suspect were presumably there, too.

"I was."

"Was everyone at PP&W invited?"

She pursed her lips, obviously parsing the question for possible pitfalls before answering.

"I wasn't in charge of the guest list, but I would say it was likely everyone from the junior partners on up were invited."

"And that would be about…how many people?"

"From the firm? Well over a dozen. In attendance overall? I would guesstimate between two and three hundred."

"And all of the Powers family was there?" Ethan pushed.

Ms. Fraser met his gaze challengingly. "Everyone except Tyrone's former wife, Natalie."

Something in her tone implied she wanted to add a "so there" to the end of her sentence. And perhaps she should have. After all, she'd handed him an alternative suspect on a silver platter.

"Does the former Mrs. Powers live in the area?"

Sheriff Stenton shook his head. "Last I heard, she was in Little Rock."

"Do you believe that the former Mrs. Powers would have any reason to travel from Little Rock to Bentonville to harm her ex-husband?" he asked.

Ms. Fraser gave him an odd look. "Regardless of what her feelings for Tyrone may have been, Trey Powers was her son, Lieutenant."

The tips of Ethan's ears burned with chagrin. For a moment, he'd been so focused on the widow and the ex-wife of one victim, he'd completely forgotten the second. The man who—until he'd been shot—had been this woman's client as well.

But rather than backing off, he dug in. "What was Trey Powers's relationship with his mother like?"

Michelle Fraser actually rolled her eyes at that. "She doted on him. He was her everything. And the feeling was mutual."

"And his relationship with his stepmother?"

"Lieutenant, we've already established Mrs. Powers didn't have any form of maternal relationship with her husband's grown son. The two were cordial with one another."

"Cordial," he repeated, but she simply held his gaze and her tongue.

Ethan decided to switch tactics. "Back to the security system… If there's a similar setup at the lake house—and we'll have to see if there were the same technical difficulties there—I don't suppose you know if it's possible to get in touch with Senator Powers to get permission to access the footage?"

She shook her head. "I'm sure the family's personal attorney, Harold Dennis, will."

"And where is Mr. Dennis?" Ethan persisted.

"I'm hoping he's in a plane on his way back from Barbados. I'd be happy to let you know as soon as I've had word from him." She shifted her attention to the sheriff, then back to him. "My client has made arrangements to stay at a local hotel. I know you'll want her to be close by," she said flatly.

"Yes, we do."

"I'm surrendering her passport into your keeping as a gesture of good faith," she said, handing over the slim booklet.

There was an awkward silence. Her stance niggled at him. She looked prepared for anything—to charge in, dash out, throw herself over a body, whatever. It was odd. He could understand her wariness. She was, after all, an attorney, and therefore suspicious of anything anyone said. But the readiness Agent Reed had noted was also apparent. He made the mental note to look deeper into Michelle Fraser's background. Something about her didn't quite ring true.

When he didn't take the proffered passport, the sheriff gently removed it from her hand.

"We appreciate your client's cooperation, ma'am," Sheriff Stenton said, filling the conversational abyss. "You've been very helpful."

Stenton slid a glance in his direction, and Ethan forced himself to perform the necessary niceties. These were important people. Influential people. He'd been sent here to keep the investigation running smoothly. He needed to pocket his antagonism now; otherwise it might trip him up later.

"Yes, thank you, Ms. Fraser. And please give our condolences to Mrs. Powers again. The Criminal Investigation Division and all state police resources are at her disposal. We will catch whoever did this."

Her raised eyebrows told him that she heard the note of threat in his statement, but otherwise her demeanor remained cool and calm as she nodded to them both and said her good-byes.

Once the door was closed, Ethan turned his attention back to the sheriff. "I didn't have a chance to speak to the coroner yet. What's the ballpark on the time of death?"

"Based on lividity, he's guessing they've been gone over 24 hours," Sheriff Stenton replied. "We'll be able to nail that down once he gets them to the morgue."

"So we're looking at any time from Saturday morning to, let's say, Sunday noon," Ethan said as he contemplated the view beyond one of the floor-to-ceiling windows. "The houses are not very close together, but we're still not talking large amounts of acreage. The community is gated." He turned to look over his shoulder at Stenton. "Is the guard-house staffed 24/7?"

The sheriff nodded. "They say it is."

"Is there also video surveillance on the vehicles entering and leaving at the gate?"

"I didn't think to ask that," the older man admitted. He scribbled something on his notepad. "I'll follow up."

"We know these gated places aren't as secure as people think they are. Could be delivery drivers in and out of here at all hours of the day and night. Most of the time they simply wave cars they recognize through." He crossed his arms over his chest and let his gaze fix on one of the mature trees they'd obviously worked around in building the home. "How old is this community?"

"Don't know exactly."

Behind him, Ethan heard the scratch of a pen on paper. "I assume that anyone that lives in this neighborhood probably runs in the same social circles as the Powerses?" The sheriff grunted, and Ethan turned to check on him. "No?"

"There are layers to the layers, if you know what I mean," Stenton responded.

"The Powers family would be in the top layer," Ethan ventured.

"Yes, but they don't always stay there. Even before William Powers was elected to the Senate, they were heavily involved in politics."

"You mean they mixed and mingled with the common folk, too," Ethan concluded.

"Yes. The gala thing they had Friday night would have been a mixed bag."

"How do you mean?"

"Most of the people who live around here probably were invited," he said, gesturing toward the window. "The top layer, let's say. But there would have been a lot of other people in attendance. People they'd know because it was to their advantage, but not necessarily friends you'd invite for dinner."

"Do you think that Mr. and Mrs. Powers were the kind of people who entertained at home?"

The sheriff shrugged. "There's a huge dining room table but could be for show. I'd think in his business he probably did have to entertain some. I know he fundraised for his brother's political campaigns."

Ethan nodded as he digested that. "So Tyrone Powers was a man of the people like his brother," he concluded with a sarcastic edge.

Stenton chuckled. "Not quite so down-to-earth as Senator Bill," he said, matching Ethan's jocular tone. "But he came down off the pedestal when he needed to."

"And his relationship with law enforcement?"

The sheriff closed his notebook and held his hands up in a helpless gesture. "Until this bit with the son happened, really not much of one at all. Their firm isn't the type to handle those 'If you've been injured in an accident...' cases."

"No billboards on highways?" Ethan asked.

"They barely have their name on the front door of the place." The sheriff got to his feet with an exhaled groan. "Lieutenant Scott, this is gonna be one hell of a mess. There's going to be a lot of tightrope walking, and I'm glad it's you and not me who has to toe that line."

"Good thing I stretched before coming," Ethan said, regarding the older man. "Are you sure I'm not stepping on your toes taking over like this?"

"Are you kidding me?" Stenton let out a mirthless laugh. "I'm up for reelection next year. I'd run out and buy a bow for this case if I thought I could get you to take it off my hands faster."

Ethan smiled at that. "I understand. I'll need some of your deputies on occasion and will definitely be looking to you for some insights, but don't worry—I don't mind making some people mad, if we need to. That's what I'm here for."

He clapped the sheriff on the shoulder, then nodded to the double doors. "Let's head back to the scene and see if anybody's come up with anything good. I wanna take another look before they roll the bodies out."

"You've got a strong stomach, Lieutenant Scott, I'll give you that," Sheriff Stenton said with grudging admiration.

"I don't know about that, but I got a strongly worded order from my commanding officer to make sure I get this thing sewn up tight," he said as the sheriff opened the door for them.

"I hope you've got a good hand with the needle," Stenton commented when they stepped back into the busy corridor.

Ethan watched the crime scene team move through the house. To any outsider it might look like chaos, but he knew every single person there had a purpose. As they made their way to the den at the back of the house, he tried to keep out of their way.

A thrill of purpose shot up his own spine. Some men hunted animals. Arkansas was a playground for people who wanted to catch deer, ducks and even bears and elk in their sites. But there was only one type of prey he was interested in. He liked to catch the people who preyed on other people.

The first thing Ethan noticed when they reentered the crime scene was the television. In all the hustle and bustle, no one had bothered to turn it off.

NewsNet broadcast in the background, the drone of the commentator filling the room as news of the gruesome scene they stood in the midst of scrolled across the bottom of the screen.

Reporters were following Senator Powers through an airport, cameras and microphones surrounding him as he walked with his head down and hand up to shield his face.

The headline in the crawl read: *Senator William Powers returning to Arkansas following the discovery of two family members gunned down in their own home.*

Ethan watched the bodies of those two family members being zipped into bags for transport, his mouth thinned into a line. On the screen, the senator's handlers shouted "no comment" as they attempted to flank the bereaved politician.

But before they cut away, Senator Powers looked up, his gaze boring directly into the camera lens. The man looked haggard and more than a little annoyed.

"I do have a comment," he announced, speaking over the shouts of the reporters and his handlers alike. "I want to say here and now that my brother and nephew's killer will not get away with murder. The person who did this will be caught, and she will face justice."

Ethan and Sheriff Stenton exchanged a look. "I didn't mishear that, did I?" Ethan asked quietly. "He said 'she,' right?"

Beside him, Sheriff Stenton pulled out his notebook and scrawled another hasty note. "Yes, sir, he did. He most definitely said 'she,'" he responded grimly.

Ethan shot him a sidelong glance. "Put the passport someplace safe, Sheriff. And let's assign around-the-clock surveillance to Mrs. Powers's hotel." He turned back to the television, where the cameras followed the senator's progress through the doors to a Jetway. "We'll need to get in touch with the family attorney ASAP. Find out who benefits most from Tyrone's passing, particularly now that the son is out of the way, too."

Sheriff Stenton stiffened. "Pretty sure it's going to be one of the women, are you?"

"He said *she*," Ethan replied, his eyes still locked on the screen.

Stenton shook his head again. "I still don't see the wife doing this one, but when there's a bucketload of money involved, people never fail to surprise me."

"That's funny," Ethan replied grimly, turning to face the man beside him. "I'm never surprised what people will do for a bucketload of money."

Chapter Four

The hotel Kayla Powers retreated to was a medium-tier entry presented by a national chain. Still, it was the best the town had to offer. Though a half dozen major corporations called Northwest Arkansas home, five-star hotels were thin on the ground. Michelle took in the generic decor and her lips quirked. She assumed the sliding half door that separated the bed from the seating area was what qualified it to be called a suite.

Her client had changed into clean jeans and a long-sleeved top she continually pulled over her wrists and hands. The cop in her couldn't help wondering whether the gesture was born of a compulsion to hide her hands from view, but the woman in her knew better. Without asking, Michelle walked over to the thermostat and nudged the temperature up a couple of degrees. Her client was on the verge of shock. She wasn't having some kind of Poe-inspired reaction to the fact that she'd murdered her husband and stepson.

"They always keep these rooms so chilly," she said, her tone casual. Glancing over at Kayla, she asked, "Is there anything I can get you?"

"No. Thank you. I appreciate you being here," the other woman murmured.

Kayla sat perched on the edge of the couch, so Michelle

dropped down into the chair opposite her. "Don't worry, Hal should be back shortly. I'm sure he booked the first flight out that he could get." Kayla told her she'd tried to reach Harold Dennis after calling Senator Powers, but had been unable to contact him.

"He's flying private," Kayla corrected.

"Excuse me?" Michelle asked, a frown creasing her brow.

"I believe he and Bill flew out on a private jet. A client's plane. Hal was going to drop Bill off in DC so he could make the junket, then head for the island."

Michelle resisted the urge to shake her head at the thought of somebody "dropping a person off" in their private jet. She'd been around these people long enough that she should have been accustomed to this level of excess.

"Oh. I hadn't realized."

But if Harold had taken a private jet to Barbados, he would be back in Arkansas as soon as possible, Michelle reassured herself.

"Either way, he'll be here soon, and he'll know how Tyrone would have wanted things done."

"I know how he wanted them done," Kayla affirmed, "and I don't think Harold is going to be much help."

There was an edge of weary bitterness in her client's words, but when their eyes met, Kayla's were clear and direct though red-rimmed from crying.

Michelle leaned in. Sometimes the best questions were the simplest ones. "What do you mean?"

"I mean that Ty and Harold were not always seeing eye to eye on things. Haven't for the past couple years. Harold's a little more Bill's guy, if you catch my drift. I think he even stays in touch with Ty's ex."

"Trey's mother?" Michelle asked, buying a little time to slot bits of information into place. She wasn't entirely sure that she was picking up all the nuances of the dynamic between the two Powers brothers, but she got the gist of her role here.

Harold Dennis wasn't going to swoop in and rescue her from babysitting Ty Powers's widow. Not if Kayla had anything to say about it.

"Yes. His mother, Natalie."

"I see," she said noncommittally, leaving the door open for Kayla to expound. She needed more data, but like everyone else, she'd forgotten that the woman seated across from her was more than a trophy wife. "Yes, I've met her."

"Right. Because of Trey."

"Because of Trey," Michelle confirmed.

"I've been thinking… I'd like you to stay on as my personal attorney," Kayla stated bluntly.

"I'm not sure how Harold—"

"Harold might resist, but I get to say who my attorney is, and I want that to be you."

Michelle closed her eyes for a moment, absorbing the implications of what Kayla was asking her to do. Not only would she be defying the man who she assumed would be taking over the reins at PP&W, but also, if she did so, she'd be taking prime time away from the mission she had hoped to complete this week.

She was supposed to be punching her ticket out of Arkansas, not getting herself even more entrenched in the mysteries and messes the Powers family managed to make of their lives.

"Tyrone and I drew up new wills," Kayla said quietly. Michelle looked over to see the younger woman twisting her fingers into knots, her head bowed.

"New wills?" she prompted.

"His previous will designated Natalie, Trey's mother, as Ty's secondary beneficiary," Kayla explained. "After we were married, he wanted to change it."

"Naturally," Michelle said encouragingly.

"But Harold always put it off."

"Because Tyrone wanted to put you in his will?"

"Trey was still his primary beneficiary," Kayla said a shade too quickly. "But there were also some changes on how he wanted to handle the business of the firm."

Michelle slid to the edge of her seat. "Changes that will impact...?" She left the last part of her question dangling, making it clear she expected her client to fill in the blanks for her.

"In the previous iteration, Harold Dennis or Del would step in to act as managing partner in the event of Ty's death. At least until Trey was ready to take over the reins."

"Del? Senator Powers's son?" Michelle frowned. Delray Powers hadn't struck her as much of a force in the firm. As a matter of fact, she often forgot the quiet tax attorney was actually part of the same family as the more dynamic Powers men. "Are you saying Delray Powers would be in charge?"

"If Tyrone died, Hal would manage the transition until Trey was ready to take over. If Trey were to die, then Del would take over as managing partner until the next generation could step in. That is, unless Senator Powers saw fit to give up his political career and come back to the practice of law."

"And in this new will?"

"Well, it's not going to make me look very good," Kayla admitted, meeting Michelle's gaze. Her lips twisted into a self-deprecating smile. "The new will designates me as the managing partner of Powers, Powers & Walton." She drew a deep, shuddering breath. "In perpetuity, unless Senator Powers opts to come back to the firm."

Michelle slumped deeper into the chair. "I see." She paused for a moment. "When were the new wills drawn up?"

"Over a year ago."

"Right. Okay," Michelle said, nodding as she digested the information. "But why then?" she asked, knowing it would be the first question the police asked once they found out about the changes made to favor the widow. "You've been married longer than a year."

"Like I said, Harold put him off and I think they both forgot. Then, Ty had an episode," Kayla said, her voice quavering though her gaze remained direct. "His heart. He thought it was a heart attack, but turned out to be angina. It was enough of a scare to spur him into rethinking his affairs."

"I see."

"It all comes to me," she said.

Michelle stared hard at the other woman, trying to detect even a glimmer of triumph or pride in the simple statement, but she saw none. Her client was stating facts. Facts that were not going to reflect favorably on her once the police were made aware of them.

"Okay," Michelle said quietly, her mind reeling as she sorted through the various options on how to approach this newest dilemma.

"I think we should get out in front of it," Kayla said with careful deliberation.

Michelle's thoughts were trailing along the same lines, but she was curious about her client's willingness to continue laying all of her cards out on the table. "What exactly do you mean by 'get out in front of it'?"

"We need to tell the police about the will before it's read and enters probate. I want them to know I'm aware that it won't reflect well on me and that I am continuing to cooperate as best I can."

"Who else knows about the will?" Michelle asked, her eyes narrowing.

"Only the people we asked to witness and notarize it," her client replied quietly.

"People who I assume have no connection to PP&W?" Michelle asked bluntly.

Kayla nodded. "We used a friend of mine from law school

to draw up the papers. She works for a firm in Little Rock," she said. "Anderson & Associates. Two of the partners witnessed our signatures." She looked up. "Tyrone was wary of how interconnected everybody is up here. He specifically wanted an outside firm with no ties to either the Powers family or the Waltons."

"Difficult to find in this state," Michelle commented.

"True," Kayla said with a short, sharp laugh. "My friend graduated from University of Arkansas Law, but she's from Oklahoma originally and did her undergrad there. The partners in the firm where she works are both graduates of the U of A at Little Rock."

"I see. Not the caliber of institution that fits the PP&W recruiting profile," Michelle concluded.

"Exactly. Tyrone was well aware of the network in which he operated. He also was cognizant of all the treachery inside it. He was fairly certain Harold was trying to push him out at the firm."

"Push him out? Could he do that? I mean, Tyrone is a name partner. He inherited the lion's share in the firm, didn't he?"

"Push him out as managing partner, I mean," Kayla clarified. "Harold was convinced that he could run the place better than Ty could. And though he'd never say so out loud, I think Bill resented the amount of sway Ty's position gave him in the area."

"The amount of sway?" Michelle repeated, incredulous. "He's a sitting US senator. Who would have more sway?"

"Ty had more say in the day-to-day running of the family business. As the elder, he not only inherited the name, but he was also given controlling interest in the firm. That's no small thing. Everyone who is anyone up here uses our firm."

"How much of an ownership differential are we talking?"

Kayla shrugged. "Our prenup only addressed what I could expect from the portion of the family trust Tyrone controls.

I've never seen the details on it, but I know that Bill was far more financially dependent on Ty than he wanted to be. Maybe a 60-40 split?" she hazarded.

"Wouldn't that still leave Bill a very wealthy man?"

"I know his divorce from his first wife cost him quite a bit," Kayla said softly. "He never stops complaining about it even though they've been divorced for nearly twenty years."

"Didn't your own husband's first wife take a good bite out of his net worth?" Michelle asked, hoping the blunt question would startle more truth out of her client.

"Definitely. But he had more to start with, so it didn't hurt as much. Plus, Tyrone was actively generating income for the firm. Bill and Anthony Walton had to step back in order to fulfill their new positions as senator and Judge. Bill is reliant on his salary as a public official and had to report his income from the firm in accordance with congressional guidelines, which limits income earned outside of his public salary. Needless to say, his public income did not allow for the lifestyle he was accustomed to living in, so Ty covered a lot of his personal expenses."

"And he always has to be out fundraising." Michelle considered. "Not only did he have to ask his brother for funds to live, but he has to ask the public for funds to run."

"Exactly," Kayla confirmed. "And he's not nearly as gracious about the personal contributions as the public ones."

Determined to get the conversation back on track, Michelle leaned forward again. "Harold doesn't know about the new will either," she concluded.

Kayla shook her head. "There's a copy in our safe at the house, one in Ty's office safe and one on file with the firm who helped us execute them."

"Who has access to those safes?"

"I have access to the safe at home. I'm not sure about the office. It's possible Trey had access to both of them," Kayla conceded. "I'm fairly certain Bill did not. And like I said, Ty didn't trust Harold entirely."

"So, I'm assuming you want me to approach the police with this information about the revised wills before it would naturally come to light," she said, raising an inquiring eyebrow.

Kayla nodded. "It's like with what happened at the house. I have nothing to hide. We have our reasons for drawing up the documents we did, and it was done quite a long time ago."

"You are aware that gunshot residue can't prove anything conclusively, and most law enforcement agencies in this state don't even ask for it, aren't you?"

"It can prove that I have not been anywhere near anything that discharges gunpowder," Kayla reasoned. "Offering the samples can't hurt me. I did nothing wrong, though I'm sure there are some people who have already tried and convicted me."

"What makes you say so?"

When their gazes connected again, Kayla's eyes were clear and direct. A blue so pale it was almost translucent.

"I know what people think about me," she said flatly. "I know what my old friends at the firm say, and I know what the biddies in society say. I know what everyone says. They think I set my sights on Tyrone because of who he was and what he had, but I loved my husband, Michelle." Clasping her hands together, she gave a helpless little shrug. "People can believe it or not, but I really did love him. And he loved me. We were a good match, and we were happy. Happier than some people could stand."

The last sentence took Michelle by surprise. "What do you mean by that?"

Kayla sighed. "Not everybody was happy to see Tyrone so content with his life. Even people who should have been."

Michelle heard the resentment ringing through each word

the woman spoke. She'd spent enough time in Trey Powers's company to understand exactly how entitled the young man was. "You mean Trey."

Kayla inclined her head slightly. "Yes."

"I thought you said you two got along. He told me that you did."

"I thought we did." The words came out in a voice thick with pent-up emotion. "I guess that makes me more foolish than I ever thought I was."

Michelle watched as the younger woman dashed a tear from the corner of her eye. "You think Trey was only feigning his friendship with you?"

It wasn't a stretch. Trey Powers was one of those guys who used the people and things that were placed in his path, then forgot about them the moment they were depleted.

"I suppose you ought to tell the police this as well," Kayla said, swallowing down the emotion that made her voice tremble. "Trey said some fairly ugly things to me at the gala Friday night."

"What sort of ugly things?"

"Oh, the usual stuff. Gold digger. Sleeping my way to the top. Some hateful comment about how he'd have to get Harold to double-check and see if I actually was a member of the Arkansas bar or if I faked my way into the firm to get to his father."

"He said all this without provocation?" Michelle probed, knowing that it wouldn't be unusual for the young man to do so without reason, but she had to ask.

"No provocation from me," Kayla said, stiffening her spine. "People were talking about him, though. Gossiping about the charges pending against him and debating whether they thought he was guilty or innocent." She snorted. "How can anyone ever apply the word *innocent* to Trey Powers in any context? The man was born a piece of work."

"People at the gala were talking about him, and he lashed out at you because—" Michelle prompted.

Kayla threw her hands up. "Deflection? I don't know." She shook her head hard. "People love to talk about me, so maybe he thought if he turned the focus in my direction, they'd stop looking at him so hard. Either way, I told him I didn't appreciate being the family punching bag."

"And what did he say to that?"

Michelle didn't have any difficulty conjuring up the numerous ugly things Trey Powers could have trotted out. As handsome and cool as the young man was on the outside, on the inside he was seething with molten hot vitriol. He resented everyone and everything that ever stood in his way of getting exactly what he wanted in life.

"He made some comment about how I wouldn't have to worry about being a member of his family much longer, if things kept going the way they were going." The desolate expression in Kayla's eyes made it clear Trey's words had struck home with her.

"He believed you and his father were having difficulties?"

Kayla shrugged. "I don't know how, but I suppose so. The worst part was that he said it loud enough for everybody around us to hear." She gave a bitter laugh. "All of a sudden, they were no longer talking about the charges pending against Trey. Mission accomplished, I guess. By the time we left that night, everybody was eyeballing me as if it was the last time they'd have to see me in one of their ballrooms."

"Did you speak to Tyrone about it?"

"I tried to on the way home," Kayla confessed.

"What did he say?"

"He dismissed it all. Said there was nothing wrong with us. That we were settling into a normal marriage, and people love to gossip. He was upset with Trey," she said, adding a pointed look for emphasis. "He didn't appreciate his own son using him to deflect, I guess."

"How did you and Tyrone leave it?"

"We simply…left it." Kayla opened her hands in a helpless gesture of futility. "We went home, we got ready for bed, he kissed me good-night and within minutes he was snoring."

"And you?"

Kayla flashed a self-deprecating smile. "I went down and finished off the bottle of Chardonnay I'd left in the fridge after lunch."

"Had you had much to drink at the party?" Michelle persisted.

Kayla shook her head. "Not nearly enough. Ty didn't like me drinking in public. Apparently, Natalie had a tendency to get a little too far into her cups and run her mouth at social functions. It was one of the things he told me from the start would be a deal-breaker."

"And the drinking thing…" Michelle asked leadingly.

"As far as I know, Ty wasn't aware. Or didn't care as long as I didn't do something to embarrass him."

"But you were upset after the party," Michelle stated simply.

"Well, sure I was. I mean, I'm not supposed to embarrass him, but it doesn't matter if his son humiliates me? I was angry."

"So you took off the following morning to punish him?" she hazarded.

"Partially." Kayla huffed. "I guess it was more like I wanted to see if he'd even notice I was gone."

"Did he?"

"I got a text Saturday evening. After he realized he hadn't seen me all day long. He'd had a round of golf scheduled and was up and out early. And truthfully, it wasn't too unusual for us to go a whole day without seeing each other. I guess I should be happy he did notice eventually."

"What did you tell him?"

"I said I was tired and needed to get away, so I went to the lake house."

"And he had no problem with that? He didn't want to join you there?"

Kayla winced. "Truthfully? I think he was a bit relieved. Ty is…was drama avoidant. I'm assuming he invited Trey over so he could lecture him on proper family decorum in public settings, yada yada."

"Was Tyrone the type to lecture?" Michelle pressed.

The corner of Kayla's mouth kicked up. The stare she leveled on Michelle spoke volumes. "We're all attorneys. Lecturing is what we do."

"Good point."

"Listen, I know what the optics are here. I'm the second wife, the social-climber-turned-closet-drinker who stands to end up with a lot more than most people would think I'm entitled to," she said.

Her delivery smacked of the calm and measured cadence used in closing arguments, and Michelle was growing too aware of Kayla's background in criminal defense. Feeling a need to pace, Michelle rose, rubbing her palms together as she tried to gather her thoughts.

"I realize it goes against the grain to give up information to the police right off the bat, but I'm telling you, I have nothing to fear here. I did not do this," Kayla assured her.

Michelle sighed and stopped pacing. "I believe you didn't kill them, but I am not on board with the 'nothing to fear' part," she said frankly. "What if someone is trying to set it up so you *do* look guilty? What if there's enough circumstantial evidence for them to put together a cohesive case for a grand jury? It's what happened with Trey in the Mallory Murray case. They piled those circumstantial bits up until they were a mountain too big for anyone to ignore."

Kayla nodded. "I understand. But there are two big differences between me and Trey."

"What are those?"

She held up one finger. "One, I didn't do it." She added a second finger to form a victory sign. "Two, I am not going to even attempt to hide anything from the authorities. As far as I'm concerned, they have full access to every facet of my life."

Michelle pursed her lips and dropped back into the seat across from her client. "Even the personal stuff? Your worries about your marriage? The drinking?"

"Full access."

Nodding, Michelle digested her client's plan for mounting her defense. It was as good a plan as any. Trying to hide evidence and avoid questioning by the police sure hadn't done Trey Powers any favors. "I suppose you want me to pay Lieutenant Scott a visit and convey your intention to continue to cooperate fully?"

Kayla nodded. "Yes. And you have my explicit permission to share the personal, private information I have given you, if you think it will help them move past me as a suspect. I realize as the spouse, they have to give me a good, hard look, but I also don't want them to let the trail grow too cold while they do."

"Noted." Michelle stood and grabbed her bag. She gave the generic hotel suite one last appraising sweep. "Do you want me to bring you dinner—"

She turned back to find her client had curled up in a ball on the end of the sofa, a throw pillow clutched to her chest. Gone was the clear-eyed attorney who wanted to make certain the investigation was steered in the right direction. In her place was a young, vulnerable widow who appeared to be alone in the world.

"I'm okay," Kayla insisted, even though it was clear she was not.

"Is there anyone I can call for you? A friend? Your parents?"

Kayla shook her head. "My parents are on a cruise. I've spoken to them, and we checked flights from their next port of call, but it would take them the better part of two days and four flights. They're scheduled to be back in port in three days, and since we can't hold any kind of funeral or memorial until the coroner releases the bodies, I told them not to rush back."

Michelle twisted the strap of her bag around her hand, feeling torn about leaving Kayla to her own devices after such a traumatic day. But they weren't friends, and a friend was what Kayla needed at that moment, not an attorney.

"How about a friend? Is there someone who might come stay with you?"

Kayla's lips twisted into a sad smile. "I've been moving in Ty's world the past few years, and even before that, I mostly hung out with other attorneys from PP&W. Most of my school friends have gone to Little Rock or elsewhere. And the people up here..." She drew a shaky breath, then let it go. "I'm not sure I have any I can call my own."

Sympathy tugged at Michelle's gut, but she tamped it down. She and Kayla were not friends, and to even attempt to step in as one now would be disingenuous. "Okay, well, you have my number if you need anything."

"I do. Thank you."

Michelle passed the overpriced mini bar as she headed for the door. Gripping the handle, she turned back. "I hate to say this at such a time, but it really would be best if you tried to keep a clear head for the next few days."

Kayla didn't even turn to look at her. "You mean you want me sober," she said baldly. "I don't know that I can promise that."

Biting her lip, Michelle shifted into negotiation mode. "Can you keep it to the room? I mean, it might not look too good if anyone were to spot you hanging out at the hotel bar."

She heard the other woman's harsh chuckle, but Kayla still didn't turn to look at her. "Sure. Absolutely."

The affirmation was quiet but firm. As Michelle opened the door and stepped into the corridor, she heard her client say, "I've gotten really good at drinking alone."

Chapter Five

Ethan sat back in the squeaking chair he'd requisitioned from a desk the clerk told him was currently unoccupied. The office he'd been offered at the Benton County Correctional Complex was not much bigger than a broom closet, but at least it had a door. He hated trying to work in a warren of open cubicles.

His laptop sat open on the desk, but it was his phone that kept drawing his attention. He hadn't expected a phone call from Michelle Fraser first thing in the morning. Frankly, hearing her voice on the other end of the call had freaked him out. He couldn't help wondering if she had somehow sensed he'd spent a good portion of the previous evening digging into her background info.

The information he'd found showed her to be nothing more than what she claimed to be—a highly qualified attorney working for the area's most prestigious law firm. She'd done her undergraduate work at Boston College and graduated from Harvard Law. After graduation, she'd worked as an associate in a boutique law firm in Boston, then a midmajor in Philadelphia, before making quite a name for herself in corporate defense at a large firm in New York.

The partner track at a firm the size of Colins and Preston was arduous and fiercely competitive. Maybe it made sense for her to jump ship and move to Northwest Arkansas when PP&W came calling. She'd come in as a junior partner, a fact that had to tick off at least some of the more senior associates. But none of that explained why she made his cop radar ping.

He sighed and pulled up the document where he'd added a page of facts the defense attorney supplied to the Powers case notes. She'd been as cooperative as her client, informing them of Kayla Powers's hotel information as soon as she'd seen the shaken widow settled. She'd answered the few questions he'd wanted to clarify from his notes without hesitation or any sign of dissembling.

It wasn't until she'd requested to meet with him in person to give some of her own thoughts on the investigation that he remembered she knew both of the victims well. She'd confirmed Trey had been her primary client in the months since his arrest in connection to Mallory Murray's death. And as a junior partner and the lawyer defending his only son and heir, she'd had extensive interaction with Tyrone as well, Ethan imagined.

Though he was convinced there was more to Michelle Fraser than met the eye, Ethan still didn't like the widow Powers for the double homicide. But he couldn't base an investigation on gut instinct. Until more evidence came to light, Kayla Powers had to remain their primary suspect.

He rocked back in his chair, laced his fingers behind his head and stretched his chin toward the ceiling, hoping to ease some of the tension in his shoulders before Ms. Fraser arrived.

But it wasn't meant to be.

A sharp rap on his door startled him from the stretch. His arms fell to his side and he jerked upright in his chair. The woman standing in his doorway smiled one of those closed-lip, "caught ya" kind of smiles. He was struck anew by how unlike his vision of a corporate attorney she was. Sure, she wore a suit, but this one was a sky-blue color that made her eyes pop. A plain white blouse dipped low enough to give a tantalizing peek of clavicle, but nothing so revealing as cleavage. The chunky blonde streaks that framed her heart-shaped face came to a point at her chin. She wore tasteful jewelry and low-heeled pumps and carried an expensive-looking leather satchel he assumed doubled as briefcase and handbag. "Oh. I didn't expect you to get here so quickly," he said, trying to play it cool as he lowered the lid of his laptop.

"I'm sorry. I didn't mean to startle you. I live on this end of town so I was nearby. I know it's early, but I imagine it's going to be fairly chaotic at the office today, and I wanted to be sure I spoke to you before I got caught up in it."

He turned to the chair across from the desk. "Please, take a seat."

She settled into the hard wooden guest chair that had been in the office when he took it over. He watched her every movement carefully, trying to get a better read on the woman. But she gave little away. She set her bag on the floor at her feet, then sat back. She held no note pad and carried no phone or laptop, though he was sure both were in the bag. Instead, she folded her hands neatly in her lap, the small smile firmly in place as she met his gaze directly.

He wished he didn't find her calm competence so intriguing. She and her client were doing everything they could to make his job easier. He simply didn't understand why.

"My client asked that I come here to speak to you directly about some of the circumstances around the business of PP&W. There are some incidents that may come to light in the coming days."

"Incidents?" He sat up straighter, automatically reaching for a pen and the notepad. He preferred to keep things analog when having a conversation. He found people were more forthcoming when he had a pen in hand and his eyes on them, rather than his head down typing. Plus, maintaining eye contact allowed him to get a better read on the person delivering the information. "What sort of incidents?"

Ms. Fraser sighed, and he surmised she was feeling torn about her client's strategy of full cooperation. He couldn't blame her. People often acted against their own best interests. As a lawyer, he'd seen more than his share of defendants insist on taking the witness stand against counsel's advice and common wisdom, but it was difficult to convince someone that they might not be the best narrator of their own story.

"I'm told Mrs. Powers and Trey had a bit of a run-in at the Powers Family Foundation gala the night before she left for the lake house."

"Told by Mrs. Powers?" he prompted, wanting the clarification.

"Yes."

"What kind of run-in?"

She sighed again, and the attorney in him felt for her, even as his cop fingers clutched the pen tighter. Whatever she had to share would not cast her client in the best light.

"Apparently, some of the guests were openly discussing the case against Trey Powers. Though I can attest he was generally a fan of the limelight, he must not have cared for the speculation circulating the ballroom. My client believes that he intentionally said some harsh things to and about her in an effort to deflect the attention from himself."

"What harsh things?" Ethan asked.

"He insinuated that Mr. and Mrs. Powers were having marital issues. He also insinuated that Mrs. Powers had married his father to gain access to a society she never would have had a foothold in on her own merit. And, of course, the privilege that comes with the kind of money and connections the Powers family enjoys."

"What does your client say about these allegations?"

"My client admits that she and her husband were no longer in the honeymoon phase of their marriage, but they were still on solid ground. Both led busy lives with interests they did not share and that often separated them. They were—" she paused here, choosing the next word carefully "—evolving," she concluded.

"Fighting?"

She shook her head. "Not according to Kayla. More of a settling-in, is the way she made it sound."

He raised an eyebrow, prompting for more.

"Mrs. Powers says they didn't fight. Apparently, his marriage to Trey's mother was somewhat…volatile, so if Kayla and Tyrone disagreed on something, he tended to walk away. I get the impression communication may have been difficult between them, but I don't—" She hesitated for a moment. "Lieutenant, I've spent a lot of time around the Powers family in the past few months. I saw nothing of an aggressive nature in the dynamic between Mr. Powers and my client. Not even passively aggressive. If anything, they took particular care with each other."

He made a quick note of that assessment, then shifted gears. He'd delve deeper when he spoke to the widow herself.

"And your take on her relationship with your now former client? You said their relationship was, uh, cordial?" he asked, drawing the word out.

In this capacity, her impressions carried more weight. She was hip-deep in the Powers family drama, but most of her immersion would have come from her defense of Trey, not Kayla.

She nodded.

"But was it contentious?"

She straightened her spine. "In all the time that I was representing Tyrone Powers the third against the allegations brought against him, I never heard him disparage or denigrate Kayla Powers," she answered carefully. "I don't believe they were close, but I never witnessed or heard of anything acrimonious between them."

"Until that night," he inserted.

Ms. Fraser nodded. "Exactly. Mrs. Powers was shocked and hurt by the things my former client said the night of the gala. And according to her, her husband had no desire to play referee between his wife and his son. They discussed it on the way home from the gala, but once they reached the house, Tyrone refused to discuss it any longer."

"And you were at the gala?" he asked, shifting gears in hopes of throwing her off her game.

It didn't work. "I was for a short time. I made my appearance, spoke to some of my colleagues and a few acquaintances, but I'm not much of a party person. I left as soon as the senator departed."

"To fly back to Washington on a private plane with your boss," he said, wanting her to be well aware he had listened carefully to everything Kayla said the previous day.

"Correct. Except Harold Dennis is not technically my boss. He's the family's attorney. We both report directly to Tyrone... Reported," she corrected. "I guess everyone is assuming Harold will handle the firm now."

"I see." He made another quick note about PP&W's structure, then shifted again. "So you missed the dustup between Trey and Kayla Powers."

"I did."

"Still, a public squabble at such an important event for the family... Add that to the insinuations Trey Powers made—I have to believe your client would have been extremely upset," he stated.

Her bright blue eyes widened slightly. "I didn't think it was your job to deal in supposition, Lieutenant."

He inclined his head to acknowledge the hit but didn't let off the gas. "She wanted you to tell me this for a reason."

"Yes. She *was* upset—both by the things Trey said about her and Tyrone's refusal to defend her. I think it's reasonable for any spouse in such a position to be upset."

"Perhaps," he conceded. "Did they go to bed…angry?"

"They went to bed…agitated," she corrected. "My client was upset and she couldn't get to sleep. Once her husband was asleep, she got up and went to the kitchen for something to drink. When she awoke the next morning, Tyrone had left for an early tee time."

"So the last time your client saw her husband alive…"

"He was snoring in his bed," she stated without hesitation.

He wrote the word *snoring* on his notepad. His gut said this wasn't the only bit of information Ms. Fraser had to share. He also couldn't shake the feeling there was something she was holding back about her client's weekend activities. Placing the pen down on the pad, he looked up expectantly.

"And?"

"And what?" she asked, her brow puckering.

"Is that all you came here to tell me this morning?"

She stared back at him, one eyebrow lifting as their gazes clashed. "I gave you a significant piece of information."

The corner of his mouth twitched, but he fought the urge to smile. She was good at this game, but so was he. "You did. As I'm sure you and your client are aware, it's always good to get out in front of the gossip before we can hear it from someone else."

She inclined her head. "Things like little tiffs at public events do have a way of coming out eventually."

"They do."

Ethan watched with interest as she shifted on the hard wooden chair. He could practically see the gears meshing in her head as she decided how best to approach whatever else she had on her mind. But he was a patient man. And he had a feeling whatever it was, it would be worth the wait.

His intuition didn't lie.

"There will also be an issue with Tyrone Powers's will," she stated coolly.

He picked up his pen again, made a note of the change in subject matter, then turned his attention back to her. His heart raced with anticipation. He could only hope his expression didn't betray his heightened interest. "His will?"

She nodded. "Mrs. Powers informed me yesterday she and her husband had new wills drawn up by a firm in Little Rock." She paused as if searching her memory, but he could tell the name was on the tip of her tongue. "The Anderson law firm—Anderson & Associates—drew up the papers and witnessed their signatures."

"Anderson & Associates," he repeated as he wrote the name out. "Why not their own firm?"

He looked up as he spoke, but immediately regretted asking the question. It hurt to have a woman as challenging as Michelle Fraser look at you as if you barely met the intellectual equivalent of a piece of used chewing gum.

"Never mind. He didn't want his firm involved," he stated flatly. "I assume you're sharing this because the new will favors your client. And the fact that it was drawn up at another firm likely indicates it will meet resistance from within PP&W."

"Correct on both counts." She gave him a small smile, and Ethan couldn't help but feel slightly vindicated. "The new document kept Trey as the primary beneficiary, but changed the secondary."

"And I assume the new beneficiary is Mrs. Powers."

"It isn't unusual to make one's spouse a party to one's estate," she replied, her tone noticeably icier than it had been. "I am told the previous iteration still had Mr. Powers's first wife, Natalie Powers, named as successor to her son."

"Do you know if Mr. Powers had a particular reason to engage another firm?"

"According to my client, Mr. Powers was not entirely comfortable working with Harold Dennis."

"The family's attorney who is not technically your boss," he murmured as he made notes.

When he looked up, he found the corners of her mouth turned up in a smile and those brilliant blue eyes glinting with repressed humor.

"Exactly."

He lowered his pen and gave her his undivided attention. Then he asked his favorite question. "Why?"

Regret twisted his gut when her smile faded and the line bisecting her eyebrows reappeared, but he squashed the sensation. He wasn't here to make this woman happy—he was here to find out who killed two members of a very prominent family. A family who had her so ensnared in their web, it was hard to tell if she was party to their plots or hapless prey.

"Why what?"

Her response jolted him. He was used to being the one who asked questions. Still, he'd been intentionally vague, and she was an attorney. Ethan shouldn't be surprised she didn't fall for his usual tactics. So he went the direct route.

"Why does your client want me to know she and her late husband had doubts about the family attorney?"

"Because she has asked me, not Harold, to represent her."

He leaned back, purposefully softening the tension between them. "What's it to me who represents her?"

She narrowed her eyes as if testing the weight of his feigned nonchalance. "Because we both know Mr. Dennis is about to descend on this scene, and I can guarantee he won't be as cooperative and forthcoming as my client and I have been." With that, she gathered the handles of her bag and rose. "You have my contact information. My client instructed me to assure you she will continue to do everything she can to aid in your investigation."

Ethan remained seated, though it went against the very strict manners his mother had drilled into him as a child. If his years as an attorney and an investigator had taught him anything, it was the value of being willing to cede the higher ground when there was no immediate advantage to holding it. Instead, he cocked his head to the side and looked up at her, prepared to launch one last arrow in an attempt to throw her off her game.

"Except she won't tell us why she really went to the lake house."

Ms. Fraser blinked, and if someone had asked him to testify under oath, he'd swear he saw a hint of her sly smile tug at the corners of her mouth. "I told you. She was feeling vulnerable and wanted some alone time."

"Was she hoping her husband would go chasing after her?" he challenged.

She shrugged. "Perhaps. I can't really say what her hopes were. I only know what she has told me."

"Do you believe her?"

"Does it matter?" she shot back.

He liked the way she handled herself so nimbly. As much as he wanted to catch her flat-footed, she managed to parry each attempt he made. A part of him wished he could go up against her in court.

"Your messages have been delivered, Ms. Fraser," he said, inclining his head with mock deference. "If your client asks how it went, tell her I gave you top marks across the board. I don't know this Harold Dennis from a hole in the wall, but I cannot imagine he'd be half as fierce as you."

She gave a little snort as she hitched her bag onto her arm. "Don't underestimate Hal Dennis, Lieutenant. Men don't end up in positions like his accidentally."

"You mean he grew up aspiring to be seated at the right hand?" he asked, but his jovial tone came across as snide, even to his own ears.

"Sometimes a strong right hand wields more power than a figurehead." She turned to leave the tiny office, her shoulders squared. "Thank you for your time."

"Thank you for your cooperation," he returned, matching her flippancy.

She glanced back. "You mean my *client*'s cooperation," she said, flashing a tight smile that didn't reach those icy eyes. "I counseled against bringing you more information. I told her to let you do your job."

"I'd expect nothing less from a good defense attorney." Pausing for a moment, he gave her an insincere smirk he'd been told was nothing less than condescending. "And I hear you're the best in town."

"Oh, isn't that nice. I'll miss Special Agent Reed. Bless her heart, she worked so hard to bring a case against Trey Powers, and now…" She heaved a sigh. "Let me know if my client can be of further assistance, Lieutenant. Happy hunting," she added, almost as an afterthought.

He sat frozen for a moment, too stunned by those last two words to do anything but watch her wend her way through the maze of cubicles beyond his precious door.

Happy hunting.

A shiver ran up his spine and prickled his scalp. He ran his hand through his hair, trying to calm the sensation as his mind raced.

That wasn't something attorneys said to one another. The lawyers didn't come into play until after the police had done their job. She was exhorting him to do his. And not only because her client was their prime suspect.

He'd wager money Michelle Fraser had once been a hunter as well. Not for game, but for bad guys. But not only had she switched from law enforcement to the practice of law, she'd gone over to the dark side.

An occurrence even more rare than a lawyer stepping into cop shoes.

Reaching for his phone, he called Special Agent Grace Reed again. She was the one who'd planted this seed in his mind. Now, Michelle Fraser was standing between his office and the apprehension of a possible murderer. Again.

"Scott here," he said when she answered. "Listen, how deep did you dig on your background on Michelle Fraser?"

"Well, I ran a background check, of course," she began hesitantly. "Verified her credentials with the bar, studied some of her more recent cases, but I didn't go much deeper," she admitted.

He nodded his approval as she spoke. She'd done nothing more than he would have in compiling a basic dossier on counsel for the defense. "Right, why would you?" he interjected.

"Do you think I should have?"

"No, but I do think your observation about her acting more like a cop than a lawyer is spot-on. Kayla Powers has retained her to be her personal attorney."

There was a beat of silence. "She has?"

"Yes."

"Not Harold Dennis?"

"No," he confirmed.

"Interesting," Grace responded.

Ethan smiled as he heard the sound of a pen tapping travel through the line. "Isn't it?"

"Harold Dennis will not like that," she concluded, and he could almost see her turning the implications over in her mind.

"Mrs. Powers claims her husband didn't trust Mr. Dennis entirely," Ethan informed her.

Agent Reed barked a short, bitter laugh. "They did a good impression of presenting a united front whenever I saw them."

"I'd like to dig deeper on Ms. Fraser and Mr. Dennis. Do you have time to help me?"

He heard the soft intake of breath on the other end of the call and sensed that he'd caught the usually sure-footed agent off guard. Probably because he could have ordered her to help, but that wasn't Ethan's leadership style. He'd heard tales of his predecessor's bullying. But Ethan believed one got the best out of people when they operated from a position of empowerment, not fear.

"I, uh, yes," she said, quickly recovering. "Yes, Chief. I'd love to help."

"Thanks. I appreciate it. I have my hands full up here, and I know there's no one better suited to be my backup on this," he said, meaning every word.

Up until the previous day, Agent Grace Reed had been their resident expert in all things Powers-related. He wasn't about to waste those months of work simply because his boss made a decision based on pressure and politics.

"Thank you, Agent Reed. I know the events of the past couple days must feel like a bad case of whiplash, but I promise you, I know who my best resource is on this, and I don't squander resources. Follow your nose on Fraser. Maybe she's from a family of cops? Whatever. It's early days so we don't have much to go on except gossip and our guts at this point, but I'd rather listen to intuition than a bunch of opinions from people with agendas."

"Gotcha. I'm on it," she said, and he smiled at hearing her usual brisk confidence restored.

"Thanks. I'll be in touch."

Ethan ended the call and leaned back in the chair, grasping his wrist and raising his joined hands to his forehead as he closed his eyes. He replayed the entire encounter with Michelle Fraser, trying to put his finger on exactly what it was about her that made his neurons fire. Sure, she was physically attractive. Striking in both her style and manner. But Agent Reed was right about the cop signals.

Happy hunting.

He smiled as he lowered his hands and sat up slowly, wondering if the intriguing Ms. Fraser knew those two simple words might have put her dead center in his crosshairs.

Chapter Six

The door to Powers, Powers & Walton was lettered with tasteful script. It had barely closed behind her when the firm's re-
ceptionist, Bailey, chirped, "Hold, please," into her headset
and rose from her chair to catch Michelle.

"Mr. Dennis asked to see you in his office as soon as you
came in," the fresh-faced young woman informed her in a
grave tone.

Michelle fought the urge to smirk at the "Mr. Dennis"
portion of the message. It had taken Harold Dennis weeks
to break the young woman of the habit of referring to him
as "Uncle Hal" to associates and clients alike. Then, she'd
explain how Harold Dennis wasn't really her uncle, but that
he'd known her mama and daddy, "Like forever," so he was
like an uncle.

"Thank you, Bailey," she said as she breezed past the
young woman's command console. "I'll put my things away
and head up to his office now. If you'll let him know?" she
called over her shoulder.

"Sure will," Bailey replied, reverting to her usual chipper
disposition. As if the firm's founder and his son hadn't been
discovered murdered the day before.

Michelle nodded a few hellos but didn't break stride, her
eyes fixed on her office door. The more senior attorneys

kept offices on the upper floor, so she knew she had a little time before her presence was expected. But she could feel the gazes of the other employees lingering on her back. They couldn't know about Kayla's decision to choose her over Harold Dennis, so she assumed they were waiting to hear if she had any insights about the murders themselves. She almost made it to her door before one worked up the nerve to ask directly.

"Michelle," a young man called out to her in a voice so raspy it broke.

She fought the urge to cringe. Chet Barrow was as obnoxious and entitled as his friend Trey had been but lacked a filter and self-awareness. Something that worked against him, both at work and as Trey's ally. Still, he was a bright attorney when he applied himself, and the guy did sound truly upset over the loss of his friend.

Her hand gripping the door handle, she turned to find the ambitious young attorney standing beside her, uncharacteristically disheveled, all traces of feigned cool stripped away. She couldn't help softening toward him.

Chet had followed Trey around like a puppy. Emulated almost everything Trey was or did, from his haircut to his choices in shoes and neckties. The only difference was that while Chet came from a family with some money, he didn't have the seemingly unlimited funding the Powerses did. Which meant he didn't have exactly the same expensive wristwatch and cuff links the police believed would help prove Trey Powers had killed Mallory Murray.

"Hey, Chet," she said by way of greeting. "How are you holding up?"

He shook his head, and his perfectly coiffed hair flopped over his wrinkled brow. "I just can't… I can't wrap my head around it."

"I know," she replied with genuine sympathy. Opening

the door to her office, she strode to her desk, knowing Chet would follow her in.

"It's just so unreal."

Michelle didn't bother telling him she'd been at the crime scene with Kayla Powers and it was all very real. Everyone would know that by now. She placed the tote that contained her laptop in the bottom drawer of her desk, then opened the center drawer and withdrew a key she palmed under a container of breath mints.

"I know. I have to head upstairs to meet with Hal right now," she explained, pulling a face to convey the dread she truly felt. She popped a mint into her mouth, tossed the container back into the drawer, then locked the desk down as if she did so every time she stepped away from her office. "Can I catch up with you later?"

"Oh. Yeah. Sure," he said, backing out of the office as she moved toward the door.

She slipped the key into the pocket of her jacket, then offered a wan smile. "Thanks. I hate to give you the rush, but I'm sure Bailey has already informed Uncle Hal that I'm on the premises, so…"

The use of the nickname the associates had adopted the first time it slipped from Bailey's lips made the corners of Chet's mouth twitch. "Right. Better get up there," he said, stepping aside as she pulled her office door closed behind them.

She didn't bother locking it. The notes she'd been accumulating about the firm and the defense of both Trey and Kayla Powers were in the bag she took everywhere and secured in the locked desk. "I'll check in with you later," she said, but she didn't mean it.

Michelle had every intention of avoiding interaction with as many people as possible. She'd spoken to her intermediary with the Bureau the night before and they agreed time was of the essence. The Powers family tragedy would play out as it needed to with or without her. She'd get what she needed from the firm's database and get the heck out of there as soon as possible.

Heads swiveled away, and people tried to pretend they weren't trying to catch any snippet of conversation they could. Michelle lifted a hand in farewell, then headed for the open-riser staircase that led to the second floor of the building. The entire interior of the PP&W offices had been renovated many times since it was first established, but the firm held onto the essence of the sleek mid-century modern design of the building. The staircase was a testament to that aesthetic. The soles of her pumps clicked on the mica-flecked faux marble installed sometime during the Kennedy administration. Now, sleek cables provided support for the staircase, but from old photographs she knew that once upon a time the spindles had mimicked the curved rails used around the reception area.

The second floor was comprised of four large corner offices, each with a seating area for an assistant, and comfortable couches for clients to relax on while they waited.

She turned left and walked toward the office on the southeast corner of the building. Its view was the least desirable of the four, but it still beat the street level parking lot view most of the lower floor's offices provided.

Harold's longtime assistant, Nancy, was seated at her post. When Michelle approached, the older woman nodded and said, "Go on in. He's expecting you."

"Thank you," Michelle said, flashing a quick smile.

She wrapped two knuckles against the door and turned the handle. "You wanted to see me?" she asked as she poked her head through the opening.

Harold Dennis stood from his chair, motioning her forward with one hand while he clutched the receiver of his desk phone in the other. She entered the office and closed the door quietly behind her, staying near the opposite side of the room until he finished his phone call.

"Sorry about that," he said, placing the phone back on the cradle.

"No problem." Michelle started forward.

Harold came out from behind the desk, extending both hands as if to embrace her. Her steps faltered. While they had a cordial working relationship, they certainly weren't on hugging terms. Then again, two of the firm's own had never been murdered before.

Thankfully, Harold stopped short of a full-on hug, instead gripping only her upper arms and giving them a gentle squeeze. "This is just horrible," he said, shaking his head.

"Yes," Michelle agreed. She looked up and noticed that his salt-and-pepper hair had been freshly barbered. Searching her memory, she tried to recall if he looked this perfectly groomed at the gala just a few days before.

"I keep trying to think of something more to say about it, but for the first time in my life, I'm at a complete loss for words," he admitted. He gestured her toward one of the leather upholstered chairs situated in front of his massive desk, and Michelle wordlessly accepted the invitation to sit. To her surprise, Hal dropped down into the other chair rather than resuming his spot behind the desk.

"I can't imagine how it must have been for you and Kayla," he said, his voice dripping with concerned sympathy.

"I won't lie, it was pretty shocking," she confessed. "You know I've seen a lot of things, crime scene photos, that sort of thing." She shuddered. "I've even been on a few scenes, but never one so…" The word *fresh* sprang to mind, but she didn't care to use it. It implied a shorter timeline than would behoove her client. "Active," she said at last.

"No doubt," he said, nodding along. "I can't believe it."

Michelle couldn't help noticing he didn't seem to have even a hint of a suntan. No time, maybe? Had he gotten off the plane, gone directly to accommodations only to hole up with his laptop on what was supposed to be a vacation? He would have had at least a full day to enjoy the beach and all the splashy sunshine of Barbados. Even if he were an ardent sunscreen user, surely he would have picked up some color. A slightly sunburned nose, a pink line along the part in his meticulously styled hair?

"And of course, I saw Kayla this morning," Hal stated, interrupting her line of thought.

"Did you?" She shouldn't have been surprised that he would go directly to Mrs. Powers upon his return, but Michelle couldn't recall telling him where her client had been staying.

"Kayla called me and told me that she would feel more comfortable with you representing her in this matter." His tone was matter-of-fact, but Michelle heard a slight edge in his statement.

"I hope you don't mind. I'm certainly happy to step back if you have an objection, but I think in this case she feels more comfortable talking to a woman." It was a nonsensical argument given the situation, but one that Michelle often found effective when dealing with men. Particularly men of the previous generation. Once she played the woman-to-woman card, they generally backed off pretty quickly.

"Yes." He blinked twice, then nodded. "And it would be very difficult for me, given how close Tyrone and I were."

Michelle did nothing to give away her doubts on that particular topic. "Yes, she mentioned that to me. She doesn't want to put you in a difficult position."

"Well, I know that with you she has the most brilliant counsel PP&W has to offer," he said with an ingratiating smile. "Otherwise, we wouldn't have entrusted you with young Trey's defense."

He closed his eyes and let out a heavy sigh. "It's impossible to believe he's gone as well."

Michelle kept any snarky commentary about Trey Powers's escape from justice to herself. She, more than anyone, was supposed to presume the young man had been innocent until proven guilty.

Then, like magic, Harold sat up straight, his expression clearing of all hints of sadness and becoming all business. "Kayla tells me you've met with the gentleman from the Criminal Investigation Division." It wasn't a question but a statement of fact.

"Yes. His name is Ethan Scott. Lieutenant. Apparently, he's Grace Reed's direct supervisor."

Dennis, having been involved in all the pre-arrest interviews between Special Agent Reed and Trey Powers, was well acquainted with the other agent's name. "Ah, I see."

"As such, I think it's safe to assume he has access to all of the information the CID gathered in the investigation of Trey in the Murray case. I am also of the opinion they'll be looking at the family dynamic with a somewhat jaundiced eye."

Hal inclined his head. "I agree. Go on."

"Against my counsel, Kayla Powers submitted to voluntary testing for gunshot residue, fingerprinting, clothing analysis and has made it clear that she intends to cooperate with the state police investigation in any way she can."

"Going over the top to prove her innocence," Hal commented dryly.

"I believe she *is* innocent. I think she's submitting whatever evidence she can provide to clear her name in hopes that the police will move past the obvious spouse as suspect and move on in their investigation into who may have done this to Tyrone and Trey."

"Yes, time is of the essence," Hal agreed, though his expression remained stony. "Not only do we need to see the killer brought to justice, but we also want to mitigate any blowback this may have against the firm."

Michelle's surprise must have shown on her face before she could mask it.

"Ms. Fraser, Michelle, you know that I'm good friends... was good friends..." He drew a deep breath, then plowed on. "I am good friends," he asserted at last, "with both William and Tyrone Powers. And as their friend I owe it to both of them to be sure that the family firm and the legacy it was intended to be for both Tyrone's and William's sons continues untarnished."

"Of course."

"I don't mean to sound unfeeling, you understand, but I do also have a responsibility to look to the future and to guard our presence."

"Yes. I understand."

"You'll keep me apprised of any further contact between Mrs. Powers and Lieutenant Scott? Or any other member of law enforcement, for that matter?"

Michelle heard the note of finality in the question and placed her hands on the chair arms to rise. "Yes, sir."

"Thank you for taking this on," Hal said as he rose as well. "I know that your expertise will be a great comfort to Kayla in the days to come."

Michelle nodded. "I'll be in touch with the coroner's office about when they might be able to release the bodies so that arrangements can be made."

"Thank you again."

Anxious to escape, Michelle skirted the chair and headed directly for the door. But before she could turn the handle, he called after her. "Of course, in this case we may have to start the process of distributing Ty's responsibilities and assets. I know we have a copy of his will on file. We'll have to make arrangements for a smooth transference of management."

Michelle froze for a moment, then turned back to him, ready to test the waters. "I assume you'll be acting as managing partner in the interim?"

"Me?" He chuckled and shook his head. "Oh, no, that will fall on young Del's shoulders, I'm afraid. But I will be here to provide advice and counsel as needed," he added with a reassuring smile.

"Oh, yes, Del."

She wasn't surprised to hear that William's son would be considered next in line to manage the firm, but she thought Hal Dennis might possibly use this opportunity to make a power move. She'd been wrong. Doing her best to keep her expression neutral, she nodded and twisted the door handle. "Yes, I'll make certain he knows that I'm here to help in any way."

"Thank you, Michelle."

With that, she made her escape. Her pumps clattered on the marble steps as she hurried back to her office, but she didn't bother shifting her weight to her toes to muffle the noise. She had a lot of work to do and not very much time to accomplish it all. This moment of transition could prove to be critical in both of her cases. She needed to act now, while the firm operated in a vacuum of grief and uncertainty. This would be her best chance to catch them in the act.

Back in her office, she unlocked her desk, opened the drawer and extracted her laptop. She logged in, but rather than opening one of the many legal documents that populated the screen as the system awoke, she typed in a command that allowed her to access the network's operating system.

Working in incognito mode so her digital footprints would be covered, she logged into the financial database where the firm's financial transactions were stored. The pattern she'd been following for the past nine months appeared to be un-interrupted. She exhaled in relief. She was able to retrieve the same information using a remote access key, but doing so off-site left a digital footprint larger than a yeti.

While she was here in the office, she was just another at-torney logged into the network. The next few days would be crucial. If the pattern didn't change in the wake of Tyrone Powers's death, it could signal that he—and for that matter, his son—were not involved in the fiscal malfeasance she'd uncovered. After all, dead men could do no bad deeds. That would narrow her list of suspects precipitously. And, if Kay-la's assertion that Hal Dennis was more William's man on the inside checked out, it might give her the firepower she needed to prove her case.

Logging out of the operating system, she slid back into de-fense attorney mode. Opening the file she'd begun on Kayla's behalf, she started typing up notes about her meeting with Lieutenant Scott earlier that morning while they were still fresh in her mind.

Fifteen minutes passed before she was interrupted.

"Knock knock," a male voice called from the open door-way.

Michelle looked up to find Delray Powers standing on her threshold. On instinct, she lowered the laptop screen as she rose from her chair. "Oh, come in, Del," she said to cover her shock at seeing him there. Only then did it occur to her that she should have thought to visit him following her meet-ing with Harold Dennis. Then again, she and Del had never had very much interaction other than some mildly friendly chit-chat. Still, condolences were in order, and she'd blown right past them.

"I'm so sorry," she said sincerely. "I should have come to see you—"

"No worries," he assured her, his voice creaking a little

bit. "I just got here myself. Uncle Hal suggested that I come down here and..." he trailed off with a shrug. "I guess reassure people?"

Michelle's heart went out to the young man. He wasn't even thirty by her best guess, but now the weight of this firm would rest squarely on his shoulders. At least for a few days. A part of her couldn't help wondering how he'd react when Tyrone's new will was revealed.

"Of course." She crossed the room and extended her hand. When he took it, she enclosed his with her other hand. This was about as touchy-feely as she was willing to get with a colleague she barely knew. "I am so sorry about your uncle. And Trey, of course. I know you two were close."

A lie. Trey had been nothing but disdainful toward his cousin, but now was not the time to poke at old wounds.

"Thank you."

The bewildered expression on the young man's face told her the response was prompted by ingrained manners more than genuine gratitude for her condolences. He clearly had no idea what to say beyond those two words, and she had nothing more to offer than the usual platitudes.

"I know you're probably feeling overwhelmed," she said, taking a step toward the door. When he backed up, she fought the urge to smile. He wanted out of this conversation as much as she did. "If there's anything I can do to help..."

"Uncle Hal says you're representing Kayla," he stated flatly.

"He called me the minute he got off the phone with Kayla and asked me to step in and help...handle things. I assured him—and now you as well—that I will do my best to keep the firm's name separate from the family's personal tragedy as much as I possibly can."

"Thank you," he said again.

Michelle saw no reason to draw things out. "I know you

must have so much to do. Thank you for coming in. Your presence will be a comfort to the associates."

As if awoken from a daze, he nodded eagerly. "Yes, I, uh, I was going to go on and, um, make the rounds."

She inclined her head. "Of course. Please let me know if there's anything more I can do to help."

With another somber nod, Del backed away, lifting his hand in an awkward half wave. She counted to ten before walking to the door to be certain he'd moved on. When she spotted a cluster of Trey Powers's sycophants gathered around the cousin her late client had openly mocked, she closed her office door without a qualm.

Then she locked it.

There was work to do and a power struggle on the horizon. Her days at PP&W would be numbered regardless of who was in charge, and she refused to leave without getting what she came for.

Reaching into the depths of her tote bag, she pulled out the burner phone she picked up at the local superstore on her way home from getting Kayla Powers settled at her hotel. The clock was ticking on this investigation, and she needed to update her contact at the Bureau.

Chapter Seven

Ethan dawdled as he and Sheriff Stenton followed Harold Dennis's assistant to the staircase. The first floor of Powers, Powers & Walton was abuzz with purpose. The hubbub was a marked difference from the hushed silence of the executive level where he'd met with Tyrone Powers's family attorney. He scanned the warren of desks in the open-floor-plan office, but his gaze didn't linger on the bullpen for too long. Michelle Fraser was not a cubicle dweller. She had to be behind one of the many closed doors encircling the open office space. As if he conjured her, one of those doors opened and she stepped into the corridor. His steps slowed as she turned in his direction.

Had someone told her he was on-site, or was this mere coincidence?

"Excuse me for one moment, please," he said to the woman leading them down the last of the steps. "I'd like to have a word with Ms. Fraser, if I may."

The sheriff glanced back up the staircase, then at Harold Dennis's assistant, his expression wary and his posture uneasy. "Do you need me to come along?"

Ethan shook his head. "No, thank you. I know you have a lot to do. Don't let me keep you." He offered the older woman an ingratiating smile. "I can see myself out from here. Thank you again for your time and your assistance, Mrs. Ayers."

He and Sheriff Stenton had questioned her along with her boss. Dennis was the only one of the firm's senior lawyers in the office. According to Mr. Dennis, William Powers would be arriving in town later in the afternoon.

"Oh, it's just Nancy," she said, giving his arm an absent-minded pat. "And please let me know if I can be of any further help," she assured him. "It's so hard to believe," she repeated for what had to be the tenth time. She pressed the crumpled tissue she balled in her fist to her nose and glanced away.

Ethan tipped his head down to acknowledge her pain. "I know, and we are so sorry to have to impose on you at such a time. I'm sure you understand. Every minute is a precious commodity in a case such as this."

"Absolutely," she said in her soft drawl. She gestured toward Ms. Fraser, then turned her attention to the sheriff. "I'll see you out, Bud, uh, I mean, Sheriff."

"Much obliged," the older man replied without missing a beat.

Ethan and Stenton exchanged nods and farewell, both knowing they'd be meeting again sooner rather than later. When he started for Michelle Fraser's door, she began walking in his direction, meeting him halfway. For a moment he wondered if there might be a reason she didn't want him to come to her private office. Surely, she knew it would be better if the two of them were to speak in private.

No sooner had the thought formed, she swept an arm to her right in a gesture of invitation. "Lieutenant Scott," she said by way of greeting. "Please come inside."

Ethan turned and saw she was inviting him into a small conference room. A glass wall exposed a table large enough to seat six people comfortably, eight in a crunch. There was a small bar at the room with a built-in mini fridge and a single-serving coffee maker.

He followed her into the room.

"Can I offer you a cup of coffee? Some water?" she asked as if he were a client coming in for a consultation.

"No, thank you. I had a cup upstairs as I was meeting with Mr. Dennis."

She nodded and pulled out a chair and gestured for him to do the same. "I thought perhaps you might come in to see him this morning," she said in a neutral tone. "Things have been fairly strained around here today, as you can imagine."

"I would expect them to be," he said evenly. "Have you spoken to your client again since this morning?"

She gave her head a brief shake and stopped as if uncertain she was giving the correct answer. "Not since I've spoken to you," she confirmed, holding his gaze steady. "Why? Is there something I need to discuss with her?"

"No, not necessarily." Ethan took in the view of the Benton County courthouse afforded by the narrow floor-to-ceiling windows. "The state crime lab sent back a report on the gunpowder residue and clothing. It's preliminary, of course, but there were no surprises."

"By no surprises you mean—" she left the sentence hanging.

He lifted a shoulder in a shrug. "We both know gunshot residue testing is highly inaccurate in most cases. The only thing it proves conclusively is the person submitting to the testing had been in the vicinity of a gunpowder discharge."

"And my client has not been in the vicinity of a gunpowder discharge," she asserted.

"The tests confirmed as much."

"And the bloodstains on her clothing? The testing confirmed the blood was smeared onto her clothes, but not fresh, am I correct?"

It was his turn to nod. "Correct."

"And since we've stipulated the presence of my client's fingerprints in the room where the victims were discovered, it's difficult to prove she had anything to do with their deaths. In the absence of a weapon, that is," she amended, lifting a single eyebrow as if challenging him to produce a weapon.

A part of Ethan wished he could, if only to wipe her smile off her face. But unfortunately, not one shred of the evidence they'd collected thus far pointed to Kayla Powers as the murderer.

"I assume you've asked your client to compile a list of people who may hold grudges against either her late husband or Trey Powers."

"I have." She folded her hands on the table in front of her. "I have to imagine we have a number of the same names on our list. Perhaps we should collaborate, Lieutenant, rather than work around or against each other."

Ethan eyed her cautiously. This wasn't the first time a defense attorney had tried to go with the useful and cooperative ploy to mask their client's sins. But both he and the sheriff agreed they did not believe the widow had anything to do with these grisly deaths. Of course, their personal opinions didn't mean they weren't going to continue to look at her long and hard.

"We would appreciate any and all cooperation you can give," he said neutrally.

"I think you'll find we've been more cooperative than most people in my client's position would have been."

"Most people don't have the privilege of having an attorney on-site almost immediately upon the discovery of a crime," he shot back.

"Ah, but I was only called in to offer emotional support. You forget, my client is an attorney herself."

"Isn't there some saying about the attorney who represents

themselves having a fool for a client?" he asked, certain the jab would hit home with her.

"There absolutely is. But my client didn't retain herself as an attorney, she retained me. But I can assure you even in those harrowing moments before I was able to get to the scene—well, Mrs. Powers is a bright woman who knows how to handle herself."

"So, you'll share your list with me?" he asked, hoping the change in tactic would throw her off-balance enough to catch her off guard.

No such luck.

"I already said we would, Lieutenant,"

"If we're working in a spirit of cooperation, can we drop the formalities? I'm Ethan." He leaned in, locking gazes with her. "May I call you Michelle?"

"Absolutely," she said easily.

He sat there, momentarily transfixed by her piercing blue eyes.

"My client has nothing to hide," she stated boldly.

"I don't believe your client is guilty of these murders. But I do believe she's hiding something. I believe you may be as well." He leaned back as he waited for her to digest both simple statements. He could almost see the cogs turning in her mind. "What is your client not saying?"

"I cannot tell you without her permission, but I can assure you it has nothing to do with the commission of this crime."

Instinct told him she was being truthful, but all assurance aside, they both knew the lack of a better suspect left Kayla Powers at the top of his list.

"Okay, so I'm listening. Tell me—who do you think might possibly have a motive to do this?" he challenged.

She leaned back in her chair and drew a deep breath, letting it go slowly and deliberately. "Honestly? If he weren't one of the victims, I would have said Trey Powers," she confessed in a low tone.

"He was your client," he challenged.

"Yes. In a different case. And I think we both know Agent Reed did an excellent job of piling up enough circumstantial evidence to bring him to court, but I doubt whether the government could have proven their case beyond a reasonable doubt."

"And now we'll never know," he said grimly.

"Correct. We will never know."

"Off the record, and for what it's worth—there is no record anymore since the prime suspect is now deceased—do you think he did it?"

"Killed Mallory Murray?" she asked.

It was a stalling tactic and they both knew it, so he waited her out.

"I believe Ms. Murray met an untimely death on Table Rock Lake while boating with Trey Powers," she said, choosing each word with exacting care. "I believe she was knocked off the boat by a blow to the head. And I believe no attempt to rescue her from the lake was made."

"So you would go with negligent homicide," he said in summation. "Do you think she fell off or was knocked off?"

"I have no idea." She gave her head a slow shake. "Of course I have seen the reports from the crime lab, the coroner and the reconstruction by experts, but I still can't say for certain. I don't think any jury would have been able to convict him of more than negligence."

"Though he purposely drove the boat back to the family slip, swore his coworkers to secrecy and claimed not to have seen the victim the night she disappeared?" he pressed.

"All moot points. He'll never be tried for this case now. And likely, Mallory Murray's brother will never find any satisfaction within the judicial system." She tucked her chin to her chest, then shook her head. "It doesn't make me happy. I've met Matthew Murray. He's a nice man and a good prosecutor. I know he and his sister were not close, but no one deserves to lose a family member under such circumstances."

Ethan placed his hands together and leaned in. "So, we can't point the finger at Trey, and Mrs. Powers is presumably exonerated, at the moment." He added the last with a direct stare. "Who's next on the list?"

He watched as Michelle Fraser chewed the inside of her cheek. It was actually the first time he'd seen her look nervous about anything, and it intrigued him.

At last, she cast a pointed look at the ceiling. Ethan did his best to keep a straight face. "Somebody here at the firm?" he asked cautiously.

"It's possible. I told you the deceased and my client had drawn up revised wills. My client believes some of the members of senior management would not be pleased by his directives."

"And by not pleased, you mean royally ticked off." Ethan rocked back on the chair, hooking his arm over the edge of the seat back. Was she accusing one of two men with seemingly airtight alibis of double homicide? "But how? Mr. Dennis was in Barbados, and Senator Powers on the other side of the world."

"Has anyone checked the flight plans?" she asked. "Do we know for certain Harold Dennis ever landed in Barbados?" Folding her arms in front of her she gripped her elbows as she leaned closer to the table. "I'm told the corporate jet they borrowed had already returned to Arkansas. He claims he flew commercial home, which is why it took him so long to get back. If the jet had waited there, he could have been back within hours of Kayla Powers discovering the bodies. Instead, he had to wait for a flight."

She said the last part with enough derision to make his

ears prick out. Michelle Fraser didn't like Harold Dennis. Oh, it was nothing overt, but something in the way she spoke of him made her irritation more apparent than she would probably like.

"I will make a note to follow up with the client who loaned the senator and Mr. Dennis the jet for the trip," he assured her as he pulled his phone from his pocket and quickly typed a reminder to do so.

"Anyone—"

A rising crescendo of voices bounced off the glass. He and Michelle turned in unison toward the front of the office in time to see an immaculately dressed woman clad all in black enveloped in a stout hug by Nancy Ayers. Even though the woman was locked in Nancy's embrace, Ethan got a decent look at her. Tasteful but expensive jewelry, a rock the size of hail on her hand and artfully streaked hair twisted into an elaborate yet sedate style. The associates hung back, but some of the older members of the PP&W staff pressed forward.

"Oh, here we go," Michelle said under her breath. "Here's one for your list," she said, turning her attention back to him.

"Who is she?"

"Lieutenant, you're about to meet Natalie Powers Cantrell, Tyrone's ex-wife and Trey's mother."

Ethan rose, pivoting to get a better look at the woman surrounded by the staff of the firm. He couldn't help wondering if Kayla Powers would receive the same warm condolences.

As if reading his mind, Michelle gave a soft grunt of displeasure. "All hail the returning almost widow."

His head swiveled away from the crowd to the petite woman now standing beside him. "You don't like her."

"Let's say Trey didn't come by his sense of entitlement all on his own." She gave a wan smile. "Mrs. Cantrell insisted on joining a few of my meetings with Trey as we prepared his defense."

"I hear she got quite a settlement in the divorce," he said, nodding as he recalled all of the information he had on Tyrone's first wife. "And remarried, I assume?"

"Remarried well," Michelle provided. "The Cantrell family is one of Little Rock's oldest and most revered—as I am sure she'll let you know within the first five minutes of conversation," she added.

"Ah. So she took Tyrone's money then married more money."

"Money does tend to attract money. Of course, the Cantrells swim in a much larger society pond. Up here, the Powers family was at the top of the heap. I'm told in Little Rock, there's more jostling for position."

"I can imagine."

"Come, I'll introduce you," she offered, waving a hand at the glass door.

As they approached the diminishing knot of people, she leaned in and spoke softly, "I'm not exactly sure how this will go…"

Before he could respond, two of the associates jumped back as if they might be radioactive, but Nancy took a step closer to the impeccably coiffed woman. Natalie Powers Cantrell was a beautiful woman. She wore the glow of a woman decades younger, likely due in equal parts to wealth and good health. But her countenance was cool and closed off. Despite receiving so many heartfelt embraces, she carried an air of the untouchable. Perhaps it was a defense mechanism, he allowed. After all, the woman was suffering through not one, but two losses. But there was a stillness in the way she held herself that seemed off to Ethan, though he couldn't put a finger on exactly why.

"Mrs. Cantrell," Michelle said as she approached, interrupting his observations. "I am so sorry for your loss. Losses," she said, quickly correcting herself.

Ethan wondered if the slip had been a calculated one on the sharp-eyed attorney's part, but he didn't dare look away from Natalie Powers Cantrell. Something told him he needed to watch this woman closely if he wanted to catch any flicker of emotion.

"Mrs. Cantrell," he said, offering her his hand. "I am Lieutenant Ethan Scott of the Arkansas State Police Criminal Investigation Division. You have my condolences."

"Thank you." The older woman lifted her chin and looked him straight in the eye. Without looking at Michelle, she spoke in a low voice vibrating with anger. "You have some nerve, switching from defending my son to the woman who murdered him."

"Mrs. Cantrell—" Ethan began, but Michelle cut him off.

"I took the cases assigned to me by Harold Dennis," she interjected, her tone calm and soothing. As if this wasn't the first time she'd had to convey this message to the other woman. "If either Trey or Mrs. Powers felt the representation I provided was not adequate, they were free to fire me and choose another attorney."

"*Mrs.* Powers," Natalie Cantrell said, practically spitting the name from her mouth. She flashed a furious look at Michelle, then refocused her attention on him.

Ethan fought the urge to shift his weight as she gave him a once-over likely meant to make him feel like he'd been dressed down. But he stood his ground. "Mrs. Cantrell, I assure you, with the help of the local authorities, we are giving this case our full attention."

"Can you understand why one might wonder why you're here fraternizing with her—" she paused to cast Michelle a withering glare "—attorney. Such as she is."

To her credit, Michelle Fraser didn't flinch. Nor did she take the bait. Instead, she turned to him with a pleasant smile and said, "Thank you for keeping me up to date, Lieutenant. Please let me know if my client or I can further aid the investigation."

She pivoted on her heel and walked back to her office, unperturbed by the stares following her.

The woman beside him cleared her throat indelicately. When he turned back to Natalie Cantrell, he found her watching him with narrowed eyes and snapped back into business mode.

"Our investigation is ongoing," he said stiffly. "As I am sure you are aware, time is of the essence. If you wouldn't mind answering a few questions?" He glanced over at Harold Dennis's assistant, and gave her an appropriately somber nod. "We can all go back up to Mr. Dennis's office, if you would be more comfortable."

Without a response, Natalie Cantrell turned and strode toward the staircase he'd descended, leaving Ethan and Nancy to follow in her wake.

Chapter Eight

"I can't say I'm surprised," Kayla said dryly. "After all, Trey was her pride and joy."

They were seated opposite each other in the hotel suite once again, but this time, the room seemed to be strewn with Kayla Powers's possessions. If she didn't know the police still had the house cordoned off, Michelle might have wondered if she'd gone home to pack more than the overnight bag she'd left with. But then she noticed the price tag attached to the thick cashmere throw draped over the arm of the sofa.

Her client had gone out to shop, and the realization struck Michelle with a bolt of panic. She couldn't blame the woman for indulging in a little retail therapy, but the optics of a new widow out buying up creature comforts would not play well.

"Kayla, have you been shopping?" She added what she hoped came across as a playful little grimace to the end of the question to soften the judgment in her tone.

"I needed to pick up a few things. I didn't pack much and…" She trailed off as they both surveyed the room. "This place is so beige."

The impulse to scoff at such a comment coming from a woman who decorated a room in fifty shades of white was strong, but Michelle refrained. Instead, she nodded understandingly. "I get you. But maybe you should make a list of things you need and I can bring them to you?" Michelle hated the hesitancy she heard in her suggestion and pushed through it to a place of certainty. "Anything at all. I can bring it to you."

"If I'm going to be held prisoner in this room, I may as well call Lieutenant Scott and ask if they have an open cell for me," Kayla said coolly.

Michelle pulled off the kid gloves she'd been using with her client. "That's where you'll end up if people see you out shopping for anything other than a black dress."

"You said Lieutenant Scott confirmed they had no hard evidence."

"And you know as well as I do how quickly the circumstantial can pile up. You know we have to manage the narrative in order to do so."

"It's cold in here and I can't get the temperature to come up," she complained, her voice edging into whine country.

Eager to head her off, Michelle held up a hand. "I totally get it. I run a heater under my desk in the summer because they freeze me out with the A/C in the office, but it's better if you limit how much you're out in public. At least for a short time."

"One of the deputies took me to the house to collect clothes for Ty," she said quietly.

"But, the coroner—" Michelle began.

"I know, but I had to do *something*," Kayla insisted. "Anyhow, I looked in my closet and realized I have black cocktail dresses, but nothing appropriate for funeral services."

"I see." Michelle softened her tone. "So, you went shopping for a dress and figured you'd pick up some other things while you were out. Makes sense."

Kayla bit her lip and looked away. "I don't know if I can go back there again. The house," she clarified in a whisper.

"Understandable."

"And I know this place is temporary, but I needed something to make it feel less…" She ran her hand over the plush throw, tears welling in her eyes. "I know I shouldn't be out shopping. I know better."

Michelle softened. "I get it. You wanted something to feel normal. Comfortable."

"Nothing will ever be normal again," Kayla said flatly.

"A new normal," Michelle suggested.

"I hate that saying," Kayla snapped.

Done coddling her client for the day, Michelle pressed her hands to her knees and rose. "Okay, fine. Well, you do know better. If there's anything you need, text me a list."

Agitated, Kayla twisted the glittering ring Tyrone Powers had placed on her finger. "I'm trapped here."

"No, you are free to come and go as you please. But keeping a low profile is a better strategy for keeping those freedoms in place." She picked up her bag, and hoisted it onto her shoulder. "Harold Dennis said something about needing to read the will sooner rather than later in order to ensure a smooth transition for the firm. I don't think he has any idea about the revisions made."

"If Natalie is here, and William arriving today, they will likely move on to probate the will before the bodies are even released. Ghouls," she added, reaching for the bottle of water she'd placed on the side table.

Michelle sank back down into the chair. "Do you have access to a copy of the new will?"

"I asked the firm we used in Little Rock to send a copy via courier."

"Excellent."

"They'll challenge its validity," she said grimly. "They'll say I drew it up and forged Ty's signature without his knowledge."

"Most likely, but you said there was also a copy in Tyrone's office safe. If they try to reject the document, we can always go to Tyrone's safe. You haven't been in there recently, have you?"

She shook her head. "No. Truthfully, I avoided going to PP&W after Ty and I married. It was too uncomfortable. For everyone," she added.

"Because you went from colleague to the boss's wife."

"Not many people knew about my relationship with Ty before we got married."

"And you didn't have a big wedding?"

She shook her head. "No. Our families. Plus Harold, of course."

"Of course."

"Judge Walton performed the ceremony."

"And it took place at…"

"The lake house." She gave a rueful smile. "Until Trey got into trouble, I thought of it as a place where happy things happened." She glanced down at her ring, then back up again. "I had my first real conversation with Ty there." Her bottom lip quivered, but she held it together. "He had a cookout and I'd won a case for a friend of his, so he invited me. I don't think he believed I'd actually show up, but…"

"You did."

"I did."

"And the rest was history," Michelle concluded.

"People don't believe it, but the rest was a love story." She paused as if considering her point. "Except those are supposed to have a happy ending, aren't they?"

Exhaling loudly, Michelle looked her client straight in the eye. "I believe you, and I promise I'm doing my best to get you the happiest possible outcome under the circumstances."

Kayla slumped in capitulation. "I know you are. I'll stay put unless I clear it with you first."

Michelle stood again, her tote still clutched to her side.

"I'm not your mother or your keeper. I'm your attorney, and as such I advise you to focus on making arrangements for your husband. You can figure out what comes next in terms of where you'll live and what you'll do later. Let's focus on getting through this week. Okay?"

Kayla nodded. "Yes. Okay. Good plan."

Feeling far more reassured than she thought she'd be, Michelle started for the door. "I'll check in with Lieutenant Scott in the morning, if I don't hear from him sooner."

"Okay," came the dull, but compliant, response from behind her.

"And, Kayla," Michelle said, pausing with her hand on the door handle and looking back. "Watch the wine. I have a feeling we're both going to need all our wits to run this gauntlet. We need to make sure everyone is looking for the real killer." She waited until her client turned to meet her gaze. "You can fall apart later, if you need to."

"Oh, I'll need to," Kayla said with a short, harsh laugh. "But I'll wait."

Their gazes met and held. Michelle saw the sharp, savvy attorney who'd captured Tyrone Powers's heart. "I have a feeling you're stronger than you give yourself credit for being," she announced as she opened the hotel room door. "I'll call you later."

She pulled her phone from her bag as she hurried down the corridor to the elevator. She was composing a text to her paralegal at PP&W when she stepped off at the lobby two minutes later.

"Ms. Fraser! Michelle!" someone shouted the second her heel hit the tile floor.

"There she is," another voice called.

The sound of hurried footsteps pulled her attention from the phone's small screen. But as she watched the small knot of reporters approach, phones and recorders in hand, she quickly looked down again.

"Is it true you're representing Kayla Powers?" one called out as she tried to speed walk past them.

"Isn't that a conflict of interest since you were counsel for one of the victims?"

"What does Senator Powers think about your defending Mrs. Powers?"

She kept walking, only peeking out from under her brows to be sure she was on course for the most direct route to the front door.

"Senator Powers arrived this afternoon, but there's been no indication he's paid Mrs. Powers a visit," a persistent young man said, pressing in close as he jostled alongside her, his phone thrust directly under her chin. When she stumbled over one of his feet, she had to grab onto the reporter on the opposite side to keep from going down. Drawing to an abrupt halt, she took advantage of their surprise to straighten her shoulders and collect herself. She waited there on the all-weather mat inside the hotel until she was sure she had the undivided attention of the reporter who'd tripped her and all his colleagues before speaking.

Looking down at the recording devices thrust into her personal space, she waited until a full five seconds had ticked by before opening her mouth.

"There is an active and ongoing investigation of a tragic double homicide taking place. I have no comment beyond that," she said succinctly.

Then, she pushed through their outstretched arms and strode out the door, practically daring members of the media assembled in the nondescript lobby to try to read something into her simple statement.

She got into her car and locked the doors. Thankfully, none

of the reporters had followed her out. They knew who their quarry was. They wanted a shot at the widow, not the lawyer.

She started the car, adjusted the air vents to blow on her heated face, then exhaled long and loud. Taking a moment, she shot a quick text to Kayla warning her about the media camped out in the lobby. Then, sliding low in the driver's seat, she rummaged in her bag until her fingers closed around her second mobile phone. She placed a call to her contact, but when someone knocked on her window, she jabbed so hard at the button to end the call that the phone squirted from her grasp and tumbled to the floorboard.

Looking up, she found Ethan Scott staring down at her, his brow furrowed with concern. Michelle glanced nervously back at the hotel entrance, then lowered her window a crack. Gesturing to the passenger seat of her car, she said, "Quick, get in."

Those thick brows shot straight for his hairline. "Get in?"

"There are reporters in there," she explained in a rush. "Get in and we can talk without someone seeing us."

He complied without argument. While he circled the car, she grabbed her bag from the seat she'd offered to him and shoved it to the floor between her legs. She'd have to find the burner phone later. And pray her contact didn't break protocol in a fit of worry and try to call her back.

"I hope this isn't some elaborate ploy to abduct me," he said as he opened the passenger door.

She rolled her eyes, but caught the dropped phone under the heel of her shoe and subtly pushed it under the seat. "You walk in there and you'll wish you'd been abducted," she replied, hooking a thumb at the entrance to the hotel.

"Why?"

"The jackals have found her," she replied grimly. "Frankly, I'm surprised the press has left her alone until now." Then she turned to face him, eyes narrowing. "You wouldn't have been attempting to speak to my client without me present, would you?"

He pressed a hand to his chest as if she'd wounded him with the suggestion. "Me? No. Wow. Where's the trust? I thought we had a better relationship," he said, his tone light.

She didn't let off the gas. "Then what are you doing here?"

"I came looking for you. I called your office and they said you were out at a client meeting. I used my powerful deductive reasoning skills to figure out which of your clients might need on-site consultation and here we are." He paused, his expression becoming serious. "I'm sorry. I shouldn't be joking about this. How is she holding up?"

Michelle sat back, eying him skeptically as she weighed how much truth she'd include in her answer. "I think shock and reality are battling it out for her."

He nodded. "Understandable."

"She's trying to make arrangements, but she can't do much yet."

Ethan drummed his fingers on his leg. She realized he was uncomfortable. She waited, looking for other tells as the silence stretched taut between them. He'd said he had come there looking for her. He would have to be the one to initiate the conversation.

"Mr. Dennis and Mrs. Cantrell both seem to be under the impression your client did this."

"And what would be her motive?"

He shrugged. "Pick one."

She held his gaze. "They don't know the will has been changed."

"Which will no doubt add fuel to their fire." He propped his elbow on the door and turned to rub his forehead. "Good call beating them to the punch by telling us."

"As my client has told you, she has nothing to hide."

He fixed those probing gray eyes on her again. "She hid the existence of a new will."

"From people who have a vested interest in the law firm, not from the police."

"I understand the reasoning, but either way this new will is not going to play well for your client."

"You let me worry about how to handle my client," she snapped. When he blinked in surprise, she took her tone down a notch. "I'm sorry. I know you didn't have to come here. I am all too aware we could, and probably should, be taking a far more adversarial approach to all this." She gestured to the hotel parking lot. "This isn't the best place for detailed explanations, but let me apologize for snapping at you. I've had a number of people try to tell me how I should be doing my job today, and it's put me on the defensive."

Ethan had the grace to let her off the hook. "Which is understandable for a defense attorney." He glanced over his shoulder at the hotel entrance. "And you are correct. I shouldn't have approached you in the parking lot…or climbed into your car," he added with a rueful smile.

She chuckled, then gave her head a slow shake. "You want me to pull out of here and drop you off on the other side of the hotel." It was a joke, of course, but to her shock, Ethan seemed to be giving the plan real consideration.

"Actually, it probably couldn't hurt."

She stared at him dumbfounded as he twisted in the passenger seat, surveilling the parking area. "Are you serious?"

"How would it go over with your boss if someone told him they'd seen me get out of your car in front of the hotel where Mrs. Powers is currently in residence?"

"Not well," she conceded.

"Take your 'not well' and multiply it by ten and you'd have my captain's reaction."

"Then why did you get in the car?" she asked, curious.

On the surface Ethan Scott came across as straitlaced as any state police investigator, but there was something off about him. He didn't seem to approach his investigation with the linear kind of reasoning one usually found in cops. He seemed more like a guy who liked to find angles. The type to play devil's advocate.

"Because you told me to." When she fixed him with a bland stare, he shrugged. "I was curious."

"About?"

"You," he responded without missing a beat.

"Me?" she asked, instantly wary.

"I can't quite figure out how you fit into the PP&W puzzle," he said, glancing back again. "Probably not a bad idea to drive out of here."

Michelle checked her mirror and saw one of the reporters had come outside to smoke. "Yeah. Okay." She waited until she'd backed out and made a right turn onto the street before pressing again. "What do you mean how I fit in?"

Ethan's head swiveled when she passed the street that would take them to the rear of the hotel. "Is this turning into an abduction?"

"It's a conversation. Your turn to answer my question," she prompted, slowing for a traffic light.

"As you know, I met with Harold Dennis, Delray and William Powers and Natalie Cantrell today."

She nodded. "Yes, and...?"

"They didn't mention you."

She wasn't surprised to hear it, but she forced herself to lift her eyebrows. "Mention me in what context?"

"Any? All?" he replied. "They had a lot to say about Tyrone and Trey, of course, and much of the discussion revolved around Kayla Powers. But they never mentioned you, and that struck me as odd."

Michelle considered her response. Obviously, he was working his way around to something. Leading her somewhere. Almost as if she was a witness. "Why, do you think?"

He gave her a half smile, then nodded to the light to indicate it had turned green. "Since you've abducted me, I'm going to need to be fed. Can we go through a drive-through? I'm starved."

She nodded to a fast-food outlet ahead. "Will this work?"

"Perfect." When she made the turn into the drive-through lane, he pivoted in his seat to look directly at her. "You are an associate of their firm representing the woman they all believe to be capable of committing a double homicide. One which happened to include a man you were representing until the day he died." He hummed softly, then shook his head. "Seems to me your name would have come up at least once. The omission was glaringly obvious."

"Perhaps they don't see my counsel as a threat," she hazarded as they moved forward in line.

"Yet you were good enough for them to hire away from your East Coast firm. Good enough to handle the defense for the heir apparent," he pointed out.

"Honestly, I don't think anyone expected me to get Trey Powers out of his mess unscathed. They were all about distancing the firm from the Murray case and minimizing the impact his trial might have on their reputation. He was removed from the list of junior partners and his photo deleted from the website."

He remained quiet. As the seconds ticked by, a shiver ran up her spine. The car ahead of them moved and she let off the brake enough to roll up to the menu. "What'll it be?"

"Number one combo. Sweet tea to drink," he replied, without even glancing at the board.

She placed his order, then added an unsweetened tea for herself. His mouth kicked up in a half smile as he pulled his wallet out of his hip pocket. "You're definitely not from 'round here."

"Because I don't want a half gallon of corn syrup added to my drink?"

He nodded, his expression sobering. "Unsweet tea, the accent, the absence of excessive use of polite address—"

"Lack of what? I'm polite," she retorted, affronted.

"Gratuitous use of *sir* and *ma'am*," he clarified as he handed her a crisp bill to cover their tab.

"Oh, let me." She started to reach for her bag, but he waved her away.

"I can cover your Yankee tea."

"Yankee tea," she muttered as she rolled up to the window and thrust his money at the young woman hanging halfway out. She settled their drinks into the cup holders, then passed the bag to him. Before pulling away, she beamed a sunny smile at the restaurant employee. "Thank you, ma'am," she said in an exaggerated drawl. "Y'all have a great day now, hear?"

Ethan let out a startled bark of laughter as she pulled away. "Please don't do the drawl—it's horrible," he chortled.

"My accent is dead-on," she insisted.

"Your attempt at an accent is dead wrong."

Michelle couldn't help but smile as she checked to pull into traffic again. "Make sure you get the right drink," she instructed as he unwrapped a straw and jabbed it into a lid.

"Don't worry, I'm not drinking your brown iced water," he assured her.

He pulled the container of fries from the bag and offered it to her. She waved the fries away with a brisk, "No, thanks," though her mouth watered as the scent filled the car. She'd make sweet potato fries with her dinner, she decided there and then. "Okay, well, abduction's over," she said as she took the first right turn and headed back in the direction of the hotel.

Ethan had extracted his cheeseburger from the bag and was unwrapping it with undue care. "Who are you really?"

He asked the question in such a conversational manner she almost answered truthfully, to see if he'd believe her. But she'd impulsiveness trained out of her by the Bureau long ago. "What? Do you think I'd divulge my superhero alter ego without a credible threat against the galaxy?"

She slowed for a stop sign, then signaled to turn onto the street behind Kayla's hotel. Rather than responding to her pathetic attempt at a joke, he took a healthy bite out of his burger. The ticktock of her turn indicator filled the yawning silence. At last, he reached for his cup, stuck the straw in his mouth and swallowed the bite with a deep draw on the straw.

"I think you're a cop. Or you were a cop," he amended, staring down at his lunch with a scowl.

She gaped at him as he stuck a probing finger under the top bun, extracted a pickle slice and dropped it into the bag. Heat filled her chest, raced up her neck and set her ears aflame. "What? Why?" she sputtered, then, recovering a shred of her shaken composure, made the turn with her face averted. "I mean, what would make you think so?"

"I'm a cop," he answered as if the answer should have been obvious. "Like recognizes like."

"I'm an attorney," she said, adding a scoff of laughter. "Did you forget?"

"Nope." He took another bite, then chewed thoughtfully as she approached the rear of the hotel. "But I think you're also a cop. Grace Reed does, too."

He added the last part on as if it were the final nail in his argument.

"I don't know why—"

Before she could deflect even further, he pointed to a service drive leading to the lot where hotel employees parked. "Here is fine."

He closed the wrapper around his burger and dropped it back into the grease-stained bag. He was pulling his fructose-laden tea from the cup holder before she had drawn to a complete stop.

"Listen—"

"No, I get it," he interrupted. "There are things going on here I don't understand. I'm all too aware of what I don't know," he grumbled. But when he looked up, his eyes were sharp and direct. "But whatever it is, you can trust me with it."

"I don't know what makes you think there is anything," she said, waving her hand in airy dismissal of a ridiculous idea.

"My gut is rarely wrong," he announced, his expression grave. "My gut and Grace's?" He shook his head. "No way you've fooled us both."

She opened her mouth to protest, but he turned away, pulling at the door handle. "All I wanted to tell you is I see you," he said as the door swung open. "We see you," he corrected. "And we're all on the same side."

"I don't get where this is coming from," she protested, but it sounded weak to her own ears.

"Like recognizes like," he repeated as he climbed out of the car, leaving the tantalizing scent of fried potatoes in his wake.

"And because you're a cop, you think I might be, or have been one, too?" she asked, tilting over the steering wheel as she bent to peer up at him. She'd thought he might be a little unconventional in his thinking, but now she was wondering if she'd underestimated how far off the typical cop mark he fell.

Ethan shook his head. "Not because I'm a cop."

"Okay," she said, drawing the word out into multiple syllables. Tired of the cat and mouse, she asked the direct question. "You got something more than hunches in your back pocket?"

"You can trust me, Ms. Fraser," he repeated.

"So you've said. Because we're all cops," she added dryly. "Allegedly."

"Right. And because I'm a cop who is also a lawyer." He backed up a step, then turned to make his way up the service drive, fast-food bag and cup clutched in one hand. "Like recognizes like," he called over his shoulder.

Michelle stared after him, the shiver she'd felt earlier turning into a ball of ice in the pit of her stomach as she watched him walk away without looking back.

Had she been made?

Was her cover blown?

He'd met with the senior partners at PP&W. Did they know? Did Ethan Scott know for certain, or was he bluffing to see if he could make her blink first? The same thought ran through her head on a continuous loop as she pulled away from the curb. She swung a wide left turn on the first street leading away from the hotel. Beneath the heel of her shoe, the burner phone she'd dropped earlier vibrated, but did not ring.

Her contact at the Bureau sending a message to check on her welfare no doubt. Two blocks down, she pulled over and fished the phone from under the seat. The screen read only—

What do you want for dinner?

Biting her lip, she inhaled deeply before she typed out the reply chosen to assure her contact she was alive and unharmed.

Pizza is fine.

Once the message was sent, she pressed the hand holding the phone to her hammering heart.

Chapter Nine

Ethan stared at the forensics report filling his computer screen, practically willing it to offer up a suspect, any random suspect, but no such luck. All of the fingerprint and DNA evidence collected at the crime scene could be matched to the victims or the same handful of people—Kayla Powers, Senator William Powers or Harold Dennis.

The senator and Mr. Dennis were away at the time of the murders.

He ran his hand over his mouth, pulling at his cheeks as he closed his eyes. He'd been looking at the report so long, it felt like the information was emblazoned on his eyelids. He scraped his palm over his jaw and added the rasp of the day's growth of beard to the list of things prickling him. At the top of the list stood Michelle Fraser and her cagey, but selectively forthcoming, manner. Even her presence on the list rubbed him the wrong way. He had a double homicide on his hands and zero time to be chasing hunches down rabbit holes.

He opened his eyes and clicked on the email with the grainy camera footage they'd been able to obtain from the security company for the lake house. The file had been edited to only the time frame he'd requested when he'd submitted the request through Senator Powers's local offices, but included both interior and exterior views. He'd asked Grace

Reed to review it while he was conducting interviews. She'd written a detailed report of all the video footage, including time stamps for reference. She'd also summed the whole thing up succinctly:

> "This woman was barely coherent enough to get to the bathroom on her own. There's no way she drove to Bentonville, shot two grown men and left the scene without leaving any additional evidence."

Ethan was only on the third of the time stamps referenced by his best investigator and already inclined to agree. The odds of Kayla Powers rousing herself from the drunken disarray captured on the security footage, driving miles of winding mountain roads to commit the crime and leaving again without anyone seeing her or any record of her coming and going were beyond slim. Not only was the woman stone drunk for most of the weekend, but she also never made it past the lake house's expansive great room with its expansive view, priceless artwork and twenty-four-hour security. Other than the bathroom breaks Grace Reed referenced, Kayla Powers was within camera range nearly the entire weekend.

So if he ruled Mrs. Powers, the senator and Harold Dennis out, he needed to come up with other options. He drew the yellow legal pad he used to take notes closer and tried to open his mind to the alternatives.

At the top of the list was the possibility of a hit carried out by a professional. Though such events were not as prevalent as Hollywood would have people think, they were not unheard of. Money always talked, and dead men told no tales.

He listed Senator Powers, but drew a line through the name. Not only were there several witnesses to his presence on the congressional junket, but everyone also had video footage of a man in an airport half a world away.

Harold Dennis didn't strike Ethan as the type of man who liked mess, but first impressions were not always accurate. The private jet he and the senator had flown on had returned to Arkansas the following day, but getting his hands on flight plans on a private plane heading for an island nation would be a stretch. And, though the lawyer was giving the appearance of full cooperation, there had been holes in his alibi. Holes he didn't seem inclined to sew up tight enough for Ethan's satisfaction.

Dennis was divorced. His children were grown. He lived alone and was traveling alone. According to Ethan's interview notes, no one had met him at the airport. He had planned to stay at a private residence booked through a concierge travel service. The same company had left a car parked at the airport for his use. The car he'd left parked in the same spot from which he'd retrieved it when he boarded a commercial flight back to Arkansas. It seemed like a lot of gyrations for a man like Harold Dennis.

He then listed Kayla Powers. Like it or not, she was still the person with the opportunity and access, even if he personally felt the odds of her committing the crime were extremely low. Then again, she would have the means to hire it out.

He drew an arrow from her name to the professional, then added a question mark. He had a team working the couple's financials. He'd lean into the murder-for-hire angle. He'd also take a closer look at Natalie Cantrell.

She had seemed eager to volunteer the names of people who'd seen her in Little Rock over the course of the weekend, and she would have been a more likely suspect if Trey Powers hadn't been killed as well. He could see a woman like Natalie using some of Tyrone's own money to off her ex and put her son in the driver's seat. But no matter how brittle the ex-wife came across, her adoration of Trey was something universally acknowledged. The only way he could see her being involved was if the set-up had gone tragically wrong.

Ethan flipped through the pages of notes he'd made so far. The only persons he'd interviewed, but whose fingerprints hadn't been found at the scene, were Senator Powers's son, Delray, and Nancy Ayers, the ultraefficient assistant Tyrone and Harold shared.

He sat back and stretched. His neck popped as he rolled it to work the knots out of it. The greasy fast-food burger he'd had earlier sat heavy in his stomach, even hours later. His conversation with Michelle continued to weigh on him as well.

He was the kind of guy who asked direct questions. He didn't like spending time wondering when questions could be asked and answered. Still, he couldn't help wondering about the mysterious Ms. Fraser. He wasn't exactly sure what kept holding him back, which made him feel off kilter.

He snatched up his phone and placed the call.

She answered on the second ring. "Detective Scott," she greeted. "Working overtime?"

"Yeah, well, the clock is ticking," he said brusquely.

His terse tone zapped the teasing note from her voice. "What can I do for you?"

"Who are you, and what are you working on?" he asked without preamble.

There was a long pause. "I thought we'd already covered this, but my name is Michelle Fraser, and I am an attorney. I represent Mrs. Kayla Powers, who found her husband and stepson dead at the marital home after returning from a weekend away."

"You're a cop."

"No, you're the cop," she replied with exaggerated patience. "I am an attorney for a firm called Powers, Powers & Walton. You have a nifty leather wallet with a badge on one side and an identification card saying you work for the Arkansas State Police. Ringing a bell yet?"

"Before you became an attorney," he persisted.

"I went to law school."

"I have your résumé," he said tersely.

"Then why are you asking me questions?"

"There's a two-year gap."

"I traveled. It's not unusual," she answered, shortening her delivery to match his.

"Grace and I think you're a cop."

There was an infinitesimal pause, but he'd swear it was there. "Wow, we've gone straight to conspiracy theories," she drawled. "Do give Special Agent Reed my best."

"What are you working on?" he pushed.

"Essentially the opposite of what you're working on," she shot back.

"No. You're trying to help us solve this, right?" he persisted.

"Because it behooves my client to do so."

"Behooves," he mocked. "Is it an alphabet agency?"

"I have no idea what you mean, but I did master the alphabet well before kindergarten."

"Do you work for an agency known by an acronym?"

"Most people call it PP&W."

He harrumphed and instantly regretted his pique because the break gave her the opening she needed to redirect his line of questioning.

"I will tell you Harold Dennis has called a meeting with all your favorite people for tomorrow morning at ten."

"Called a meeting for what purpose?"

"He said succession planning for the firm, but since both William Powers and Natalie Cantrell are present and accounted for, I would not be surprised if it includes a reading of the will he intends to submit to probate."

"And I assume you and your client plan to be in attendance to submit the more recently, uh…" He stumbled to a stop. *Executed* was the only word coming to mind, but in light of the manner in which the victims had been killed, he hesitated to use it. "The will Mr. and Mrs. Powers had drawn up in Little Rock," he concluded.

"Precisely."

"And you anticipate trouble," he surmised.

"I don't think any of them will be excited by the change, no." She gave a short laugh. "I don't expect a fistfight, but I also didn't expect to be drawn into the middle of a double homicide investigation."

Unable to resist, he tried one last time to get a straight answer out of her, "What did you expect to be working on?"

A beat passed before she replied, "Trey Powers's defense, of course."

"Of course." He sighed and squeezed the back of his neck to release some of the tension gathered at the base of his skull.

"Anyhow, since you called, I thought I'd let you know."

"Did you know your client drank herself blind drunk while she was up at the lake house over the weekend?"

"I told you she'd had some wine."

He gave a derisive snort. "Your definition of *some* and mine differ by about three bottles."

"What's your point?"

He sighed and sat back, his shoulders slumping.

"No point. I can tell you I've clocked your client at about 99.5 percent innocent."

"What's holding you back on the other 0.5 percent?"

"Oh, you know, the usual… Pesky things like motive, opportunity, proximity, access…"

"She wasn't the only one with all of those things."

"But she was the only one who claims to have been alone for the entire weekend."

"Right, but now you have video evidence of where she was and what she was doing."

"Maybe she has a look-alike stashed somewhere, and she set up this whole elaborate scheme to cover her tracks. Isn't that how it usually goes on TV? How do I know she doesn't have an evil twin?"

"You're tired. Call it a day," she suggested, her voice gentle.

"Don't be nice to me now," he ordered gruffly.

"I've been nice to you all along," she chided. "I'm a nice person."

"You're a cop," he murmured. "I feel it in my bones. I read it in every move you make. Who are you, and what are you doing here?"

"I think we've talked enough for one day," she said softly.

"Michelle—"

"Ethan—"

"You can tell me. You can trust me." When she didn't respond or immediately dismiss his offer, hope flamed in the pit of his stomach. "Maybe I can help."

"You can't help me. You have enough on your plate," she reminded him. "Don't worry about me and what I have going on."

"I can't help it. I need to know."

"No, you don't," she replied in a matter-of-fact tone. "It's absolutely none of your business."

"If it's tied to this investigation—"

"I can assure you it's not."

"But there is something," he said, sitting up straight in the chair as they both realized he'd boxed her in. When she didn't speak, he pulled the phone away from his ear to make sure the call was still connected. Three seconds ticked by before she spoke again.

"Keep your eyes on your own paper, Lieutenant Scott."

"Maybe we can help each other," he insisted.

"You can help me by figuring out who actually did this. It was not Kayla Powers."

"Are you looking into something connected to the firm?"

"Good night, Ethan," she said abruptly.

"Michelle, wait—"

But it was too late. She'd ended the call. Without giving himself a chance to think about it, he redialed. This time when she answered, she sounded frustrated and edgy.

"I have nothing more to say, Lieutenant Scott. I can't state it any more clearly. Unless you have reason to call me concerning my client, leave me alone."

"I'm sorry, but I—"

"We are not birds of the feather. We're not team players. We're not partners." She bit off each short sentence, her tone clipped and final. "You have your mission here, and I have mine. And if, by chance, they were to ever intersect, I wouldn't need to come to you for help."

She ended the call again, and this time Ethan did not try to call back. Instead, he lowered his phone and pushed away from the modular workstation wedged into the corner of his hotel room.

Michelle Fraser was doing something more than practicing law. She was more than another attorney on the PP&W roster.

Grace's instincts had not been wrong. Neither were his.

Michelle Fraser was a cop, but the knowledge was no comfort to him. Rather than feeling validated by the knowledge, he felt a tremor of fear pass through him.

Clearly, whatever she was doing, she was operating alone. Undercover? Most likely. Her résumé had been impeccable and airtight. Those two years easily explained away with travel. He knew plenty of lawyers who'd gone off on one last adventure before settling in for the long slog toward partnership. But she was wrong. They were alike in more ways than she'd ever know.

She was a cop masquerading as a lawyer, and he was a lawyer who found his calling in being a cop.

THE FOLLOWING MORNING, fueled by a sausage, egg and cheese croissant and an extralarge coffee from the local doughnut shop, Ethan settled in at his borrowed desk in the Benton County Correctional Complex and began making phone calls. The first he placed was to Grace Reed.

"C.I.D. Agent Reed speaking," she said briskly.

He chuckled at her formal greeting. "Don't you ever check your caller ID?"

"Always."

"You answer every call so formally? Even if it's your sister?" he challenged.

"Especially if it's my sister," she replied without rancor. "Can't have her forgetting which one of us is the badass."

"Absolutely not," he agreed.

"What's up, Chief?"

"I got a half-baked admission out of Michelle Fraser yesterday."

"Admission of what?"

Aware he was treading into unknown territory, and that someone with even a tenuous connection to the Powers family might be listening, he kept his messaging cryptic. "She may be something more than she appears."

"More than a smart, savvy attorney paid handsomely to defend the sleazebag kids of people with far too much money?"

"Exactly."

"Hmm. How half-baked was the admission?"

"On the doughy side. I asked if she liked alphabet soup, and she told me she was too busy with her current mission to enjoy it."

He heard the tap-tap-tap of Grace's pen as she parsed his meaning. "Interesting. A real workaholic, huh?"

"Might have been a habit she picked up after law school. You know, in those two years she was traveling abroad."

"Oh, traveling abroad," Agent Reed repeated with exaggerated nonchalance. "No doubt."

"You know some employers like to be sure their new hires are well traveled and well trained."

"True."

"Maybe see if she started her journey in DC or Virginia?"

He didn't need to explain to Grace that DC might mean connections to the FBI or ATF, but Virginia would likely point to a background with the CIA or DEA.

"I'll poke around and see what I can find." He could hear a pen scratching on paper as she made notes. "Anything else I can do for you?"

"Yeah. Harold Dennis. Can you collect all you have on him and forward it on to me?"

"Mr. Dennis?" Grace was clearly surprised by the request. "Sure, but wasn't he out of the country over the weekend?"

"Yes. Something else I need to follow up on. He and the senator flew out on a private jet owned by a company called DevCo. D-e-v-c-o," he spelled. "They're a client, and they let the senator and Mr. Dennis have the use of their jet. Can you or Thompson reach out to see what we can do to check flight plans, confirm passengers onboard, whatever we can get?"

"Will do," she said in her usual brisk tone.

Ethan was relieved to hear it. Their initial conversations about the case had been stilted, but as they got deeper into it and Grace realized he'd be coming to her as a resource, she seemed to relax. He couldn't blame her. She'd done an incredible job investigating Trey Powers and the circumstances surrounding Mallory Murray's death, then had the rug pulled out from under her. He would have hated handing over his files to any other investigator as well.

Feeling they were on firmer footing, he took a chance on teasing her. "Wanna trade places with me?"

"Um, no. That's a negative," she replied, but he heard the smile creep into her tone. "I'm happy to stay in the bullpen this inning, Chief."

"I'll touch base with you later," he said, then ended the call.

Before he could put the phone down, it rang in his hand. He checked the screen, grimacing when he saw Captain Will Hopkins's name. "Scott here," he answered, instinctively reaching for his pen.

"Ethan," his boss said briskly. "How are things going?"

A dozen disparaging answers sprang to mind, but Ethan squelched the urge to reply with any of them. "Things are slow to develop. Did you receive my progress report?"

"I did, but it didn't contain as much actual progress as I'd hoped," he responded, his tone dry as dust.

"There hasn't been as much as I'd like either, sir."

"Tell me about the widow," Hopkins ordered.

Ethan knew the boss was asking for something more than he'd put in his initial report. The head of Company D was a big believer in instinct, and thankfully, he seemed to trust Ethan's. As succinctly as possible, Ethan gave him the rundown on Kayla Powers's background, the few opinions he'd collected about her time at PP&W, general impressions he'd gathered about the couple's marriage, and then rounded it out by reminding his superior that Mrs. Powers had not only been fully cooperative, but also essentially exonerated by the video footage supplied by the security company. "All in all, sir, she's only a person of interest due to a lack of alternatives."

"Yes, I'm with you," the head of the division responded. "Who else is on your short list?"

Ethan stifled the urge to laugh at the terminology. His list was so short, it came down to only one person without an airtight alibi. Still, he had to give the boss something. "Well, I'm left with Senator Powers's son Delray, Mr. Powers's ex-wife, Natalie Cantrell, and Harold Dennis at the moment." He paused for a breath. "Truthfully, I can't see any of them pulling the trigger, though."

"You think we have a murder-for-hire situation?"

"It's possible," Ethan hedged. "No forced entry, no robbery or even the attempt to make it look like one."

"Plenty of people with money," Captain Hopkins chimed in.

"Yes, but not the bottomless pockets Tyrone Powers had," Ethan said musingly. "They're reading a will this morning."

"So soon? Have the bodies even been released?"

"No, sir, but I gather there are some questions as to the future of the firm, not to mention Tyrone Powers's personal estate—particularly since his only child is dead."

"Right," Will Hopkins said thoughtfully, drawing the word out. "Well, maybe the disposition of his assets will shed some light on who stands to benefit most."

Ethan knew who the winner of that particular lottery would be, but he did not say anything about the will Michelle Fraser had alerted him to. He wanted to wait to see how the morning's proceedings actually played out before passing the possibility of a probate war up his chain of command.

"Yes, sir. Hopefully, this family meeting will be what we need to get to the truth."

"Keep me informed, Scott," the older man ordered.

"I will, sir." With that, he pulled the phone away from his ear and checked to be sure his superior had ended the call before blowing out a gusty breath. Checking the time, he saw it was nearly the appointed hour. A quick glance at his notifications showed a new message from Michelle Fraser had arrived.

Heading in to the office. Any chance you might "coinciden-
tally" swing by for another round of interviews while this
is happening? I've got a feeling this might go sideways.

Without thinking twice, Ethan grabbed his keys and ID
from the desk drawer and rose. The message gave him the
impetus he needed to follow his gut. He was one step out the
door when Sheriff Stenton called out to him.

"I'm on my way out," he answered, hooking a thumb toward the door.

"Walking and talking," the sheriff replied, not breaking
stride. "Did you hear they're reading Tyrone Powers's will
today?"

The sheriff puffed a little as they fell into step, but he
didn't slow.

"I did. How did you?"

The older man huffed a laugh. "Don't let the population
explosion fool you. This is still a small town."

"I guess so."

"Seems a little fast to be readin' a will," Stenton observed.

Ethan nodded. "Sounds to me like a few people have a lot
at stake. I was heading over there to interview some of Trey
Powers's, uh, colleagues," he said, recalling the list of close
associates Grace had included in her background information.

The sheriff nodded. "A good idea. Mind if I ride along?"

Ethan glanced at the man beside him and spotted the same
tension in the sheriff's jaw as he felt coiling in his own belly.
The sheriff's bells were ringing, too. And though he'd long
grown accustomed to working on his own, for once Ethan
was glad he wasn't the only one whose cop radar was pinging.

And the knowledge he, Sheriff Stenton and Michelle Fraser were all on the same page only confirmed his hunch.
Whether she'd admit it or not, the woman had cop blood
pulsing through her veins.

He hit the crash bar on the exit door and held it open for the sheriff. The older man shot him a wary look. "I have a feeling today is going to be a doozy."

Ethan nodded as he jogged two steps to catch up again. "And I have a feeling you're right, Sheriff."

Chapter Ten

Michelle picked Kayla up at the hotel the following morning and delivered her directly to the front door of PP&W. As they walked through the offices, staff and associates greeted her with polite solemnity, but not with an excess of warmth. Michelle cast a sidelong glance at her client as they started up the staircase. Kayla's slender hand trembled on the rail.

"Are you okay?"

Kayla nodded, but her response was a whispered, "Of course not."

"What can I do?"

"Nothing." Her client's smile was tremulous as they proceeded up the staircase at an unrushed pace. "I… I laid off the wine last night."

"You did?"

"And now I'm thinking I could have used the fortification."

"I don't see how a hangover would help."

"It would be a distraction," Kayla said grimly. "But I thought I'd better be clearheaded for this morning."

"Smart thinking. You're going to need all your wits about you in the next few days." Michelle gave a soft chuckle as she caught Kayla's wry glance. "Okay, probably weeks," she amended. "We only need you to hold it together for now. Then you can fall apart. Or, if you want or need help when this is all over, we'll tackle whatever issues you need to deal with when the smoke has cleared."

Her gaze fixed on the top of the stairs, Kayla nodded. "My thinking exactly."

They reached the second floor, and Nancy hurried over from her desk to greet them, her arms outstretched. Michelle couldn't help noticing it was the exact same way she'd greeted Natalie Cantrell the day before. She hung back, feeling the weight of the packet of paperwork sent from Little Rock in her tote bag. To her surprise, Kayla not only accepted the older woman's motherly embrace, but also seemed to melt into Nancy's arms. Unlike Natalie Cantrell, who'd held herself stiff and apart in the scene Michelle had witnessed the day before.

As she watched Kayla extricate herself, it occurred to Michelle she hadn't offered her client much in the way of consolation. Where to draw the line was one of the tricky parts of her job. Her actual job. Life undercover often meant she was immersed in a particular world for years of her life, but the nature of what she did made close relationships impossible.

"Good morning, Nancy," she said as the older woman relinquished her hold on Kayla. "Harold asked us to come in to speak with him about some firm business."

Mrs. Ayers's perfectly coiffed hair bobbed as she gestured to the large conference room that took up much of the wall opposite the staircase. "Oh, yes," she said in a rush, "please come on in. Everybody is waiting," she added, then winced.

"Everybody?" Kayla asked in a tone so innocent she might as well have been cast in the role of cartoon princess.

"I mean—" Nancy started to stammer.

"I'm sure Harold has asked William and Del to be here as well," Michelle said, cutting in smoothly.

"Oh. Of course," Kayla said, sounding mildly befuddled by the notion of the other partners of the firm assembling.

Nancy led the way to the conference room door, then paused with her hand on the nickel-plated handle. "The coffee service is set up, and there's water on the table. I've had some breakfast rolls brought in. If you need anything at all, y'all let me know."

"We will," Michelle responded. "Thank you."

Kayla flashed another shaky smile. "Yes. Thank you, Nancy."

"Of course, sugar. Anything you need. Anything at all, you let me know."

The older woman pushed the door open and announced them. "Mrs. Powers and Ms. Fraser are here," she said briskly.

Michelle stepped into the room behind her client. To her credit, Kayla didn't shrink back at the sight of Natalie Cantrell seated at the long mahogany table. Senator Powers, a younger, more ruthlessly preserved version of his older brother, stood at their entrance. His son and Harold Dennis hastened to follow suit.

"Oh, don't get up on our account," Kayla said, trying to wave them into their seats.

But William Powers was already on the move. With his gaze locked on his sister-in-law, he circled the end of the long table and came to stand in front of Kayla, his arms outstretched for an embrace.

Kayla hesitated only for a moment before stepping into the hug. "I'm so sorry," she whispered, her voice breaking on the sentiment.

"I think I'm supposed to be consoling you," the senator replied in a voice rough with emotion.

Michelle hung back, observing their interaction with the detached interest of a person watching a stage performance. Senator William Powers, urbane and polished to a high sheen despite the horrid circumstances, appeared to be every inch the grieving sibling hoping to console his distraught sister-in-law.

A woman he barely stopped shy of calling a murderess on a cable news network.

Michelle couldn't help wondering what he truly thought of his brother's marriage to someone nearly a quarter century his junior.

She took another step back as both Harold and Del approached Kayla. One by one, they exchanged brief embraces and air kisses. Words were murmured on both sides, but it was hard to gauge the level of sincerity.

Only Natalie Cantrell remained true to form.

Seated at one of the high-backed leather chairs, she pivoted enough to watch the proceedings, but didn't bother to rise from the chair. Nor did she voice any platitudes. Michelle couldn't help but admire the woman for her ability to stay true to herself at a time when most others rushed to put their best foot forward.

The men filed back to their chairs, and Kayla made eye contact with Tyrone's previous wife. To Michelle's surprise, Kayla inclined her head in the direction of the still-seated woman. "My condolences," she said, her voice husky and raw.

Natalie Cantrell looked momentarily taken aback, but was quick to recover. "My condolences to you as well," she replied, but her words came out clipped and insincere.

Michelle directed Kayla to the chairs Hal Dennis had pulled out for them on the opposite side of the table from Tyrone's brother, nephew and ex-wife. It was clear to see the battle lines were drawn.

Harold cleared his throat. "I know this seems distastefully soon to be discussing, but I feel it's in everybody's best interests if we make sure the firm stays on stable footing as we navigate our way through this difficult time," he began.

Michelle sat back in her chair, fighting the urge to smile

as she realized he sounded like a Hollywood depiction of a southern gentleman lawyer.

"There's already been some speculation, and I have to admit, jockeying," he added, his tone dripping with disdain, "among the associates."

"Let me guess. Chet Barrow thinks he should be the next in line for junior partnership, since he was the closest to Trey," Michelle said dryly.

"Chet Barrow is a fine young man from an excellent family," Natalie said, leaping to the ambitious young lawyer's defense.

Harold silenced them both with a stern glare. "I won't name any names because everybody is operating under strain these days. Nor will I tolerate anyone casting aspersions on other people's ambitions. Having ambition is a positive attribute in our line of work, not a detriment. Either way, I prefer to give people the benefit of the doubt. Stressful situations don't always allow individuals to show their best colors."

Michelle shot Kayla a glance but the younger woman sat still. Frozen. Obviously waiting on pins and needles for the real fireworks to start.

"But discussions such as this are why I think it's important to establish at least a temporary hierarchy within the firm. Therefore, for the foreseeable future, I will be acting as managing partner until such time as Delray feels comfortable in taking over the role," he said, nodding deferentially to both the senator and his son.

Michelle zoomed in on Del. The young man's face showed nothing more than solemn acceptance of the new role thrust upon him. Or was it resignation?

"We appreciate your willingness to step into the breach," Senator Powers said, his sonorous voice echoing in the large conference room. "I know Del here—" At this point he clapped a hand onto his son's shoulder. Michelle didn't miss Del's surprised reaction. "Well, he's a fast learner, and I believe he'll pick up the mantle of leadership quickly. We'd hate to place an undue burden on you for any extended period of time, Hal. I know you've had an eye on retiring soon."

"It's no trouble," Harold Dennis said graciously. He opened the leather dossier in front of him and placed his palms flat on the surface of the gleaming table. "As a matter of fact, I'm only following the directives given to me by Tyrone himself when we drew up his last will and testament."

"Excuse me," Michelle interrupted. "Can you tell us when the will you're referencing was executed?"

Harold seemed taken aback by the question. "The date?" He shook his head in bewilderment, then flipped to the last page in the file. "This will was signed and witnessed on six years ago, when Trey joined the firm. Why?"

"Witnessed by?" Michelle prompted.

"Myself, and Nancy Ayers," he answered in a clipped tone. "Again, why do you ask?"

At this point Michelle pulled the heavy manila envelope from her tote bag. The seal was intact, and the address embossed on the upper left-hand corner showed it to be from Anderson & Associates in Little Rock.

"I ask because I believe you are referring to an outdated will," she stated calmly.

"What? How can that be?" Natalie Cantrell demanded, her head swiveling as she switched her glare from Michelle to Harold, then back again.

"Mr. and Mrs. Powers had new documents drawn up after they were married." She offered Natalie Cantrell a small, tight smile. "As one would expect after a divorce, of course."

Across the table William Powers assented with a soft, "Of course," though his jaw clenched tight.

Del looked confused, and Natalie visibly upset.

"I have no knowledge of such a document," Harold Dennis said stiffly. "I've been handling Tyrone's personal business for nearly thirty years, and he's never said a word to me about changing his will after he and Natalie separated."

Michelle slid the sealed envelope across the glossy table. It came to a stop short of Harold Dennis's leather portfolio. "Mr. and Mrs. Powers opted to engage outside counsel for the purposes of revising their instructions. Anderson & Associates in Little Rock."

Harold Dennis looked down at the envelope. The corner of his upper lip twitched up when he read the name of the small, boutique firm, but he caught the sneer before it could take hold. "I've never heard of this firm," he said in a tone so officious it could almost make one believe if he hadn't personally approved the creation of the other firm, it couldn't exist on this earthly plane.

"One of my friends from law school is a partner there," Kayla said, speaking up for the first time since they'd been seated. "Tyrone wanted to use somebody from outside of the PP&W family. He wanted his wishes to be captured by someone wholly without bias or a stake in the firm."

If she had chosen her words to be incendiary, she hit the mark. Almost immediately Harold, William, Natalie and Del started sputtering and spouting their indignation. Michelle let them go for a moment before raising her hand in a call for silence.

"If you'd like, you can go ahead and read the document you prepared six years ago—you are more than welcome to—but I think you'll see these new papers are much more recent." She turned to Kayla. "When did you sign the new documents?"

"April of last year," she answered without hesitation.

"This is highly irregular," Harold protested.

Michelle cocked her head and wrinkled her brow as she studied the older man. "Is it? Seems to me as family counsel you should have suggested he rewrite portions of his will when his first marriage ended."

"Yes, well, yes. He should have come to me to make the changes."

She shook her head. "But he isn't required to. I know a number of attorneys who use counsel from outside their own firms to draw up legal documents. It saves a lot of hassle in the event those documents are later disputed."

"What are the terms of this new will?" Natalie Cantrell demanded.

Kayla opened her mouth to speak, but Michelle quieted her with a gentle hand pressed on her arm. "Mr. Dennis has the documents. Let's let him read them aloud now so there can be no question as to how your late husband wished to proceed from here."

The four people seated across the table stared at her, frozen by shock and displeasure. At last, Harold Dennis snatched up the envelope, stuck his index finger under the flap and ripped it open.

The thick sheaf of papers inside indicated Tyrone had indeed spelled out his wishes in great detail. But given what Kayla had told her about the terms of the will, most of those details would be lost to posterity, since Trey was deceased as well.

"I, Tyrone Delray Powers, Junior…" Dennis began, his eyes scanning far ahead as his words trailed off.

Natalie Cantrell leaned in. "Well? What does it say?"

Harold held up a finger to stay her questioning as his eyes moved faster and faster across the pages. "Trey would have remained primary." He flipped one sheet over, shaking his head as he read onto the second page of the document. "I don't—" he muttered as he continued to read.

"What?" Senator Powers demanded, all overblown civility gone.

"She gets it," Harold said more clearly, shaking his head and reading as quickly as he could. "She gets it all," he said, his voice rising in disbelief.

He flipped another page and Michelle craned her neck to see if he'd reached the signatory statements and the notary's declaration about entity. Ignoring the detailed addendum stacked below those all-important first pages, he flipped back to the beginning.

"Damn it, Harold, what do you mean?" Natalie Cantrell demanded.

Harold finally looked up and met the other woman's gaze. "He left it all to Trey, of course, but then in the event Trey predeceased him or died before the will could be processed through probate, he has left everything to his…wife." He spoke the last word with such raw bitterness Michelle felt Kayla flinch beside her. "Kayla Powers is to take over as managing partner of PP&W effective immediately."

Natalie slapped a hand on the table. "We'll contest it," she said without hesitation.

"On what grounds?" Michelle demanded. "You and Mr. Powers are long divorced. As a matter of fact, you remarried within months of the paperwork being filed. Your son has, unfortunately, died before Tyrone's will could go through probate. You have no material interest here."

"She coerced him," Natalie accused.

"Prove it," Michelle challenged, keeping a quelling hand on her client's arm. "No judge is going to overturn a properly witnessed will favoring a current spouse in favor of an ex. I believe, under the circumstances, it could be argued Mr. Dennis was negligent in not ensuring Mr. Powers amend his will prior to last year." She fixed her gaze on Natalie Cantrell. "Truthfully, I'm not sure why you are here."

"It's none of your business why I am here," Natalie snapped back.

"Actually, it is," Michelle responded coolly.

"Who are you, anyway?" Natalie swiveled toward Harold, then William. "Isn't she an employee of this firm? She should be fired for such..."

When she paused, grasping for a word, Michelle couldn't help providing her own answer. "Truth telling?"

"Insubordination," the other woman spat out.

"Ah, but I would have to fire her, and I don't want to," Kayla said, her tone calm and firm.

"Now, Natalie," Harold said in a patently consoling tone.

"You told me I was named in Ty's will as a beneficiary," she blurted.

"Ty's outdated will," Kayla murmured under her breath.

"Of course, Tyrone had every right to draw up a new will after the divorce was finalized," William said, smoothly inserting himself into the confrontation. "But by 'everything' you can't mean all of Tyrone's assets, both business and personal," he said with such an air of jocular disbelief one was almost tempted to chuckle along with him.

"I mean all of it," Harold said. He flipped the document back to the first page and picked it up and practically tossed it into the senator's lap. "He has left his interest in the firm, the entirety of his personal estate, as well as his share of the family trust and all of its holdings, to Kayla Powers."

"My, my, what an advantageous marriage you've made," Natalie Cantrell drawled.

Kayla shook her head. "It was never supposed to come to me. Trey was the intended heir. You can see by the attached codicils I was only ever supposed to get the spousal portion of any assets accrued since our marriage. There's a will in there for me as well, which stipulates any interest in the firm and family assets were to revert to the family trust if we had no children of our own to inherit."

"Which you do not," Natalie said with a sneer.

"We do not," Kayla confirmed, her voice soft. But she sat up straighter in her chair and looked the older woman straight in the eye. "But you could not honestly believe I was going to allow him to leave you in place as the secondary beneficiary."

Kayla turned to Harold, effectively dismissing her predecessor.

"And you as the family attorney should have advised Tyrone to amend his will long ago. You didn't, and your lack of oversight was one of the reasons he chose to retain outside counsel. Ty wasn't entirely certain you had his best interests at heart."

"Now, you listen here," Harold Dennis said, rising from his seat.

"How do we know this isn't something you drew up yourself?" William asked, the razor-sharp implication of the question slicing through the tension in the room.

Kayla turned to stare at the man who'd embraced her so warmly mere minutes earlier. "Excuse me?"

William Powers looked up, his gaze appraising as he seemed to take his sister-in-law's measure for the first time. "How do we know you didn't fabricate this document?" He shrugged. "It seems convenient you happen to have a copy of a will nobody else has heard of on hand. One my brother didn't even discuss with me, much less with the family attorney," he said, nodding to Hal. "It seems oddly convenient."

Kayla gaped at him. "Convenient?"

"Perhaps a poor word choice," said the senator with a conciliatory gesture, but the sentiment rang insincere. The man was a career politician; words were his bread and butter. "Coincidental?"

"What are you saying?" Michelle asked, raising one eyebrow.

"I'm saying there's no proof this will is not a forgery," he replied, as easily as if stating the time of day.

"There's a copy of it in the safe in Tyrone's office," Kayla said firmly.

"How do we know you didn't place it there after Ty was killed?" Senator Powers shot back.

"Because I haven't been in this building for months. Check your security footage. Check the hotel's footage. Every minute of my life has been accounted for since I came home and found my husband and his son brutally murdered in my home," she retorted, her voice quaking with rage.

"Who all has the combination to the safe?" Michelle asked, though she already knew the answer.

"Tyrone, and I believe Trey," Kayla replied.

"Do you?" Michelle asked.

She shook her head. "No, but he did tell me where he kept a list of his passwords and such hidden."

"Would Mrs. Ayers or any other member of staff have reason to access Tyrone's office safe?" Michelle pressed, looking from one person to the next.

"The safes were for our personal use," William replied stiffly. "We were not supposed to keep firm business in there."

"But obviously, there would be some instances where those lines might be blurred," Michelle asserted. Pushing back from the table, she rose. "Shall we go look for it?" she asked her client.

Kayla nodded mutely and began to rise.

"But it would prove nothing," Natalie said as the others followed suit. "Even I know where Tyrone kept his combinations and passwords written on a piece of yellow legal pad under the pencil divider in his center drawer," she said as they filed out of the conference room.

Michelle saw the corner of Kayla's mouth kick up, and wondered if it was because her husband had indeed been a creature of habit, or if she was about to prove Tyrone's ex-wife wrong. When they reached the door to the corner office, Nancy Ayers rose from her seat, a look of puzzled concern furrowing her brows. Harold Dennis brushed past the assemblage and reached for the door handle.

"Mr. Dennis—" Nancy said as he attempted to open the door and found it locked.

He looked over at the flustered woman, annoyance written all over his face. "Why is this door locked?"

"Because I asked it be locked and kept locked while our investigation is still active," a deep male voice said from one of the adjacent seating areas.

They turned almost as one, and Michelle saw Ethan Scott and Sheriff Stenton pushing out of their seats.

The lieutenant gave her a wry smile as they approached. "The sheriff and I thought it best to secure both offices. I'm sorry. I thought Mrs. Ayers might have mentioned it."

"There wasn't, um…" The woman stammered to a stop when Dennis glared at her. "You didn't tell me you needed to go in there."

"It's okay. You can unlock it now if you would, Nancy," the sheriff said genially. "I don't want to get you in hot water with your boss."

"We need access to Tyrone's wall safe," Harold Dennis said coolly, straightening to his full height as the lieutenant and the sheriff joined them. "On private firm business."

"It's okay," Kayla Powers said quickly. "They can come in with us."

With her head bowed, Nancy Ayers took a ring of keys from her drawer and sidled through the center of the knot to get to the door. The second they had access, the older woman shrank back so as not to be caught in the stampede. Michelle hung back to walk in with Ethan Scott.

"You're missing an interesting morning," she said in a low voice.

"I wish I'd been invited," he murmured back. "Looks like all the cool kids were."

"Okay, where is the combination?" Harold Dennis called, clearly in a hurry to get this exercise over.

Natalie Cantrell walked over to the large antique desk she'd selected to furnish the office nearly twenty years before and slid the center drawer open. But when she lifted the pencil tray, her preternaturally smooth brow puckered slightly. "Oh."

"Yeah, I told him that wasn't the best place to hide things," Kayla said, for the first time in days sounding like the bright, self-assured woman she was. "Try the bottom left drawer. There should be a file folder marked 'C. Klein Briefs.'" Michelle looked over at her sharply, but her client's smile had turned soft and misty. "He thought it was funny."

A moment later, Harold Dennis pulled out a manila folder with a neatly printed label marked exactly as Kayla had said.

"It is funny," Michelle whispered to her client, knowing she would need to bolster her through this last part.

"It's full of blank paper," Harold reported.

"One page is not blank," Kayla assured him.

The older man fanned the pages, then froze when he flicked past one with a neat column of numbers, phrases, nonsense words and other alphanumerical combinations. Without speaking, he withdrew it from the file and let the rest drop to the floor where the papers scattered at his feet. Paper crunched under the soles of his hand-tooled leather shoes as he moved to a painting of a riverbed in the autumn and swung the frame aside.

Michelle and Ethan exchanged a glance at the other lawyer's direct approach, but said nothing. They watched as the older man twirled the old-fashioned dial on the square wall safe.

Then, as the door swung open on well-oiled hinges, they

all took a step forward, crowding to see into the small, dark space.

"Well, I'll be," Harold whispered, almost to himself. Michelle elbowed her way past Natalie Cantrell in time to see his hand close around a sealed envelope made of the same heavy paper stock as the one sent from Little Rock. When he drew it out into the open, she caught sight of the Anderson & Associates logo and return address.

Then a flash of something metal caught the morning light coming through the blinds as it fell to the floor with a heavy thud.

A collective gasp rose from those assembled when they saw the handgun that lay on the floor.

Chapter Eleven

Ethan stepped up behind Michelle and leaned in to catch a glimpse of what the others were staring at, transfixed. A dull grey handgun lay on the thick Aubusson carpet, its barrel pointed directly at the feet of Kayla Powers. Michelle stared at the weapon, incredulity written all over her face. He couldn't blame her. It was as if her client had been chosen in some bizarre game of spin the bottle.

"Well, I'll be," the sheriff said under his breath.

"Nah," Ethan answered softly. "Too obvious."

Michelle lifted her head as if sensing danger, then turned to look at him. Before she could say anything, he asked, "Mrs. Powers, to your knowledge did your husband own a handgun?"

Kayla stared at the gun, her eyes wide. "Yes," she whispered at last. "Ty owned a number of guns. I know he kept a handgun at the house. He has hunting rifles, a crossbow..." She looked up, her brow puckered in confusion. "Do those count?" Then, as if she'd caught herself as soon as the words escape, shook her head. "No. Yes. Of course. He has all the usual array of hunting equipment. As I'm sure you saw when you searched the house and garage."

Sheriff Stenton nodded. "Yes, and we did catalog the gun kept in the wall safe you indicated in the master suite."

"Do you have any idea if this particular gun might have been a part of your husband's collection?" Ethan persisted.

Kayla shrugged. "He could have kept one here for all I know." She lifted her hands palm up in a gesture of futility. "I don't know why he would, but he could have."

Out of the corner of his eye Ethan saw Harold Dennis flex his knees as if to stoop down for a better look at the gun.

"Don't move," Ethan ordered in such a commanding tone the older man immediately froze in place. "I mean, you can stand up but please, everybody back away from the weapon. We don't know if it's secured."

Satisfied the assembled were following directions, Ethan stepped past Michelle and braced a foot on either side of the handgun and stared down at it. "Looks to be a semiautomatic," he called out to the sheriff, who'd worked his way past the others. Squatting down, he cocked his head. "No magazine in it. Do you have any gloves on you?"

The older man unsnapped one of the many compartments on his utility belt and extracted a pair of purple latex gloves. "Got a bag, too," he said as he handed over the gloves. He pulled out a small square of clear plastic and unfolded it to reveal a startlingly large evidence bag.

"Thank you," Ethan said as he took the proffered gloves and bag. "I'll need a pen or something to lift it." He shifted on his haunches, dropping one knee beside the weapon in order to pull on the gloves. Aware of the rapt attention from his audience, he called out, "I'd appreciate it if everyone could move to the other side of the room, but nobody leave."

"Here," Michelle Fraser said as she thrust an ornately engraved metal letter opener in his direction. He looked up at her in surprise. She hooked her thumb toward the desk. "I grabbed it off the desk."

"Thank you." He set the letter opener down next to the gun, pulled on the latex gloves and freed his phone from the case clipped to his belt. He took several photos of the gun in the position in which it had landed. He also captured the array of papers now scattered about the office floor and a surreptitious snap of the group of witnesses gathered now on the other side of the desk.

"I need to make sure it's completely disarmed," he explained as he lifted the gun, gingerly taking care not to handle the stock or the trigger. He knew as well as anyone it was incredibly difficult to lift decent fingerprints off a gun thanks to advances in anti-corrosion technology, but on the slim chance there were latent prints on this one, prints that did not belong to Tyrone Powers, he was going to do his best to preserve them if he could. Holding the weapon with the muzzle pointed down he opened the chamber and found a nine-millimeter bullet in place.

"Sheriff?"

"Yes, sir?" Stenton replied promptly.

"No magazine, but one in the chamber," he reported as he removed the bullet and did a visual check to be sure the barrel was clear. "Weapon has been disarmed."

Placing the gun gently back on the rug, Ethan took more photos of both the gun and the single bullet. When he was satisfied, he slipped the letter opener through the firing mechanism to hold the gun close enough to inspect it. "Appears to be a Glock 17. All serial numbers and markings intact," he relayed to the sheriff, who stood beside him taking notes. He slid the gun and the bullet into the evidence bag. "Mrs. Powers, we will be taking this gun into police custody for ballistics testing."

"Understood, Lieutenant," Kayla replied. "Do whatever you need to do."

"You know what you need to do. Didn't you see?" Natalie Cantrell said, sliding in closer to Senator Powers's side. "It was pointing right at her when it landed."

Ethan fought the urge to roll his eyes. "Coincidence, Mrs. Cantrell," he answered in a no-nonsense tone. Holding the bag closed in his gloved hand, he rose to his full height and turned to Harold Dennis. "Was this what you were looking for in the safe?"

The older man startled at the question. "What? No." He shook his head so hard his perfectly barbered steel gray hair almost moved. "We came to see if there was a copy of the will Mrs. Powers presented to us. She claimed there has been a copy kept in Tyrone's safe."

"I see." Ethan nodded to the envelope the older man clutched in his hand. "Is that what you were looking for?"

Harold Dennis raised his hand as if he had forgotten he'd been holding the thick envelope. Ethan could see the logo for a Little Rock firm stamped on the corner. He wanted to see how this drama was going to play out. "If Mrs. Powers already presented you with a copy, why did you need a second copy?"

"Because they believed I was presenting them with a forgery," Kayla Powers replied tartly.

At last, Michelle seemed to find her voice. "We came in here to prove the copy of the will presented by Mrs. Powers to Senator Powers and the rest of those gathered here today was indeed legitimate. They had their doubts, so we came to see the copy Mr. Powers kept in the safe here as he had told his wife he did."

"There should also be a copy in our safe at home," Kayla informed them, her voice husky. "I had the firm messenger the copy we gave to Mr. Dennis this morning."

Michelle stepped in. "There were some questions as to the validity of the document, but I believe finding its duplicate here today should put those doubts to rest."

"I'm not sure we can say so entirely," Senator Powers said gruffly.

Kayla turned to her brother-in-law. "Bill, do you want to fight me on this? You can if you want, but you know I'm going to win. And you're going to look like the man who's picking on a widow. Are those the optics you want to have coming into an election year?"

"Don't you threaten him," Harold Dennis said, bristling.

"I didn't threaten him," Kayla said with a scoff. She pivoted to face Ethan. "Lieutenant Scott, did you hear me threaten the senator?"

"No, ma'am," he replied, and looking each of the men in the eye, he shook his head slowly. "Her statement was not a threat. She was merely saying a family squabble would not look good in the public eye given the circumstances."

"Particularly when the bodies haven't even been released to have services," Michelle pointed out to them. "Some might consider the purpose of this meeting to be unseemly, given the timing."

"Harold, Bill, please," Kayla began. "I understand this isn't what you believed would happen, but let's be honest, no one ever dreamed we'd be in this position—"

"Oh, someone dreamed," Mrs. Cantrell cut in. "Someone dreamed about exactly this outcome. Someone killed my son in hopes of this happening," she insisted, her voice growing shrill. She whirled on Ethan, her head thrown back and her throat taut with rage. "Aren't you going to do something? Anything?" she demanded. "Arrest her!"

Ethan scowled at the woman, but empathy won out over the impatience her imperious tone stirred. "At this time, we have no evidence—"

"Oh, for the love of all that's holy!" she cried, throwing her hands in the air. "Can you believe this? The woman is found covered in blood, two men dead in her own home. No sign of a break-in. Yet you have no evidence it was her. No evidence at all."

"Now, Mrs. Cantrell," Sheriff Stenton interjected, his tone thick and smooth as warm honey. "You know we can't divulge everything we know."

"You don't know a damn thing, Bud Stenton. My daddy always said you didn't have the sense God gave a goose."

Ethan stared wide-eyed as Natalie Cantrell's soft moonlight and magnolias drawl disappeared, only to be replaced with the slightly twangier hill-country accent more like Stenton's and Nancy Ayers's.

It hadn't occurred to Ethan that at least some of the people in the room had more or less grown up together. Harold Dennis was older than the Powers brothers, but by less than a decade. He, Michelle Fraser and Kayla Powers were the outsiders in this group.

And Kayla and Delray Powers were the two with the most at stake, if what Michelle told him about the wills were to hold true.

It was time for him to deal with the two of them, one-on-one.

While the others squabbled, he turned to Michelle Fraser. "Would you and your client please accompany us to the office?" When she nodded, he turned to Delray and asked, "You, too, if you have the time?"

"No one is under arrest here, am I correct?" Michelle asked, her tone cautious but confident.

Ethan shook his head. "No one is under arrest. I would simply like the opportunity to talk to each of the principal beneficiaries of the two wills." He turned back to Delray. "You're welcome to bring an attorney of your choosing along if it would make you feel more comfortable."

"I'll go with you," Harold Dennis said, breaking away from the other conversation.

But Del shook his head. "No, Uncle Hal, would you stay here, please?" He glanced over at the door as if he expected a better candidate to walk through. When no one appeared, he drew a deep breath and gave the older man a confident nod. "I think it would be better if you were to stay here in the office. Rumors will be flying around, and we need somebody steady at the helm now more than ever. If you would stay here with my dad, I don't mind accompanying the lieutenant to the sheriff's offices." He turned to Michelle. "I won't ask you to sit with me, though, because I don't want there to be any possibility someone would say you had a conflict of interest. Who would you recommend I bring?"

"If Chet Barrow is here, I think he would be a good choice," Michelle told him. "He needs something to focus on, and despite his posturing, he is a bright kid. He'll help you navigate anything you feel uncomfortable talking through."

Del nodded. "Good call."

"I'm assuming you'll want to follow us in your own vehicles?" Ethan asked.

"Yes," Michelle said briskly. When Del nodded, Ethan turned to Sheriff Stenton. "Okay if I leave you here to secure the scene?"

The sheriff was already ushering Senator Powers and Natalie Cantrell to the door. "I'll stay on-site until my deputy is here. Join you shortly."

Ethan nodded. "Sounds like a plan."

He approached Nancy Ayers's desk, his most affable smile in place. "Ma'am, could I prevail upon you to get some sort of a tote bag or duffel bag I might use to carry this out without drawing attention to myself?" He raised the bag containing the handgun for her to see.

"Oh!" She fluttered a hand to her chest, then nodded. "Of course. One moment."

Ethan watched her paw through desk drawers. At last, she pulled a canvas tote bag with a grocery store logo from her bottom drawer. "Will this do?"

Then, before he could reach for it, she nearly snatched it back. "Wait, what am I thinking? You need something better than this to carry something like—"

"Actually, no, it's perfect." He extended a hand for the bag. "If I walk out of here with a machine gun case people might start talking."

The older woman gave a nervous laugh, then thrust the bag into his hand. She pressed her palm to her heart again and shook her head. "Right. I'm sorry. I was being ridiculous," she babbled. "I can't believe what's happening—"

"Totally understandable," he said soothingly. "And you weren't ridiculous, you were helpful and I appreciate it," he said sincerely. "Can I count on you to help the sheriff secure the area?"

Nancy straightened as if he'd pinned a deputy's star to her floral blouse. "Absolutely."

"Thank you, ma'am."

With a small, tight smile, he took the tote bag containing the handgun from Tyrone Powers's safe and marched to the stairs, trusting all the interested parties would soon follow.

"You're saying you didn't know the contents of either last will and testament before Mr. Dennis called the meeting?" Ethan clarified, leaning in to look Del Powers straight in the eye.

"Asked and answered," the annoying young lawyer with the over-styled hair seated next to Del replied in a dismissive tone.

They sat in the closet of an office he'd been using at the county detention center. Since this was an informal interview, all parties agreed it was okay to leave the door open so the room wouldn't feel too closed in.

Thankfully, Del ignored the man who'd introduced himself as Chet Barrow and answered. "No. Not exactly. I mean, I always knew at some point it would be Trey and me running the place, but I never expected to be the managing partner," he said, giving his head a slow shake. "It's like when you're the prince who's born third or fourth in line to the throne, you know?"

Beside him, Barrow gave a snort, but no further comment.

"You mean a line of succession?" Ethan hazarded.

Del nodded. "I figured it would pass to Trey and eventually he would have a couple of kids and they'd jump in line ahead of me." He gave a short, sharp laugh. "My whole life is planned out for me to work my way down the ladder."

A loud guffaw escaped Barrow, but he made no objection to his client's commentary.

"I've never considered myself a particularly ambitious person." Del shrugged. "There wasn't any competition between Trey and me."

"No?"

The younger man gave them a wan smile. "I knew from the time we were kids it was never supposed to be me. Trey was the anointed one, and I was happy to go along for the ride. Nobody expected much of me and as long as I showed up where and when I was told and didn't do anything to make my dad look bad... Overall, it's been a pretty good life."

Ethan considered his statement for a moment, doubt niggling at him. He was so ambitious; it was hard to imagine someone so admittedly...not. "And even now you don't want to be the one with all the power?"

Del gave a short, humorless laugh. "No."

"You sound pretty sure," Ethan said, instantly skeptical about anyone who would be so cavalier about tossing away wealth and the access money can buy. Then again, he hadn't been born with either. Del Powers had, and he would never want for either. Maybe if you always had influence and were confident you always would, you might not feel the need to fight for more. Being a Powers was a given in Del's life, regardless of who was actually running the law firm.

But something about Del told him the young man was not entirely confident about his position in the family.

"Tell me about your relationship with your cousin Trey."

"My relationship with Trey?" the young man asked, clearly surprised to be asked about anything so personal.

"Yeah," Ethan said, trying to keep the conversation on a more casual footing. "You were about the same age. Were y'all close?"

Del eyed him with a lawyer's skepticism and slid a glance at the man beside him before he answered. "We didn't run with the same crowd, but we weren't *not* close."

Ethan fought the urge to laugh at the backbends the guy was willing to do to avoid saying a simple *no*. "When you say he ran with a different crowd, how would you characterize your cousin's friends?"

"His friends?" He paused for a moment as if weighing the harm in answering. "I don't know many of them well."

"Your impressions, then." He flashed a coaxing smile. "I'm not asking for testimony. I only want to get a feel for who he was running with. Were they serious or partiers?"

Del snorted, and Chet rolled his eyes. "I think you know they were partiers," Del said, his ears turning red.

"And you're not?"

The young man sat up, and Ethan knew he'd delivered the perfect strike to the kid's masculine ego. "I can party if I want to. I choose to do other things with my time."

"Right, of course." Ethan lounged back in the chair. "What sort of hobbies do you enjoy?" he asked, but his attention was drawn to some movement outside his office door.

He spotted Kayla Powers and Michelle Fraser taking seats not far away from where he was speaking to Del.

"I hike a lot," Del said with a shrug. "Fish, hunt. The usual."

"Boating?" Ethan prompted, though his attention remained divided.

"Not as into the boating as Trey was," Del answered briefly. "I prefer nonmotorized watercraft. Canoes, kayaking, that sort of thing."

"Oh, yeah. Me, too," Ethan said, forcing his attention back to the young man seated across from him.

"Sure you do," Chet Barrow muttered. "Can we move this along?"

Unfazed by the other attorney's impatience, Ethan kept his focus on Del. "I grew up not far from the Buffalo River. I consider it my happy place."

Del nodded as if he understood the feeling entirely. "I like going up to the lake house, but I'm happier paddling around in the coves than speeding around on the lake."

Ethan thought about the sleek red ski boat Trey Powers had been driving the night Mallory Murray went overboard and ended up drowning in Table Rock Lake.

"Were you with your cousin the night of the boating accident?" he asked.

"Objection," Barrow spouted, sitting up out of his slouch.

"We aren't in court, counselor," Ethan said evenly. "It was a simple question, and Mr. Powers's response would in no way incriminate him."

Del shook his head. "No, I wasn't with them the night of the accident. As a matter of fact, I was out of town the whole weekend."

Ethan nodded. "Oh, right." He flashed a sheepish smile. "I think I remember reading as much in the report."

"I told the detective in charge of the case when she interviewed me."

"Grace Reed," Ethan said with a sage nod. Chet Barrow grunted at the mention of the name, so he couldn't resist pushing a bit. "She's one of our best."

"Is this relevant to the disposal of Tyrone Powers's estate?" Barrow asked officiously.

Ethan didn't answer. Instead, he let the tense silence stretch until Del shifted in his seat.

"I have to agree with Chet. I don't know what any of this has to do with Uncle Ty's will," Del said briskly.

Shrugging, Ethan allowed him to steer the conversation back at last. "I'm more concerned about your uncle's death… Your uncle and your cousin's deaths…" he amended. "Do you know if maybe your cousin was keeping company with anyone who would have wished him ill?"

"We've already covered this ground, Lieutenant," Barrow interjected.

Del opened his hands in a gesture of futility. "I told Agent Reed and Sheriff Stenton everything I know about the people Trey hung around. Granted, there were a lot fewer these days than there were before his arrest, but he still had a pretty substantial circle of friends." He put a little emphasis on the last word, and it made Ethan look up sharply.

"But you don't think they were good and real friendships?" he hazarded.

"Calls for speculation on a topic Mr. Powers knows nothing about," Barrow interrupted.

"I'm asking his opinion, and again, we are not in court," Ethan returned calmly. "But feel free not to answer if it makes you uncomfortable, Mr. Powers," he added, cutting a glance at the young man beside him.

Del glanced at Barrow, then sat up straighter. "I don't think Trey was interested in developing good and real friendships, Lieutenant. My cousin was all about appearances. That's why he was so upset the night of the Powers Family Foundation gala."

"How would you know?" Chet asked, his tone dripping with disdain.

Red flags of color lit Del's face, but the young man didn't back down. "You can go, Chet."

Barrow's jaw dropped. He was clearly not accustomed to being dismissed. "What?"

"Go ahead and head back to the office. I'll be back shortly."

The attorney opened and closed his mouth a couple of times, before curling his lip into a sneer. "You know what? Okay, fine."

Ethan scratched his jaw, than crossed his arms over his chest, trying not to be too obvious in his gloating as the young attorney gathered his things, muttering under his breath the whole time.

Del remained silent, too, a look of stubborn stoicism blanking all emotion from his face as the other man fumed. In his studied nonreactivity, Ethan could see exactly how Del Powers had survived in his cousin's shadow.

When Barrow was gone, Ethan propped his elbows on the desk and leaned in. "Trey was upset the night of the gala. People were talking about him."

Del nodded. "People have been talking about him for months, but I don't think he expected them to have the guts to do it at a function sponsored by our family."

Ethan nodded as if digesting the notion. "It would be galling."

"I'm sure you've heard he said some unkind things to Kayla," Del said with little inflection in his tone.

"Yes. She told us they had exchanged some words at the Foundation gala."

"More like Trey had some things to say, and Kayla stood there and took it," Del said succinctly. "Believe me, most of the time it's easier to let it roll right off you."

"You don't seem to bear the same animosity toward Mrs. Powers as other members of your family do," Ethan observed quietly.

"I didn't realize anybody bore any animosity toward Kayla at all until the past couple of days," Del said with a shrug. "Uncle Ty seemed happy. I thought Dad was okay with everything. He didn't raise any objections when the two of them got married."

"Do you think your uncle would have hesitated if your father had objected?"

Del gave a short laugh. "Lieutenant, my father might be a US Senator, but he was still the second son," he said, fixing Ethan with a pointed stare. "Who do you think held the balance of power in the Powers brothers' relationship?"

"I assume you mean your Uncle Tyrone."

"Bingo."

"Were you surprised Trey turned on Mrs. Powers at the gala?"

"Surprised?" Del shook his head. "No. Not surprised. Trey was feeling backed into a corner, and whenever Trey didn't get his way, he had a tendency to lash out. Kayla happened to be standing nearby, but it could have been any one of us in the line of fire."

"You realize you're the only member of your family who isn't pointing the finger at your uncle's second wife," Ethan said bluntly, hoping to throw the young man off-balance with his candor.

"I'm not *not* pointing a finger either," Del answered blandly. "Aunt Natalie was also no saint. She likes to sweep in here and act like she was the woman usurped, but she was the one who left Uncle Ty. She had a better offer on the table."

"From everything I hear, there is no better offer than to be a member of the Powers family."

"In Northwest Arkansas, maybe," Del answered, letting his derision for how the family was perceived show plainly on his face for a brief moment. "But let's be honest here, Lieutenant, this is a small pond. We may be big fish up here, but anywhere else outside our sphere of influence?" He shook his head, then looked away. "It's a big world out there. Most of us don't stray outside of our little corner of it often. We like being the big fish in the small pond, and stepping out, even if it's someplace as middling as Little Rock, only reminds us of how small we are in the big picture."

"I understand." Convinced he'd fished this particular small pond enough for the time being, Ethan extended a hand. "I appreciate you coming down here to talk to me one-on-one."

Delray Powers shook Ethan's hand, then rose, buttoning the jacket of his bespoke suit in a single practiced movement. "Any information on when we might be able to proceed with arrangements?"

Ethan gave him a weary smile. "I'm afraid that information will go directly to Mrs. Powers, but I'm sure she'll be in contact to make certain everything is done to the family's satisfaction."

"I know it's all circumstantial and you don't have anything hard to go on at this point," Del began, then darted a glance at the door. "But you have to admit it's all pretty coincidental, don't you?"

"Sometimes a coincidence is simply a coincidence," Ethan stated. "My job is to determine whether enough of those circumstances add up to something real and tangible. If they do, and we can find proof to back up our suspicions beyond a reasonable doubt, you can bet we will hold the responsible party accountable for their actions."

Del bobbed his head. "Thank you, Lieutenant. I'd better get back to the office and see what I can do to smooth Uncle Hal's ruffled feathers."

"Your feathers are remarkably unruffled," Ethan said as he stepped around the desk to see the other man out.

"Hard to miss what you've never expected to have, Lieutenant," he said, sending a wan look at Michelle and Kayla as the two men left the small office. "PP&W was never supposed to end up in my hands, and frankly, I'm somewhat relieved it never will."

"Never say never," Michelle Fraser said as she rose from her perch on the edge of a cubicle desk. "If someone has their way it could be passing into your hands faster than you ever imagined." She flashed a half smile. "I saw Chet leave. You doing okay, Del?"

"Yes. There was no reason to keep him here."

"He's shaken," Michelle said, and Ethan couldn't help but admire her kindness. He couldn't say he'd be as patient with the obnoxious young attorney. "He would have done anything for Trey."

"I think we're all trying to get our bearings," Del allowed.

Michelle glanced over at Kayla, then back at Del. "Nice summation, counselor. Now, do me a favor and make sure I still have a job to come back to this afternoon?"

"You still have a job," both Del and Kayla responded without hesitation.

The four of them shared a laugh, then exchanged hugs and handshakes once again. As they watched Del walk toward the exit, Ethan asked, "Sheriff Stenton still keeping the peace?"

"I asked him to hang back for a few minutes to give us a chance to talk to you alone," Michelle answered, her eyes fixed on Del's retreating figure.

"Oh?"

Kayla rose from the desk chair, her expression as curious as his must have been. "You can't be seriously worried about your job," she said, her brows knit.

Michelle sighed heavily, then hooked a hand through an arm of each of them, turning them back to the glorified broom closet Ethan was calling an office. "No. But I do need to talk to you about my job," she said as she urged them forward.

Ethan stepped aside, allowing them to precede him into the room. "Oh?"

"Yes. Close the door if you would, please," Michelle asked as she propelled Kayla to a chair.

Ethan followed her instruction, then waited until they were both settled into their chairs before circling the desk and re-claiming his own seat. He watched as the bright, sharp attorney seated across from him drew a deep, surprisingly shaky breath. "You aren't quitting are you?" he cajoled.

"Quitting? No." She grimaced as she looked over at Kayla. "Or, well, maybe. Sort of."

"What do you mean?" Kayla demanded.

Something coiled in his gut, but it was the good sort of anticipation. "Go on," he prompted.

"I think, in light of this morning's revelations, and the possibility of a power struggle taking place within the walls of Powers, Powers & Walton, the time has come for me to talk to you both about my real job."

Chapter Twelve

"Your real job?"

Michelle could feel Kayla's probing gaze as she asked the question, but she was unable to tear her eyes from Ethan Scott. The corner of his mouth twitched and she had the distinct impression he was smothering a smug smile. She couldn't blame him.

He'd been right about her all along.

While she never intended to blow her own cover, the events of the morning made her realize she was going to have to call an audible in order to be able to wrap up her case the way she wanted to. Kayla Powers was in charge, for now, and she had Kayla on her side. If Tyrone's wills got tangled up in probate, it was entirely possible a judge would appoint a mediator or a third party with no familial connection as managing partner of PP&W until the will situation could be unraveled.

Michelle couldn't wait. She needed to get the information she'd come for and get the heck out of there.

With Kayla at the helm, Michelle figured she could simply ask for the access she'd been trying to gain for the better part of a year. And with Ethan Scott and the Arkansas Criminal Investigation Division backing her up, she might be able to exonerate her client while shutting down what could possibly be one of the larger illegal campaign finance schemes currently operating in the States.

To do all that, she had to admit Ethan Scott and Grace Reed had been right about her all along. She was a cop down to the soles of her feet.

Recruited by the Federal Bureau of Investigation while still in law school, she worked for the Bureau for the better part of those two years she claimed to have been touring Europe. As a forensic accounting expert, she'd become the Bureau's lead investigator working with the Federal Election Commission.

Senator William Powers's seemingly unlimited war chest of campaign funding was a hot topic in DC oversight circles. Not many people expected to find wealth in a state like Arkansas—particularly not in the rural Ozark Mountain region.

Sure, everybody knew the state was home to the world's largest retailer, but they were unaware the area was also home to massive shipping and logistics companies as well as food processing conglomerates. When she first started looking into the possibility of campaign finance violations in Senator Powers's organization, she'd been surprised as well.

It had taken some convincing to get her elitist East Coast superiors to realize there was money flowing through them there hills.

"I am Special Agent Michelle Fraser, on loan from the FBI and working for the Federal Election Commission's investigatory branch," she said in a low, confidential tone. "I have been working undercover at PP&W in an attempt to discover how the firm was circumventing election contribution laws and feeding Senator Powers's campaigns with unreported contributions."

Kayla sucked in a sharp breath, and Michelle turned to look at her client. "I assure you I am a qualified attorney who is fully prepared to mount any defense you might need against any charges brought against you in the death of Tyrone Powers Junior and Tyrone Powers the third," she stated unequivocally.

"You were investigating him?" Kayla asked, sounding wounded by the idea.

Michelle shook her head. "No, ma'am. I don't believe your husband was directly involved in any kind of impropriety. I can't say if Trey might have been. My investigation hasn't allowed me access to the encrypted files we need to see exactly who was moving money between accounts."

Ethan Scott leaned forward, propping his forearms on the edge of the desk and threading his fingers together. "What can we do for you?"

Michelle didn't look away from Kayla. "I need your help. I'm afraid the window of opportunity may be closing on both of us."

"What do you mean?" Kayla asked.

"It's clear somebody is trying to frame you for these murders," she stated bluntly. "I don't know if the killings themselves were committed by a professional or by someone you know, but I will bet dollars to doughnuts the gun that dropped out Tyrone's safe this afternoon is the same weapon used to kill both men."

She chanced a glance in Ethan's direction and found him nodding. "I agree," he said. "I've asked them to expedite the ballistics on it. But the gun won't give us anything more concrete than we already have."

Michelle and Kayla both nodded. As defense attorneys they were well aware getting usable, conclusive evidence from a gun was unlikely. They'd be able to determine if the gun had been fired recently, but not exactly when. They could match bullets to those used to kill Tyrone and Trey, but not whether they came from a particular gun. And everything people saw on television about the ability to lift clear finger-prints from a gun was largely fiction.

"It could give you more circumstantial evidence," Kayla said softly.

"And it is starting to pile up." Michelle reached over and gave the other woman's wrist a reassuring squeeze. "I believe whoever is involved in the campaign finance scheme may be connected to the murders."

"Always follow the money," Ethan Scott said gravely.

"Exactly."

"But how? You've been at PP&W for years," Kayla said, her bewilderment evident in every word. "Wouldn't you have figured it out by now?"

"I never said it was easy. The biggest hurdle has been my inability to work freely within the firm's mainframe system," Michelle assured her. "PP&W has a far more sophisticated data security system than most law firms. Running into their maze of technology was one of the things that tipped me off about the firm's involvement."

"You're some kind of computer genius, too?" Kayla asked, incredulous.

"I did my undergraduate work in information technology. I'd originally planned to go into copyright and patent law with an eye on working in the tech industry."

"But then the Feds came calling," Ethan interjected. "Who wouldn't choose a graded government salary over the pittance those struggling social media moguls are paying?"

Michelle shot him a quelling glance, but kept her focus on Kayla. She could exchange snarky commentary with him later. Right now, she had to convince the new managing partner of PP&W to give her carte blanche.

"I'm close. I'm so close, but I'm restricted as to the time I can spend on the firm server without drawing suspicion."

"I'm still trying to wrap my head around the whole thing,"

Kayla said wonderingly. "I saw your résumé. I told Tyrone you looked like a good candidate. I convinced him female defense attorneys go over better with juries. So much for trusting my feminist instincts."

"Your instincts were right," Michelle said without a trace of rancor. "I am a damn good defense attorney, as my track record has proven. But yes, the résumé you saw was...in-complete."

"Obviously," she said dryly.

"Kayla, I've been working my way up in this firm, gaining the trust of people like Harold Dennis and your husband so I could get this far. We have an opportunity here," she said, maintaining direct eye contact with her client. "With your say-so, I can access any file I may need and get out. If I've narrowed it down correctly, I should be able to have all of the data I need to determine exactly who is involved and to what extent."

"What do you want from me?" Kayla asked.

"I need you to clear the decks for a day, maybe two."

"And by clear the decks you mean...?" Kayla's brows rose.

"I mean close the firm for a couple days. Tell everyone you're taking the rest of the week off out of respect for Ty and Trey, and to allow the family to prepare for the services."

She turned and looked at Ethan Scott. "Any time line on when the bodies might be released?"

"Probably within the next 24 to 48 hours," he responded. "I can put in a call."

"Tyrone wanted to be cremated," Kayla said blankly. "They're not going to allow me to do so this quickly."

Ethan Scott nodded. "We would ask you to transport the bodies to a local funeral home to be held until the coroner's report is complete, but if you wish to conduct a memorial service there's no reason to delay. I would advise against an open casket."

Kayla shuddered. "No," she whispered. "I don't care what Natalie says about Trey's service, but I don't want anyone to see Tyrone the way I saw him."

"Do you agree it would be a good idea to close the firm for a few days?" Michelle pressed.

Kayla's gaze snapped to hers. "Is this actually happening? Am I about to take the helm of a sinking ship?" she asked.

"Not necessarily," Michelle was quick to interject.

"Tyrone took such great pride in the family firm. His father built it. He couldn't wait to hand over the reins to Trey one day," she said, her voice breaking. "I'm glad he's not here to hear all this. I'm glad he won't have his heart broken this way."

Michelle turned back to Ethan. "Do you see where I'm going with this?"

He nodded. "What do you need from me?"

She shook her head. "I need you to continue with the murder investigation as you would normally. I need Kayla to remain the primary suspect as far as the world is concerned, but I also need you to start looking in other directions as well."

"The possibility of a professional hit had crossed my mind," he admitted. "And one ordered as a cover-up of some kind would lend credence to the theory."

A soft whimper escaped Kayla, but Michelle didn't have time to soften their conversation to protect delicate feelings. "A distinct possibility. This is why I need to dig into the money. I need to see if all of it's going to the senator's campaigns, or if it's being shunted through there as a front for something else."

"We're going back in there," Kayla said. "To the office?"

"We have to. You have to establish you are in control of the firm."

"I don't feel like I'm in control of anything at the moment."

She barked a short laugh of disbelief. "Until five minutes ago, I thought you worked for PP&W."

"Technically, I do. And I know I don't have to tell Lieutenant Scott this, but in case you don't understand exactly what happened here, I went off script. If my superior finds out I revealed myself and my mission to the two of you, after two years of deep cover, I would most certainly be out of a job."

Kayla nodded, but her dazed expression left plenty of room for concern.

Michelle shot Ethan a look, wondering if she'd done the right thing by taking them into her confidence. He gave her a brief nod of reassurance.

"What's your plan?" he asked brusquely.

"I'll need access to the offices while everyone else is gone. I'll probably need some sort of cover story for the actual IT department. I'll dummy up a notice of a scheduled maintenance outage on one of the main software systems. One that's network-based, rather than an internet portal."

Ethan pursed his lips. "Sounds reasonable, but don't those usually happen in the overnight hours?" he asked, concern furrowing his brow.

Michelle shrugged. "Wouldn't be the first all-nighter I've pulled and probably won't be the last."

"It won't be safe for you to be in there alone late at night," he stated flatly.

"It's a law firm after hours, not a highway underpass. I'm probably safer there at 2 a.m. than I am at 2 p.m.," she said, casting a sidelong glance at Kayla.

"True," the other woman murmured, though she was clearly lost in thought.

"I'll come down there with you," he insisted.

She shook her head. "You'd be a hindrance. If I'm caught down there alone, I can say I couldn't sleep and was working on a case file. How would I explain your presence?"

"I need to get out of the hotel," Kayla said, giving voice to what had been preoccupying her, oblivious to their conversation.

"We can arrange a cleaning company for the house," Michelle offered, grateful to pivot away from Lieutenant Scott's daydreams of crashing her undercover party at PP&W.

Kayla wagged her head back and forth. "I can't go back there. We'll have to have it done, but I'm not going back there. Ever."

"Perhaps you'd be more comfortable renting a house," Ethan suggested. "Maybe one of those owner vacation rental situations?"

"Maybe," Kayla said, her voice soft and raspy.

"Or you could rent a place on Beaver Lake," Michelle suggested. "Maybe find a little peace and quiet in the middle of all this."

"The lake," Kayla repeated, her head jerking upward as if yanked by a string. "I could go to the lake house."

Michelle started when she realized what her client was truly saying. "You mean you want to go to the Powers family lake house?"

Kayla nodded. "Yes. After all, Ty did leave his interest in it to me. It's partially mine now, by law. Or it will be when we're though probate. If I'm going to bluster my way into running the firm in the interim, I might as well go for the house, too."

"Wouldn't you rather be closer to town? Arrangements will need to be made, and—"

"I can work with Nancy on the service. Trust me, once I say 'go,' there won't be much for me to do other than show up at the time she tells me."

Michelle had no doubt of that. But she had big doubts about Kayla staying at an isolated house nearly an hour away.

"Do you think it's such a great idea to be in a property

you hold jointly with Senator Powers?" Ethan asked, voicing her concerns.

"Particularly after his reactions this morning," Michelle chimed in.

Kayla's eyes sharpened as she looked first to her, then Ethan. "If you think about it there should be no safer place. I can make it known to everyone in the family I intend to use the house for the foreseeable future. Bill will avoid me for fear of being seen in the company of the suspicious widow. But I don't want any of them to be able to say they were unaware I was in residence. Given this morning's confrontation, if something…untoward were to happen to me, they would automatically be on the suspect list. As for my place on the list, the police are well acquainted with the security system and what it's capable of capturing. I can give them full access to monitor my whereabouts via the security company."

Ethan and Michelle exchanged a glance. Still, Michelle felt uneasy about her client staying alone in such an isolated spot. "Would you agree to having a sheriff's deputy on-site with you?"

Kayla let one shoulder rise and fall and then gave a negligent shrug. "Sure. They can have access to the guesthouse."

Ethan pulled out his phone. "Let me talk to Sheriff Stenton. Not only do we need to keep up the appearance you are still our primary suspect—"

"Which technically, I am," Kayla interrupted.

He tilted his head as if conceding the point. "Technically, you are. Either way, I agree, I'd feel better about you being out there if there was an officer nearby."

"Truthfully, that makes three of us," Kayla admitted. "Admitting as much makes me sad. I've never been afraid to be alone at the lake house. It was always a haven for me."

"We don't have any reason to believe you'd be in danger out there," Ethan was quick to reassure her.

Michelle was forced to agree. "I'd say you're in no greater danger there than you would be here. At least there, you'd have some protection from the press. Maybe you should consider hiring a temporary guard for the gate."

Kayla shook her head. "I'll go out there with whoever the sheriff can spare. If the press finds me, then I'll address the security issue. For the time being I'd like to keep this as low-key as possible."

Michelle nodded. "I understand."

She shifted in her seat uncomfortably, feeling oddly torn between her two worlds. Part of her didn't want to care about Kayla Powers or the people she left behind at PP&W, but now she was almost out, she had to admit they did matter to her. And those feelings were damn inconvenient. She'd forgotten how hard it was to be two people at once. Other than the brief moments when she had contact with her relay agent, there were times when she could almost forget she wasn't simply an attorney who specialized in criminal defense, working for PP&W.

But she was more, and those worlds were about to collide.

"I'll make sure we get you settled at the lake house, and you have everything you need." They shared a pointed look. Out of the corner of her eye she saw Ethan sit up and take notice, but she rushed on in hopes of covering. "Groceries, anything like that. If you want me to pick up any additional clothing from the house—"

Kayla shook her head. "I have clothes at the lake house. I should be good for a while."

"Then we need to head back to the offices and make it clear you plan to be the one in charge. I have a feeling the longer we leave Harold Dennis to his machinations, the more entrenched he'll become."

Kayla drew a deep breath, then nodded. "Not sure how

much deeper he can bury himself in PP&W business, but yes, we need to make it clear he can't simply wave me away."

"And you'll make the announcement about the firm to be closing for the rest of the week?"

Kayla nodded and pushed from her chair. "Yes, I'll tell those with active cases to plan on working remotely if they can't get a continuance."

"Then I'll make sure the email concerning a network outage goes straight to the IT manager. When Benny brings it to your attention, sign off on him distributing the information to the rest of the firm."

As they rose, Ethan Scott did as well. "When do you plan on going into the offices to access the files?" he asked, directing the question specifically to her.

"I can't be sure. Aside from scheduling the outage, I need to lay some groundwork first."

"Will you let me know when you're going in?" he asked.

"Probably not," she answered, meeting his gaze squarely. "I can handle myself, Lieutenant Scott."

"I have no doubt you can, Ms. Fraser," he said, emphasizing the use of the title rather than her actual rank. "But all of us need backup at some time."

"If I do, I'll let you know."

"Best answer I can hope for, I guess," he said dryly. Gesturing to the door, he added, "I would appreciate it if both of you ladies would keep me in the loop as far as any information you come across relating to my investigation."

"Of course we will," Michelle assured him.

Kayla hesitated at the door. "I don't want to be one to cast aspersions on other people, but might I suggest you both take a closer look at the client that owns the private plane Bill and Harold used the night of the gala?"

"The client?" Ethan asked, clearly on high alert.

"Yes. It is a relatively new client called DevCo. Harold

brought them on board. They are a real estate development company. I'm not sure exactly what was going on with them, but something about their business made Ty uncomfortable."

"He said as much to you?" Lieutenant Scott persisted.

Kayla nodded. "Not explicitly, but he made comments about them. I know he felt some of their practices might not be entirely aboveboard."

"You say Harold Dennis was the one who brought this client into the firm?" Ethan asked as he walked back to his desk to make a note.

"Correct. They're based out of Oklahoma, I believe, but they have a lot of property in Northwest Arkansas. If I recall correctly, the man who owns it made his money in oil, but his son has a passion for the land business."

"Names?" Ethan asked.

But Kayla only shook her head. "I can't recall them at the moment." She gestured to her head. "It's kind of a mess up there right now, but if they come to me, I'll let you know." Eyes widening, she glanced at Michelle. "Or they'd be in the client files. It shouldn't be too difficult for you to get their information."

"I'll look into it," Michelle promised.

Ethan set his pen down. "I'd appreciate that."

Michelle frowned as she turned back to Kayla. "Do you believe this was one of the things making Tyrone uneasy about Harold Dennis?"

"I think Harold saw himself as a rainmaker for the firm. This was a big-money client. He told Ty they might be his ticket to retirement. Or so Ty told me," she added with a wry smile. "But if you know anything about the Powers family, you know they consider themselves to be the big shot real estate tycoons around these parts." Her lips twisted into a smirk. "It could have been nothing more than Ty feeling his throne was being threatened."

Michelle thought back to the research she had done on the Powers family and how they came to amass the generational wealth they now enjoyed.

The first Tyrone Powers had started from humble beginnings—worked as a logger, then a builder, and put himself through law school before making his way in the world by representing the interests of landowners and other entrepreneurs such as himself. He'd made friends with all the area movers and shakers and considered himself to be one of them. It was a sense of entitlement he'd passed on to both of his sons.

"Thank you. I'll follow that money trail, too," she assured Ethan, then raised a hand in farewell. "I'll keep in touch."

"Please do," he replied, his voice soft but his gaze penetrating.

Michelle escorted her client through the municipal building and back out into the parking area surrounded by razor wire. Once they reached Michelle's car, they strapped in, waiting for the vents to deliver some much-needed cool air. When she glanced over and found her client eyeballing her, Michelle leaned back. "What?"

"There's some kind of connection between you and the lieutenant," Kayla said, unable to keep the amusement from her voice. "At first, I thought it was nothing more than basic pheromones. I mean, the man is not hard on the eyes," she said slyly. "But now I see it's…"

When Kayla didn't go on, Michelle couldn't resist asking. "See what?"

"There's something more there than simple attraction. More like an understanding."

Michelle thought back to Ethan's insistence they were of a like mind. She was still ruminating when Kayla interrupted with her conclusion.

"You are similar, I guess. You both take the same direct

approach with people. There's little fancy footwork with either of you."

Her assessment startled a laugh from Michelle. "Gee, thanks."

"I actually meant it as a compliment," Kayla said with her soft laugh. "You know how it is with most attorneys. We'd rather dance a jig around a topic than give a direct answer."

"But not you," Michelle pointed out. "You couldn't give the police evidence fast enough."

"Because I know my conscience was clear and my life is on the line," Kayla shot back. "Obfuscating would only make me look even more guilty than they were inclined to believe I was already."

"True."

Michelle backed out of the parking space without making further comment on her client's observations. She had enough to worry about in the next forty-eight hours. Everything she'd been working on for the past two years was coming to a head. She couldn't dwell on thoughts of Lieutenant Scott, or whether they might actually be as alike as he believed them to be. She had to find the key evidence she needed to make her case, so she could get back to her real life.

Whatever it would look like after this was done.

Chapter Thirteen

Michelle punched the code Kayla had pulled from Tyrone's files into the alarm system. The vestibule of the PP&W office was lit by nighttime security lights. Beyond them, the hulking shadows of furniture loomed in the yellowish pools of light cast by low wattage bulbs. She kept close to the walls so as not to cast shadows of her own. Not for the first time, she was grateful she'd been assigned an office away from the wall of windows facing out onto the county courthouse. The other attorneys fought for them, but the interior space suited her needs. And on this particular occasion, it saved her from having to commando crawl through the deserted office space.

Like a cat burglar out of a television show, she was dressed in black from head to toe. She even had a black ball cap pulled down over her hair. As she unlocked her office door she wondered if she would keep the funky hair color she'd selected for this particular persona or go back to her own natural shade of dirty blond.

Inside her office, she hit the thumb lock on the knob and hurried to her desk. Rather than taking a seat in the chair she pushed it aside and dropped down to the floor where she extracted her laptop from her bag. She spent the next few seconds booting up, making sure she had power connected and plugging an old-fashioned Ethernet cable into the dongle she attached to her computer. She wanted a hardwired internet connection to ensure a smooth data transfer.

True to her word, Kayla had gone back to the PP&W offices and walked in as if she had been born the boss.

Senator Powers and Natalie Cantrell had already departed, according to Nancy Ayers. The nervous assistant had not seen Del return to the office even though he'd left the sheriff's offices well before they did. No doubt he was touching base with his father off-site.

Only Harold Dennis had remained in the building, his door closed. She nodded to the deputy sitting in a chair outside Tyrone Powers's former office. Nancy informed them a team had come in to process the office for evidence. A single strip of yellow police tape was now stretched across the doorframe. She'd left Kayla in Nancy's capable hands and run down the stairs to her office to start setting up the bogus network outage.

Now, as she keyed her way into the server, Michelle marveled at the skill with which Kayla had handled Harold Dennis. At first, the older man had been contentious. He'd been unwilling to leave his office, claiming he had known Tyrone his entire life, and he'd be damned if he'd leave his protégé's legacy to a woman who married her boss.

Kayla remained calm. She'd explained to Harold that she felt no animosity toward him, nor did she understand where his hostility toward her was coming from. She flattered him, telling the older man she needed his experience and expertise, though Michelle was certain Kayla was more capable than anyone wanted to give her credit for.

Like the entitled man he was, Harold had eaten it up. When Kayla floated the idea of closing the offices for the remainder of the week so they might pay homage to the family and use the time to make the appropriate arrangements for the memorial services, he readily agreed.

Michelle hummed softly to herself in the darkness, shaking her head at the remembrance of the older man's clear duplicity. The offices might be closed to the public and clients, but it was clear Harold Dennis would not be abandoning his post anytime soon. Which is why it was necessary for Michelle to do her work in the dead of night.

Poor, beleaguered Benny Jenkins, the firm's IT guru, usually spent his days beset by attorneys who somehow managed to blow up their laptops. He liked to grumble about how the attorneys could be smart enough to handle extensive schooling yet couldn't remember to update their security software or log out of the VPN when not actively using network resources. In other words, he was more than amenable to the suggestion of any kind of break.

She'd dummied together an email using the logo of one of their main database providers, then sent it from a cloned email address. He'd replied to the account she set up and confirmed the supposed outage was scheduled to take place that night.

To anyone else it would appear the systems were down, but Michelle had an entire team of IT professionals locked in and ready to start going at the security on the server as soon as the appointed hour rolled around. The minute her contact gave her the heads-up they were in, she'd start doing her own digging.

Satisfied she'd set herself up for success, she braced her back against the wall and closed her eyes. All she could do now was wait.

Only six minutes had elapsed since the scheduled outage had begun when her phone buzzed. She snatched it up and pressed it to her ear. "Hello?"

"We're in."

"So quickly?"

A chuckle reverberated in her ear. "We're good at what we do."

Michelle exhaled and then grinned. "And thank goodness. Thank your team," she said as she watched her screen fill with data. "I'm in, too. Have we started the upload to the secure server?"

"The upload is almost complete. I had them run it first."

"Ten-four," Michelle replied.

"Let me know when you're out and we'll restore service."

"Will do," Michelle answered, already distracted by the columns and letters and numbers filling her screen.

She ended the call and watched as the transfer of files to the portable hard drive she brought began. The countdown on the computer itself claimed it would take fifteen minutes. She hated hanging around any longer than absolutely necessary, but Michelle wanted the assurance of having the PP&W records in her pocket. She figured this would be her only shot at the files; therefore she could indulge herself in the belt-and-suspenders approach to securing this data. No one would be coming into the office at 1 a.m. Particularly not when Natalie Cantrell had set her son's memorial service for bright and early the following morning.

Michelle couldn't help wondering if it was because Mrs. Cantrell was anxious to get back to her life in Little Rock as quickly as possible. She didn't seem to be concerned about the inconsequential amount of money Tyrone had stipulated for her in the codicils nobody had bothered to read in Harold Dennis's office. Michelle had been surprised to discover Tyrone had left a part of his estate to the woman who had left him, but Kayla seemed to be utterly unfazed by it.

"A total Ty move," Kayla said with a shrug. "He felt a responsibility for everyone and everything around him. I used to tease him about suffering from oldest child syndrome."

Michelle watched the green progress bar move millimeter

by millimeter across the screen. What would records show? Would she find a piece of the puzzle she'd been missing? Would Tyrone Powers prove himself to be as innocent as his wife believed him to be? Was fear of discovery the reason Tyrone and Trey were killed? Would they be able to single out a payment to a possible killer?

She couldn't help thinking about Harold Dennis and the private jet. She'd found DevCo's corporate information easily enough and passed it along to Ethan Scott, but she hadn't heard anything more. But since Kayla had planted the seed about Harold Dennis, she couldn't stop wondering about him.

For decades he'd been the power behind the throne—first, as a young man working for the senior Tyrone, then as the mentor who helped Tyrone III grow into the role. Did he resent being the power behind the Powers family? Or was he simply what he appeared to be—a man destined to do other people's bidding?

A heavy clunking sound broke the still quiet of the sleeping building. Michelle sat up, drawing her legs in, prepared to spring to her feet, but the noise did not come again. She glanced up at the ceiling, then let her gaze travel over the wall to the door. The building was far from new. It was entirely possible what she'd heard was merely a function of the ancient heating and cooling system.

She didn't call out. If there was someone else on the premises, she didn't want them to know she was there. Instead, she lowered the lid of her laptop to a forty-five degree angle to minimize the glow of the screen, and pushed it deeper into the chair well.

Then, she reached a hand into her bag, drew out her service weapon and waited.

All too aware of the slash of dim light the frosted glass running the length of the office door allowed, she angled herself against the desk facing the wall she'd leaned on moments before.

But no other sound came from the space beyond her locked door.

Her heart rate had returned to normal when she heard a different noise. This one was not the metallic *thunk* of machinery. It was more of a scuffling, scratching sound. On alert again, she gripped her weapon tighter, her eyes fixed on a strip of light on the wall. If anyone came near her door, she'd see a shadow in the diffuse light.

She stared hard at it, barely willing to blink in case she missed a hint of movement.

Behind her, the laptop whirred softly. Shifting her weight, she ducked her head and raised the lid. The download had passed the 50 percent mark. Checking her watch, she saw ten minutes had passed since the transfer started. She eyed her phone, tempted to call in to double-check on the upload to the cloud. This was simply a backup to the backup, she reminded herself. Was it worth the heart palpitations?

But she couldn't bring herself to pull the plug on it when it was so close to being complete. She was simply a little spooked.

Pressing back against the desk, she wondered if she should have asked Ethan Scott to come with her. Not because she needed some big, strong man to help her complete her mission, but more to act as her backup. A human thumb drive, of sorts. After all, a person could never have too much backup, right? And if backup also came with broad shoulders, a handsome face, some dry wit and a nine-millimeter, all the better, right?

She chuckled at her own reasoning. Then she amused herself by imagining tucking the handsome cop into her bag alongside her laptop, phone and firearm, and oh so casually strolling out of the PP&W offices once and for all. But though she had envisioned her exit over and over throughout her assignment, it failed to tickle her as much as she thought it would. She would miss Kayla, with her disarming mix of vulnerability and cut-to-the-chase sensibilities.

And Ethan Scott?

She'd likely never lay eyes on the man again. He was based in Arkansas. Born and bred in the Ozarks, and proud of it. She was a former military kid who'd never called any place home for more than a few years.

Her time in the DC area was the closest she'd come to putting down roots, but while her network spread wide, those roots didn't go deep. She kept in touch with a handful of her former classmates from law school, even fewer from her undergrad. She had a colleague or two she knew well enough to grab a drink with when she'd worked in the office, but no doubt their lives had moved on while hers had gone undercover.

When the idea was first pitched to her it sounded so intriguing. There was nothing she loved more than putting together a puzzle. This assignment seemed to have her name written all over it. Not only was she able to use her investigative and legal skills—she could also tap into her knowledge of technology.

Leaning over, she checked the progress bar and smiled when she saw the download was nearly finished. Another glance at her watch reassured her she would indeed have her backup for backup, and then she'd get out of there.

Out of there.

Ethan had asked her to text him when she left the office. She'd warned him it would be in the middle of the night, but he claimed he didn't care. There was no reason to interrupt his night. Not when she'd be heading straight back to her place to dive into data.

She tilted the screen back and watched as the last few

kilobytes of data were transferred from the network to the flashing drive. The message she'd been waiting for popped up. Her download was complete. She ejected the drive and retracted it, then sent the agreed-upon text to her contact to let her know she was out.

Insomnia sucks. Taking a pill.

But as she went to drop the memory stick into her bag, something stopped her. The urge to check the data one more time gripped her so hard, she felt almost paralyzed. Figuring the sensation was more likely caused by the numb legs and aching back from sitting on the floor, she crawled out from under the desk. But she couldn't resist the urge to check one more time before she left.

Placing her laptop on the desk, she tilted the lid back until the screen lit her face. She plugged in the drive once more, checking the directory of files to be certain she hadn't transferred anything to the laptop itself, then double-clicked on the directory for the external source. A smile curved her lips as she watched thousands of data files populate the menu screen. She was scrolling to the bottom to see where the final count landed, when she heard the scuffling noise again.

She swore softly under her breath, ejected the drive and dropped it down the front of her shirt before closing the lid on her laptop. She saw no movement against the strip of diffused light bouncing off the office wall, but the tight coiling in her gut told her something was happening. Plunging a hand down the front of her T-shirt, she secured the thumb drive in the band of her bra.

She looped the handles of her bag over her left wrist and rose with her service weapon gripped in her right hand. She'd almost convinced herself she was being foolish, made skittish by bumps in the night in an old building, but the urge to flee was growing stronger by the second.

Then she heard the rattle of someone testing her door handle.

She dropped back to the floor and disengaged the safety on her weapon.

The hairs on the back of her neck rose as she shifted into the chair well. Seconds passed, but they seemed like minutes. She was debating whether she'd actually heard what she thought she heard when a muffled sound crack echoed through the building.

Before she could draw breath, the glass beside her door shattered into pieces. Michelle held her position, her gun at the ready.

Someone swore softly, then she heard the soft snick of a lock being turned. The office door swung open, allowing more of the dim light from the outer office to spill in. The sound of labored breathing drew closer and she held her own. Glass crunched beneath heavy footfalls. Unable to ascertain whether her intruder worked alone or had company, she decided the best course of action was to hold her position.

Sipping oxygen through her nose and barely parted lips, she waited, her hand tight around the grip of her weapon. She tensed every muscle in her body, ready to spring into action. But her intruder stopped on the other side of the desk. Then, they grabbed something—presumably her laptop— from the desk, knocking a stack of client files to the floor as they turned to leave.

Footsteps crunched on the glass again, this time moving faster. Thankfully, whoever it was seemed to be fleeing the scene. The temptation to go after the thief was so strong she had to grit her teeth to ward it off. Her computer was clean as a whistle, she'd made sure it was. Michelle bit her lip as she eased herself out of her hiding spot. The person who'd shot out the glass panel was running now, crashing through the maze of cubicles between her office and the front vestibule.

She reached the opening in time to see a tall figure also clad in dark clothing dash through the dimly lit foyer and out the front door.

Rocking back on her heels, she leaned against the door for support, panting as she stared up at the ceiling and pieced together what had happened.

A man. A man had shot his way into an office that was supposed to be empty. A tall, broad-shouldered man, she realized, forcing her brain to home in on pertinent details. Tall. Dark clothes. Broad shoulders. Not fast, she noted absently. Squeezing her eyes shut she tried to zoom in on the details. He moved quickly, but not easily. Not agile, but not clumsy either. Ungainly.

And who knew she'd be here at this particular hour? Did they think she'd leave her laptop behind with the offices closed for the day? She turned her head to look back at where she'd placed the computer. No laptop. Pressing her hand to her heart, Michelle treated herself to a great big gulp of air as she felt the hard ridge of the removable drive tucked into the elastic band between her breasts.

Okay, so someone had taken her laptop, but they'd be sadly disappointed at what they found there. She exhaled slowly and was trying to muster the energy to get up and get out when another thought struck her. Not a professional.

A pro would have made sure the office was empty. A pro would have come in and taken her out before taking her laptop.

Had her assailant been the same person who shot Tyrone and Trey? Or was he simply someone who figured out she'd been snooping around and wanted to see what she'd found. Could the two incidents be nothing more than coincidence? Not likely.

She needed to know how someone knew she would be here in the first place. Grabbing her phone, she pulled up Kayla's contact information. But her pulse roared in her ears as her thumb hovered over the call icons.

Kayla.

Kayla and Ethan were the only people who knew she'd be poking around in the PP&W computer system. But the man she'd seen dashing from the building wasn't Ethan Scott. She knew as much down in her bones.

It had to have been someone sent by Kayla—the woman with an alibi for everything.

Her stomach flipped inside out as everything she'd learned about Tyrone Powers's widow in the past two days filtered through her mind. But this time, she forced herself to strip away the presumption of innocence.

Kayla Powers was conveniently away when her husband and his son were brutally murdered in her home. There were no eyewitnesses to attest to her whereabouts. And what about the public confrontation with one of the victims before she left for the lake house? Alone. Only grainy surveillance footage obtained by a security company paid to monitor the premises could exonerate her. She claimed to have been drunk. She'd volunteered evidence and gave the appearance of full cooperation, even though they all knew the forensics testing she'd submitted to was of little prosecutorial value.

Drawing her hand back from the screen, she gnawed her bottom lip as she mulled the possibility. Acting on instinct, she pulled up Ethan Scott's contact information and placed the call.

"Are you out?" he asked by way of greeting.

"No, not exactly," she said, eying the mess around her warily.

"What do you mean, 'not exactly'?"

"I, uh, well, I was on my way out when someone took a shot at me."

"What do you mean 'took a shot at you'?"

"Well, not really at me. At my door. Or rather at the window beside my office door." She frowned as she looked at the wide-open door. "It doesn't make any sense," she said, thinking out loud. "Were they shooting at me?" She turned back to look at her desk. "Maybe they weren't shooting at me."

"I don't think I like the sound of any of this conjecture," Ethan replied shortly. "You need to get the hell out of there."

"He took my laptop."

The non sequitur must have caught him off guard because whatever was coming next in his lecture died away. "Excuse me?"

"My laptop, of all things," she explained. "I dropped to the floor, but it was on the desk. Whoever shot the glass came in, grabbed the laptop and ran."

"They took the computer and ran?"

Michelle nodded. "Couldn't have been a professional. A pro would never have left without making sure I couldn't identify them," she said, still thinking aloud.

"Identify them? Can you identify them?" he persisted.

"Not specifics," she admitted. "Tall, male, a little awkward in their movement, but I can't explain exactly how. It was shadowy, and I could only catch glimpses of him as he ran past security lights."

"Michelle, you need to get out of there now," he said in a low, urgent tone.

"The only people who knew I was going to be here were you and Kayla," she said, her mind whirring like a top.

"Get out of there," he ordered.

"Right." She nodded as the words finally broke through the haze. "Going now."

"Are you sure Kayla and I were the only ones who knew you were heading in there tonight?"

"As far as I know, yes," she informed him. Slipping out of her office, she headed for the door in the same manner in which she entered: sticking close to the walls, avoiding the lights and keeping her head down.

"No contacts at your agency?" he persisted.

"Well, yeah, they knew," she admitted gruffly. "I had an IT team working through my primary contact."

"Any chance your inside person might be the leak?"

"How do I know you aren't?" she shot back.

"You don't, but I'm not."

"Which leaves Kayla," she said.

"Possibly, but Kayla doesn't strike me as anybody's fool. If she were to tip somebody off about your presence in the office tonight or what you might be doing there, it would only reinforce the appearance of her guilt."

"I thought the same thing."

"We've got such a preponderance of circumstantial evidence pointing in her direction right now I sincerely doubt she would be the one to pile on anymore."

"So, you're saying it's not you and it's not Kayla—therefore it must be my contact at the agency."

"I'm saying it's a possibility," Ethan replied. "Are you out yet?"

"Not quite," she answered.

"I'm getting in my car. Isn't there an all-night diner two blocks up from the courthouse?"

"Yes."

"Go there, but stay in your car until I get there. Don't go inside. I'll come to your car," he instructed. "If you get the feeling anyone is following you, keep driving in random patterns, circle blocks, whatever you need to do to get them off your case."

"Ethan?" Michelle didn't like the tremor she heard in her own voice, but at the moment she couldn't even pretend to feel steady.

"Yes?"

"I know how to lose a tail."

"I have no doubt," he assured her. "I'm only saying these things to make myself feel better."

"I figured." She hesitated for a moment, then plunged ahead. "Ethan?"

"I'm here."

"I've never been shot at before," she confessed.

"No?"

"Nope. Have you?"

"A few times," he answered, his voice husky.

"I don't like it," she stated without hesitation.

His chuckle warmed her from the inside out. "I didn't care for it much myself."

She heard the sound of a car ignition. "Are you on your way?"

"I am. Are you out of the building?"

"I am," she replied.

"I'll be at the diner in less than ten minutes. Hang tight."

Keeping her head down she hurried to her vehicle parked two blocks south of the law offices. She waited until her hand touched the handle to unlock her car. The second she was inside she tripped the lock again.

"I'm in my car," she reported.

She heard a whoosh of breath as he exhaled loudly on the other end. "Good deal. Now talk me through what happened again."

Sinking back into the driver seat, Michelle pulled the car out of the spot and headed toward the diner. "I wanted to finish downloading the files to an external drive," she began.

"An external drive? I thought you were uploading to a cloud," he asked.

"I did. I wanted a backup for the backup."

On the other end, Ethan chuckled. "Why am I not surprised?" he asked wryly. "Okay, you got your backup for the backup. What happened next?"

Michelle gripped the wheel tighter as she accelerated through the next intersection. "I heard something. Sounded like someone was trying to open my office door, so I ducked under the desk. The next thing I knew, the glass was shattering. I had my service weapon in my hand, but I was hidden from view. I figured it was best to stay put."

"Unless you were planning to shoot your way out of there, I'd say so."

Michelle let off the gas as the lights of the diner came into view. "I had no plan, but you can bet I would have, if I needed to."

"I have no doubt."

He said the words with a sort of grudging admiration. They warmed her as she pulled into one of the empty spaces in front of the brightly lit building. "I'm here."

"ETA two minutes," he answered.

"Boy, that was a fast ten," she said with a huff of a laugh.

"No traffic, shots fired, use whatever excuse you want," he informed her. "Almost there."

Chapter Fourteen

Michelle stared over the rim of her coffee mug as he soused the short stack of pancakes he'd ordered with a steady stream of maple syrup. He met her gaze and tipped the syrup dispenser back to slow the flow. "What?"

She shook her head, her gaze dropping to his plate. "You're going to eat all those? In the middle of the night?"

"I think better on a full stomach," he said, brushing her concern aside with a wave of the sticky dispenser before he planted it on the table once more. "It's not like that infusion of caffeine is going to work wonders with your REM sleep."

"True." She set the heavy ceramic mug down with a thud and reached for the sweating glass of ice water the lone waitress had provided when they sat down.

"You're thinking Kayla, huh?" Rather than waiting for her answer, he set to work cutting the stack into bite-size pieces with the side of his fork. "Why would she?" he asked as he speared his first forkful.

"I keep coming back to who knew, and it was you and Kayla," she repeated. "Was it you?"

"Nope," he answered as he chewed. He paused long enough to gulp down the mouthful, then took a sip of his own water. "But riddle me this—if it was Kayla, why would she, presumedly, hire some man to break into a building she owns in the middle of the night only to steal something no one expected to be there?"

"She knew I would have my laptop with me," she argued.

"Right, but you would be there, too. If the person was there to get you, why didn't they look for you? Why would he take the laptop and bolt?"

"Well, it doesn't make any more sense for my contact at the agency to have arranged it. They already had all the files backed up to the secure off-site server."

"So maybe we're looking at this the wrong way. Maybe it wasn't you or your laptop they were looking for," he said, stabbing up another fork load of pancakes. "Maybe it was the information itself."

"Presuming someone knew I'd be there to access the data."

He chewed as he nodded. "Let me ask you this," he began as he set about attacking his plate again. "If not for the timing and our assumedly closed circle of knowledge, would you suspect Kayla?"

"No."

He looked up and found Michelle appeared to be as surprised by her ready answer as he was. "Gut check complete."

"Yeah, I guess so," she said in a bewildered murmur.

"What do you think she'd say if we showed up on her doorstep in the middle of the night demanding answers?" he asked.

She picked up her discarded coffee cup and cradled it between her palms as if needing to absorb its warmth. "I don't know." She worried her bottom lip for a moment. "Why? Do you think we should?"

He shrugged, then shoveled another forkful into his mouth. The wheels were turning in her head and he knew his impromptu breakfast might be drawing to an end. She was not going to rest until she had the answers she wanted, and he had the sense she might be ready to roll at any moment.

"You saw the footage from the last time she stayed at the lake house," she said quietly.

He looked up, raising a questioning eyebrow as he chewed. "You think she might be drunk?"

"I have a feeling she wanted out of the hotel for a reason. A little more freedom, a lot more privacy."

Swallowing hard, he reached for his water again. "I wondered if that weekend was a one-off."

"I can't say for certain, but I get the feeling it's getting to be more and more of a problem," Michelle said bluntly. "Pure speculation on my part."

Ethan looked down at his half-demolished plate of pancakes, bid them a silent farewell, then dropped his fork onto the syrup-soaked plate. "Okay, enough speculation," he announced, wiping his sticky hand on a flimsy paper napkin before reaching for his phone.

"What are you doing?" she asked as he thumbed through the screens. "It's nearly 2:30 a.m."

"No time like the present," he insisted, then pressed the phone to his ear. "Yes, hi. It's Ethan Scott," he said when the person on the other end answered. "I'm here with Michelle. There have been some developments." He paused, then looked up, meeting her wide-eyed glare directly as he answered the next question. "No, she's fine." He shifted onto his hip and pulled his wallet from the back pocket of his jeans. Extracting a crisp twenty, he waved it at their waitress, who was busy holding up the other end of the counter. "I'm calling to let you know we're heading out there. Can you send the address?" He listened for a moment, then nodded. "Great. Perfect. See you shortly."

He ended the call, thanked the woman who'd served them and slid from the booth.

"You called her," Michelle asked, scrambling to gather her things and slide from the booth.

"Yep. She sounded fine. Wide awake, too. She said she'd drop a GPS pin in a text." He gestured for her to go ahead of him. "I think we should go separately, and approach using different routes."

"How cloak-and-dagger," she commented as she pushed the diner door open.

"Says the undercover agent to the plainclothes cop," he quipped.

Her smile was slow to blossom, but when she turned back to face him, it landed like a punch to the gut. Her blue eyes twinkled in the bright fluorescent lights streaming out into the night. He was already regretting his suggestion to ride in separate vehicles. After what had gone down in the PP&W offices, he was reluctant to let her out of his sight.

But the situation called for evasive maneuvers, and he wasn't entirely certain he could handle an hour alone in the car with her in the velvety darkness of the early morning hours.

"I'm going to call you," he said, but it came out much deeper and raspier than intended.

"Okay."

"We'll be in communication the whole time, but I'm going to head north out of town on Highway 72. You take 62 directly there. I should end up only a few minutes behind you."

"And the point of this exercise is…"

"To see if either of us is followed," he finished succinctly.

"You're not the most reassuring guy in the world," she told him, her mouth kicking up into a twisted smile.

"You don't need my reassurance—you're a Fed."

"True."

"You've got this."

Michelle pressed a hand to her chest, rubbing her sternum as if needing to ease an ache there. He was about to offer a change in plan when she let her hand drop to her side and bobbed a quick nod. "Yeah, okay. Let's do this."

IF THERE WAS one thing he learned, it was that Michelle Fraser had abysmal taste in music. Okay, maybe abysmal was a bit harsh, but definitely pedestrian. He'd been able to handle about twenty minutes of whatever pop/soft rock mix she had playing in the background before he had to speak up.

"Are you listening to a playlist or a station?"

"Huh?"

He chuckled. She'd clearly been lost in thought as she drove. Probably not a good thing on a dark and twisting rural highway in the dead of night, though. "Wake up, counselor," he ordered.

"I'm awake, Lieutenant," she retorted.

"If you're awake, I have to assume the music you're subjecting me to is a choice," he said gravely.

"I can turn it off."

The music cut out and he grinned into the night. "Thank you."

"I usually don't pay much attention to the radio. I mostly listen to audiobooks in my car."

"Anything good lately?"

"So many," she answered easily. "Have you read the latest Peterman?"

Ethan grunted. "You listen to legal thrillers? Don't you ever take a day off?"

There was a pause, then she laughed. "Most of the time I listen to either romance or non-fiction, but I figured you didn't and I was trying to make conversation."

"You make assumptions," he said, feigning injury. "I'll have you know I often swap books with my mother and sisters, and I happen to be a big fan of stories with a happily-ever-after."

"Do you believe in them?"

"Happy endings?" he asked, trying not to be offended by the surprise he picked up in her tone. "Sure."

"A lot of people in our line of work get jaded."

"Which line of work are you referring to, policing or lawyering?" he asked, unable to repress his teasing smile.

"Either. Both," she answered with another soft laugh.

He wanted to keep going like this. He wanted to know more about her. "Both can be hard on relationships, but I figure when you find the right person it all works out."

"And have you?" she asked.

"Is this your coy way of asking if I'm involved with someone?"

"I didn't think I was being coy," she countered.

"Right. You weren't. And no, I haven't met the right person yet." They lapsed into silence, and afraid she wasn't going to reciprocate, he rushed in. "How about you?"

"Me?"

"Relationship?"

"Oh. No." She paused and he could almost hear her frown through the phone. "I've been undercover for two years, so no."

"And your family? Who feeds your to-be-read pile?"

"Mainly newsletters and book reviewers," she replied. "Both my parents were career army. They split when I was young, so I got shuffled around even more than the usual military kid. My mom has retired and lives in Maryland. My dad was killed in action when I was eighteen."

He winced as if absorbing the blow for her. "I am sorry," he said quietly.

"Thank you."

Another silence settled. The hypnotic hum of tires on asphalt nearly lured him in, but then he caught sight of a sign indicating a sharp right turn and forced himself to sit up straighter. "Where are you?" he asked.

"Um, at the corner of dark and desolate," she answered. "GPS says I'm fifteen minutes away, and I turn off the highway in a few miles." A beat passed. "Where are you?"

"Not far behind. I'm showing nineteen minutes and about ten miles from the turnoff."

"You're moving at a good clip," she commented.

"I grew up driving roads like this," he reminded her.

"I grew up in places with streetlights."

"I bet moving to Bentonville was a nice dose of culture shock."

"Some, but not as bad as you'd think. I like seeing stars at night."

He chuckled. "If you think you see stars in town, make sure you look up when you get to the Powers place."

"I should call Kayla and give her at least some heads-up. I need to make sure we can get past the gate. I'm assuming she has locked herself in."

Ethan frowned, not enthusiastic about ending the connection. "We could conference her in," he suggested.

She gave a soft, rueful laugh. "I'm afraid I can't, Lieutenant. She's still my client, and rules of confidentiality apply."

"I wasn't trying to—"

"I know," she said, not letting him finish his thought. "But we're almost there, and I'm a trained federal agent, in case you've forgotten."

"So you say. I never did see any ID," he answered gravely.

"I'll show you my credentials when we get to the house."

"That's what they all say—"

"I'm signing off, Ethan," she interrupted. "Thank you for keeping me company, and for helping me calm down. I'm fine now. I promise."

"Maybe wait until you turn off the highway," he suggested, loathe to end the call.

"I'm signaling for the turn now. Oh, and there are a couple of fairly sharp switchbacks before you get to it, so take it easy."

"You signaled for a turn on an empty highway?"

"I'm a law-abiding citizen. Besides, there's some guy who drives like a maniac following me, and I'm afraid I'll be rear-ended."

The moment she spoke the words, he spotted a set of headlights striping the highway ahead of him. Letting off the gas, he cringed as a beat-up old farm truck with no working taillights pulled onto the highway ahead of him.

He groaned his annoyance. "No need to worry about me following you now. You have Farmer Fred and his rusty old Ford running interference for you."

"There's someone out this early?"

"There are lots of people who start their days before dawn. Particularly people who run farms or ranches," he replied.

"I suppose that makes sense."

Propping his elbow on the door, he dropped his head into the cradle of his palm as he slowed to a snail's pace behind the rattling pickup. "Hopefully, he's moving from field to field. If not, I'll pass at the first chance I get."

"Don't rush. I'm hanging up now to call Kayla. I'll see you shortly."

Three beeps signaled the end of the call. With a put-upon sigh, Ethan eased off the gas even more to give the farmer some extra room.

He coasted along for a moment, not wanting to press the driver of the truck. The poor guy was probably sipping coffee from a container and trying to ease his way into the day. Ethan felt his own eyelids growing heavier with each passing second. Finally, impatience won out. He rubbed his temple and glared at the reflection of his own headlights in the dented chrome bumper of the truck ahead of him. "Seriously, guy? This is going to be your top speed?"

As if the driver heard him complaining, the truck slowed even more. Ethan tapped his own brakes and lifted his hand to check the speedometer. They were creeping along at less than thirty-five miles per hour on a highway marked for fifty-five.

"Okay, come on. Now you're messing with me," he grumbled.

The safety ridges cut into the pavement at the center line growled their warning as he swung into the other lane to check to see if it was safe to pass. Unfortunately, a bright yellow road sign indicated a sharp turn to the left, precluding any possibility of a safe pass on the dark country road.

"I guess she wasn't lying about those switchbacks," he mumbled as he dropped back into line behind the truck.

The driver ahead slowed even more.

Ethan hit his brakes again, making sure to leave a safe distance between his vehicle and the tailgate of the pickup truck. Part of him wished he was still a trooper on patrol. This guy deserved a ticket for the lack of operating taillights, if not the dangerously low rate of speed. The tree line thickened around them, and the inky darkness of the mountain night seemed to close in.

The road sloped downward as they headed into the lowlands where the Army Corps of Engineers had stemmed the flow of the White River enough to create the lakes that transformed Northwest Arkansas into a sportsman's paradise and a tourist playground.

Coasting down the incline, he tapped his brakes occasionally to slow his momentum. When they rounded the curve and the hill bottomed out. Ethan was about to check if there was enough of a straightaway to punch it past the truck when the other driver signaled a right turn.

Ethan expelled a gust of frustrated breath and hung back, figuring he could be patient a few more minutes. "At least your signals work," he muttered, frowning at the truck's dented tailgate. He craned his neck to scan the right side of the road, hoping to gauge how long he had to wait until the slowpoke turned off. A flash of bright lights coming from his left startled him. Ethan looked into his rearview mirror in time to see a vehicle taking the curve at a high rate of speed and bearing down on him.

Slapping at the dashboard, he activated the emergency flashers, hoping to warn the driver behind him of pickup truck's snail-like pace. But to his consternation, the headlights in his mirror only grew larger. It was another truck. This one larger, with a boxy cab and a wide flat windshield.

"What the—" He trailed off as he tapped his brakes repeatedly, then laid his palm on the horn, giving one long, loud blare in hopes of startling the driver of the pickup truck into getting a move on.

But contrary to the flashing right turn signal, the truck ahead of him swung into the left lane as if it were preparing to pass another car. All too aware of the vehicle on his rear bumper, Ethan pressed the gas pedal to the floor in hopes of shooting ahead of the ancient pickup and creating enough room for the impatient driver behind him to pass.

"It's too early for this," he growled, turning his head in hopes of getting a good glare in at the farmer as he passed. But to his surprise, the rattletrap old pickup chose this moment to lurch forward. He stayed apace with Ethan's rear quarter panel despite their ever-increasing speed.

And the truck behind him showed no inclination to slow his roll.

Another bright yellow road sign indicated a sharp turn to the right and advised a much slower rate of speed. His hands gripping the wheel, Ethan tapped his brakes in a last-ditch effort to get the truck behind him to slow before they got to the turn.

No luck.

The pickup truck started to drift back over into his lane and he floored the accelerator to get away.

"What the—" He jerked the wheel hard, skidding through the turn with his eyes partially closed. His tires squealed on asphalt. A spray of gravel shot out from under his rear tire when he caught the narrow shoulder of the road. If he made it through this stretch of road in one piece it would be through sheer luck.

Fate seemed to be on his side.

The road straightened after the turn. He spotted a wide shoulder running along some river bottom pastureland and fixed his gaze on it.

He gritted his teeth as the SUV bumped and crunched across the gravel shoulder and then slowed when he hit the softer ground under the overgrown grass along the side of the road. His vehicle jerked to a halt on a rut.

He looked up to see the bigger truck zoom past. Caught in the beams of his headlights, he could see now it was an old hay truck with a bed made of warped plywood. TDP, LCC was painted in script on the passenger door.

His breath came in short staccato bursts as he watched the truck's taillights disappear beyond the next rise. Twisting in his seat, he tried to catch sight of the pickup, but the door pillar blocked his view. He ducked his head to peer into the side mirror and saw the truck had stopped about a quarter mile back. Ethan rolled his window down and stuck his head out in time to see the driver complete a three-point turn and take off in the direction they'd come from.

Dropping back into his seat, he huffed out a rush of air as he stared at the taillights on the hay wagon. Dimly he registered an insistent female voice ordering him to return to the route. He glanced at the map display. The navigation system was imploring him to get back on the road. He blinked when the order to proceed to the route came through the speakers again. "Did you see what happened here? Give a guy a break."

Ethan drew a shaky breath and then let it seep from his lips. Forcing his shoulders down, he rolled them a couple times. "I was on the route," he complained to the disembodied voice. "Apparently, some people didn't want me to be on the route."

The moment the words slipped out, suspicion set in. On a surge of fear-fueled anger, he punched the gas and fishtailed as he steered the SUV back onto the pavement. Jabbing his thumb at the call button on the steering wheel, he ordered the voice assistant to dial Michelle Fraser's number.

She answered on the first ring. "Hello? Are you lost?"

"Not lost, but delayed," he said, checking his rearview mirror repeatedly.

"Did you stop at an all-night pancake house?"

"I did not." He bit his lip as he settled back into the drive. "Did you make it okay?"

"I'm in. Kayla is awake. I'm putting on a pot of coffee. How long till you're here?"

"Um—" He cut his gaze to the GPS. "I'm still eleven minutes out," he reported.

"You took the scenic tour?" she persisted.

"I'll explain when I get there."

His tone must have told her he wasn't in the frame of mind to joke about it because she sobered instantly. "Is everything okay?"

"I don't know," he confessed. "I don't think so."

"Are you okay?" she asked without missing a beat.

He pressed the accelerator, eating up pavement as fast as he dared to go on the narrow unlit highway. But no matter how his speedometer climbed, he never caught sight of the hay truck's lights.

The GPS interrupted his thoughts to warn him about the upcoming turn onto the road leading to the Powers family lake house. "I'll be there shortly. Are the gates open?"

"Yeah, I left them open for you."

His palms began to sweat where he gripped the steering wheel. "Close them."

"You'll be here in less than ten minutes," she argued. "There's a deputy parked out there."

"I'll call you when I'm at the gate itself. And keep the doors locked."

"Ethan, what's going on?"

"I'm not sure yet, but whatever it is, I don't like it."

"I don't like the sound of this."

"Are you closing the gates?"

"Heading back there now."

"Do not open the door for anyone other than me."

"I won't." He heard Kayla ask what was happening. "We need to close the gates. How do I close the gates?"

He heard Kayla question why and he slammed the heel of his hand against the steering wheel. "Forget the gates. Call the deputy and tell him not to let anybody but me in. Set the alarm. Stay away from the windows."

"Uh, okay," Michelle answered, sounding breathless. "We need to set the alarm."

"I armed it after you came in," Kayla replied.

"The alarm is armed," Michelle reported back to him.

"Good. Hang tight," he said, his voice taut as he turned onto the lake road.

"Talk to me."

"I had a thing with a couple of locals."

"Locals? What kind of thing?"

"I assume they were local. Who knows?"

"You aren't making any sense. Local whats?"

"Farmers, I guess? Cattle ranchers? I don't know." He exhaled his impatience and tried to marshal his thoughts. "I had a couple of trucks tag team me right after we hung up."

"Tag team you?"

"A pickup and a hay hauler."

"At this time of morning?"

"Yeah, well, I guess they start work early around here."

"But there aren't any farms around here. It's nothing but forest for miles," she argued.

"Maybe in the area immediately surrounding the lake, but I got up close and personal with a strip of pasture back there."

"What?" Michelle's voice rose with agitation. Then she must have pulled the phone away from her face because her voice was more distant when she asked, "Are there any farms around here?"

Kayla was nearby because he heard her answer, "There are some by the highway, but everything on this side is private land. Timber, mostly."

"I was still on the highway when I met up with them, but I don't think they were heading out to tend the fields."

"What are you saying?"

"I'm saying I think someone tried to run me off the road."

Chapter Fifteen

Michelle waited until they had mugs of coffee in hand and taken seats on the tall stools at the marble-topped island in the kitchen before diving in. Taking turns, she and Ethan told Kayla the story of what happened at PP&W and the decision to come to her. When Michelle got to the part where she ended the call with Ethan, she turned to look directly at him.

"Tell us what happened."

"Well, a pickup truck pulled out in front of me on the highway," he began, using the tips of his fingers to turn the mug in a slow circle. "He was going slow and I was getting pretty annoyed, but we were getting close to the switchbacks, so I couldn't pass."

"I know the stretch," she said encouragingly.

"When we reached the bottom of the hill, he had a friend join him."

"A friend?"

"Some jerk driving a truck, you know, the kind used to haul hay?" When they nodded, he tapped the rim of his mug, clearly agitated. "He came out of nowhere, barreling down on me."

"And you have reason to believe they were working together?"

"No proof, only a hunch."

"I thought you were supposed to deal in proof," Kayla said, her tone challenging. "You seem to be big on suppositions these days."

The look Ethan shot her might have frozen a lesser woman in her tracks, but Michelle was discovering Kayla Powers was no one's pushover.

"What's giving you this hunch?" she asked, hoping to keep the conversation on track.

"They seemed to be tag teaming me. The pickup truck slowed down and blocked the passing lane while the truck behind me appeared to be intent on running me over or off the road." He paused for a moment and lifted his mug and took a sip of the coffee. "I guess he succeeded at the last one."

"A strange place to do it," Kayla mused. "If you want to terrorize someone on the roads around here, wouldn't it make more sense to do it up in the hills than down in the river bottom?"

"I think it was more a crime of opportunity," he said dryly. "I don't suppose you know any of the people who own the farms or ranches around here?"

Kayla sat back on her stool and eyed him coolly. "Actually, I do."

"Can you give me a name?" he countered.

"Powers."

The name landed in the center of the room, its final consonant reverberating like the concussion of a bomb.

Michelle waded in, her scalp prickling a warning to choose her words carefully. "The Powers family owns farmland?"

"Ranchland," Kayla corrected. "And yes. It's my understanding they have for years."

"The door of the hay truck was stenciled with TDP, LLC," Ethan informed them, his jaw tight.

"Tyrone Delray Powers," Kayla said, enunciating each name with deliberate care. "Ty's father bought the land."

"So, the people driving those trucks work for you," he said, his level gaze fixed on her.

"Technically, I suppose so," Kayla answered, her stare every bit as direct.

Ethan shifted forward, his posture confrontational. "You have to understand, when suppositions pile this high it looks bad."

"It looks exceptionally bad," she replied.

Kayla's agreement seemed to throw Ethan off-balance.

"I believe it's meant to look bad." She held Ethan's gaze.

"Okay, we get it," Michelle interrupted. "But I have to say I agree with Kayla here. You have a whole pile of circumstantial evidence pointing to Kayla."

"It's getting to be more than a pile," Ethan retorted.

"And you have to admit it's slightly too convenient. All these flashing neon signs keep popping up and point at Kayla saying, 'The Widow did it!' Feels a little too easy, doesn't it?"

"Nothing about this is easy," Ethan muttered. But he leaned back, letting the stool support his weight as he rubbed an exhausted hand over his face.

"No, it's not," Kayla agreed.

"Right. We're all trying to find answers," Michelle insisted.

"I'm not entirely convinced we're all on the same side," Ethan said gruffly.

"I did not try to run you off the road," Kayla asserted, her voice crisp and tart.

"I never said you did," Ethan answered, his tone deceptively calm. "Still, it's awfully convenient people driving vehicles belonging to a ranch you own were involved in the incident."

"It's anything but convenient, and I can prove I was here the entire time," she shot back.

"Yes, having such a robust security system is proving to be the most convenient part of all, isn't it?"

"Enough." Michelle slammed the flat of her palm on the veined marble island as she slid off the stool to stand. When they both turned to look at her, startled by the outburst, she took the time to nail each of them with a hard stare. "We get it. You both have reason to be wary of each other, but bickering isn't going to get us one step closer to figuring out who killed Tyrone and Trey, nor is it going to help me figure out what kind of mess PP&W is in."

When neither of them spoke, she pressed on. "We all have a vested interest in getting to the bottom of this. I believe in working together—the three of us can cover a lot of ground. Can we set the bickering and suspicion aside for now and try to focus?"

Kayla broke first. "What do you need me to do?"

"Tell me who else knew I'd be at the office tonight."

Kayla raised her hands. "I didn't tell anyone."

"Me either," Ethan was quick to add. But then he frowned. "But speaking of security systems…does the one for the office have cameras?"

Frowning, Kayla shrugged. "He got notifications on his phone whenever someone keyed in." Her forehead creased and she closed her eyes as if trying to recall something. "There have to be cameras because he could see on his phone who'd disarmed the alarm. I remember him commenting on what a suck-up Trey's friend Chet was, putting in extra hours at all hours. He said he was going to talk to Hal about it."

"And it's possible Harold Dennis would also have access?"

Kayla sat up straighter. "I'm not sure. Probably. Maybe Benny in IT, too?"

"Ooh. Good thinking," Michelle enthused. "Let's assume someone else does. It would explain how someone knew I was there."

"But it doesn't explain why they took your laptop and left," Ethan interjected.

"No, it doesn't." She turned to Kayla. "I need to explain to you how I came to be here." She cast a sidelong glance at Ethan and drew a deep breath. "A few years ago, an interested party noticed an abnormality in some legal documents," she began, choosing her words carefully.

"Can we have it straight?" Kayla asked, rubbing her forehead. "I'm too tired for legalese. I think if we're going to get anywhere we need to speak plainly."

"I agree," Ethan said with a nod.

"Okay. Someone noticed their name was used as the principal owner of a real estate development company they'd never heard of. When they looked into it, they found it was a shell corporation set up by one of the attorneys at PP&W."

"Which attorney?" Kayla demanded.

"William Powers."

There was a moment of absolute silence as they digested the information.

"But Bill hasn't been active at the firm since he announced his candidacy years ago," Kayla pointed out.

"Yes, I know. But William Powers signed the incorporation paperwork for this company using Judge Walton's name years ago. We assume DevCo was then set up as a client, and money from an influx of real estate transactions started to flow through the firm. As a name partner in the firm, Judge Walton retains financial oversight rights. The financial end of it is pretty murky, but the upshot is, he believed the bulk of the money has found its way into the senator's political action committee and didn't want his name associated with any shady dealings. The uptick in activity combined with the transfers made into the Powers for the People fundraising account raised a red flag for the person who brought it to the complaint."

Kayla wet her lips. "Do you think Bill suspected Ty was on to him?"

"I have no idea." Michelle met Kayla's eyes directly. "But I think I oversimplified things. The way things were set up, I think this was meant to be a long game, and it involved more than your husband and his brother."

"How do you mean?"

"The company was originally registered in the name of Anthony Walton."

"Judge Walton?" Kayla said, clearly shocked by the news.

"Yes. He came across the original articles of incorporation and did a little digging around on his own. He's not entirely convinced William Powers actually filed that paperwork."

"Oh, boy," Ethan murmured.

"In the beginning, they were smart about covering their tracks, but once William Powers won his first race, things became even more convoluted, and greater sums of money started moving through the shell company. Judge Walton brought the initial transactions to the attention of the Federal Election Commission, who reached out to the Bureau, and here I am."

"What are you hoping to find in the documents you downloaded this evening?" Ethan asked.

"I hope to find a clear-cut paper trail, but hope and expectation are two different things."

"What do you expect to find?"

"I think we're looking at a fairly sophisticated real estate Ponzi scheme. I'm not sure if Senator Powers is the one at the top of this pyramid, or if someone was using his name."

"Either way, I expect to find he's had some low-level associate handling most of the transactions," Kayla hazarded.

"I agree," Michelle said with a nod. "If he is involved, he'd want to be as far removed from the pipeline as possible."

"But Ty…" Kayla frowned. "Do you think this might be why Ty was so wary of Harold Dennis?"

Michelle shook her head. "It's possible. So far, I haven't been able to find any direct interaction between Tyrone and the company in question. The only thing that feels off to me is the senator hasn't done anything to distance himself from the company we're investigating."

"I'm almost afraid to ask," Ethan said, raising both eyebrows.

"DevCo," Kayla whispered.

Michelle nodded a confirmation, turning her attention to Ethan. "What did you find out about the flight plans for the private jet?"

"As far as we can tell, the jet left Northwest Arkansas Regional, made a stop at Reagan National in DC, then flew on to Barbados as stated. It returned to the private hangar at NWA Monday morning."

"Any luck getting a passenger manifest?"

Ethan shook his head. "Stonewalled."

"Most likely because the person you're asking is the person who desperately wants to hide the information."

"But we know Bill went on to Europe," Kayla interrupted, "but Harold…"

Michelle inclined her head. "Yes, Harold. Mr. Dennis managed to fly into and off the island without seeing anyone. He supposedly had to wait to fly back commercial." She cast a sidelong glance at Ethan. "I don't suppose you were able to find him on any commercial flight manifests?"

"The request for information is still out there." He drew a deep breath, then blew it out. "But the airlines and the FAA aren't always quick to share such information. I had to go through Homeland Security to even submit the request."

"And Bill sits on the Senate Homeland Security Committee."

"A convenient coincidence," Michelle drawled.

"Where does that leave us right now?" Kayla asked, her voice husky with fatigue.

"It leaves me in need of a computer and a couple of hours to poke around and see if I managed to swipe anything useful while I was in the office."

"You can use the computer in Ty's office. It's a desktop, but he has full access to the PP&W server."

"I'd rather not use one so connected to PP&W if I can help it," Michelle interjected with an apologetic wince. "Logging on from Ty's might leave a great big footprint."

"I have an ancient laptop around here somewhere," Kayla said, gesturing vaguely. "I'll have to find it and the cord. I mostly use my phone for everything these days."

"If you would look for it, I'd appreciate it," Michelle said firmly. "I'll use Tyrone's desktop if we have no other option, but I'd prefer to have something not connected to the firm's network in any way."

Kayla stood up. "I think it might be in one of the closets upstairs. I'll see what I can find."

The moment she left the room, Ethan turned to look directly at her. "It might be best to use Tyrone's computer after all. What if it isn't someone at PP&W? What if you access the data from the cloud, and it's somebody within your agency?"

"Let's see what Kayla can come up with before we go there, but you don't need to worry about my data."

"I don't?"

"Nope." She reached into the front of her shirt and extracted the thumb drive from the band of her bra. Holding it up triumphantly, she beamed at him. "I always make sure I have backup."

ETHAN AND KAYLA dozed in chairs on opposite sides of Tyrone Powers's spacious home office. She couldn't blame them for sleeping. There wasn't much for them to do other than sit and watch her scan through column after column of data, looking for patterns.

As usual, she let her mind drift as she worked, musing over the absurdity of building such a sumptuous office into a vacation home, but she figured the rich got to be rich because they never stopped working at it. Kayla did say they often entertained clients at the lake house, so Michelle supposed it made sense for Tyrone to have a place to talk turkey while the rest of the world worked hard at having fun.

Ethan jerked upright on a soft snore, and she smiled at the screen as he mumbled an apology, shifted in the tufted leather club chair and drifted off again.

The laptop Kayla had unearthed from a closet was a PC. It appeared to be a few years old, but barely used. She'd plugged her thumb drive into the port and said a prayer to the tech gods she'd grabbed everything she needed.

She worked steadily for a couple of hours, oblivious to her own lack of sleep. Adrenaline coursed through her veins. The answer was close. So close she could almost reach out and grab it. She only needed to let her mind take her to it.

Leaning back in Tyrone's huge leather chair, she curled her knuckles against the bridge of her nose, closing her eyes as she smoothed the arc of her brows. "Relax. You've got this," she whispered to herself.

Embarrassed she'd spoken the words out loud, she sat up and opened her eyes, checking to see if either of her companions heard her little pep talk. But the only sounds in the room were the occasional whir of the laptop fan, Kayla's soft breathing and Ethan's occasional grunts and snorts.

As quietly as she could, she rose, grabbing her coffee mug from the coaster on the desk. She padded into the kitchen, checking the night sky beyond the wall of windows at the back of the lake house. She had an hour, maybe a bit more before the sun started to rise. They'd have to leave within two hours to make it back to Bentonville in time for Trey Powers's memorial service. Time was of the essence, but Michelle was loath to leave before she found the key to the data.

With a fresh mug of coffee, she tiptoed back into the office and resumed her seat. Neither Ethan nor Kayla twitched an eyelid. A part of her envied them their ability to catch a nap at this time. Even if she wanted to, she was too keyed up.

Too close.

She took a sip of the strong black coffee and placed the mug carefully back on the coaster. The soft clink of ceramic on the stoneware coaster was as loud as a starter pistol in her mind. The sound brought her back to the sharp crack of the gunshot and the glass sidelight.

Shaking her head, she shelved all thoughts of what had happened in the PP&W offices for later. Right now, the night was slipping away from her.

Covering her eyes with the palms of her hands, she took three deep breaths before allowing herself to look at the computer screen again. The brief respite did the trick.

The moment she opened her eyes it became clear—the same sequence of five numbers leaped out at her over and over.

It was the employee ID number the server logged each time a specific person accessed a file.

Most associates at PP&W—heck, most employees around the world—failed to realize their every keystroke could be monitored. When Michelle began to fully comprehend what she was seeing, she wanted to kiss Benny in IT square on the lips for his diligence. She also wanted to kick herself. She should have hacked into the firm's human resources files while she was in the server.

With a few taps at the keyboard, she entered a command to isolate only the repetitive employee ID number. With the filter applied, the pattern of moving money into one specific account then immediately out of it into another was so apparent she wanted to weep. She recognized the DevCo client number from the research she'd done on the company. The account receiving the funds was a bank account number familiar to everyone working the case of William Powers's bottomless war chest.

She'd found the pipeline into Powers for the People.

"Bingo," she said softly.

Ethan startled as if she'd shouted. Lifting a hand to rub his eyes, he asked, "You found something?"

"I did," she said, unable to contain the quiver of excitement in her voice. "I found transfers of money into DevCo and the same number out to the Powers for the People contribution account."

"No kidding?" Ethan launched himself from the chair and came around the desk to join her. He braced one hand on the back of the chair and the other on the desk as he leaned in, peering at the monitor. "How do you know these are all DevCo to Powers?" he asked.

"I'll double-check the DevCo number to confirm, but I recognize the numerical sequence. I'm pretty sure it was in the company information I sent to you, if you would double-check for me," she said glancing up at him.

"Hang on." He pulled his phone from his pocket and began to scroll. A moment later, he read the number out loud.

"That's it," Michelle stated, pointing to the number repeating on the screen. "I have isolated the transactions by this number," she said, indicating the column with the employee ID numbers. "The only problem is I didn't download HR files, so I'm not exactly sure who employee 19544 is."

"There are HR files on Ty's desktop," Kayla said in a groggy voice. Michelle looked over to see the other woman straightening in her chair. "We can log in. If anybody asks,

I have every right to look at them, don't I?" she asked, her voice raspy, but firm.

Michelle smiled. "Yes, you do."

She spun in the chair to face the large all-in-one computer built into the credenza behind the desk. Kayla had powered it up earlier, but Michelle had opted for the laptop and thumb drive. She couldn't be certain who knew what, and it was better to do her research with as much stealth as possible.

She shook the mouse, and the screen sprang to life. "Do you know his password?"

Kayla moved to join them. "Yeah. It's 'Kapow.' Capital *K*, lowercase a-p-o-w." When Michelle shot her a look, Kayla blushed. "It was an old joke. Our couple name. You know, like the tabloids?"

Michelle softened as she eyed her…friend? She wasn't exactly sure when she and Kayla had crossed the line from acquaintance to client to friendship, but whatever their relationship was, the trust between them made it something deeper.

She offered a tired smile. "Old jokes are the best jokes. And *Kapow* is a great couple name."

"We thought so," Kayla whispered.

Turning back to the computer, Michelle keyed in the password and the desktop sprang to life. Michelle had fully intended to hack into whatever she needed to get the numbers, but Kayla hadn't exaggerated when she said Tyrone had everything on his computer.

The master dashboard offered up everything she could have ever wanted on a silver platter. If she had come here first, there would have been no need for a late night break-in. She wouldn't have had someone taking shots at her door or stealing her computer. She could have simply asked Kayla for access.

But she'd never been one for the easy route, she thought

with a smirk. Plus, it would have meant she had to trust Kayla enough to take her into her confidence, and people in her line of work were wary of giving too much information away.

Sighing, she clicked on the icon labeled Human Resources, and watched as the employee dashboard populated. There, four slots down from the top was the number she'd isolated.

19544.

She followed the line of data across until she saw the corresponding name.

Kayla and Ethan moved in to stand behind her and peered over her shoulder.

"Who is it?" Kayla prompted.

Michelle cleared her throat and shot a glance at Ethan before answering. "It appears our winner is… Harold Dennis."

Chapter Sixteen

After Trey's memorial service, Natalie met mourners at a gathering at the historic Peele Mansion and botanical gardens. She'd invited Kayla and Michelle to avoid gossip, and they'd accepted in order to preserve the illusion of congeniality in the family. With a glass of water in hand, Michelle wandered through the rooms of the old house, marveling at what people once considered fashionable wallpaper and doing her best to pretend she wasn't watching Harold Dennis's every move.

She, Kayla and Ethan had split up, agreeing it wouldn't look good for the three of them to appear overly friendly. Michelle had been grateful for the relative peace of the memorial service. She hadn't slept a wink since her brief nap prior to her visit to the PP&W offices, and fatigue was quickly overtaking her.

Cruising past the brunch buffet laid out in the mansion's dining room, she filled a plate with miniature quiches, some cheese and a selection of bite-size pastries. Protein and sugar would see her through. She certainly didn't need any more caffeine. She'd been jittery all morning.

She was scanning the room when she saw Ethan pull his phone from his belt and accept a phone call. Kayla stood in the small library, making small talk with a few PP&W associates. Michelle noted she'd stayed as far away as possible from the front parlor where Natalie Cantrell held court.

Harold Dennis, Senator Powers and Del all danced attendance on the older woman, pointedly ignoring the presence of Tyrone's widow and heir. Michelle smirked. Those men underestimated Kayla. Had from the beginning. Only Del had the grace to say a few words to her, and he'd broken away as soon as his father caught his eye. Watching the interaction, Michelle couldn't help but think Tyrone Powers had done exactly what he'd needed to do to ensure the future of his firm.

"Ms. Fraser."

Michelle jumped, then flashed a weak smile when she recognized the older man with the commanding baritone. "Judge Walton. How are you?"

The judge shook his head. "Terrible thing. This whole business."

Michelle couldn't help wondering if he knew she was the one sent in to investigate his suspicions. It was possible. After all, someone had to have pulled some strings to be certain she was the candidate Tyrone Powers and Harold Dennis selected to replace Kayla. Still, in all the interactions she'd had with the judge who had been a name partner before ascending to the bench, he'd never given a hint of inside knowledge.

"It is," she concurred, aware she'd taken too long to respond. "I'm sorry, my mind was elsewhere," she said, flashing an apologetic smile. "How are you doing, sir?"

His mouth twitched into a smile. "We've already covered the niceties," he reminded her.

"My apologies," she said, a blush creeping up her neck. Glancing down at the plate she held, she shook her head. "I think I need to eat."

He nodded. "A good idea. There are some lovely spots in the garden if you need some quiet as well."

She flashed him a grateful smile. "An excellent idea. Thank you, Your Honor."

"Thank you," he replied with a pointed stare. At her puzzled frown, he tipped his head to the side. "For putting up with the family circus. For helping poor Kayla. I know Tyrone would be beside himself at the thought of anyone suspecting her, even for a moment. He trusted her implicitly."

"Oh, well, good," she stammered, thrown by the mere existence of someone who didn't want to throw her client under the bus. "It's been my pleasure to get to know her."

"Not to speak ill of the dead, but I'd wager it has been more pleasurable than dealing with your last client." He sighed. "If Natalie has her way, Trey will be canonized a saint by the end of the week. And they aren't even Catholic."

A burst of laughter escaped her, drawing the attention of some of the others in the room. She averted her gaze when she saw Harold Dennis step out of the parlor, a grave expression creasing his face.

Judge Walton adroitly pivoted so they were facing away from the other man's censorious glare. "I knew Trey from the day he was born, and I loved him, too, in my own way. But I wasn't blind to what he'd become. I know you had an uphill battle ahead of you with him. I also know Matthew Murray and our justice system. Sad to say for Matthew's sake, you likely would have won Trey's battle for him. And I think we both know the victory would have been a testament to your skill rather than his character."

"Yes, sir."

"Go eat," he said with a kindly smile. "You look like you need some respite."

"Thank you, Your Honor," she said, giving him a wan smile as she ducked past him and headed for the doors to the gardens.

She found a wrought iron bench situated in the shade of a hedge and sat down, grateful to be off her feet, though she didn't dare kick off her black pumps. Her body and brain were in shut-down mode, and she didn't know if she could consume enough energy to push through.

Balancing the plate on her lap, she popped a couple of cheese cubes into her mouth and chewed. Her water was almost gone. She should have grabbed a refill before making her escape, but the encounter with the judge had thrown her. Extracting her phone from the small purse she carried, she pulled up Ethan's contact information and typed out a quick text.

I'm hiding in the garden trying to eat. Would you grab me some water? I'm flagging.

"Hello."

Michelle jumped and the plate filled with food slid from her lap to the ground at her feet. She followed its progress, a low moan of frustration seeping from her lips. Then her gaze landed on the polished black wing tips in front of her.

She looked up to find Harold Dennis staring down at her, his stance wide, his arms crossed over his chest and his face lined with disapproval.

"Your client was accessing confidential files from Tyrone's computer," he announced without preamble. "Until a judge rules on the probate, she has no right to those files."

"Until a judge deems a person's most recent will invalid, the executor has every right to access all assets held by the deceased within reason." She tilted her head as she looked up at him. "Did you skim over the part where Tyrone named Kayla Powers executor as well as secondary beneficiary?"

"I don't know what you think you're doing, but—"

Not liking the confrontational tone of his voice, Michelle surreptitiously pressed the call button for Ethan, then slipped the phone into the pocket of her black suit as she rose. "Oh, I think you know exactly what we're doing, Harold," she countered.

Sure she had her feet under her, she lifted her chin to meet his gaze. "Who is the principal owner of DevCo?"

"Excuse me?" His frown deepened. "Why are you asking questions about my client? Don't you have enough on your hands with defending yet another murderer?"

Harold Dennis had never hidden his disdain for the practice of criminal law. When the children and grandchildren of longtime clients found themselves in trouble, he'd been more than happy to pass those cases off to an associate. Taking his discarded casework was how Kayla had carved out her niche within the firm and paved the way for Michelle to step in. She wondered if he realized her presence in his firm was truly a monster of his own creation.

No. Men like Harold Dennis only indulged in the kind of crime that allowed them to keep their hands clean.

Or did they?

Standing toe to toe with the man who thought he called the shots in her career, Michelle decided to go for broke. "Who owns DevCo? And why are you moving money through them to Senator Powers's campaign accounts?"

"I don't know who you think you are—"

"I know who I am," she interrupted. "I'm Special Agent Michelle Fraser working on behalf of the FBI and the Federal Election Commission, and I believe you, Harold Dennis, have been moving money through dummy accounts in order to circumvent campaign finance contribution restrictions. We also think some of that money has been used to finance the senator's personal expenses."

"You're delusional," he said with a scoff.

"I didn't imagine the paper trail you left behind," she responded. "We have all the transactions and they were all done using your PP&W login. You left a digital footprint."

"Somebody must have hacked my computer," he said with a dismissive wave. "Those sorts of things happen all the time. Technology is not as secure as we'd like to believe it is."

"Oh, I know," she said taking a step closer to him. "But I also know the firm's financial data was on a heavily encrypted server, and it took quite a few IT experts to get through the firewalls, but we did it. Benny deserves a raise, by the way."

His jaw tensed and his eyes turned frosty. "You have no proof."

"I have proof like you would not believe," she replied. "Years and years of transactions. We've had a whole team working on this since well before I came here. If you were hacked, Harold, you've been getting hacked for approximately five years."

He laughed, but there was little humor in the sound. "You think you have proof, but you're wrong. Go ahead and file your little report. Whatever data you stole from our company has been…compromised."

Michelle felt a single sinking feeling in her gut. Ethan hadn't been wrong about her contact at the agency. And she hadn't been wrong to make a duplicate copy of those files.

"It seems a lot of things around here have been compromised," she challenged. "Your ethics, your morals and your willingness to get your hands dirty in order to get what you want."

"What is it you think I want?"

"Control of PP&W, for starters," she answered with a shrug. "But we all know you can't have it permanently."

She took another small step closer, craning her neck as she gazed up into his angry face. "You'll always have to settle for being the power behind the Powers family, but never the one who actually wields the power. It has to be frustrating."

"You have no idea what you're talking about."

"Is that why you killed them? Tyrone and Trey?" she jabbed her finger into his chest. "You thought you knew what was in Tyrone's will. You thought you would be managing partner for the foreseeable future, possibly for your entire lifetime if you could keep William in office and Del under your thumb."

"I won't listen to this nonsense. You're lucky I don't sue you for slander," he added, pitching his voice low and menacing.

"You're lucky you're not in jail for murder," she shot back as he turned on his heel and started back down the garden path.

Michelle cleared the edge of the hedge and looked to her left. Sure enough, Ethan Scott stood nearby holding a bottle of water. "You catch everything, Lieutenant?" she called out to him, not breaking stride as she followed Harold back to the house.

"Every word," Ethan replied, falling into step beside her. "I've asked Grace Reed to reach out to the FEC and the FBI. I'll have to figure out who he's got working for them on the inside."

Harold Dennis spun around as he reached the top of the shallow steps leading to the house. "If you don't stop following me, I will file a complaint for harassment. Judge Walton is right inside."

Michelle huffed a laugh. "By all means, let's go in and talk to the judge. Let's ask him who brought me here."

Harold burst through the doors, causing a commotion

among the assembled mourners. Michelle trotted to keep up as his long strides ate up the distance between the garden door and the front parlor. Michelle couldn't help noticing his gait didn't match the awkward lope of the assailant who had stolen her laptop.

Harold stopped in the foyer outside the main parlor. He pointed theatrically at the front door. "I'd like you to leave right now," he ordered, his booming voice cutting across the hushed conversations.

Kayla emerged from the small library, as Natalie and the senator rushed from the parlor.

"Harold, for heaven's sake," Natalie said, glancing nervously at their guests.

"What's going on here?" Senator Powers demanded. "Harold, this is hardly an appropriate—"

"Tell her what's appropriate," Harold almost shouted, spittle flying from his mouth as he jabbed one finger in Michelle's direction.

Ethan stepped in. "I believe what would be appropriate at this moment would be to ask you to accompany me down to my office so we could have a little conversation, Mr. Dennis," he said in a congenial tone.

"I'm not going anywhere with you."

"Don't make me arrest you in front of all these people."

Harold sneered. "Arrest me? On what charges?"

"I believe we can start with fraud and campaign finance violations," he said, sliding a glance at Michelle for confirmation. When she nodded, he raised both eyebrows as if challenging the other man to say whether he'd had enough.

But Harold Dennis didn't know when to give in. "You have no evidence," he said, enunciating each word.

"I don't know who you think you have in your pocket, Harold, but I have this."

Michelle reached into her suit pocket and pulled out a thumb drive.

It wasn't the one with the data downloaded from PP&W files. The original was locked in the safe in Ethan's hotel room. But Harold wouldn't know as much. "I made a backup copy of all the files."

Harold's face blanched. Natalie Cantrell and Senator Powers stepped up beside him, but their expressions were clouded with doubt.

"What about campaign finance?" Senator Powers demanded.

"The political action committee Mr. Dennis established for you prior to your first campaign, Powers for the People?"

"Yes," he replied, still looking puzzled.

"Haven't you ever wondered where the bulk of those contributions come from?"

"The same place most contributions come from," the senator answered readily. "Individual citizens, interested businesses, organizations who support the policies I support as a legislator."

"And you've never wondered how there was no ebb and flow in the cash flow coming into your accounts?" Michelle asked.

William Powers shook his head. "I'm not an accountant. I don't audit the books. As for the rest, I assumed Tyrone was keeping the balance on an even keel."

"Tyrone," Harold blurted, his voice thick with derision. "Your brother hardly lifted a finger to ever help you in any of your campaigns."

"That's not true," Natalie and Kayla answered almost in unison.

"And you," he said, turning on Kayla. "You couldn't be

content to guzzle your wine and spend his money? You have to make a grab for the firm?"

"I did no such thing," Kayla shot back.

"You had him name you executor of his will and managing partner," Harold cried. "If that isn't cause enough for suspicion, I don't know what is," he said to Ethan.

"It was indeed cause," Ethan assured him. "But, as you mentioned earlier, we haven't found any evidence Mrs. Powers had means, motive or opportunity. You, on the other hand—"

"I was—"

"Faking a trip to a Caribbean island so you could claim to be out of the country when you made your grab."

"What? How? I flew down there after dropping Bill off in DC," he asserted.

"And flew back the following morning," Ethan countered. "We've spoken to the pilot and attendant who crewed the plane y'all used. It's a sort of private plane timeshare, isn't it? One purchased by the company you established in Anthony Walton's name on behalf of William Powers."

"What?" The senator startled at the mention of his name, but Judge Walton stepped forward, unruffled.

"I am the one who found the articles of incorporation," he said firmly. Fixing his most judicial gaze on the senator, he asked, "Did you file them on behalf of a company called DevCo using my name as principal?"

"What?" William repeated. "No. Of course not."

"They were submitted with your name," Judge Walton calmly responded.

"But they were entered into the PP&W system by Harold Dennis," Michelle interjected smoothly.

"Mr. Dennis, who saw absolutely no one in Barbados before returning to Arkansas on the morning after Tyrone and Trey Powers were found murdered," Ethan added. "The flight attendant said he overheard you arguing with someone on the phone. He said he assumed the person on the other end of the line was a woman because you kept telling the other person whatever they'd found meant nothing." He paused to let the possibility of witness testimony sink in. "But it wasn't a woman, was it? It was Tyrone. Your friend. The man you mentored. He was about to topple your house of cards and you couldn't let it happen."

Harold Dennis's face was nearly purple with rage, his fist clenched tight at his sides, but when he spoke his voice was calm. "Again, where is your proof?"

"I don't have it all together yet," Ethan replied with a casual shrug. "But you know who does?" Wearing a smile Michelle'd swear was filled with pride, he pointed to her. "She does. We'll start with fraud, it's as good a foundation as any." He turned to face her and inclined his head, brows lifted. "Do you want to do the honors, or should I?"

The warmth in her face slid down to her heart, then settled in her belly. She'd been right to press dial when she found herself alone with Harold Dennis. She'd needed backup and Ethan provided it.

Gazing up at him, she realized she was content to be done with it all. "You know what? This is your backyard. You bring him in; we'll work out the rest from there."

"I'll take him," Sheriff Stenton volunteered. When Michelle and Ethan turned to him in unison, he gave them a paternal smile. "You two look beat, and it's going to take a couple hours to get him processed, anyway."

"A couple of hours?" Harold Dennis cried. "It does not—"

"Maybe longer," the sheriff said, talking over the indignant man. "Cuffs, or you coming along peacefully?" he asked Hal.

"You will not cuff me," Hal retorted. "And I want my attorney."

"Oh, sure," Sheriff Stenton answered easily, hooking a big hand through Harold Dennis's elbow. "Which one you want?" he asked, gesturing to the assemblage.

The PP&W associates turned away almost as one—like a school of fish sensing the approach of a predator.

Harold swiveled to shoot a pleading look at William Powers. The senator raised his hands to indicate he couldn't risk touching Harold's predicament. "Hal, what have you done?" he asked as he took Natalie's arm and stepped back.

Harold's jaw set into a thin line, but Michelle caught the sheen of moisture in his eyes as he fixed his gaze on the mansion's front door. "Let's get this farce over with," he said stiffly.

Sheriff Stenton turned back to Michelle and Ethan. "Get some rest. I'll call when he's ready to entertain visitors."

Anxiety twisted her gut as they followed the sheriff and her suspect out into the wide veranda of the old mansion. "I should go with him. I'll need to get someone from the Bureau field offices in either Tulsa or Little Rock, and—"

She didn't realize she'd been twisting her hands together until Ethan placed his hands over them to still her movements. "The sheriff is right. We won't be any good to anyone until we get some rest and clear our minds. Make a call to get someone here, but then shut it down for a moment." He gave her clasped hands a gentle squeeze and her gaze flew to his. "We've gotten this far. We'll sort it all out once we can think straight."

"Right."

Her hands felt cold when he took his away, and she quickly

stuffed them into the pockets of her suit jacket. She ran her thumb over the plastic stick drive she'd used to call Dennis's bluff. Ethan had been the one to suggest it. He'd been right. Working together, they made a good team.

Once they'd seen Harold loaded into the back of the sheriff's SUV, Ethan nudged her in the direction of her own vehicle. She turned to look up at him as they stood on the curb. "Have I thanked you yet?"

"Thanked me?"

She shrugged. "You helped nail my investigation, but yours is still—" She let the thought drift away on the breeze.

"Ongoing," he supplied firmly. "But I think you may have helped with it as well."

"You think so?" she asked, tipping her chin up to meet his gaze.

He nodded, then opened the driver's door for her. "I'm hoping I can convince you to work with me on it some more."

"I'm happy to help however I can," she said as she stepped into her vehicle.

"Great. Text me after you've slept some, and I'll meet you down at Stenton's offices. Harold should be good and riled up by the time we get there," he said with a grin.

Michelle couldn't help smiling back. "Just where we want him," she agreed.

He backed up to allow room for her to close the door. "See? I told you. Like recognizes like, Ms. Fraser. I knew you were a cop down to your bones."

She rolled her eyes and reached for the door handle. "Yeah, yeah. You were right, Lieutenant."

"See you in a couple hours," he called as she closed the door.

Michelle drew in a deep breath as she started the car. Ethan raised his hand in a half wave, then started for the side street where he'd parked his vehicle. She watched him go, her stomach still twisting and the quiet of the car's interior filling in all the space around her.

"Right, but will I see you after that?"

Chapter Seventeen

Their reunion at the Benton County Correctional Complex wasn't going as Ethan had anticipated. As a matter of fact, they hadn't been reunited at all. He'd seen several people dressed in standard issue Fed suits come through the offices, but hadn't caught so much as a glimpse of Michelle.

Alas, he'd had more than his fill of Harold Dennis, and his lawyerly non-answers.

Sheriff Stenton must have sensed his growing frustration, because when the dinner hour approached, the older man volunteered Ethan for the food run.

"You're running on empty, son. Get out of here, breathe some air, make whatever call you keep checking your phone for," he added with a teasing smirk. "Old Hal in there isn't going anywhere. The Feds have their hooks in him nice and deep, thanks to Ms. Fraser."

Ethan must have jolted at the mention of her name because Stenton laughed. "Go. Get out." He rocked back on his heels and crossed his arms over his chest. "You might oughta try the Daisy Dairy Bar if you haven't already. Real popular place."

"Is it?"

"Heard your friend Ms. Fraser say she was real partial to their pineapple shakes," the sheriff informed him. "Me,

I'm more of an onion ring man." He gave his rounded belly a pat. "But Mrs. Stenton is on one of her health kicks, so it's salad for me."

Ethan eyed the older man through narrowed eyes. "The Daisy Dairy Bar?"

"Mmm-hmm," Stenton hummed, looking off into the middle distance.

Smiling at the man's lack of acting skills, Ethan ducked his head in defeat. "Pineapple milkshakes, huh?"

"That's what I heard."

Checking his phone as he stepped out into the bright sunshine, Ethan growled when he found no texts or calls from Michelle. He hadn't been expecting a big gushing thank you, but he thought after all they'd been through over the course of the week, he'd at least rate a goodbye message.

"Hello."

His head jerked up, and he saw Michelle Fraser leaning against his SUV, and two foam cups sitting on the hood. She'd stripped off her suit jacket. The sleeveless blouse she wore exposed softly curved arms. The tight black skirt clung to her rounded hips and stopped just above her knee. She looked good. Tired, and a little rumpled, but good.

Almost too good.

He had to remember she wasn't likely to stay in these parts now that her case was wrapping.

"Fancy meeting you here," he said, unable to conjure up anything more original.

"I texted Bud and told him you needed a break," she said as she pushed away from the side of the vehicle.

"Oh, you did, now?" He raised both eyebrows. "Bud, is it?"

"We bonded over our love of the Daisy Dairy Bar." She smiled, then reached for one of the cups. "I wasn't sure what flavor you liked best, but I figured I couldn't go wrong with good old vanilla."

He accepted the cup and paper-wrapped straw. "I like most anything, so thank you." He nodded to the cup beside her. "I'm guessing you're having pineapple?"

Her eyes widened and she nodded in grim understanding. "He's giving away my secrets."

"Not all of them," Ethan assured her.

"Only the most important ones," Michelle said as she lifted the cup and placed the straw to her lips. She drew on it greedily, and Ethan's mouth went dry. "I didn't peg the sheriff as the type who'd give away the key to winning a woman's heart so easily."

"Is that the key?" he asked, his voice gruff.

"One of them," she said, color tingeing her cheeks as she ducked her head. "How's it going in there?"

"He had pretty much shut down by the time your team was done with him," Ethan said, unwrapping his own straw and jabbing it into the lid.

"Yeah. Sorry about that," she said with a grimace. "If it makes you feel better, he didn't give up much for us either."

"But you have your evidence," he reminded her.

"We do," she conceded.

"Catch any heat?" He took a sip of his shake, trying to play his question off as casual concern.

"Some," she said with a shrug. "Got a bit of grief about breaking cover, but once I relayed our suspicions about my point of contact, it diverted their attention."

"As it should. So, uh—" he looked away as he mustered the nerve to ask what was really on his mind "—what's next for you?"

"I'm not sure," she said, sipping at her shake again. "I think..." She glanced over at the razor wire-topped fence.

"I think I'm ready to live aboveground for a while though, I can tell you that much."

"No more undercover work?"

"No." She bit her bottom lip. "I think I'd like to have a life, you know?"

He nodded. Unable to stand the distance between them any longer, he moved to lean up against the SUV beside her. "I think you've earned it."

They stood side by side for a full minute, neither of them moving or talking.

"Where do you think you'll go?" he asked.

At the same time, she said, "I think I'm going to take some leave."

"Oh, sorry. Go ahead," he said.

"No, uh…" She laughed. "I'm not sure. I think I'll be staying here for a while."

"You are?" he asked, turning toward her.

She smiled and nodded, pivoting in his direction. "Yeah. I mean, I have an apartment here and a job… I think."

"You mean with Kayla?"

"We haven't discussed anything formally, but I figure she's going to need some help," she answered.

"I might need some backup with this nasty double homicide I'm working," he grumbled.

"Wow. I had no idea I'd be so in demand. I'll have to sort out what I'm going to do about the Bureau. Anyone who says juggling multiple jobs is easy is really a clown."

"You're killing me here," he confessed in a grumble.

She looked up, her bright eyes lighting with pleasure and mischief. "Am I?"

"You know you are."

"How am I supposed to know—"

He set the cup on the hood of the car, then snaked an

arm around her waist to pull her close. "You know because I know."

"And like recognizes like, Lieutenant?" she asked, tipping her head back, an inviting smile twitching her mouth.

"Yes." He dipped his head, his mouth mere millimeters from hers. "You and me. We're alike."

"Yes, we are," she agreed. Then she lifted up onto her toes and closed the distance between them.

Her mouth was soft and sweet, and the tangy, tropical taste of pineapple clung to his lips even after they broke the kiss. He held on to her, not willing to step out of the bubble they'd created in the midst of murder and mayhem. Needing to stay in the happy place they'd found in each other for just a moment longer.

"One more," he whispered. "It's going to be a long night, and I'm going to need backup if I'm going to make it through."

Michelle smiled as she wound her arms around his neck. "Better make it two. You might need backup for the backup."

"Good thinking," he murmured as he lowered his mouth to hers again. "Very. Good. Thinking," he said, punctuating each part of the compliment with a kiss.

When she pulled back with a sigh, he pressed his forehead to hers. "I think I'm supposed to go to this dairy bar place and score some illicit onion rings for your friend, Bud. Want to ride along?"

Michelle shook her head as she snagged her cup from the hood of the car. "Can't. We're interviewing the senator next," she informed him. "But here." She reached into her ever-present tote bag and pulled out a grease-stained white bag. "I've got you covered."

* * * * *

AGENT COLTON'S SECRET INVESTIGATION

DANA NUSSIO

I dedicate this story to my readers, who make this career of storytelling possible. Thank you for allowing me into your lives and for connecting with the characters who escape from my mind onto the page. I so appreciate you for sharing their pain, their hopes and their triumphs and for smiling along with me when they earn their happily-ever-afters. I am grateful to those of you who ask bookstores to stock my books, place them on your online preorder lists and leave reviews when you've finished enjoying them. This one's for you!

Chapter One

Deirdre Colton shielded her eyes as the dust her rental car and the wind had kicked up on the ranch's ridiculously long driveway smacked her in the face. She elbowed the door shut, kicked the dirt with her new cowboy boots and brushed off her mouth with the back of her hand. Great. She'd already seen more of the desolate Wyoming countryside than she'd hoped to in two lifetimes during the drive from the airport in Casper. Now that she'd reached her destination, just outside Laramie, she could taste that parched earth, too.

Shivering, she zipped her jacket up to her throat, convinced that the weather app had skipped a few details when it predicted a high of nearly seventy degrees. That wicked wind made it downright chilly for May.

"Deirdre, you're not in DC anymore."

She adjusted both her sunglasses and her attitude. Even if everything she'd seen so far in the Cowboy State made her long for the constant activity around Capitol Hill, for morning jogs through the National Mall and for the black-mud coffee in the DC FBI field office—well, not that—she had a job to do. This time it involved more than just an investigation, even if this lead could help her assist a team of Colton cousins in solving a missing-persons case *and* allow her to capture an alleged serial killer. It was critical that she be the one to make this arrest. Her future with the bureau might depend on it.

The property that spread before her looked nothing like the location she'd pictured for this career-defining moment. But then, she'd had no reason to expect something like Harmony Fields Ranch, a place that appeared from nothing around it like those occasional crusty peaks that jutted from the miles of flat land along the interstate. The massive log-and-stone house itself could have been the centerfold in one of those snazzy home and garden magazines. It held court above the property with two sparkling walls of windows peering out over the ranch buildings and a raised deck that hugged the whole second floor.

At the trunk, she unlocked her .40-caliber Glock 22, stowed it in her FBI cant holster and positioned her jacket to cover it. Then she carefully scanned as much of her perimeter as she could see without binoculars or a rifle scope. Whether the place appeared deserted or not, she planned to follow at least some of her protocols.

A collection of newer wood outbuildings stood in the distance with letters *HF* woven into the patterns of their green shingles. Beyond those, fenced fields stretched in all directions, cattle grazing over them looking like black specks on the straw-colored ground. The sign out front even said there was a petting zoo here, too, but someone had to be exaggerating there.

The whole display proclaimed that Maeve O'Leary's long-lost stepson had found success out West.

Just as Deirdre's gaze shifted to the open doors of the largest barn, a cowboy stepped away from the building, a stereotype in hat and boots. Her muscles immediately tightened, senses on alert, as she tucked her phone in her pocket and tugged her jacket to cover her weapon. The man observed her for several annoyingly long seconds and then sauntered her way. No, *swaggered* was more like it, given the slight bow in his legs and his unhurried approach. As though he had nowhere else to be. Only his scuffed boots, well-worn jeans and the flannel shirt—rolled sleeves straining above his elbows—countered any assumption that the guy lazed around all day. And with that wary look beneath the brim of his hat and the handgun holstered at his hip, he appeared anything but relaxed.

Deirdre pressed her left elbow against the holster at her hip, her senses on alert. Though she'd planned for only a witness interview today, like always, she needed to be prepared for situations to change faster than the speed of pistol fire. Especially here in the Wild West, where she worried that her quick-draw skills were a bit rusty.

The cowboy stopped a few feet in front of her, standing taller, his shoulders broader than the impression he'd given from across the lot. With that closely trimmed beard and mustache, he could have ridden out of one of those fifty-year-old Westerns she'd become an expert on during her bouts of insomnia, which were too frequent lately. Good thing she didn't go for the young-Clint-Eastwood shtick, she decided, as the man squinted back at her, his eyes gray rather than Clint's blue. That flutter in her belly had to be indigestion from airplane snacks, though she couldn't explain the Ennio Morricone spaghetti Western score playing in her head.

"Good afternoon, ma'am."

The music cut, and her stomach settled into a hard lump. Yes, she was supposed to be in her work zone, but who had the guy just called *ma'am*? At thirty-three, she didn't look a day over thirty, in her opinion. Could manage twenty-seven if she bothered with powders and creams. Which she didn't. The cowboy blew right past her affront, anyway, yanking off the hat and giving that sweaty crop of chestnut-brown hair a brisk rub before repositioning it.

"May I help you with something?" As his gaze dropped from her face to her feet, skipping the whole part in the middle, a smile spread on his lips. "Directions to a Western outfitter in Laramie, perhaps?"

Deirdre frowned. Why she'd thought buying those boots would make her look like she fit in on a ranch, she couldn't say, even if they were the cutest pair, with traditional round toe, cowboy heels and fancy stitching. The jeans and waffle Henley top didn't seem like good ideas now, either. She *didn't* belong on this ranch or in this part of the country, though she could say the same about most places in her life. But after hours in planes, shuttles and automobiles just to reach this destination, she wasn't in the mood for the man's pithy comments, either.

"This is the Harmony Fields Ranch, isn't it?"

The cowboy's smile disappeared, his eyes narrowing. He shot a glance at the house before looking back to her again.

"That's what it says on that enormous arch you passed," he said, his words clipped.

"Good. Then I'm at the right place. I'm looking for Micah Perry."

His chin lifted slightly. "You've found him. I'm at a disadvantage here, though. You know who I am, but I don't know…"

He gestured to her and then lowered his hand to his side, keeping it relaxed but within easy reach of his firearm. She couldn't help wondering if everyone in that part of the country greeted visitors with such suspicion.

"I'm FBI Special Agent Deirdre Colton."

She slowly withdrew her badge from her jacket pocket and held it out to him. He stared at it a few beats and then nodded.

Though he tucked his thumbs through his belt loops in a casual pose, his gaze flicked to the house a second time, and he shifted already-dusty boots in the dirt. "How can I help you, Officer? I mean, *Special Agent.*"

His unease shouldn't have struck Deirdre as odd. Guys she met in social situations seldom said things like "that's cool, so pass the pretzels" when she told them where she worked. Their reactions usually fell more under the category of How to Scare Off a Guy in Sixty Seconds. Her ex, Brandon, would have made his exit in less than thirty, which had only made applying to the bureau more appealing to her after their Big D.

Something about Micah's response struck her as different than any man she'd met, though. As though he'd been expecting her to show up at Harmony Fields. Had someone at the field office gotten wind of her plan and tipped him off? Had she miscalculated the risk in conducting her cross-country, not-quite-sanctioned investigation?

"Is there someplace we can talk? I'd like to ask you a few questions about—"

"Can't you just take your report out here?"

He sneaked a third peek at his home, and this time the tiny hairs at Deirdre's nape stood on end. Who or what was inside that house? She steadied her breathing while calculating her next move, her eyes trained on his hands in case he went for his weapon. Sure, she'd made the rookie mistake of going in without backup, but he was supposed to be a witness. A *victim*, even. Not a suspect. Her failure to consider that he might be harboring a fugitive could turn out to be only one of her mistakes today, but it would be the biggest. And the deadliest.

"I think it would be better if we spoke inside."

Deirdre braced herself for him to demand a search warrant, though that would be the *least* problematic action he could take. She reached for her phone to make the pointless call to 911, since the authorities would never reach her in time to assist, but Micah's confused look made her hesitate. As she started to demand to know who was inside the building, a strange sound, like a cry, startled her. She clicked her teeth shut. The odd noise seemed to have come from Micah's belt. He unclipped a little receiver and stared into the even tinier screen.

"Is that a *baby monitor*?" She pointed to the device, but since he didn't look up, she lowered her arm.

Without answering, he stomped toward the house, still watching the screen. She had to jog to keep up with him, her left foot smarting from the blister already rubbing at her heel.

"What's he doing up?" Micah grumbled to himself as he walked. "He should have napped another hour."

"There's a *baby* in there?" Why had she even asked? She pretended not to notice the incredulous look that Micah gave her. The sound of crying. A baby monitor. *Napped.* Of course there was a baby, the existence of whom hadn't popped up in any of her research. With investigative skills like hers, no wonder she was on thin ice with the bureau.

He stomped on until he passed one of the six-by-six deck pillars and opened a slider on the ground floor. "Why'd you think I wanted to talk outside?"

Micah had just gestured for her to precede him inside, but now he stepped in front of her to block her entrance.

"How is it that you don't know about my son? No one told you about him?"

It was Deirdre's turn to squint. "Your son? And who would have told me? I think there's been a misunderstanding."

"You've got that right. A big one. Why would anyone send a federal agent out here? Especially one from the East Coast."

"How did you know—" she began, but she didn't bother finishing. Whether or not his words made sense to her, she couldn't have been a bigger fish out of water on this land, more than a thousand miles from both the Pacific and the Atlantic. Even the cowboy realized that.

"You never said what you were here to ask me about."

"Your stepmother," she blurted and then pressed her lips together. What was wrong with her? She could go toe to toe with any of her fellow special agents—male or female—so what was it about this cowboy that unnerved her? Could the fact that she needed his help so badly be crippling her effort to secure it?

The rancher stared back at her as though he'd seen a ghost, his jaw slack. He closed his mouth just as another cry poured from the monitor still in his hand. He held up an index finger. "If you'll excuse me."

Without waiting for a response, he stepped through the open doorway and closed the slider. It wasn't a bad place to be dismissed, with her choice of chaise lounges and patio dining and conversation arrangements, but she had no way of knowing if he would even return. That was one way of avoiding an FBI interview, she supposed, and a new one to her. On the other hand, she'd done a lousy job of starting this conversation, and now she would have to come up with another plan to get him to speak with her.

Just as she'd started back to her car to regroup, the sound of the door slide brought her back around. Micah stepped outside, and a toddler with sweaty dark hair and a red, tearstained face peered out at her from his dad's arms.

"This is Derek." Then he gestured to her. "And this is Special Agent Colton."

Deirdre pasted on a smile. "Hi, Derek."

The toddler buried his face in his dad's chest, another reaction that didn't particularly surprise her. She'd never had the touch with kids. They probably realized she was more frightened of them than they were of her, so they wisely kept their distance. After a few seconds, though, this particular little boy turned his head and peeked back at her. Automatically, Deirdre covered her face with her hands and opened them like a pair of doors. What made her do that, she couldn't say, but it worked for others who had success with children, so she gave it a shot. The child's eyes widened, and a smile disturbingly similar to his father's spread on his lips.

"I have nothing to say about *Ariel Porter.*"

Deirdre startled at Micah's words, and she shifted her attention back to him, missing neither the alias he'd mentioned nor that he'd ground out the words when he spoke it.

"Now, Mr. Perry, I've flown all the way from Washington, DC, to speak with you, so please give me a chance to tell you about my investigation."

"I'm sorry for your wasted trip. As I said, I don't want to talk about *her.* I haven't seen or spoken to old Ariel in the more than fifteen years since Dad died. I can't help you, so I don't want to waste your time. Or mine."

"Just try to answer a few questions. I'm sure you'll be of more help than you think."

He shook his head. "Thanks for stopping by."

Deirdre's thoughts raced. Her only witness—and possibly her only chance to save a career that dangled by a thread—would be gone in seconds. Her heart thudded as she scrambled for something to say that would, if not stop him, at least slow him down before he returned inside and locked the door.

"Don't you mean Maeve O'Leary?" Deirdre hated the desperation that had sneaked into her voice and hoped he couldn't hear it, too.

"Who?" Micah had just opened the door again and stepped across the threshold, but he jerked his head to look back at her.

Her lips pinched. "Maeve—"

"I heard you. I just don't know who you're talking about. Look, it sounds like you've received some faulty information, but now I *know* I can't help you." He shook his head when she started to interrupt. "We're not even talking about the same person."

"Unfortunately...we are."

The cowboy turned to fully face her and waited for an explanation. If his arms weren't already filled with a wiggling toddler, she figured he would have crossed them, too.

She began carefully, well aware that her words ripped new holes in his already tattered memories and that a victim would be forced to relive a tragedy made worse with new revelations. "Ariel Porter Perry is an alias of a woman whose real name is Maeve O'Leary. One of several aliases, our investigation is beginning to show."

"Is your investigation also revealing that she *murdered* my father?" Micah lifted his chin as though daring her to contradict his claim.

"Yes, we believe that O'Leary was responsible for the death of Leonard 'Len' Perry."

He slowly lowered his chin. "Took you long enough to figure it out."

Deirdre accepted his criticism with a nod, though she didn't deserve to be its target. She needed answers from him, and she would do whatever it took to get them. "Yes, we have found some problematic areas in the original investigation."

"That's what you call not following up after she drained my father's accounts, sold the house and vanished? Wonder how anyone could have overlooked something so insignificant."

At that, she shrugged, though she couldn't help drawing her shoulders closer to her ears. Sure, someone had made mistakes, but she couldn't help the temptation to come to the defense of fellow peace officers. The blue wall of silence was a thing for a reason.

"We also believe there is at least one more victim. Another *husband*. Possibly more."

Micah opened and closed his mouth twice, his shock obvious in his rapid blinking. She should have delivered those bombshell details in smaller, more digestible bites, but he wasn't exactly being a cooperative witness, and desperation made her spill the whole story.

"A *black widow killer*? You're saying that Ariel—I mean this Maeve…"

"Yes." She nodded for emphasis. "Now would you be willing to answer a few questions?"

The cowboy took two steps backward, as if he wanted to put distance between himself and the woman who'd just set fire to his past.

"I already said I don't know—"

"Are you unable to help? Or just *unwilling*?" Her accusation hung heavily between them as she stared up at him in disbelief. After everything she'd just told him, how could he still be reluctant to help her?

"Want juice," Derek announced, breaking the silence.

The toddler reached up and splayed his pudgy hand over his father's whiskers.

Micah covered the child's fingers with his own and slowly slid the hand from his face. "Just a minute, buddy. Let me—"

"Juice!" The word came out as a plaintive whine this time, and the child wiggled, trying to get his father to put him down.

"Looks like someone needs some juice," Deirdre said. The distraction probably wouldn't be enough to convince her potential witness to change his mind, but it gave her a moment to scramble for another plan. Only she was running out of ideas. And hope.

When Micah lowered his son to the ground, the child shot

off for the stairs and then scrambled up the steps in a hands-and-feet approach.

The cowboy yanked off his hat and then waved with it at the staircase.

"Guess you'd better come inside."

Chapter Two

His breath coming in short gasps that had little to do with the stair climb, Micah caught up with his son in the kitchen. Already, Derek was busy adding fresh handprints to the collection always present on the bottom third of their stainless steel refrigerator. Though the child could reach the handles on the side-by-side doors, at least he hadn't mastered opening them yet.

"Juice. Puleeze." The child drummed his hands on the refrigerator door as if his dad needed help locating his favorite drink.

"Just a minute, kiddo."

Micah needed a moment himself to digest the information their guest had just dropped on him. He'd barely had time to register the news so far, and his whole body shook from the resounding clash of suspicion and truth: His heart pounded in a plot for escape from his chest, and his hands were so sweaty they would have slipped off the handle if he tried to open the refrigerator door.

His father really *had* been murdered? He was right all along? Though Micah had known it in his heart, the agent's announcement had sharpened the truth to a wicked point, and her revelation that Ariel—*Maeve*—might be a black widow killer as well pierced the layers of nearly healed scars.

Dropping his hat on the quartz countertop of the island, he bent at the waist and gulped mouthfuls of air. He had to get control, for Derek at least. Straightening, he closed his eyes and opened them again, hoping to clear the fuzzy edges of his new reality. It didn't work.

If only learning that law enforcement officers were finally pursuing the woman who'd destroyed his family could give him some relief. He wouldn't get off that easily. The regret he carried for fleeing west instead of fighting harder after the county coroner had listed his father's death as from natural causes pressed down on him now, heavy and damning. The police might have failed at their jobs, but he was Len Perry's only son. He'd let his father down and allowed his stepmother to get away with murder.

He shook his head, trying to force the thoughts from his mind. Nothing he said or did could make up for his choices then, anyway. And right now, he couldn't afford to look at past mistakes when he needed to focus on the current threat to his ranch, and, more importantly, to his own son. Dread formed a knot and settled heavily in his gut. Would he fail to protect Derek as he once had his father? He ground his teeth, jutting out his chin. He would never let that happen. Whoever was sabotaging Harmony Fields would have to get through him first.

"Daddy!"

Micah blinked, pulled from his dark thoughts to glance down at Derek. The child clung to his jeans just above the knees now, a tantrum already building toward an impressive crescendo. His own self-flagellation would have to wait. His son's needs came first. Always. He chose not to consider whether his father had ever believed the same about him.

"Almost there, buddy."

He scooped up Derek and deposited him in the highchair. The toddler started pounding on the tray before Micah could lock it in place. Soon, he had the child settled with a firefighter sippy cup filled with juice, and he'd scattered a handful of O-shaped cereal over the tray. Only then did he glance over to find their uninvited guest standing in the kitchen doorway. He'd let her inside downstairs before he'd edged off his boots, but he couldn't wait for her while she'd struggled to remove hers. Not with a frustrated two-year-old running loose in the house.

Now the special agent leaned against the wood in her stocking feet, one set of toes rubbing against the opposite heel.

"Guess you found the kitchen."

"My advanced FBI investigation skills at work there," she said dryly.

Her hazel eyes appeared to take in every detail of the room, from the black farmhouse sink to the fancy pecan built-in pantry and range hood cover that Leah had insisted on during their home construction. Strange how those upgrades seemed even more frivolous as he viewed them through the stranger's eyes.

"And I guess *you* averted a crisis." Deirdre pointed to Derek, who was mowing down his snack as quickly as his chubby hands could grasp the O's. When she waved at the child, he lifted his grimy hand and opened and closed it to wave back.

The fist that had gripped Micah's chest since they'd come inside loosened by degrees. At least the agent hadn't immediately leaped into her list of interview questions, which she probably assumed he'd agreed to by letting her in the house. He couldn't help with her investigation. He'd run as far as he could from New York City after his dad's death and buried those memories so deep it seemed as if they'd happened to someone else. With just a few words, the FBI agent had reopened the Earth, forcing him to see and feel it all again.

To delay the conversation, Micah sprinkled a few more pieces of cereal on his son's tray. "A snack can make a lot of things better."

"I have to agree with Derek on that." She watched him for a few seconds longer and then shook her head. "I don't know how you parents do it."

"What? Hand out snacks? We do it fast."

Until that moment, the agent had reserved her smiles for his son, but she turned one on Micah, her full, rose-colored lips curving and her heavily lashed eyes crinkling at the corners. For a flash of a moment, he forgot why they were even together in his kitchen. Warmth spread beneath his rib cage, his mouth so dry that he was tempted to steal Derek's juice. He turned his head to short-circuit the strange connection. What was that all about?

Appearing to have missed the jolt of electricity altogether, the agent stepped around the L-shaped bar that formed two sides of the kitchen's perimeter and then past the wrought iron bar stools that lined it and into the great room. As she smoothed her hand over the buttery leather sofa he'd chosen himself and her gaze moved from the floor-to-ceiling windows to the stone fireplace that stretched nearly as high, Micah couldn't help watching *her*.

Weren't female FBI agents supposed to be buttoned-up middle-aged women with no makeup and their hair in tight buns? Didn't they blend in with dark jackets, sensible shoes and an everywoman diligence? If those things were true, then Special Agent Colton had clearly missed the memo.

To be fair, she'd tied her dark blonde hair in a knot of some sort. She didn't appear to be wearing cosmetics, either. But nothing could have prevented her oval face, heavily lashed eyes and flawless light pink complexion from making her stand out in a crowd. Her fitted shirt and those curve-hugging jeans probably didn't fit the agency dress code, either.

And, for that matter, no one would have referred to those sexy boots that she'd left on the mat downstairs as *sensible*.

Deirdre stood at the base of the staircase, her gaze moving from first the baby gate at the bottom and then the wooden handrail and metal balusters that led to the balcony above. Unfortunately, her position offered him an unobstructed view of her perfect, round behind. To his mortification, she swung around and caught him appreciating said benefit.

He didn't miss her crossed arms and pursed lips as he averted his gaze, suddenly needing to check on his son. As if she would ever buy that. What was wrong with him, anyway? That his senses were out of whack after the news the agent had dumped on him was no excuse for gawking at her. He didn't gawk. He didn't even *date* these days, since the women he'd met couldn't accept that he and Derek were a package deal, and his son deserved a stepmother who actually wanted him. Anyway, if he were interested in female companionship, an FBI agent tracking his father's murderer would never be his first choice. Or even his twentieth.

"You have a beautiful home," she said after a long pause.

"Thanks. We like it." He turned her way but stared at his hands folded in front of him. That the agent had still offered her inane compliment instead of telling him where to stuff his wandering eyes demonstrated just how desperate she was for information about his stepmother. Details he probably couldn't give her, even if he wanted to.

"Do you live here with your son and your...partner?"

"Just my son," he answered automatically over her politically correct inquiry. "My, uh, *wife*—that's Derek's mother—passed away two years ago."

His throat thickened with emotion as it did whenever he shared his sad story. Deirdre shot him a questioning look, but her focus moved on to his son in the chair. She drew her brows together as though weighing the child's age against the information he'd supplied.

"Car accident. Derek was only six weeks old when it happened." He would tell his son the gentlest version of that story when he was older.

"I'm so sorry." Deirdre grimaced, her investigator's impassive expression falling away briefly before she put it back in place.

"Thanks." He nodded his appreciation as he'd done with dozens of friends and even more strangers in the past two years. No one knew what to say, and he knew even less how to respond.

"Do you have a babysitter or a nanny to help with him while you work on the ranch?" She gestured to the windows and the fields beyond them.

"I have off and on, but they keep leaving for better opportunities in town. I do have a cook, who comes in once a week, and a cleaning service once a month. And the neighbors help out when they can."

"Still, it must be hard."

The muscles at the back of his neck tightened, her pity harder to take than her earlier disdain. "It's not perfect, but we do the best we can."

He lifted his chin and glared at her the same way he had others who'd dared to question whether he could care for his own child. "He's my son."

She nodded and cleared her throat. "Apparently, my intel about you wasn't nearly as good as I thought it was, either, since I didn't know he even existed."

"Don't you hate it when that happens?" He'd meant it both as a joke to lighten the tense moment and a quick step away from memories where grief and betrayal were bound together with an unforgiving rope. Some of those details from the time of his wife's death no one needed to know.

"I'm not wrong about Maeve O'Leary. And I'm not wrong about your father. Or *you*."

"Me? What does this have to do with me?"

"You might be Maeve's only surviving victim."

"I'm not a—" He shook his head, the term ill-fitting, yet the truth of it squeezed in his chest. He'd been just a kid, an adult only by a few days along with eighteen candles on a birthday cake.

Suddenly, the timing of the agent's arrival and that of all the acts of sabotage to the ranch seemed less coincidental as well. Could they be connected? Could the suspect behind all those crimes on Harmony Fields be none other than his step-*monster* herself? The idea was absurd. If Ariel, aka Maeve, was a black widow killer, he wasn't another husband she could strangle in her web. But the possibility of connection still niggled at the back of his mind. Could this smart, lethal adversary have found out about his success out West and followed her insatiable need for money right to him and his son? And if she had, could he stop her before she killed again?

"I really could use your help," Deirdre said, breaking the long silence.

He shook his head. "Look, I appreciate your confirming what I already believed about my dad. And I'd like to see my stepmother pay for her crimes as much as anyone, but I've already told you I don't know anything—"

"About Maeve O'Leary," she finished for him and then sighed.

"I'm sorry. Really. I wish I could help. I'm also tied up with problems of my own around here." He tried to ignore the truth that he was failing his father again, but with Derek's safety at stake, he had no choice. "In fact, when you pulled up, I thought you would be—"

He stopped as the sound of crunching gravel filtered in from outside. The agent must have heard it, too, as she immediately crossed to the wall next to the windows and peered outside. "Were you expecting someone?"

"If I'm guessing right, that's Sheriff Richard Guetta." He stepped behind her and glanced down at one of the familiar white SUVs from the Albany County Sheriff's Office with black and yellow lettering on the side.

She jerked her head to look back at him. "You called the *sheriff*?"

"That's what I was trying to tell you. I was waiting for him to come by and take a report. *Another* report on whoever's been sabotaging my ranch." He shook his head, smiling over his confusion at her arrival. "Sheriff Guetta had agreed to come out himself this time since so many things kept happening, but I thought it was overkill for him to send the FBI."

Her expression tight, she kept watching the vehicle on the driveway below. After the sheriff's recognizable mop of prematurely white hair appeared over the top of the SUV, Deirdre turned back to Micah.

"I get what you meant now." She sighed and then pushed her shoulders back. "This isn't going to go well."

"Why is that?"

She'd slid another look at the window, but now she met his gaze directly. "Because I'm not exactly supposed to be here."

"What do you mean 'not exactly'?"

"Not at all."

Chapter Three

Deirdre shifted in her seat as Sheriff Guetta turned the kitchen bar stool sideways so that he faced her instead of the countertop, his black uniform slightly rumpled but the seven-pointed star above his heart shiny. Her face felt hot. Her chest tight. She'd had no choice but to give a quick overview of her story, and she now sat stuck like a convict, waiting for the guillotine blade to drop. Okay, maybe not that extreme, but the sheriff now had the power to end her career, and she was sweating while awaiting sentencing.

The law enforcement officer didn't seem to be in any hurry to continue his questioning, watching her instead with unnerving pale blue eyes. He took a sip from the iced tea glass that Micah had rested in front of him. No way would she be able to swallow if she took a drink from hers. She recognized his tactic. She'd used it herself dozens of times to keep her interview subjects off balance. It was equally effective on her, she decided, pressing her shoulder blades against the metal back of the bar stool.

Guetta leaned forward and rested his elbows on his knees, his fiftysomething spread spilling slightly over his fully outfitted duty belt. Finally, he spoke.

"Now let me get this straight." He paused again to flick his lollipop stick from one side of his mouth to the other, hinting at an attempt to beat a tobacco habit. "You have exactly *zero* approval for this cross-country journey you made to get a witness statement. In fact, you're not assigned to this case, or *any* case, because your boss benched you for coloring outside the lines."

Deirdre shot a look to Micah, who stood next to the highchair, wiping his whining toddler's hands and face and pretending not to listen to every word she and the sheriff said. His rapid blinking gave him away. She didn't owe the rancher any answers, even if he probably had as many questions as the sheriff did. Micah could have given her the heads-up that law enforcement was on the way, after all. And, though she'd at least tried to tell him about her investigation, he still hadn't agreed to help her.

She purposely turned her stool away from him to focus on the sheriff. "My issue with the bureau wasn't as bad as you're making it sound. My superiors and I just had a disagreement about my approach in pursuing a suspect. Someone wanted for heinous crimes, I might add. And one we were able to detain without any further loss of life."

"Well, that's something," the sheriff said.

At least someone understood that, since no one in the DC field office had appreciated her efforts. *You're welcome.* If she'd come out and said those words that had been burning on her tongue at the time, she probably wouldn't have a job to save right now.

"Sounds like a suspension to me," Micah pointed out.

"I wasn't *suspended.*"

Deirdre shot an annoyed look at Micah, surprised to find him standing on the other side of the bar now, holding Derek, instead of across the room near the refrigerator. As the toddler wiggled in his arms, again trying to get his father to put him down, Micah trapped her with a condescending look. Who was he to judge her? Had he never made a mistake before? Had he never had a wonderful idea that turned out to be not so great? Even if she'd gone a little off book by taking a side trip to Wyoming, at least she'd been tracking his father's killer, which was more than officers from any other agency had done on this cold case in a long time.

"What do you call it, then?" Guetta asked.

Her cheeks burned, but if she had any hope of weathering this situation, she had to come as clean as possible.

"My superiors referred to it as 'forced leave' while I remain under investigation. And, technically, this trip is a *vacation*."

"Sounds like splitting hairs to me," the sheriff said with a chuckle.

"But you know how important that distinction is." At least she hoped he did.

The sheriff gestured to Micah as if to include him in the conversation. "A *suspension* would have required her to forfeit her badge and weapon. And she still seems to have those."

Deirdre pressed her elbows to her sides to feel the reassuring presence of her holster, but it offered no comfort now. With one call to Washington from the sheriff, her badge could disappear. She stared at her hands as all that work she'd put into her job for the past three years—and the two years of testing and training before that—floated away like smoke through an open window.

Micah pointed to the holster nearly concealed at her hip. "You carried that thing on the plane?" He waited for her nod. "How did you even do that when you're supposed to be on 'vacation'?"

"By jumping through a lot of hoops, I would guess," Guetta chimed.

Deirdre gestured to the sheriff. "What he said. But also, FBI special agents are technically always on duty, even when traveling for personal business and even when the bureau isn't paying for the flight. If I had checked my weapon and something happened on the flight that I possibly could have prevented, there would be hell to pay."

The sheriff held both hands up, palms out and fingers splayed, an incredulous look on his face. "What's funny is you put yourself in the doghouse for not following orders, and you plan to get *out of trouble* by conducting an off-books investigation and single-handedly bringing down a serial killer."

When he put it that way, it did sound ridiculous. The sick feeling in her gut confirmed that suspicion. But since she'd already flown across the country and driven over even more of it while searching for information, she had to at least try to defend her plan. Her only hope was the lawman's pity, and she would be naive to depend on it.

"Anyway, I'm also helping my cousin Sean Colton, of the NYPD Ninety-Eighth Precinct, and his team with *their* investigation."

"Your cousin?" the sheriff asked.

Though she understood that he was trying to rattle her, she couldn't seem to avoid the blur. "Second cousin. His late dad, Kieran Colton, and my father, Eoin, were *first* cousins."

She waited, her throat tight, wishing she'd avoided specifically identifying the two men. Maybe this far from Virginia no one would recognize her high-profile politician father's name, but she couldn't guarantee it, since he loved publicity almost as much as the womanizing that kept him in the news. Good thing she caught no recognition in either man's gaze. Today was already bad enough without bringing dear old Dad into it.

Micah gestured with a circular motion for her to get on with her story, and then he started it for her. "You said this team you're helping is trying to find a missing person, who happens to be their family friend."

She narrowed her gaze at him. What had changed? Had the rancher decided to support her now, instead of just judging her? She couldn't decide whether to be grateful or suspicious, but since distrust better fit her DNA, she went with that. She adhered to the Benjamin Franklin quote that "God helps those who help themselves," and in her experience, people never lifted a finger for anyone else without something in it for them.

"Yes. The prominent psychiatrist Humphrey Kelly," she said, clarifying his comment, anyway. "If he hadn't stepped up after Kieran Colton's death, the four siblings wouldn't have been able to stay together."

The sheriff planted his elbows on the counter, folded his hands and turned his head to look right through her.

"So, when you found a link between that case and a potential serial killer that you could make a splash by arresting, you agreed to help your cousins out, even if that meant going rogue."

She held her hands wide and blew out a breath. "You're right. I didn't think it through. But since I'm here—"

"Since you're here," he repeated, "we'll have to deal with the FBI agent who just can't follow the rules. That'll mean having a little chat with your superiors back in DC."

Her gut clenched as her last bit of hope flitted away. Her career, the only thing she'd ever done without her father's express direction and approval, was over. *He's my son.* As Micah's words from earlier replayed in her thoughts, she wondered if her own dad had ever felt that kind of vehement bond with her. He certainly wouldn't now.

"That's enough, Richard."

Micah's stern voice shocked her as much as his stance. With his arms folded over his chest, he stood staring down the lawman as though he had no sense at all. He couldn't talk to a police officer like that. He'd even called him by his first name. She braced herself, looking back and forth between them, waiting for one to throw a punch. Or, worse, draw a weapon. She didn't know what to make of Micah clearly taking her side this time—or her temptation to appreciate it just a little. The last thing she needed was a cowboy with a hero complex coming to her aid and getting one of them shot.

Guetta threw his head back then and laughed in a full-belly way that would have been great to share if she weren't the butt of his joke. When Micah's lips lifted as well, a sign that the men were friends, she ground her teeth hard enough to unsettle years of orthodontia.

"What is this? I don't have time for your jokes." That she couldn't turn her rental around now and drive back to Casper, ignoring posted speed limits, frustrated her even more.

The sheriff chuckled for a few seconds longer and then wiped the corners of his eyes.

"Look," he said, when he finally stopped laughing, "I manage a department with forty-five officers covering nearly five thousand square miles of land. To say we're stretched pretty thin is an understatement. You think I have time to waste tattling on a rogue agent whose work is outside my jurisdiction?"

"You mean you're not going to contact the special agent in charge?"

"Why would I do that when I have an allegedly competent investigator, who's on vacation and has decided to be a *volunteer* to help us out on a case?"

"I haven't volunteered for— Wait." She stopped as some of the puzzle pieces fell into place. "I'm already here on an investigation. Two, really. You don't expect me to assist on one of yours, too, do you?"

She looked from the grinning sheriff to the rancher, who watched the other man with a guarded look.

"You're not serious," she said, though he clearly was.

"You're attempting to blackmail a federal agent into doing free investigating for your department?"

"Will you be reporting *me*, then?"

Deirdre opened her mouth and closed it. She couldn't go to the agency about him without falling on her weapon and figuratively pulling the trigger. And if she didn't agree to work as an unpaid investigator for the sheriff's office, he could still report her. She swallowed, feeling the squeeze all the way down her throat as the jaws of a trap snapped around her.

"Besides, I'm not that big a fan of the feds," Guetta admitted. "Whenever we get a big case, someone from the Denver office charges in like the Lone Ranger to take over."

Her lucky day—now she was stuck in the middle of a turf war with someone who'd probably watched as many Westerns as she did. She'd dealt with officials from local agencies who bristled when she'd arrived to take charge of investigations deemed federal but never from a disadvantage like this.

"I don't think this is a good idea," Micah said.

Well, she agreed with him on that one thing. The sheriff turned to the rancher.

"Think about it for a minute, Micah. You've phoned in how many reports now? Half a dozen? A baker's dozen? I even agreed to drive out myself today because we still haven't figured out who's targeting your ranch. A fresh pair of eyes on the case couldn't hurt. I know how much you want to protect your son."

Micah immediately ducked around the end of the bar to check on Derek, who sat on the floor next to a toy box, pulling out a fire truck, then a xylophone, then a teddy bear and then a whole box of plastic building blocks and dumping them all on the floor.

"But she's an outsider," he said when he looked back to them again. "She doesn't know Laramie from Colorado Springs. She doesn't know how things work around here."

Guetta pinched his chin, causing the few days' growth of white whiskers to flutter. "Could be a good thing. As I said, fresh eyes. And if Quantico did its job, she also should be handy with that firearm she's packing."

"I'm standing right here, you know," Deirdre said, crossing her arms.

The toddler raced back into the kitchen, awkwardly balancing a hard plastic pickup truck and a police car of the same material in his arms. He dropped them next to Deirdre's stool and kicked off his own demolition derby, complete with zooming engines and crash sounds.

Deirdre looked up from the child first, but when Micah lifted his chin and met her gaze, his worry palpable, something unfamiliar, tender even, spread in her chest.

"Maybe Richard has a good idea," he said.

She cleared her throat, pushing away emotions that had no place in her job. Or life. "You kidding? It's a terrible idea."

"Worse than your showing up on my property today without approval from DC?"

She answered with a shrug. Why did they have to keep bringing that up?

He rested his elbows on the counter and folded his hands as the sheriff had done before. "How about we make a deal?"

"Deal?" She wasn't exactly in a strong negotiating position.

"If you assist with the sheriff's investigation and help us find out who's targeting us, I'll tell you everything I know about my late father's wife."

She should have been happy. Though he'd agreed to give her the interview she'd flown across the country for, it had become an empty victory. "You've already said you don't know anything about her."

"I'll try to think of something." He gave her a close-lipped smile. "It's the best I can do."

She didn't answer, but he didn't need her to. They both knew it was an offer she couldn't refuse.

The sheriff stood up from his bar stool. "Remind me not to negotiate with you, Micah. You drive a hard bargain."

Again, Deirdre gritted her teeth. If the two of them fist-bumped, she would scream. She swallowed and then dived in. "I don't know anything about your case."

"That's because we just spent all of this time talking about yours," the sheriff pointed out. "It seems to be a campaign to frighten the Perry family off the land. At least so far."

He gestured from Micah to Derek in a signal that he believed the situation would escalate.

"Let me see. Someone cut the fences and released the horses from the pasture. Twice. They opened the doors to the petting zoo in the middle of the night, setting all the animals free." He gestured to Micah. "What am I forgetting?"

Micah started ticking off items on his fingers. "He ransacked our house while Derek and I were at the feed store. Several thousand dollars' worth of damage there. Then there was a suspicious fire in one of the storage sheds."

"We've been hoping to catch the trespassers in the act, but that hasn't worked out yet," the sheriff added.

Except for the arson and the breaking and entering at the house because of the amount of damage, most of the crimes could have been misdemeanor level so far. She would have said so, too, but she doubted it would go over well.

"Are you sure it's not kids messing around? You also said 'he.' Are you certain the suspect is male?"

"I'm not certain, but the buffet that someone turned over in the great room weighed a ton." Micah pointed to an empty space along the wall where the piece of furniture had probably been located before. "Still waiting for a new one to be shipped from the manufacturer."

He shifted his hand to point at the driveway. "The rabbit

hutch in the petting zoo wasn't light, either. Whoever it was destroyed that, too."

She winced at the image of the scared bunnies scattering and hated to ask the next question. "But still no loss of life, right?"

"Not directly. But if you count that he locked all the dogs in my office and then set two of the rabbits free without protection against the foxes that prey on the defenseless around here…" He paused to shrug. "Well, it wasn't pretty."

Deirdre shivered involuntarily. What was the matter with her? She'd been on the scene of some fairly gruesome homicides, but just the thought of someone hurting those poor bunnies infuriated her. She hoped Micah would miss that, but the look he gave her suggested that he didn't miss much.

"And if you find that disturbing, just consider that whoever is doing these things has been inside the house where my son sleeps."

Her gaze lowered to the child on the floor, oblivious to the possible danger around him as he played. She couldn't help it; she shivered again. Just the thought that someone who had a problem with Micah might target his child sent ice through her veins. The child looked up at her then and hit her with one of his cherubic grins.

"Dee-Dee!" he announced, pointing right at her.

"It's Special Agent—" Micah started to correct, but she waved him off.

"Dee-Dee is fine." A little too pleasant, she hated to admit.

She leaned far over, and of its own accord, her hand reached down to ruffle his baby-soft hair. An unfamiliar warmth started somewhere in her chest and spread down her arm to her hand and fingers. So this was what her coworkers meant when they talked about how easily children climbed inside their hearts. Of course, she couldn't let anything happen to that sweet little boy, but she needed to guard herself around him, too. If she lost her professional distance and became too attached, she would be of no help to either him or his father.

"It does sound like someone is trying to scare you away," she said, hoping Micah missed the lingering thickness of emotion in her voice. "Do you have any enemies? Anyone who would have a reason to take this land away from you?"

"Not anyone I can think of."

He glanced across the room to the staircase instead of looking at her. She was tempted to tell him that this would go a lot faster if he didn't lie, but she would mention that later.

"I'll need you to come up with a list, anyway. If you already gave one to the sheriff's office, you'll need to dig deeper. Look at anyone who might have a beef with you—the guy at the feed store who was angry because you took his parking spot. The high school classmate your girlfriend dumped to date you."

He met her gaze and looked away. She immediately regretted bringing that one up, since it sounded like she was looking for his dating history, but spurned lovers were classic suspects for revenge crimes.

"I'll make a list," he said, still not looking at her.

Ready to change that subject and unable to sit still any longer, she headed into the kitchen to retrieve her messenger bag from where she'd left it, next to the closed basement door. When she returned, she set it on a bar stool next to the one she'd been sitting on and pulled a notebook and pen from it.

"What report were you filing today?" she managed as she flipped the notebook open. Maybe if she put herself back in her regular routine for taking witness statements, she could escape some of the strangeness of dealing with this one.

"Someone cut the fence in the pasture, letting fifty head of cattle escape this morning before the first feed. My neighbors and I spent half the morning corralling them again. That's why Derek was late getting down for his nap."

"And he didn't sleep as long as you'd hoped," she said, recalling his words earlier.

He nodded. "He's going to be a pistol by dinnertime."

"Or before," Guetta agreed. "That's my cue to get out of here."

The sheriff crossed through the great room in several long strides.

"Wait," Deirdre called after him as he reached the front door. "Weren't you taking a report?"

"You can take notes and photos when Micah shows you the damage. I'll file the report later from my office." At her confused expression, he added, "We have computers there. Real internet, too. Not even dial-up."

"I never said—"

He lifted a hand to ward off her comments as he opened the door. "I'll catch up with you again tomorrow."

Deirdre's breath caught. "And you're expecting me to *be here* tomorrow?"

The sheriff held his hands wide. "How else are you going to figure out what's going on with this ranch?"

He pointed out the door to her rental car. "Let me guess— you planned to get your witness statement today and take off on a plane tonight."

"The red-eye," she said with a shrug.

"You were optimistic about convincing the witness to co-operate, weren't you?"

"I'm good at my job. Usually."

The sheriff grinned back at her. "Looks like you'll have to reschedule."

"I don't even have a place to stay. And the last hotel I saw was—"

"About thirty-five miles from here," Guetta finished for

her. "Good thing Micah here has a ginormous house with plenty of empty guest rooms."

"That's not going to work." Even if she were okay staying in the home of a cowboy she'd been checking out earlier, she'd already broken enough rules today without agreeing to be a houseguest of a potential witness.

"I have to agree with Special Agent Colton on that one," Micah said.

"Might as well call me Deirdre," she grumbled.

When Micah didn't answer at all, the sheriff chuckled. "You two appear to be capable adults. I'm sure you can handle being together in this house without turning into bags of hormones."

"That won't be a problem." Great. She'd just made it sound like it would be.

Micah shot her an uncomfortable look and then coughed into his elbow. "Of course, that wouldn't be an issue, but wouldn't your place be a better choice? Special Agent Colton—I mean, Deirdre—probably didn't bring any luggage. Maybe your wife and daughters have a few things she can wear?"

"Clearly, you haven't been to my house lately. With three teenagers grumbling around, I wouldn't wish that estrogen bomb on anyone. Even a disobedient FBI agent." Tilting his head to the side, he pointed at Micah. "Anyway, don't you still have a few things from your—"

"Fine. She can stay here," Micah blurted before the sheriff could say *wife*.

"We'll figure something out."

"I'm sure you will."

Guetta let himself out, and Deirdre could have sworn she heard him laughing as he strode along the deck to the stairs and the drive below.

Chapter Four

Micah was sure he'd been to libraries louder than the quad cab of his pickup as he drove with Deirdre to the north pasture to photograph the most recent damage. Derek's uncharacteristic silence in the car seat behind him hinted at a catnap that would only add to his grouchiness later. After a peek in his rearview mirror to check on his sleeping son, Micah frowned. He couldn't blame Deirdre for being less than talkative as well. She didn't care about the newest round of sabotage to his fence lines, no matter how many head of cattle had made a run for it that morning. And no matter what the sheriff had said, she was no volunteer.

Why he'd made the situation worse by ganging up on her and bargaining with his offer of help on her investigation, he couldn't say. The last thing he needed as he tried to determine who'd been targeting his family was an investigator who didn't play by the rules. Special Agent Colton found no gray areas off-limits when she tracked a suspect. For her, the ends always justified the means. But did they, really? She'd told him and the sheriff about the investigation that put her in trouble, but she hadn't said whether her unconventional methods had caused problems for that case when the suspect went to trial.

Was she really all that different from his stepmother or

his late wife? Okay, maybe it wasn't fair to lump an investigator who broke some rules to stop a murderer to an *actual serial killer*. Also, since she still appeared to be breathing in the passenger seat, Deirdre clearly hadn't abandoned her husband and newborn only to die in a car accident during her grand exit. Still, whether their situations were exactly alike or not, he couldn't afford to rely on someone whose moral code offered as many offshoots as theirs had.

You have no choice. He squeezed the steering wheel as the truth washed over him. In their lack of options, he and the agent were the same. Already, the events of sabotage on the ranch had escalated since someone had first broken the latch on the corral gate and allowed the horses to visit his back porch and munch his flowers. He was fooling himself to assume that the situation wouldn't grow more dangerous until whoever had been targeting them got whatever they wanted. Only he had no idea what that was.

To prevent his sweet little boy from getting caught in the crossfire, he would have to do whatever it took. Even if that meant collaborating with an FBI agent whose definition of *right* stretched so far outside the right/wrong lane that it required escort cars with posted Wide Load signs and flashing lights.

His fingers tightened again, causing the steering wheel to bite into his palms. He might have to work with Special Agent Colton, but that didn't mean he had to trust her. Beautiful women had already wreaked enough havoc in his life and those of his whole family, thank you very much. He didn't bother trying to tell himself he didn't find Deirdre attractive. If that episode before the sheriff's arrival hadn't been proof enough, now his whole body hummed with nervous energy that had more to do with her nearness than today's sabotage incident or even the news about his stepmother. Whatever it was, it needed to stop right now.

"I'd prefer not to wear your late wife's clothes, if you don't mind."

As Deirdre's words fractured the silence, catching him thinking things that were so far out of bounds that the sidelines had vanished, Micah jerked his shoulders. He tried to play off his awkward move by including it in an even more graceless stretch, but as her words sank in, he pressed into the headrest instead. Leah's clothes.

"Good thing, because I donated them a long time ago."

Immediately, he regretted the words that escaped before he could stop them. Though he kept his eyes on the dirt road ahead, he could still feel her gaze, warm on the side of his face. Why had he put it like that? Did he *want* her to ask more questions about Leah? He couldn't blame her for being curious about him disposing of his wife's possessions so soon. Some widows and widowers clung to their late spouses' things, even holding on to items they couldn't justify—like socks—for years. His temptation to tell a stranger that the situation had been different with his late wife made no sense. How could he explain that he'd needed to purge rather than cherish basic reminders of her?

"I don't know why Richard even suggested it," he added when he couldn't hold still under her scrutiny any longer. "You're at least three inches taller than Leah was."

He forced himself to use her name and hoped Deirdre didn't notice the effort it had required. She resettled his extra hat that he'd loaned her earlier on her lap. It was too big, but she had to wear something out in the fields.

"Probably forty pounds heavier, too," she said after a few seconds.

"Much less than that," he said automatically and then frowned. He'd all but admitted that he'd sized her body up against his memory of Leah's. "It's not that. It's just…you know, your job. The fitness regimen. You're—" he paused, grasping for words "—sturdier."

Her laugh came out low, slow and more sensual than she probably realized. Parts of him weren't nearly as naive to that power.

"Now that's a descriptor every woman dreams that someone will use when referring to her," she said in a dreamy voice. "*Sturdy.*"

Micah dampened his lips, never letting his gaze leave the windshield. These waters were already too muddy for him to try to clarify further without risking getting lost in the soup. No way would he tell her what all that *sturdiness* did for him, either.

"I'm sure I can find you something to wear."

With a quick peek to the side, he caught her watching him, an incredulous expression on her face.

"You think *we* wear the same size?"

This time he blew out a breath. "No. I—"

Deirdre swiped a hand at the dash in front of her. "Aw, just kidding. You're probably right, anyway."

Not even close. Somehow he managed not to say it out loud this time. He peeked out the side-view mirror. Everything he said to her seemed to be a mistake. Not only had he drawn attention to the uncomfortable intimacy of her being forced to share his wardrobe, but now he'd also painted in his own mind the image of the agent's feminine curves brushing the inside of *his* clothes. She probably was wondering if the pants and shirts he would give her would even be clean. He hadn't missed her disdain as she'd spoken of her journey to his ranch. The agent was no fan of the West. And more than likely cowboys like him in general.

"We'll run into Laramie later this afternoon, so you can pick up a few things."

"At the Western outfitter?" At his side glance, she grinned. "You mentioned it earlier."

They both knew he'd been making fun of her when he'd suggested that. "I was thinking about Gary's Farm & Fleet. Closest big shopping mall is back in Casper. But if you still think you need more barn dance gear, we can—"

"No, no. Gary's it is."

He didn't even try to hold back his smile this time. "Great. You'll love the place."

Her silence told him how much she believed that.

They drove slowly over the last half mile of bumpy road, and then he pulled his truck to the soft shoulder. He pointed through the windshield to the field off to the east.

"This is the area that received the damage this morning."

She glanced up and down the fence line, which, at least in this area, remained intact.

"How come I don't see any cattle out in the pasture?"

"Since there's a *gaping hole* in the fence, we had to move them to the weekend pasture. They do love to find a break in the fence line and head off on adventures."

She closed her eyes and shook her head. "Right. I didn't think about that."

Micah threw open the truck door and jumped down from the step. Deirdre hopped out as well, meeting him near the tailgate.

He couldn't resist a grin as he pointed down at her pristine boots. "I hope you don't mind getting those dirty. We're going to have to walk. Just a half mile or so."

"We have to *walk*?" She squinted until her eyes were tiny slits.

He pointed to tall grass along the fence that they would have to follow to reach the area of damage. "We could have taken the horses, but I wasn't sure you could ride."

"You could've asked."

"I'll remember to do that next time." He noted that she still hadn't said whether she had any experience sitting a horse. "Anyway, I thought city slickers were used to walking in your concrete jungle."

She gestured to the dry grass. "That doesn't look like concrete, and believe me, I would never walk that far in *these* boots." Like earlier, she rubbed the pointed toe of one against the heel of the other.

"Blister?"

She lifted both shoulders and let them drop. "One of those, and a raw place on my calf where the top of the boot rubbed. I should have known better than to wear them."

He stared at her boots for several seconds, surprised that she'd admitted to her mistake. In her field of work, where male agents probably outnumbered females at least three to one, it probably didn't serve her well to admit any form of weakness.

"You'll break them in. If they're a great fit, you don't get blisters at all."

"Guess I didn't pick well." She kicked at the dust and then winced.

"Do you mind if I ask why…?" He gestured to her whole getup, reminding himself not to linger on his favorite parts of it. His memory adeptly filled in the blanks.

"Thought it would help me fit in better."

He tried not to smile and could tell how badly he'd failed from her frown.

"How's that working for you?" he managed.

"Other than the blister and the cowboy who thinks I'm a comedy skit, just dandy."

"I'm not laughing. Well, not really."

"Thanks." She pointed to the rear window of the truck cab, where the back of Derek's car seat peeked around the sides of the rear-seat headrest. "You don't plan to leave him in there, do you?"

"With an FBI agent right here watching me? Not a chance."

After lowering the tailgate and lifting the flip cover on the truck bed, he pulled out the child-carrier backpack. He used the pack's kickstand to prop it on the ground outside the truck door.

Deirdre followed him around the truck bed, appearing to watch every step.

"You mean you would if I weren't here?"

"Well…" Grinning, he held his hands wide and then shook his head. "You're too easy. You know that?"

Her eyes widened. She had to know that he'd meant *too easily fooled*, but what he'd said sounded like something else entirely.

"No. I never leave him in the truck. Even when it's only going to be a few minutes and it's really tempting."

"That's good to hear."

Her question should have offended him more. Not for the first time that afternoon, she seemed to be evaluating whether he was a good parent. He couldn't help but to respect someone who had his son's best interests at heart, even if she'd admitted that she knew nothing about caring for children.

He pushed back his hat and stared up at the sky. "On a sunny day like today in the low seventies, the temperature inside that closed cab would climb to over one hundred degrees in about thirty minutes. There's not a job I can think of on the ranch that takes less time than that."

She nodded as though satisfied with his answer and then pointed to the backpack on the ground. "That looks like something you'd be wearing for a hike, not a day in the fields."

"Works in a pinch. We have to get creative sometimes on days when I can't find childcare."

He reached into the cab and unbuckled Derek's car seat.

The child grunted and groused as Micah worked the harness straps to release his legs and arms.

"You said something about coming out here on horseback. You don't ride with him—" Deirdre stopped and pointed over her shoulder to her back.

"Why not?" Micah chuckled until her eyes widened with alarm.

He had to stop with the ranch jokes. She might have experience in investigating crimes and tracking serial killers, but here on Harmony Fields, she was greener than a spring calf still getting its footing.

"I don't do that, either."

"Then how...?"

She squinted at him as he lifted his still-lethargic son and propped him on his hip.

"It's been a little tricky, but the truth is there's no safe way to take a baby on horseback. Other than maybe a gentle circle around the corral."

"So what do you do with him when you have to go out in the fields?"

"My neighbors are always happy to watch him for a few hours so I can get some work done."

"Didn't you say they also helped you corral the cattle this morning after they escaped?" At his nod, she added, "I can't believe they do all that. I don't even *know* my neighbors in my condo complex outside DC."

"It's different around here. We're all so spread out. We count on each other when something comes up. We're not just neighbors. We're friends."

"You're lucky to have that support system."

She stared off into the distance, making him wonder if she had one of those herself, or even any close friends.

"Sometimes one of the ranch hands will do babysitting duty when it's my turn to ride the fences, or lately, check out more damage," he said, trying to draw her back from wherever she'd gone.

She grinned when she turned back to him. "Now that I really can't picture."

"You kidding? Some of those guys are my best childcare providers." Swaying back and forth to comfort his child, Micah frowned at her. "You should know better than to discount a whole gender in possible performance on a certain job."

"I was thinking more about guys more comfortable roping a two-hundred-pound steer than diapering a twenty-pound human, but point taken."

"Make your steer about a thousand pounds heavier and I'll concede *your* point."

Until then, Derek had still been slumped against his shoulder, but as Micah glanced down, the toddler opened one eye as a test. Slowly, he lifted the other lid and studied Deirdre warily. Then he lowered his gaze to the backpack, stationed on the ground.

"No ride," he announced, clasping his legs around Micah's waist.

"Just for a little bit, buddy." Micah gently peeled Derek away from his side and aimed the child's feet at the two leg holes in the backpack. The toddler kicked his feet and shook his head, the game becoming an upside-down version of whack-a-mole, without the bat. Only by bracing the contraption between his legs could Micah prevent the whole thing from falling with his son inside.

"No!"

Even with his seat planted and his father snapping the harness straps over his shoulders, Derek still protested. He yanked off the New York Yankees baseball cap his father had put on him, held it out and dropped it on the ground.

"I wish I could get to ride around in that cool pack."

Deirdre's words must have surprised Derek as he let his tennis shoes touch the ground and peered between his dad's legs at her. Micah lunged for the hat and lifted the backpack, baby inside, onto the tailgate. He had to hold on to the contraption to prevent it from toppling over.

"I really like your fancy hat, too," she said.

"Yankees!" Derek announced.

When Micah plunked the cap back on his son's head with his free hand, Derek patted the top several times.

"Not the Wyoming...? Not the Cheyenne...?"

Realizing her questions were for him, Micah glanced up from where he was sliding his arms into the backpack straps. He grinned at her furrowed brow. "I'll save you from having to list every city. There isn't a single pro sports team in the state of Wyoming."

She leaned her head to look from the boy to his dad. "New York, then?"

Micah hefted the pack onto his back, securing the waistband first and then snapping and adjusting the straps at his sternum. "You can take the boy's dad out of Manhattan, but you can't take Manhattan out of—"

"The boy's dad," she finished for him. "But isn't the new Yankee Stadium in the Bronx?"

"Must you be so borough specific?" he asked with a grin.

"What about the Mets?"

"The *who*?" Even a former New Yorker like him knew that those team allegiances were formed in the crib and held until the grave.

She shook her head. "Never mind."

He shouldn't have made her smile. Certainly not laugh. When she turned both on him, the force connected like a sucker punch. His throat tightened and warmth spread across his hips, right where he'd anchored the backpack. Then lower.

Worse than even that, his knees buckled, and he practically dumped his precious cargo.

Deirdre shot over to him and gripped his upper arm, compounding his humiliation. He could have sworn he'd never looked at a beautiful woman before.

"You sure you got that?" she asked after a few seconds.

He flexed his biceps, both so she would release him and because he hated hoping that she wouldn't. She did, slowly lowering her arm to her side.

"I'm fine. I just tripped." He looked past her, hoping she wouldn't call him on his lie.

As she started to step away, Derek reached out and grasped the short ponytail that Deirdre had tied her hair in before their drive into the fields. She pulled back, surprised, but the toddler only continued to stare at his hand, where her light-colored strands had spilled through his fingers. Micah tightened his jaw. Whatever statement it made about a man's character that he could be jealous of his own two-year-old, Micah had to admit that all those negatives applied to him. He shoved his hands in his pockets, wishing his fingers didn't ache to feel all that softness for himself.

"I want Dee-Dee," Derek announced.

Deirdre's gaze flicked to Micah's and then away, her cheeks pink. And though he'd worn a hat all day, his face still felt sunburned. In advocating for himself, the child had unknowingly spoken of his father's wants as well—the kind that Micah had no business having.

"I'm carrying you, buddy," Micah said when he found his voice. "Deirdre will be right there with us."

"No. Dee-Dee can carry me."

"You're *my* little boy. It's my job to take care of you."

Hoping if they got started that Derek would be distracted enough to forget his demand, Micah marched into the grass toward the fence corner. Deirdre fell into step beside him.

"You see. We'll all be there in no time," he assured his son.

"I sure hope so," Deirdre answered for them all.

Since she was pretending not to be in pain as she walked, he tried not to notice her tight expressions every time she stepped on a rock.

"Dee-Dee, carry me. Dee-Dee, carry me."

"She can't do that. You're much too heavy—"

"Too heavy for whom? Me?"

Micah winced as he realized he'd said the exact wrong thing to this woman, who probably had often experienced others questioning her strength and abilities.

"I'm sure you could do it. There's just no reason to. You're already doing so much for us. You don't need to prove—"

At her glare, he forgot whatever he'd been about to say.

"Here. Hand me the pack." She reached out her arms and waited.

"You know, it's not always good to reward a child for making demands."

Instead of answering, Deirdre, who had to be the most stubborn woman he'd ever met, continued to stretch out her arms. Finally, he unbuckled the chest strap.

"You're going to regret this decision."

"No more than anything else I've done today."

She had a point there. He unbuckled the belt and allowed her to help him out of the backpack straps. Once she'd settled the pack on the ground, kickstand open, she turned away and let him slide the contraption over her arms. She widened her stance to accept the weight when he released it and then buckled and tightened the waistband and cinched the side straps.

Derek giggled the whole time, but he seemed to know better than to thrash his head around and unbalance her.

"Ride with Dee-Dee," he called out with glee.

"Hope you're ready for this." Forcing himself not to look back and risk the temptation to help her, Micah started off again.

She marched along beside him, her shoulders back, her chin lifted.

"Just show me where to go. We need to get this handled so we can move on to the other case."

"Up there. Past that hill." He pointed to an area that he knew from experience was farther away than it appeared.

Deirdre didn't wait for him to lead and marched ahead, her slight limp from earlier barely perceptible now. She had to be in pain. His aching shoulders knew how much that pack and the toddler inside it weighed. But she would never admit to what she probably thought of as weakness, even if she had to crawl back to the truck. As she powered on, Micah grinned and tried to keep up. He couldn't help but like Special Agent Colton a little more.

"Now that's an interesting new development."

Crouched low in a conveniently located stand of trees, the spectator shot a glance around to see if the words had been overheard. A chuckle replaced the silly gasp that preceded it. No need to be concerned. There were no humans around for miles besides that rancher and his guest, who traipsed together across the field to examine today's damage.

The newest gift. The freshest warning.

Good thing local police had bumbled every bit of this investigation so far, like a collection of circus performers squeezing into a clown car without doors. *Investigations*, plural, the viewer corrected with a grin. And this new officer, whoever she was, would probably be just like them, complete with white makeup and a red nose.

Sinking back to ensure that the brush provided an effective cover, the viewer adjusted field glasses that were showing their age and watched the pair's progress across the field through the scratches. Earlier, the sheriff couldn't get his squad car off Harmony Fields fast enough. He'd left clouds of dust and rock in his wake as he made his escape.

The sheriff must have left the case in the hands of this newcomer, but she'd already proven herself a simpleton by letting Micah trick her into hauling his kid on her back. The rancher had always been too clever for his own good, but on this, he didn't seem to be able to take a hint.

At least his success would be of benefit soon.

Harmony Fields. Even the name was laughable. There would be no harmony on that land until Micah Perry packed up the kid and rode away as fast as one of those horses could carry them.

But his time was running out. Polite hints could only work for so long. Then people just vanished. Without a forwarding address. Or a proper goodbye.

Chapter Five

Deirdre dumped several packages on the overly ruffled bed in a guest room, which featured lace or doilies on every available surface. If she weren't so worried that she would sleep right through dinner, she would have taken a swan dive into that mess of pillows, too, even if the room looked like the top of a '60s wedding cake.

"You're going to regret this decision." She repeated Micah's words from earlier and made a mean face in the dresser mirror.

Oh, she regretted it, all right, but no way in hell she would admit that to him. Just like she hadn't gushed with gratitude when he'd reclaimed the backpack and his son so that she could take notes and use her phone to photograph the crime scene. She rubbed the back of her neck, the aching muscles at its base still nothing compared to her burning feet, and then started pulling items out of the shopping bags.

Gary's Farm & Fleet had met her expectations for fashion shopping à la feed store, but at least now she had a couple of outfits to get through the next few days, and she wouldn't have to wash out her panties and sports bra and go commando every night. The pink fuzzy slippers that she'd also found in that miniscule lingerie department and the pair of slip-on sneakers from the closeout display near the checkout were bonus buys.

A knock at the door caught her attention just as she set aside the fleece shorts and T-shirt that would serve as her pajamas.

"Yes?" she called out.

Micah pushed the door open and leaned his head inside.

"I just wanted to make sure you're comfortable. Is the guest room okay?"

She nodded, though she suspected he hadn't selected a single item inside it.

"Is there anyone you should call to let them know you won't be returning tonight? Boyfriend? Girlfriend? Spouse? Or boss?"

Deirdre crossed her arms but shook her head. "No boyfriend. *Ex*-husband doesn't care where I am. Never did."

She squeezed her arms tighter, not sure why she'd told him so much. Or why he'd asked. Beyond being utterly pitiful, her personal life was none of his business. "And you already know I can't tell my boss."

His lips lifted, though he appeared to straighten uncomfortably in the doorway.

"Then you have everything you need?"

"I think so."

"I would *hope* so."

He grinned as he gestured to the new Resistol hat and the huge pile of clothes and toiletry items she would never use again after this trip, even if she'd bought a cheap duffel to haul it all home. Ranch chic just wasn't her vibe. Still, she appreciated his sacrifice in joining her on the shopping spree. He'd spent the afternoon chasing Derek down aisles, past everything from horse feed to beekeeping gear to tractor parts while she'd picked through the limited selections. He'd even been forced to intervene during an impressive toddler meltdown while she'd tried on a few boxy shirts and some pants, all before he had to hurry back to the ranch to help with the cattle's dinner feed.

He cleared his throat and pointed to the insulated rubber work boots she'd set next to the bed.

"You're going to love those boots. More comfortable than the ones you've been wearing. We wear those instead of the Western style for a lot of our work." He held his hands wide. "Well, except for anything on horseback. They don't fit well in the stirrups."

She couldn't help grinning over his rambling, but she couldn't blame him for being uncomfortable standing at the door of her assigned bedroom for the next few days. She wasn't feeling superconfident herself. How are they supposed to stay in the same house when she couldn't help watching him every time she thought he wasn't paying attention?

"I still don't know why I needed them, though," she said, returning to the safe subject of her footwear. "I'll only be here a few days. And, technically, I'm not working on the ranch."

"Clearly you've never been on a ranch before. *Everyone* works here."

She tilted her head and studied him. "Why do I have the sneaking suspicion that the sheriff blackmailed me to stay here because you're short on ranch hands?"

As the low rumble of his chuckle tickled through her skin, she crossed her arms to protect herself from its intoxicating roll.

"Nah. Richard told you he needed extra manpower—er, *person* power—to help on this investigation. Harmony Fields is taking up more than its share of time and resources from his department. Your being here to offer an extra pair of hands on the ranch is a bonus."

She followed his gaze to the pair of leather work gloves he'd insisted she would need. Then, as she recognized that they were both staring at the bed she would sleep in, the room becoming a little too cozy, the air too warm, Deirdre pivoted to glance past Micah's legs, looking for his son.

"What happened to Derek?"

"Why? Haven't you seen him? I thought you had him." Micah looked over his shoulder, his eyes wide when he glanced back.

Just as Deirdre shot toward the door, Micah grinned.

She planted her feet and crossed her arms. "Funny."

"I'm a good dad, you know. At least, I try to be." He gestured over his shoulder and then twisted his arm to peek at his watch. "I have a show on for him in the family room. I figure I have about thirty minutes. Forty-five, max."

"For what?"

"Before the witching hour."

"Witches? Not knocking on anyone's religion, but I didn't sign up for a conversion."

"No conversion involved. It's that late-afternoon period where toddlers are too hungry, too tired, too *everything*, and their world implodes."

"Sounds like a blast."

"Clock's ticking. You have enough time to hit the shower." He pointed to the guest room's attached bath. "Towels are in the cabinet. Water heater's generous. I'll get started on dinner."

Her whole body was already melting with the idea of hot water pouring over her head and her sore muscles when his last words sank in. As if it weren't bad enough that she would be staying at the home of a potential witness, now he planned to *cook* for her, too.

"Oh. I figured we'd just get something delivered."

He'd started to turn away, but now his head swiveled back. "From where? Gary's?"

She pursed her lips. Obviously, she'd said something ridiculous again. Food delivery had to be a foreign concept out here. "I think Gary has gotten enough of our business for one day."

"I agree. Oh, I forgot."

Micah disappeared from the open doorway for a few seconds. When he returned, he stepped all the way inside and rested a box of adhesive bandages and a tube of antibiotic gel on the short bookshelf near the door. "Thought you might need these."

"I don't," she began but didn't bother finishing. He already knew about the blisters.

"Remember, *tick, tick, tick*." He pointed at his watch and closed the door behind him.

For several seconds, she stared at the first-aid products, not sure what to think about how he'd spent the afternoon taking care of her needs. She was supposed to be independent. Self-reliant. Strong. So she shouldn't have liked being taken care of that way. She didn't know what to make of the fact that she did. A little too much.

DELICIOUS SMELLS OF basil and oregano and the clang of banging metal greeted Deirdre twenty minutes later as she headed down the stairs. She found the sources of both scent and sound in the kitchen, where something wonderful simmered on the stove and the little musician on the floor banged another saucepan with its lid and a serving spoon.

Despite her plan to behave as if she'd turned the homes of every witness she'd ever interviewed into bed-and-breakfasts, she couldn't help hesitating in the kitchen doorway. She hated conceding the upper hand in any situation, and Micah's advantage here was several arms, legs and a few torsos above that. She braced against the doorjamb, waiting for him to rub in that point.

Instead, Micah, who'd changed into a brown University of

Wyoming T-shirt with gold letters and a bronco-riding cowboy on the front, glanced over from the stove and smiled. He
appeared more relaxed now that they weren't speaking in her
bedroom, and she could agree with him on that.

"Feel better?" Micah called out over his son's drum solo.

"Yes, thanks," she shouted back.

Only Derek chose that moment to cut his performance,
and her words reverberated off the walls. Both Perry guys
stared back at her, one with curiosity, the other with mischief.

"Glad to hear it," Micah said.

His gaze skimmed over her T-shirt and shorts more slowly
than necessary, and just as they had when she'd caught him
checking out her butt earlier, nerve endings that had no business reacting at all sizzled and popped.

"Nice slippers," he said after a long pause.

Humiliation washed over her as even her toes tingled under
his notice, but she planted her hand on her hip and frowned
to cover her discomfort. If only this were as effective as the
slippers had been in masking the bandages on her feet. "Hey,
these are my recovery shoes."

He gave her footwear another glance but lifted his gaze
just as the shivers started working themselves up again.

"Hungry?"

"Starving." She didn't bother denying it. Those airplane
snacks hadn't exactly stuck to her ribs, and if she didn't eat
soon, she might cry louder than the toddler had in his tough-
est moment of the day.

She pointed to the two pots on the stove. "What is that?
It smells amazing."

"Just spaghetti."

"Basghetti! Basghetti! I'm hungry!"

Derek leaped up from his pans, letting the lid and spoon
clang to the floor. Then, with a moan that could have kicked
off an acting career, he wrapped his arms around his father's

legs. Pressing his lips together as if holding back a smile, Micah shuffled toward the counter, his son still clinging to him like a koala on a branch.

"Here, let me handle this," he said to Deirdre. "We're on borrowed time."

He swung his son up on his hip and deposited him in the highchair, positioned at the head of the rich wood table in the alcove dining area. The table was already set for dinner with casual dishes, paper napkins and two huge red wineglasses, all out of reach of the highchair's occupant.

"It's almost ready, buddy." He reached down to brush back Derek's hair.

Once he'd wrestled wiggling legs into the safety strap and reluctant arms into a pocketed bib and locked the tray in place, Micah used his foot to straighten the plastic beneath the highchair. He hurried back to the stove to dump cooked pasta into a colander in the sink.

"Witching hour?" she couldn't help asking, using his term from earlier.

"It arrived early today." With efficient movements, he doled out a small portion of noodles on a cowboy plate. "Thought he'd make it to the end of the program. Not so much."

Though Micah wouldn't see it as he stirred the pot of sauce, Deirdre nodded, aware that her arrival had been at least one of the things that had thrown the child off his schedule.

The cowboy moved around the kitchen with the deftness of a short-order cook, chopping up his son's pasta, mixing in a tiny bit of sauce and delivering it to the table, along with a toddler-size fork. Derek went to work on his plate, using the utensil and sometimes his hands to guide food to his mouth. Red streaks quickly appeared on the tray, a few stray noodles landing on the mat.

"Anything I can help with?" Deirdre asked, not entirely sure she wouldn't eat with that same gusto and mess when her plate finally arrived.

"I have it under control. You can take a seat if you like."

Soon, Micah had two plates of pasta and sauce on the table, both topped with freshly grated Parmesan. Deirdre eyed the food, trying to hold back attacking at least until the cook took a seat. Manners were of no concern to Derek, who'd already finished his dinner and sat sated, smearing drips of sauce in circles on his tray.

Micah pursed his lips and then shrugged, signaling he'd picked his battles and would let that one go. Taking his son's plate with him, he slipped back into the kitchen and returned with two small plastic cars and an already open bottle of Sangiovese. He dropped the cars on Derek's tray, right into the mess, and then held out the bottle.

"I forgot to ask if you drink wine, if you drink at all or if you'd like some of this."

She looked from the bottle to his face and then back to the bottle. Now wine, too? She'd already broken so many rules today that any witness statement she obtained from him could only be used as background, since it wouldn't be admissible in court. Having a drink with him now would only add to her tally of shame, so what the heck.

Decision made, she lifted her oversize glass. "Yes. To all three."

"Well, set that down if you expect me not to spill this everywhere."

Once she followed his instructions, he tipped the bottle, giving her only a stingy restaurant pour despite the promising size of the wineglass. Not that even a generous home version would have helped to calm her nerves, anyway. She doubted that anything could.

"Looks like you're an expert," she said as he filled his own glass, twisting the bottle to avoid the drip.

"Surprised I even remember how to do this."

"You don't usually drink?"

"Not wine. More a beer guy if I have anything." He set the bottle aside and brushed his hand over the smooth wood tabletop. "Can't remember the last time I even sat here. Derek has his own chair, and I eat most of my meals standing at the bar."

"You're still standing now, too," she pointed out. "But you also seem to be a busy guy. I don't see how you ever find time to sit down."

"Occasionally, I do."

Micah pulled out his chair and dropped into it, rolling his shoulders, as though this had been a long day for him, too. He glanced from his plate to Deirdre's and then to his son, playing contentedly in his chair. "Hey, this is nice."

"Yeah, it is," she admitted before she could stop herself.

That was the problem. It was *too* nice. Cozy, like it had been in the guest room. More intimate without the necessity of a bed. Like a sweet little family dinner where she'd cast herself as the wife and mother. She blinked away that ridiculous daydream, her lungs tight, as if someone had vacuumed all the oxygen from the room. Her face felt hot, the wine only responsible for part of it.

She focused on the thick wood beams that created the dining area and suspended the balcony above them. When she'd taken in every inch of those, she lowered her gaze to her plate and lifted her fork to twirl it in the pasta. Anything to delay having to meet Micah's gaze again.

Where had that vision come from, anyway? She wouldn't have recognized a real family dinner if one popped up and took a big bite of her spaghetti. Now, photo-op dinners staged for campaign ads, she knew all about those, since they were the best family photos Eoin and Georgina Colton ever took with their only daughter. More than that, she didn't have dreams of domesticity and biological clocks. And if she hadn't already declared a moratorium on dating since marriage hadn't worked out for her, and motherhood didn't seem to be in the cards, either, she would never choose a family member in a murder case she was investigating for her prospects list.

"Thought you said you were hungry."

Deirdre startled at Micah's words, her head and fork coming up at the same time and a bit of sauce flinging across the table. It splatted on the silkscreened cowboy centered on Micah's T-shirt.

"Bull's-eye," he said with a chuckle.

"Oh, no. Sorry. Here, let me clean that up." She popped up from her seat, napkin in hand, and leaned over the tabletop, intending to do that.

Micah held out a splayed hand. "I've got it. No harm. No foul."

Continuing to chuckle, he cleared it away with a few quick swipes with his napkin. If only she could dispose of her humiliation as quickly. The ship had already sailed on her plan for looking like an in-control agent, but she would appreciate it if she could stop making a fool of herself around him.

"Sorry," she said again. "I got a little lost in my thoughts."

"Hey, I'm used to food decorations on my clothes. I have a two-year-old. I just wasn't expecting them from your side of the table." He pointed to her plate. "Now, could you eat some of that instead of teaching my son how to start a food fight?"

He twirled spaghetti on his fork and lifted a big bite but paused before putting it in his mouth. "It's really good. I promise."

"I'm sure it is."

Deirdre took his cue and twisted a bite onto her fork but

found she wasn't as hungry as she had been. Clearly, she was the only one feeling a little uncomfortable with their cozy meal, she decided as Micah put away his dinner with enthusiasm. As she took her first bite, she realized why. The savory mixture of flavors burst on her tongue and filled her mouth.

She sighed, her appetite returning. As she took another bite, her eyes fluttered closed. When she opened them again, she caught Micah watching her with something unreadable in his eyes. Though he quickly looked down at his plate, she couldn't help wondering if he was more bothered by their private little meal than she'd assumed.

"Told you it was good." He slid another bite in his mouth and smiled as he chewed.

She quickly cleared her plate and then set her fork aside. "If you tell me you just whipped that up in the past twenty minutes, I will skulk out of here in shame. I have had endless time to cook lately, and I've still barely touched the microwave."

"Being suspended probably doesn't inspire you to get creative in the kitchen."

"I'm never an inventive cook." She paused, frowning. "And, as I already told you, I wasn't suspended."

"I know. Just a forced vacation. Whatever you say."

Wanting to avoid that topic and needing time to come up with a better one, she sipped her wine and then set down the glass.

"Your crystal is beautiful. You're lucky whoever ransacked the house didn't find these." She gently rubbed her finger over the delicate rim, and then her breath caught as she realized what she'd said. While trying to steer clear of a topic that made her uncomfortable, she'd introduced one that reminded Micah of both his dead wife *and* his fears for his child's safety. Zero for two on that one.

"Yeah. Lucky."

His sad smile was bad enough, but the raw look in his eyes went beyond just contradicting his words. It touched a place inside Deirdre that she usually shielded better than her body behind a Kevlar vest. Her throat felt so thick that she had to concentrate to swallow. This had to be the same sensation someone felt after running into an active crime scene with neither weapon nor protective gear, and yet she was still tempted to step around the table to Micah, cradle his head against her and tell him everything would be all right. He knew that wasn't true. Already, he'd lost two people he loved, and now he was terrified he couldn't protect a third.

"I'm sorry. That was so insensitive."

"No worries."

But rather than take another bite, he moved his pasta around on his plate, as lost in his thoughts as she'd been earlier.

"I didn't, by the way," he said when he finally looked up.

"Didn't what? Think what I said was insensitive?"

He shook his head. "I didn't cook the sauce. I just warmed it up."

His smile returned, and Deirdre found she could finally breathe normally again.

"Remember when I said I have a cook a few days a week?" He waited for her nod before continuing. "She's a grandma and a chef wannabe. She prepares a few things fresh and then bulk cooks at home and loads my freezer."

"So, you and Derek definitely aren't starving out here on the ranch."

"We wouldn't starve without her help. We would just eat a lot more mac and cheese and frozen pizzas."

"A family after my own heart."

Micah's gaze flicked to her, and she straightened in her seat. Though she hadn't wanted him to know what she'd been thinking about earlier, she'd all but announced it by burying it in a joke. He didn't seem to notice as his attention turned to his son, who'd begun to nod off in the chair next to them.

"I'd better get someone in the bath and into a fresh diaper before he has to go to bed as a big orange monster. Have another glass of wine, and I'll be back in a few minutes."

His father's words having awakened him, Derek shook his head. "No bath."

"Yes, bath. Sorry, kiddo." Micah removed the tray and reverse-wrestled his child out of the chair and bib. "You're too dirty."

"No bath." Derek started running the moment his father set his feet on the ground.

"Wait. I've got an idea," Micah called out.

The child stopped and looked back curiously.

"Maybe Miss Deirdre would like to help with your bath?"

Micah tilted his head and lifted an eyebrow. She could only guess from his grin that her own expression showed pure panic.

"I haven't ever—"

She didn't get the chance to finish as the toddler ran full force to her, not stopping until he rammed the side of her leg. He lifted his arms over his head.

"Up."

Unable to resist those sad eyes and those chubby little hands, she reached down and hauled the little boy into her lap, sticky fingers, dirty face and all. As he snuggled against her, she couldn't help but to wrap her arms around that tiny body and lean close to breathe in his hair. An unfamiliar warmth spread in her chest and all the way to her fingers.

"Think Miss Deirdre might need another bath now, too," Micah said.

Despite his light words, he had that same sad look in his eyes, and this time she was tempted to carry the toddler to his dad and hug them both. She held herself perfectly still, hoping the impulse would pass. Worried that it wouldn't.

"So you want Miss Deirdre to help with your bath?" Micah asked his son.

Derek nodded. "Dee-Dee helps."

She stiffened as the little boy turned in her lap and touched her face with a sticky hand. *Help.* That was what she'd come to Wyoming to do in the first place. By assisting her cousins with their investigation to find missing person Humphrey Kelly and tracking and arresting black widow Maeve O'Leary, she hoped to help herself as well by proving her value to the bureau. Now that the threats against the rancher and his son had become part of the equation, she hoped to help them, too.

Only she couldn't do that if she became too close. If she'd learned nothing else in her training, she'd understood that keeping a professional distance was critical for both cases and witnesses involved. Yet, already enjoying herself as the houseguest of a witness, now she would be headed to bath time, too.

It was a mistake. She could feel it. If she got too close to them, then she might miss a clue and fail to protect either the sweet little boy or his father from whoever had been threatening them. And if emotions became involved, someone could get hurt. She worried it just might be her.

Chapter Six

Nearly an hour later, with Derek's bath and bedtime ritual completed and the clean saucepan and pasta pot drying in the sink, Micah dropped into the same seat where he'd eaten dinner earlier. He gestured for Deirdre to take the chair across from him, though this part of their to-do list promised to be more awkward than even sitting with a child between them in a big-boy bed for two whole stories.

No way would he admit just how relieved he'd been when his son begged Deirdre to read a second book to him before he drifted off into dreamland. Micah wouldn't have been able to get any words past the golf ball that had wedged in his throat while their houseguest read *Good Night Moon*, anyway. As Deirdre had sat close enough that her new floral shampoo flooded his senses and her surprisingly sweet reading voice tickled his ears, the truth had pressed on his heart that his son would never hear a story from his own mother, and there wasn't a damned thing he could do about it.

He drummed his hands on the table edge to clear his mind of those melancholy thoughts and then pointed to the empty space in the middle.

"I should have left the wine on the table." He would definitely need something to calm his nerves if he planned to work with Deirdre tonight, especially if she interjected questions about his stepmother between those about the recent events at the ranch.

Deirdre waved him off as he started to stand. "I'll get it."

She headed around the corner into the kitchen. Sounds of clinking glass and the closing of cabinet doors filtered from the room. When she returned, she carried a bottle of craft beer in each hand and had a pair of hard-plastic cups tucked under her arm.

"Best I could do." She pointed to the plastic when she'd set everything on the table, even pulling a bottle opener from inside a cup. "I couldn't find any beer glasses."

He shrugged. "Casualties from the buffet in the living room."

"I figured."

"You don't have to switch to beer on my account. But thanks for this." He pulled one bottle closer to him and reached for the opener.

"You never said you had IPAs, ambers and American lagers in there." She gestured in the direction of the refrigerator. "Right up my alley."

"What'd you expect me to have? Bottled river water?"

Her small smile hinted that her assumption hadn't been far off from that. Ignoring the cups, he drank directly from the bottle.

"Or cans." She opened her own beer and took a long pull from it.

Again, Micah pointed to the seat across from him, but instead of sitting in it, Deirdre moved to the counter and returned with the notebook and pens he'd given her earlier. She rested those on the end of the table where Derek's highchair had been stationed during dinner and lined up the chair in that spot.

When she finally sat, she lowered her shoulders and let her head hang forward. The temptation to step over and rub her neck took Micah by surprise. He gripped his hands together and stayed in his seat to avoid the impulse. Okay, he might have had as long a dry spell as one of his three bulls in the off-season—well, longer—but that didn't give him an excuse to be trying to get his hands on the special agent. For any reason. Their lodging situation was already awkward enough without having to include any of *that*, no matter how tempting it sounded.

Deirdre reached back and rubbed her own neck, briefly closing her eyes. Then she lifted her head.

"You go through that whole routine every single night?"

"Well, most nights. Sometimes when we go into Laramie for supplies, and Derek falls asleep in the truck, I just brush his teeth and tuck him into bed." He gave her a sheepish look. "One time I even put him to bed without teeth brushing. You won't report me, will you?"

She crossed her arms, tapped her lips with her index finger and stared up at the ceiling as if pondering his question.

"Well, not yet. But if I see any concerning evidence—like mismatched socks—I'll be all over that."

"Then I'll be sure to keep you far from the laundry room."

"Good idea." She pulled the notebook closer to her and clicked the pen, indicating that it was time for them to get serious. But as she tapped the pen on the paper, creating a random decoration of dots, she slid a glance his way. "I wasn't expecting Derek to ask me to read *both* stories. I didn't mean to invade on your bedtime routine."

He could admit—to himself, at least—that he'd had a twinge of jealousy, but it had passed quickly. His thoughts about how sweet she'd appeared next to his son—he didn't need to think about those.

"Can't blame him. He was just excited to have someone other than boring old Dad to read to him. Some stories probably sound better coming from a female narrator." He paused before adding, "Particularly the princess ones."

Earning the exact sour expression he'd been expecting from her, he grinned. She probably dealt with a lot of gender issues in her work, but he couldn't help suspecting there might be more to it.

"Since I would know so much about princesses, of course." She lowered the pen and used both hands to crown herself with an imaginary tiara. "Particularly ones with task-force experience and active-shooter training."

"There definitely should be more kick-ass heroines in fairy tales."

She shot a glance his way, her eyes narrowed, as though checking to see if he was joking. He must have convinced her as she returned her attention to the notebook, where she doodled tiny circles that became entwined in ink tornadoes.

"Thanks for helping with Derek's bath, if I didn't tell you that earlier. And for helping to clean up the kitchen."

"You didn't let me do much." She shook her head. "At first, I thought you were asking me to bathe Derek, not just monitor the splashing from a seat on the bathroom throne."

"Why would I expect you to do that? Because you're a woman?"

"A few of my fellow special agents might have said that. Some people think those mothering instincts are bred into us." She appeared to consider the premise for a moment. "I'm not sure I believe that."

"I don't."

Micah swallowed as Deirdre's curious gaze told him he should have moderated himself better or said nothing at all. He sat still, not ready to give more away. But she kept watching him until he either had to explain himself or run out of the room.

"I just believe that caring for a child isn't about gender," he said. "It's about determination, character and heart."

She nodded. At least she'd accepted that explanation. If she hadn't, he would have struggled to come up with a better one without telling her the real reason he believed as he did.

Deirdre pointed to the list again. "We'd better get started on this or we'll have nothing to say when the sheriff checks in on us."

"You think he'll be checking in?"

"Why wouldn't he?"

"With a competent investigator handling the situation for a few days?" He held his hands wide. "He'll probably take a quick vacation to Cheyenne or Denver."

At her shocked look, he grinned.

"Seriously, he'll probably try to catch up on his backlog of other duties. Like ordering ammunition and office supplies, overseeing receipts for patrol car maintenance, and checking to see if all the *i*'s are dotted and *t*'s crossed on police reports to be sent to the county prosecutor."

"Wow, his job sounds as glamorous as mine does."

"You mean that FBI work isn't all showing up with search warrants in your blue jackets and taking in bad guys?"

"Hardly," she said with a chuckle. "Most of the job is meticulously following the evidence and documenting everything so that we get a conviction when the case goes to trial."

She pointed to the notebook, but when she glanced down at the page, now covered with doodled tornadoes, 3-D cubes and stars, she flipped to another sheet of paper. "I still need your list of enemies, if we're ever going to get to *my* case."

"That's just the thing. I don't have any."

Deirdre started tapping the pen again, her jaw tight. "There has to be someone who doesn't like you. Someone who didn't get as good a deal as you did on a seed delivery. Or resented that you were late getting your cattle to market."

"Really, there's not a lot. That's part of what's been so frustrating during the investigation from the sheriff's office." He took a drink of his beer and shook his head as he swallowed. "In fact, a lot of people around here appreciate me for setting up the petting zoo."

She squinted at him as if he'd suddenly grown two heads.

"You mean that sign was real? You really have a *petting zoo*?"

"Of course it's real. Why would I have a sign if there wasn't one?"

She shifted her shoulders. "It just didn't seem, you know, possible. Out here in the middle of nowhere."

"First of all, we're here, so it's *somewhere*." He tried to keep the annoyance from his voice but didn't quite succeed. "And, yes, this is a rural area. That's the point. I built the petting zoo so the area children, including my own, would have a place to enjoy nearby. Admission is also free, so it's pretty popular."

"Forget appreciating you. I bet you're a local hero for that." She appeared to consider it further and then tilted her head. "But don't children who live on ranches already have a lot of exposure to animals?"

"Not everyone around here lives on a ranch. Those who do are around a lot of livestock but not *these* animals. You'll see tomorrow when you help me clean cages and pens."

She immediately shook her head. "But I'm not—"

He held up an index finger to interrupt her.

"*Everyone* works on a ranch," they said together, one with a grin, the other frowning.

What surprised him most was that she'd agreed to go along with his plan. Even if the sheriff had blackmailed her into helping with his case, Micah couldn't force her to help out with his ranch chores.

Deirdre puffed up her cheeks and blew out a breath.

"When I finally get the information I need around here, I will have earned it."

"You never know. You might end up liking the ranch and even southeast Wyoming far more than you think. All that sky. And those amazing mountain ranges in the distance."

"All that *wind*. And mucking out stalls."

At that, he laughed. "You might appreciate a breeze when you're doing *that* job."

She pointed to him with her pen. "Names. Please."

When he didn't answer, she added, "You've got to give me something. You must have had the sheriff's office look into a few people. Let's start there. Maybe it will spark some ideas."

"Guess we started with my exes."

"Okay," she said, stretching out the word. "Exes, as in plural?"

He frowned. "There've been *a few*. Mostly before I married Leah." He shot a look at her and then away. "Davis was her maiden name, but I don't think you need to put her on the list. I had to identify—" He stopped himself, shivering at the memory. No one should have to die like that, whether she'd left him or not. "You get it."

Deirdre looked up from where she'd written his late wife's name. "You said you don't have any enemies, but since your late wife can't tell us, we have to look into anyone who might have held a grudge against *her* and wanted to exact revenge on her widower or her child."

"Guess I never thought of it that way."

"Did anyone take a closer look at—" she paused and glanced down at the paper "—Leah?"

"Not yet."

She made one of her fancy stars next to his late wife's name. "When did you get married?"

"Three and a half years ago." He hated that he was tempted to tell her that the marriage had been rocky from the moment the justice of the peace's signature dried on the marriage license. She'd announced that she was pregnant within weeks. No one needed to know any of that.

Deirdre looked up at him, her pen poised in her hand, her lips slightly slack. "But you said she passed away…"

Her words trailed off as she seemed to be calculating the dates again.

"Two years ago," he filled in for her. "Everything happened pretty quickly for us. Marriage, baby, then the accident."

"Such a short time. I'm sorry."

"Barely had time to finish the house." He didn't know why he'd said it, but he regretted it even more as she lifted a brow.

"Where was she from originally?"

"Cheyenne, but I met her in Laramie when I went to get supplies."

She jotted another note in her book. "Okay, who else can we look at? Other exes? Was anyone particularly upset when you dumped her?"

"I rarely broke up with anyone. Usually, I was the dumpee."

Again, she watched him with unmasked curiosity, and this time he straightened in his seat. He had to be careful what he told her. She interviewed crime suspects for a living.

Finally, she returned her attention to her list. "But there were a few, right?"

He shrugged. "There was Lila Nichols. I only dated her for a month or two in my early twenties. Though the ranchers weren't ready to accept me as a local even after I'd bought land and started adding cattle, their daughters weren't as reluctant."

She bent her head lower, but he caught her rolling her eyes.

"Why did you break it off? Did you have a line of successors waiting in the wings?"

"No." He waited until she looked up again to answer. "I

had to back away from her because she reminded me too much of my stepmother."

"Oh."

Deirdre had deserved a little pushback for asking that nasty question, but he regretted answering that way if it made her so uncomfortable. He already had a few questions about her, and now he wanted to know about the creep who'd hurt her. What he couldn't figure out was why anything about her mattered to him.

"She slashed my tires right after that."

"That's something. Maybe she was a little like Maeve." She placed a star next to the woman's name. "Do you have any idea where I could find Lila now?"

"Right in Laramie. She's Lila Westerfield now. But she prefers people to call her Mrs. *Gary* Westerfield."

She started to write and then looked up again, her lips lifting. "You don't mean Gary of *Gary's*, do you?"

"That's the one."

"Then why did you take me to that store?" she asked. "Does she work there? Is it awkward seeing her there?"

At that, he couldn't help but to laugh. "She does stop in to see her husband, and I've seen her there, but she ignores me. Figures she got the better end of the bargain, I guess."

"So not much of an enemy." She scribbled out the star next to the woman's name. "Did you break things off with anyone else?"

"One. Kara Sullivan. The first woman I went out with after Leah's death. She was pushing for marriage from the second date, but she never seemed to want Derek around when we were together. Then, when I broke it off, she told me she hoped my son would choke and die."

Deirdre planted her hands on her hips, her mouth gaping open. "You're kidding."

"Nope. It definitely put me off dating for a while."

"Where is Kara now?" After putting a star next to the woman's name, Deirdre lifted both shoulders close to her ears and winced. "Let me guess. She's married to Sheriff Guetta now."

"She's a little young for him, but she married his deputy Jerry Jackson." At her shocked expression, he added, "It's a small town."

"And I suppose that the two of you are best friends now."

He shook his head. "She pretty much still hates me. But she's probably too busy with her new baby and a couple of stepkids from Jerry's first marriage to have time to sabotage my ranch. Besides, she likes to bring her crew to the petting zoo."

Shaking her head, Deirdre put a question mark next to the star by Kara's name. "We're back to square one. Isn't there anyone who despises you enough to make you want to leave Harmony Fields?"

"Clearly, there is, but I don't know who it could be. Now do you see why the sheriff's office has had such a tough time with all the incidents?"

Deirdre didn't answer, frowning down at the list instead. "What about when you bought the land? Did you outbid anyone?"

"No. The man who used to own the small plot of land I bought first lost it to foreclosure. But he died ten years ago. All the other adjacent pieces I purchased at a fair price from neighbors, who were happy to sell so they could retire to Florida or Arizona."

She stared at the list again and shook her head. "Other than a quick check on your late wife, we've got nothing."

"Here, let me take a look at it." He held out his hand until she passed the list over to him. "I'm really reaching here, but I'll give you a few more."

He jotted down some names, each sounding more far-fetched than the last. The businessman in Laramie who freaked out over the scratch on his pristine new SUV from Micah's pickup door. The lady at the property tax office who swore Micah hadn't paid last year's tax bill though he could produce both the receipt and the canceled check. They were little things and hardly worth the effort of sabotaging his ranch or threatening his family.

Only a single possible suspect stood out as one who might want something from him—more money—and had no scruples about taking whatever she wanted. The evil stepmother. But for some reason, he couldn't bring himself to write down the names Ariel Porter Perry or Maeve O'Leary. Inscribing either name in ink would make that threat real, and he still wanted to believe that his ridiculous suspicion was just that.

As he pushed the list back to Deirdre, his stomach knotted with the truth that his stepmother had killed before. If she believed she'd found another way to line her pockets and he stood in her way, she wouldn't hesitate to kill again.

"You can't think of anyone else?" Deirdre asked.

He shook his head.

She studied him with a narrowed gaze, as if she didn't believe him.

"You're sure?"

He pushed back his shoulders and met her gaze, forcing himself not to look away.

"No one," he somehow managed, his mouth so dry that he craved another beer.

"Then I guess we'll have to go with this. I'll stop in the sheriff's office tomorrow and get a copy of all the reports to date. Investigators must have missed something."

He swallowed, hoping she didn't notice. She had to be right that they'd overlooked some details. He could only hope that the information he'd held back wasn't the critical missing piece to the puzzle. And that he wasn't risking his own child's life in fear of fully reopening the Pandora's box that was his past.

Chapter Seven

Deirdre could barely sit still on the leather sofa, even if it was so soft that if she dozed off on it, she would probably sleep until the next afternoon. She snuggled closer to one of the couch's rolled arms as a precaution. No way she could risk being distracted if Micah took a seat there instead of the matching armchair when he returned with the coffee. Not when he finally might be ready to give her details about Maeve O'Leary. And she didn't want to kid herself about the reality that *he* was a supreme distraction.

In the kitchen, Micah continued to arrange items on a wooden tray with handles. His coffee machine must have been the slowest one ever invented. Since she should already have been given an award for her patience in waiting for the interview for *her* case, this delay pushed her to the edge. If he returned with the announcement that he wouldn't share any information until the police had captured the sabotage suspect, she couldn't be held accountable for how she would use the self-defense skills she'd acquired at Quantico to persuade him.

She leaned forward over the quartz-topped coffee table to take another look at her notebook. Only a few stars stood out next to the names on Micah's suspect list, and those were the dim kind of stars that barely peeked out of galaxies billions of miles away. How could the guy have no enemies? But unlike her dad, who had so many political foes that the family home in Virginia and his apartment in DC both required extra security, Micah said his neighbors generally liked him. Strange how she was inclined to believe him.

With a dearth of leads like this, the local investigation would progress even slower than her team's search for Humphrey Kelly. And if Micah insisted on using her progress on the case here as a benchmark on his trade for information, she might never get the chance to go home.

"Cream? Sugar?" he called from the open refrigerator.

"Black." Not that she usually took her coffee that way, but she wanted to appear all-business now. She needed information and was tired of waiting.

He carried the tray, holding two steaming mugs, a porcelain bowl of sugar cubes, a cream pitcher and napkins, into the great room only a moment later and set it on the coffee table.

"Really? I like mine so sweet that it makes my teeth ache," he said, continuing their conversation.

Justifying her earlier worry, he sat on the other end of the sofa. He lifted both mugs, setting one closer to her and one in front of him.

"Thanks."

She pulled the mug to her, warming her suddenly freezing hands. What if he was right? What if he had no information that would help her locate Maeve? Could the best lead she'd been able to locate, the one good idea for which she could claim credit, end up another dud? How could she go back to the team empty-handed? Worse, how could she return to the DC field office with nothing to prove her value?

Micah added a sizable dollop of cream to his coffee and used mini tongs to add four sugar cubes.

"Now you're making *my* teeth hurt."

He chuckled as he stirred. "And you're making me cold. I don't even have the air-conditioning on. If you're uncomfortable, I can start a fire."

Her gaze scaled the protruding rounded stones of the real-wood fireplace and then lowered to the open area at the center, a few logs already positioned on the grate, and her cheeks warmed as though he'd just lit the flame. Nope, a fire wasn't a good idea.

"The temperature's fine," she managed.

She stuck with specifics since she refused to admit how flustered she'd already felt sitting alone with him at his dining table after those sweet, unsettling moments reading bedtime stories with Derek. Though she'd hoped that the great room would give her more space to breathe, they'd only moved closer to the wall of windows with the near-complete darkness outside holding the house in its opaque grasp. If she were doing anything other than interviewing a witness, she would call this a romantic cocoon, but it felt more like a tempting trap.

After resting the mug on the table as he had, she considered for a moment and reached for the cream.

Micah smiled knowingly and stirred his own coffee again before setting the spoon on a napkin. "I suppose you want to talk about Maeve O'Leary."

"How did you guess? I've just been waiting all day for it, so maybe."

She grabbed her notebook and flipped to a clean page, writing Micah's name and the date and time at the top. Then she lifted her pen and waited.

"Do you mind if I ask you a few questions first?" he asked.

"Are you serious?" She couldn't help wondering if this was a delay tactic or a plan never to answer her.

"I've just had to tell you all about my marriage, and now

you want me to share about a subject I haven't discussed in fifteen years. One I'd hoped to avoid forever, so—"

"Fine," she said with a huff. He had a point. For her, this was just a search for information to close an investigation, but her questions involved one of the darkest and most heart-breaking points in his life. So if she planned to dig through that fragile graveyard, she needed to use a garden trowel, not a backhoe. "What do you want to know?"

"Why did you become an FBI agent?"

She frowned. This would take a lot longer than she'd planned. "Why does anyone become one? To protect the American people and uphold the Constitution."

"Did you read that off a brochure? I don't want to hear the company line. I want to know why *you* did it."

Her jaw tightened. She might have been tempted to pin the guy to the floor earlier, but now she had a whole differ-ent motive for doing it. One that would put her in the back of Sheriff Guetta's patrol car. But she needed information, and he had it, so she shared the abbreviated version.

"It's pretty simple. I didn't love practicing law as much as I thought I would, I was at a point in my life where I was ready for a big change, and I wanted to help people. So after more than two years of background checks, physical testing and training, I earned my badge."

She tilted her head and studied him. "Now, is that enough?"

"One more thing. If you want me to tell you everything I know, I think you should tell me more about this investi-gation first."

She sighed and returned the notebook and pen to the table. Of course he would want to know more than the abbreviated version she'd offered the sheriff earlier.

"I'm not supposed to give away details on an active inves-tigation. I can get in trouble—"

"More trouble than you'd already be in just for coming here to question me?"

Deirdre shrugged. That heaviness she'd felt with each questionable decision she'd made that day pushed her shoulders forward. She reached for her mug and took a long sip before returning it to the table.

"Guess if I'm already going to hell, I might as well take the freeway."

He squinted and shook his head. "What do you mean?"

"I'm going to tell you."

He offered the kind of toothy grin that probably had women from all over southeast Wyoming sashaying to the gate of his ranch. "Should I get popcorn?"

Whether or not she was tempted to swish a bit herself, she glared at him until he tucked his grin away. He gestured with a swipe of his hand for her to begin.

"Like I said earlier, my cousin Sean Colton asked me to join a team he formed to investigate the January disappearance of Humphrey Kelly. His sister, Eva, a rookie cop, and his twin brothers, Cormac, a PI, and Liam, an NYPD informant, are also on the team. He even invited my half brother, Aidan, who's a US marshal."

"So, you and your *half* brother agreed to this plan to help out a group of *second* cousins?"

"We did it because we believe in justice." Deirdre frowned, his question rankling her as much as him picking up on her label for Aidan. Why she'd included Aidan in her comment about police work, she wasn't sure. She had no idea what her only sibling believed.

"At first, the team just kept me in the loop in the event that they would need me, but then the cases became more and more interesting. Last month, Eva called to ask me to take an assignment in the investigation."

She considered for a moment and then added, "And, yes, I

was available since I'd already started my *vacation* and had the extra time."

Micah held both hands up in a sign of innocence. "I wasn't going to ask."

"You might want to remember that I'm trained to tell when people are lying."

"I'll keep that in mind." He stared into the beige liquid in the mug he held and then looked up. "You said *cases*. And more interesting how? Were they able to track down Kelly?"

She shook her head. "But they figured out that he may have engineered his own disappearance."

He set his coffee aside. "Okay, I'm intrigued."

Deirdre turned toward him on the sofa, warming up to telling the story. "Then, alongside Kelly's DNA evidence, found at his last known location—a supply closet in a Manhattan criminal courthouse—they discovered someone else's DNA. It created a strange connection between his disappearance and what should have been an unrelated murder investigation."

"Really? This is good."

"It gets even more interesting," she said. "The murder investigation just happened to have been Sean's case. One he had to pass off to another detective so he could look into Kelly's disappearance."

"That seems a little coincidental."

Dipping her head, she glanced at him from beneath her lashes. "I don't believe in coincidences."

"Me, neither."

His stark expression told her he no longer spoke about her investigation, but he blinked several times, and his smile returned.

"You should have let me get popcorn." He crossed one leg flat over the other, planted his elbow on his knee and positioned his chin in the L of his hand. "You can't make this stuff up."

"I could, but this truth is better than fiction. The DNA turned out to have come from a female relative of Wes Westmore, a New York suspect charged with the strangling death of his girlfriend."

He pursed his lips and closed one eye. When he opened it, he shook his head. "I don't get that connection. Other than maybe it had something to do with the Kelly case. Like that someone didn't want your cousin to be assigned to it."

She nodded, impressed that he'd not only followed along but also had remembered the names of those involved in the complicated web.

"You're good at this. Should I be concerned that you'll take *my* job?" Her throat tightened that she'd just joked about her position, which couldn't have been less stable these days.

He waved away that suggestion with a brush of his hand. "Just a cowboy playing some criminal armchair quarterback in the NFL off-season."

"Well, you had the right idea. We weren't sure what the connection was, either, until a psychiatric evaluation suddenly materialized in Westmore's case file, signed by Kelly and dated the day before he vanished. In the document, both digital and in the physical file, Kelly declared the defendant 'incapable of committing murder.'"

"Incapable?" Micah scoffed. "How can he say that? Depending on the level of desperation, *anyone* is capable of taking a life."

Though there were several legal definitions and a whole spectrum of motives in play with what he'd said, she nodded, agreeing with him on that basic truth. As fiercely as he appeared to love his son, she had no doubt that Micah would do whatever was necessary to shield him. No matter what it cost him.

"We believe the document was fabricated. Or at least heavily suggested. *Someone* got her hooks into Kelly to get him to write that evaluation to help in Westmore's defense."

"Westmore's female relative?"

"Yeah. The *relative*. She likely also paid another individual to sneak the document into the file." She cleared her throat, realizing she was the one stalling now.

Pushing her shoulders back, she took a deep breath and continued. "DNA analysis on the sample taken from the courthouse connected it to Westmore's mother, a widow who vanished off the face of the earth about twenty years ago."

She paused and then added the rest. "After Westmore's father died under suspicious circumstances."

Deirdre watched him, waiting for him to assemble the parts of her story. When he did, his eyes widened, and his mouth fell open.

Still, she laid it out for him. "Westmore's mother is—"

"Maeve O'Leary," he finished for her. "The black widow."

Their gazes connected, and then he looked away, leaning forward and lacing his fingers at the back of his head. After a silence that stretched so long that Deirdre could feel her heart thudding in her chest, Micah lowered his arms and looked up again.

"That's how you came to me," he said.

He slid a guarded look her way, appearing as distrustful as he had when Deirdre arrived at the ranch hours before. That she wished she could rewind their conversation to where her story had yet to involve him bothered her more than she wanted to admit.

"In a roundabout way, yes," she said. "That's how I located you."

She expected him to ask more questions, but he only watched her, waiting. When she couldn't bear the intensity of those gray eyes any longer, she began.

"I was supposed to find out anything I could about Maeve. Already, we suspected that she'd murdered Joseph Westmore, a man with a known allergy to shrimp who had an 'accidental' exposure."

Micah rolled his eyes. "Something the police at the time failed to investigate, right?"

Deirdre nodded. "Anyway, the team had also begun to suspect that she might be a black widow, so we were trying to figure out if she had other aliases and also track her down. We figured that once she no longer needed Kelly, she would kill him, too."

"What did you do to find out about her?"

"That was the hard part. We started with no photos of her, and Westmore refused to provide any. But in February, one of Kelly's former patients reported a sighting of him in Morningside Heights. He was with a woman, and both of them were in disguise. The team had the witness view footage of Westmore's female jail visitors. He was able to ID the woman as the same one he'd seen with Kelly, based on her huge eyes, even though she'd worn vivid green contacts instead of brown."

"Someone saw Maeve in New York?"

Deirdre blinked, surprised that Micah had pulled that one detail from all that she'd said. She pretended not to notice the strain in his voice, but from his worried look, she would have sworn that Micah, instead of the witness, had seen that ghost from his past.

"Her eyes were brown when I knew her." He took another sip of his coffee and stared at the grate as though he'd lit a fire after all.

Mentally recording the detail about her eye color to put in her notes later, she continued her story. "Beyond that ID, the team hit a lot of dead ends in locating her. Even an NYPD tech expert came up empty. According to the internet, Maeve O'Leary, or even Maeve *Westmore*, no longer exists."

"But you were able to find out some things about her. How did you do it?"

He appeared to have returned from wherever he'd traveled in his thoughts, and now he shifted his legs to face her and folded his hands between his knees.

"We went to the dark web."

"We?"

"The tech expert from the DC field office helped me—secretly and off-hours—using his advanced dark web know-how and some facial-recognition software," she said. "We were surprised when the biometric tool matched the photo from the jail with an older, blurry picture of a woman named Ariel Porter Perry. But we finally had an alias and were able to connect that name to a death certificate for Len Perry."

Why did she have to keep referring to the man in such sanitized terms? She was talking about Micah's *father*, someone he'd lost when he was barely old enough to vote and still too young to buy a beer. Couldn't she at least call him his dad?

"And through a search for him, you found me."

Deirdre blinked, Micah's words sounding as if he'd read her mind, but then she retraced her own comment. "Yes, we found you. We also figured that since your father's death was fifteen years ago, there might be several more dead husbands."

She braced herself for questions she couldn't answer. Already, she'd told him too much about the investigation. Far more than she ever should have shared with a crime victim. Now that he knew the truth, that she'd only stumbled upon his father's cold case while hunting for a suspect in a different investigation, he would be less inclined to help her. No one had looked into Len Perry's murder case in a decade, and even now, she wasn't focused on justice for him. Even if those answers might be a byproduct of her case, it seemed woefully inadequate.

"So Maeve's still on the run." Micah shook his head. "It still doesn't seem right calling her that."

As Deirdre reclaimed her pen, Micah tilted his head, watching her.

"Ever notice that you call her by her first name and all the other suspects by their last? Is that because she's female?"

"I don't think so," she said, shifting uncomfortably. "It's more because she's a black widow. Spiders get first names. Like Charlotte in *Charlotte's Web*."

She pulled her notebook into her lap and pointed to the page with her pen. "You can refer to her as Ariel, since that's how you knew her."

The humor vanished from his gaze.

"I *never* knew her. Neither did my dad. Her name is *Maeve*."

As Micah cradled his coffee cup and stared into the liquid that was cold now, something tightened in Deirdre's chest. She'd interviewed witnesses with sad stories before. She'd even had those moments when human emotion sneaked up to fill her throat, forcing her to stall while conducting an interview. But now she was tempted to tell him it was okay not to share his story. She couldn't do that. The team relied on her to gather this information—she was counting on herself, too—and she couldn't become soft. She had a serial killer to stop.

"Just tell me anything you can," she said instead, assuring herself again that this was the right thing to do. "Places she liked to go. Where she might feel comfortable hiding. Any detail, no matter how small, might lead us to her whereabouts."

"I don't remember any places, but I'll tell you what I can." He took a visible breath and let it out slowly. "I guess I wasn't shocked when my dad brought her home. He'd been lonely since Mom died from cancer three years before that. I knew there would eventually be someone. I just wasn't expecting *this* woman. Blonde. Tall. Slender. Beautiful—and *young*."

Lowering his head, he tightened his jaw as if gritting his teeth.

"I was a seventeen-year-old boy. Believe me, *I* noticed. She was just ten years older than I was."

She nodded, her eyes burning at the thought of his shame over his teenage hormones. "She did appear attractive, even in the few photos we have of her. As I said, Westmore refused to give us any."

"Sorry. I don't have any pictures of her," he said before she could ask. "It wasn't a period I wanted to remember."

Disappointment settled in her gut. Maybe Micah was right that he wouldn't have any information that would be helpful to the team.

"Though I found her attractive, I remember that I immediately didn't like her. It was as if she met Dad at a bar and instantly showed up with her suitcases."

"Was she mean to you?" she asked, to keep the conversation going.

"Just the opposite. She was syrupy sweet. And somehow cold at the same time. Sugar and ice. She and Dad were so different, too. He was a quiet, successful businessman, while she was—I don't know—loud and always needing to be the center of attention.

"I tried to tell him that something didn't seem right about her, but he wouldn't listen. She seemed to have him under a spell."

"How long before he married her?" she asked.

"Just two weeks after he first brought her home to meet me, they eloped. No prenup. Nothing. I wasn't even invited to the wedding. Wouldn't want to ruin Ariel's perfect getaway by having a stepson there."

"Did you at least get along after they were married?" she asked to return him to his story. The question had no bearing on the case, but she just had to know. Had to understand how he'd survived that time. She'd believed that nothing could have been worse than growing up with her parents in what had amounted to a mausoleum, but now she knew better.

"We got along as well as you could with anyone who thought you were in the way. Just a fly at her picnic. And my father always took her side. I just needed to be more understanding. More welcoming."

"That had to be hard," she said before she could stop herself.

"It was what it was," he said with a shrug. "She, on the other hand, seemed to be having the time of her life with daily shopping sprees for designer clothes, jewelry and fancy scents. Things that only benefited her. Never Dad or me. Or our apartment on the Upper East Side."

"Your dad didn't see what she was doing?"

He shook his head. "Not even during the meetings with the attorney. To make sure she and I would be cared for, *just in case.*"

"He was probably just so happy that he blocked out every hint that didn't fit with his perfect picture." She wasn't sure why she felt the need to defend a man who'd failed to put his child first, just like her father had. Both men were responsible for the choices they'd made while chasing after women.

"Maybe." Micah picked at his nails as he considered her words. "He was still in an infatuation bubble. A twentysomething who told him he was sexy despite the mid-forties dad body. As an adult, I recognize how intoxicating that had to be."

The situation Micah described matched with the cases she'd been studying of other black widow murderers. Beautiful. Fawning. Deadly. But she didn't mention that truth. He seemed to need to share more of his story, and after asking him to unlock his past, the least she could do was listen to the whole thing, no matter how uncomfortable it made her.

"Dad kept telling me that his new wife wanted to make a home for us. He used the example of how much work she was putting into my eighteenth birthday party. If she didn't like me, why would she go to so much trouble? I wanted to believe it, too, and what teenager isn't excited to turn eighteen? To be a real adult."

He took on a faraway look, staring past her to the wall of windows. Deirdre hated realizing that she'd stirred up the images he saw on that inky backdrop. Suddenly, her search for information didn't seem so important. Micah had moved clear across the country to escape the past and start a new life, and she'd followed him there to drop it all back in his lap.

"You don't have to—" She stopped herself. As much as she wanted to, she couldn't let him off the hook. She needed answers, and she owed it to him to gather information that might help bring his father's murderer to justice.

Micah didn't seem to hear her, anyway. He continued to stare, remembering.

"The party was nice," he said. "Intimate. Just *family* and a few friends. But nice."

Her heart squeezed, and her nose burned. She blinked away the emotions rolling inside her before she shed embarrassing tears right there on his sofa.

"At least you had that," she managed.

"Then, a week after my birthday, Dad suffered a massive heart attack, and he was gone."

His words struck her so much like a punch to the gut that her shoulders curled forward. Again, he didn't notice. He focused on his hands, gripped so hard in front of him that his fingertips had turned red.

"I told the police that she'd poisoned him. That it could

have been from one of those flowers and plants she grew in her plot on the building's roof or the balcony. Oleander. Foxglove. Lily of the valley. Or maybe it was one of those teas she brewed for him at night. *Something.* I knew it in my gut. But the coroner looked at Dad's heart disease history and had no trouble ruling his death as a myocardial infarction. Natural causes."

"You're probably right about the poison." She didn't know how to tell him that there was a possibility that even if his father's body was exhumed now, after all this time, testing might not show evidence of poisoning.

"What happened…after?" she asked when he didn't say more.

"We met with the attorney two days after the funeral, and he presented me with the copy of the will. Dad had left everything to her. The house. His stocks. *Everything.*"

"Didn't the attorney recommend that you fight it?"

"He did. Then my stepmother assured him everything would be okay, and she had every intention of taking care of 'my love's son.' But by the time I made it home from my first day back at school, the house was empty, sold to a real estate conglomerate for cash, the bank accounts had been drained and she was gone."

"How could she do something like that?" She grimaced over her own words. People did heinous things all the time. But somehow it was worse knowing that it had happened to Micah.

"Without a look back," he grumbled. "I had nothing except two boxes of clothes and stuff from my bedroom. She left them for me out front. Guess I was lucky to get even that."

"The bitch," she breathed and then shot a look his way, a shiver scaling her spine. What was she doing?

He didn't move, as if he hadn't heard her. Releasing her breath in a slow stream, she forced herself to record some of the details he'd given her. If she were truly investigating Len Perry's death, she would have planned to speak to the coroner, local law enforcement and the attorney who'd let them walk out of the office that day. But no one could ever make this right for Len Perry's son.

When Micah pounded the side of his fist on the coffee tabletop, causing the dishes to rattle on the tray, Deirdre jerked to lift her head.

"Six months," he said, more to himself than her.

"What do you mean?"

Micah glanced over, surprised. "Sorry." He rubbed his hand. "It's just that he'd known her for less than six months, and she killed him."

"I'm so sorry for your loss." She eased to the center cushion, no longer able to hug the couch's arm.

Seeming not to notice her movement, he nodded in the frozen way of survivors trying to bear all those offers of condolence at a funeral.

"And I didn't do a damned thing to save my *dad*."

As Micah's voice broke on the last word, something fractured inside Deirdre as well. Without stopping to consider whether she would be crossing a line of professional distance that already had so many breaks that it should have been a message in Morse code, she reached over and rested her hand on top of his. She froze, her pulse pounding, her throat scratchy. The right move would be to pull away, but the message refused to filter from her brain to her hand. She didn't even want it to.

For several breaths, Micah sat staring at their hands as well. Then, when she would have finally pulled away, he rotated his wrist and laced their fingers. His wasn't a sweet and tender touch but a squeeze that, while it wasn't painful, hinted at some of the pain he'd probably buried for years.

"We won't let her get away with it," she said.

Micah released her and, gathering the coffee mugs on the tray, escaped to the kitchen. She closed the notebook and turned to watch him pour out the warm cream, put away the sugar bowl and load items into the dishwasher.

He didn't believe her, and she couldn't blame him. The law enforcement officers after his father's death hadn't given him confidence that anyone cared about justice for him or his father. Micah's experience offered insight into his fierce determination to protect *his* son.

Well, he might not know this about her yet, but she kept her commitments, even when others didn't. She'd pledged to help him figure out who was sabotaging his ranch and endangering him and Derek, and she'd assured him she would get justice for his dad. If it was in her power at all, she intended to keep both promises.

Chapter Eight

As Micah finished filling the pygmy goats' trough and shut off the water the next afternoon, the melodic sound of Derek's laughter drifted from the outside of the enclosure. He couldn't help but grin as he opened the gate and closed it securely behind him. Around the building, past the visitors' entrance, Deirdre knelt next to his son by a section of the wood-framed hog-wire fencing that offered more secure viewing for timid petting zoo visitors.

Deirdre looked the part of a regular ranch hand now, if someone who made even work jeans, a dusty Henley and muck-baptized rubber boots look sexy could still be called *regular*. She must have left her hat somewhere again, as her twin blond braids bobbed every time she turned her head.

"Booger!"

Playing tour guide, Derek pointed to the brown-and-white-spotted goat that had pressed its snout through one of the six-inch squares right next to them.

"Are you sure his name is Booger?" Deirdre gave the child a skeptical look, not noticing that they had an audience in the barn doorway. "That doesn't sound like a nice name for a respectable goat."

The toddler nodded his head. "Booger."

"I hope he isn't offended that someone picked out a name like that for him."

"'Fended," Derek repeated with a nod.

Micah couldn't help grinning at their serious conversation. Though Deirdre said she knew nothing about kids, she was great with his son, talking to him as if he were a small adult instead of a toddler. If only she could be as comfortable with him as she was with Derek and even the goat that nibbled her fingers when she rubbed its snout.

She laughed, something she hadn't done since they'd had that intense conversation the evening before, and she'd reached out to take his hand. Her relaxed expression was a welcome change as well.She'd been cautious around him all day. How they'd managed to complete their share of chores and examine locations of prior damage around the ranch while she'd maintained a social distance and treated him like a contagious coworker, he wasn't sure.

On the other hand, he couldn't blame her for dancing cautiously around him after he couldn't accept her gesture of kindness without clinging to her like a lifeline or something. If anyone should have been embarrassed after that conversation, it should have been him. He'd shared more than she'd needed to know for her investigation.

Strangely, he wasn't sorry. As if someone had lifted an anvil off his neck, he could finally breathe. And whether or not she was actively working on his dad's murder case, with everything else going on around the ranch, he appreciated her for giving him that moment of lightness.

"If he is offended, we can just give him some extra snacks," Micah called out. "He'll forgive us."

Deirdre startled and turned her head toward the sound at the barn door. The goat chose that moment to push its head all the way through the fencing to nibble her braid. She squealed but laughed again as she stood. After swiping at the damp ends of her hair, she secured the band the animal had managed not to eat.

"His favorite snacks are watermelons or pumpkins, but hair will do in a pinch." He grinned as he approached her and his son. "But I wouldn't give him too much of that. It's not good for his diet."

"Thanks for telling me." She brushed her fingers over the bottom of her braid again. "We indentured servants need all the information we can get."

"Sure a lot of whining for someone who's serving her indenture by playing with animals in a petting zoo."

"It's a tough job, but somebody has to do it."

While Derek ran back and forth, pausing to pet any of the pygmies that poked their snouts out to greet him, Deirdre reached over the top of the fence to rub the same goat's head. When Micah realized that in that moment he would have happily traded places with that lucky animal, he turned to his task list mounted on the wall and checked off the last few items. He had to be careful around this agent or he would do or say something else that would send her rushing off to her bedroom the way she had the night before.

After he'd finished checking off items and had reclaimed his good sense, he crossed to the fence and stood next to her.

"His name is Booker, not Booger, by the way. As in Booker T. Washington."

She turned to him, surprised. "An *educated* goat that just happens to snack on hair?"

He nodded. "Has my son introduced you to any of the others?"

"Not yet."

He pointed to the black adult female, attempting to get her teeth on the bill of Derek's cap through the fencing. "She's Jane Austen. The brown one with the white dot on top of his head is Alexander Hamilton. The doe eating from the hay bale—" he paused to point to a goat with tan, white and black markings "—that's Harriet Tubman."

"What about the really pregnant one in the corner? I like her spots."

"She's Anne Frank, of course."

Her hands on the wood railing atop the fence, she glanced over at him. "Your petting zoo provides history lessons as well?"

He shook his head. "Not really. They all just have special names. When kids want to know about them, I say they can ask their parents to help them look up those names on the Internet. Learning is just a bonus."

"I thought people didn't name farm animals."

"That's because those go to market. I don't name any of the cattle." He gestured to the goats on the other side of the fence. "But these guys are pets."

"You were right that these animals wouldn't be ones that children regularly saw on the farm. Pygmy goats and miniature alpacas. Now, those look like real-life stuffed animals."

"They're not like cuddly stuffed animals, though. A few of them don't even enjoy being touched that much. And they live in a *petting* zoo."

"Must not have understood the assignment," she said with a chuckle.

"Guess not. And I might not have made the best selection for the zoo when I chose them. But they're here." He shrugged and then tilted his head, studying her. "Have you been over to see the mini lops?"

"I've been putting that one off."

"I get that. But I need to clean out the bunny hutch and enclosure before lunch, so I can take you there now." He turned back to Derek. "Let's go see the lops."

"Lops. Lops. Lops," Derek chanted as his father put him on his back and marched over to the enclosure.

Deirdre trailed behind them, clearly reluctant to visit this spot. As they approached, the tiny tan, brown and black domestic-breed rabbits with long, lopped ears skittered on both sides of the divided hutch and the equally segregated covered play yard.

"They're so adorable." She bent at the waist and peered into the fencing on top of the yard.

"Now these are the real stuffed animals," Micah told her.

After lowering his son to the ground, he unlocked a gate on the does' side of the play yard, pulled out a wiggling tan bunny and locked it again. He let the animal settle in his arms and then lifted his elbows, offering her to Deirdre. "This is Amelia Earhart. Get it? *Ear*hart."

"I get it, but I don't—" She stopped and took a step back.

"Come on. You can't be afraid of a floppy little bunny. You're a tough, highly skilled FBI special agent."

She pushed back her shoulders, as though she'd just remembered that, but finally, she accepted the animal into her arms.

"She's so soft."

When, after she'd petted the rabbit for several seconds she buried her face in the animal's fur, he couldn't help but smile. There were so many things to like about Deirdre Colton. Too many for his own good.

"Mini lops are one of the cuddliest breeds. They love to be held and brushed. Good thing, since they aren't low-maintenance pets like the goats."

Derek scooted closer to her and tugged on her pant leg. "Dee-Dee, I see Milla?"

"Of course you can see her. Do you like bunnies?"

He nodded enthusiastically. She asked him to sit crisscross on the ground and then lowered the rabbit into his arms. For several seconds, she watched him, a small smile playing on her lips, and then she stepped closer to the hutch that Micah had fashioned like a pair of side-by-side bunny hotels. She peeked into the screened windows and then rounded the perimeter of the play yard, examining it.

"This enclosure looks perfect. I don't see any damage at all."

"Can't you smell it?"

She wrinkled her nose. "Well, now that you mention it…" She shrugged.

"I don't mean the farm smells. Those are expected here. I mean the fresh wood."

With a dubious look, Deirdre inhaled. "Yeah, I smell it."

"The whole structure had to be rebuilt after someone destroyed it. This is a replica of my first hotel."

"Where you lost—" She stopped and stared at the bunnies playing in the yard.

Her melancholy touched him. He'd been pretty upset about those as well, but, like when it happened, he tried not to dwell on it.

"We added a few new friends recently. Abraham Lincoln and Mary Todd Lincoln." He pointed to a pair of bunnies in the corner of the yard.

Her sadness sliding away, she grinned, and the disconcerting thought struck him that he would do almost anything to keep her smiling like that.

"If you're inviting in married couples now, you might want to build a bigger enclosure."

"Not this time. You saw that both of them are on the left side of the enclosure, right? The *does'* side. Does to left and bucks to the right, just like in *Rudolph the Red-Nosed Reindeer.* Anyway, those two turned out to both be *Mrs.* Lincolns. A mistake from the breeder."

"Oops. Not going to change their names?"

"Why would I? They like them."

Micah stepped over to Derek and crouched down to lift the bunny.

The child tightened his hold, causing the animal to squirm in his lap. "I keep Milla."

"Remember, buddy? Gentle." He carefully loosened the child's arms. "We can't hold her too tight, or it will scare her."

Deirdre crouched next to them as well. "She sure is sweet. You're lucky that she lives right at your petting zoo, and you get to see her every day."

"See her tomorrow?" Derek asked. "Dee-Dee, too?"

She shot Micah a glance and dampened her lips. "Yes, tomorrow."

Neither of them knew how long she would be at Harmony Fields. If she were focusing only on her own case, she already would have been at the airport and maybe all the way back in DC. But as long as they still had questions on the ranch, she might be around a few more days. He should have wanted them to find all those answers right away, so he hated the truth that he hoped the investigation didn't go too quickly.

Micah finally lifted the bunny from his son's arms now that he'd loosened his grip. That served as a reminder to him: it would be a mistake for either of them to hold on too tightly to their guest.

"Right now Amelia needs a chance to go have her lunch and get a drink." He gathered the animal into his arms. "And after we're done cleaning their home, we get to have lunch, too. We're having a picnic."

"A picnic!" Derek clapped his hands, his loss of contact with the bunny forgotten. "Dee-Dee, too?"

"Of course she can come to our picnic."

Deirdre shook her head. "You don't have to go to any extra trouble for me. Really."

He carried the rabbit back to the enclosure and released her back into the play yard on the female side. "No trouble."

She followed him over to it and spoke in a low voice. "I can just make a sandwich or something. Well, if there's anything in the house to make one with, I mean. Or I can drive into Laramie to get groceries."

After locking the enclosure and checking it again, just to be sure, he held up his hand as a signal for her to stop rambling.

"It's just lunch, Deirdre, okay?"

She opened her mouth as if to argue, her shoulders lifting, but then she lowered them. "Okay."

He sent her a sidelong glance and then winked. "Around here, even indentured servants get lunch."

Chapter Nine

Deirdre took the last bite of her sandwich and wiped her mouth on a napkin, able to pause for the first time since she'd sat down to eat. She stretched out her legs on the quilt Micah had insisted they should spread on the grass under the plains cottonwood tree, though two perfectly good picnic tables sat empty nearby.

Across from her, the only one remaining of her two lunch dates lay back on the blanket, his face directed to the trees' leaves and the near-cloudless sky that peeked through it. He appeared to be asleep. The other one, finished with his lunch, chased a ball not twenty feet away, kicking it every time he caught up with it and laughing as though it came as a surprise.

This wasn't a date, she corrected her earlier thought, even if it more closely resembled a date than any of the working lunches she'd nibbled through over the past three years. It couldn't happen, anyway, no matter how tempting the idea and the company. But since Micah's eyes were closed, and he would never know, she couldn't resist watching him a little longer. She couldn't shake the tightness in her chest over that moment between them the night before, but she liked seeing him at ease like this, without the worry that creased his forehead when he spoke of his son's safety or the sadness in his eyes when he shared his father's story.

His relaxed expression was a smile, she noted, her gaze tracing the slope of his jawline to his chin and around to the other ear. The temptation to follow that same line with her fingertips and the risk that he could catch her staring made her avert her gaze. Her cheeks and neck heated as she had to fight to keep from taking another look.

Micah lifted up on his elbows and glanced over at her, but seemed to miss it all.

"Did you get enough to eat?"

She gestured to her empty plastic plate, which had once been covered with a peanut butter and jelly sandwich on white bread, baby carrots, apple slices and a prepackaged snack cake. The classic school lunch for a third grader.

"Yes. Thanks. I was starving."

"Nothing fancy." He reached for her plate and wrapper, tucking them inside the open cooler. "A good day of work outdoors will make you hungry."

"Something did. When did you even have time to pack all that?"

He closed the lid and grinned over at her. "This morning while you were still peeling your eyes open and drinking coffee with a straw."

"It's not my fault you wanted to work before the sun even crept out."

"Welcome to ranch life."

She pointed to the cooler. "Do you often have picnics out here with Derek?"

"Not often enough."

He didn't meet her gaze as he said it, and she couldn't help being pleased to think that he'd made that special lunch because they had a guest. Leaning back on her elbows, she brushed her hands over the cool cotton quilt top with a pattern of brightly colored and interlinking circles.

"What's the story with this blanket? Isn't it too new to be used for picnics?"

Sitting up, he brushed some crumbs off the cloth. "My neighbor said quilts are supposed to be used. She made it as a wedding gift. Called a double wedding ring pattern or something."

"I doubt she meant that you should throw it on the ground." She glanced away, rolling her lips. Clearly, this wasn't meant to be a special outing for her if he'd brought along the quilt meant to represent his wedding vows. Why did she have to keep bringing up subjects that reminded him of his late wife, anyway? She traced the connected circles with her fingertip, wondering if anything on the ranch *didn't* bring back memories of her.

"You're right. She probably didn't mean that. But, hey, it's a picnic, and you've got to have a blanket." Micah turned his head just as Derek barreled toward them, his ball forgotten. "Incoming."

He held out his arms, but just before impact, the toddler swerved and collapsed on Deirdre's straightened legs instead.

"Now *that* I wasn't expecting." She reached down to brush the little boy's sweaty hair from his forehead as he rested his cheek against her denim-covered knee.

"He likes you."

"I like him, too." Deirdre slid her fingers over those soft strands again. When she glanced up, she caught Micah watching her. Though her mouth went dry, her hands did just the opposite, becoming so damp that she had to brush them off on her jeans. She liked Derek, all right, but she wasn't immune to his father, either, and it scared the hell out of her.

"I like how you talk to him," Micah said after several seconds. "No baby talk nonsense. You have real conversations."

She lifted a brow. "What do you mean? How are people *supposed* to talk to kids?"

"I don't know about supposed to, but they coo at them like they would puppies."

"I don't even know how to *coo.*"

"As I said, I like the way you do it."

Their gazes connected, and a butterfly dance party started in her belly, wings tickling her insides as the sensation spread from her core to her shaky extremities. This was ridiculous. He'd offered only the tiniest bit of praise, but she'd warmed as if he'd given her a medal of honor.

Needing to escape the intensity of the moment, she lowered her gaze to the child, who now cuddled against her legs. He looked so sweet, a thumb in his mouth, eyes glazed, lashes brushing his cheek as he fought the heavy weight of his lids.

"They do have a way of winning your heart, don't they?"

At Micah's words, she lifted her head and smiled. "Guess they do."

"Then they throw up on you or throw a fit at the feed store and you remember just how hard parenting is."

She shook her head. "I can only imagine."

"And…he's out."

The child in her lap had indeed given up the fight against sleep. As she watched him, her own words replayed in her head. *I can only imagine.* The problem was she *had* started daydreaming again about what it would be like to experience all those wonderful and terrible moments of parenting. Here. With Micah and Derek. She had to stop. She needed to make some progress in the local investigation and glean any remaining information Micah could offer on her case while avoiding more of these sweet moments with him and his son.

"Should we try to take him to his bed in the house?"

"That works in theory but not in practice. He never gets

back to sleep. We're better off to let him rest here so he doesn't end up like yesterday."

So much for avoiding sweet moments. If only she could have been less giddy about having to spend more time with present company in a scene so picturesque that even a Renoir painting couldn't have done it justice.

She couldn't have been more grateful for the distraction when a pickup pulled up the dirt road near the petting zoo picnic area. A gift to get her back on track. Micah waved as two of the ranch hands drove by on their way to the main gate. Deirdre lifted her hand as well, pretending not to notice the strange look on the driver's face.

"How many ranch hands do you have working on Harmony Fields?"

Micah glanced back at her. "Just five. All men. Why do you ask?"

"Do any of them stay on the property full-time?"

He shook his head, answering her question, though she hadn't responded to his.

"All part-time. You've already met Rob and Kevin." He gestured to the dust of the disappearing vehicle. "They all have other jobs, so working here is bonus money. I'd like to get some full-time workers, but I need to have a bunkhouse built before I can do that. Now, if they have to be here overnight to help pull a calf, they sleep in the barn."

"Not the house?"

"I offer. They never accept." He studied her for several seconds. "Why are you asking all this? You don't think—"

"I just wondered why you hadn't mentioned names of any past or current ranch hands when we were putting together the possible suspect list."

He lifted a shoulder and lowered it. "You asked for enemies."

"You're telling me that you've never had an argument

with a current employee or one who left with bad blood between you?"

"Sorry to disappoint you. I've only had a few leave at all, and they did for the chance to start their own small cattle operations. The others—" he paused, spreading his arms "—they still work here."

"You must be a great boss."

He chuckled at that. "Or their tolerance for my crap is awfully high."

She doubted that explanation. Those men probably were lucky to have the chance to work for Micah Perry.

"You don't trust easily, do you?"

She jerked her head to meet his gaze. "What do you mean by that? We're talking about *you* here. You're the one who has someone targeting your ranch. Not me."

"Maybe. But you're still a little sensitive, aren't you? Makes me curious."

Deirdre shifted, disturbing the child sleeping against her legs. She sat frozen for several seconds, hoping he wouldn't awaken.

"Is it because of your dad that you have a tough time trusting?"

"What do you know about my—"

"Eoin Colton," he said to interrupt her. "It's not exactly a common name. That's *Virginia representative* Eoin Colton, right?"

Deirdre blew out a breath. "I *knew* I shouldn't have said his name. But I figured that out here nobody would recognize it."

"You mean way out here in the wilderness? Believe it or not, we get TV here. Satellite mostly. Cable coverage is shoddy." He grinned. "Usually, you would be right that I wouldn't notice it. I don't even follow politics. Takes too much energy. But you remember certain names—"

"Like those involved in sex scandals," she finished for him.

"Whew! Thanks for saying that." He made a show of brushing sweat off his brow. "I was trying to figure out a nice way to say it."

"There is no nice way."

"Well, he's had a long and successful political career despite those *moments*."

"Long enough to build quite a résumé that has nothing to do with proposed legislation," she agreed.

Micah lay back on the blanket but turned on his side this time and propped his head up with his arm. "That had to be hard on you. But aren't your parents still together? Seems like I remember seeing that."

She considered for a moment. This had nothing to do with their cases and only took time away from finding answers for either of them, but she found herself answering anyway, somehow needing him to know.

"That's part of the story. Long-suffering Georgina, standing by her man while Dad made the rounds during the legislative session." She scoffed. "The gossip rags don't even report anymore that Mom was the socialite my father had an affair with when he was first entering politics. He left his first wife, Caroline, to marry *her*."

"They don't need to bring up the old stuff when he's regularly given them new material to report on. Are you their only child?" He squinted, thinking. "Oh. Right. You mentioned a half brother."

He extended his index finger, shaking his wrist. "Wait. Didn't your dad have a child with a famous model?"

"That's Aidan. His mother is Kara Dean."

"Guess that's not the first time that happened to a political leader."

She shrugged. "My father legally acknowledged Aidan, paid child support and even gave him the Colton last name, so I guess that's something."

She paused, the thought that always left a bitter taste in her mouth souring again. "But that was because Aidan was the son he always wanted."

"I'm surprised he didn't make Aidan's mom Wife Number Three."

Micah watched her for so long that she couldn't help squirming. Derek groused in his sleep, shifted into a new position and snuggled against her again.

"I always wondered why he didn't," she said. "Well, when I learned about it. I was pretty little when it happened."

"How little?"

She brushed her hand over Derek's back. "Younger than him. Aidan's thirty-two. Just a year younger than me."

The truth that still hurt after all these years pressing down on her anew, Deirdre lowered her head. She couldn't look at Micah. Not now. She didn't want to see the pity in his eyes. Or let him see the pain in hers.

"Oh. That's tough," he said simply.

Deirdre continued to brush back the sleeping child's hair, grateful that Micah had given her a moment to collect emotions too close to the surface. As Micah shifted on the blanket to sit crisscross, she finally looked up again.

"I don't have any siblings, so I don't know what that would be like, and your situation has to be different from others', but are you and your brother close?"

His question made her smile, even if Micah had only shifted slightly from the earlier subject. She welcomed the break from discussing the skeletons her family had never been able to hide in any closet.

"We try," she said. "But we didn't grow up together. Aidan lived with his mom and stepdad, and I lived with my parents."

"But you're able to work together. You even said he's part of your team."

"You don't forget much." She grinned. "Yes, he's on the

team. He's a good US marshal. He's been with the agency nearly ten years now. An asset to the missing-person team."

"An asset, huh? Sounds like something you would write on a press release."

"It's also true," she said, frowning.

"I bet your dad is really proud of his two law-enforcement kids."

"You would think, wouldn't you?" She made a sound in her throat like a chuckle, though that truth had never been funny to her.

"What are you saying?"

Beyond the awkwardness of the conversation, she was becoming uncomfortable sitting in the same position on the hard ground to avoid awakening Derek. To ease some of the pain, she leaned back on her elbows. After a few seconds, she answered his question.

"He's proud of Aidan, anyway."

"But not you."

Since he didn't pose it as a question, she didn't answer. Anyway, there was something that she wanted to know.

"If you recognized my dad's name when I first said it in front of Sheriff Guetta, why didn't you say anything then?"

"I figured you already had enough to deal with in trying to convince Richard not to report you to the bureau."

"Then I guess I should say thank you."

He only smiled, waiting.

"Thank you." She rolled her eyes.

"How can anyone sit this way?" He unraveled himself and rubbed his calf muscle. "That feels like a torture method."

"Guess you have to be a kindergartner to appreciate it."

"It's been a while." He lay on his back again and stared up at the foliage and possibly a bit of sky.

She tilted her head back uncomfortably toward the blanket but couldn't manage the same position as his.

Micah gave her a sidelong glance. "I can move him if you like."

"It's okay. Really." She paused to watch the rise and fall of the child's chest. "I don't want to disturb him."

"You'll regret that when you have to limp all the way back to the house."

"I'll take my chances."

For a few minutes, they rested companionably without words, the only sounds coming from the rustling leaves above them and the bleating goats from their enclosure not far away. Deirdre didn't bother telling herself she could get used to lazy afternoons, just the three of them. She already had.

"That had to be really hard," Micah said, breaking the silence.

"What do you mean?"

"Growing up in that family."

Her throat immediately clogged. Few had acknowledged the truth that there were victims other than spouses in her parents' histories of infidelity, but now that Micah had said it, she felt the need to soften her version of the past.

"It's nothing like what you experienced, losing both parents by the time you were eighteen. Then the awful way it happened—"

He shook his head until she stopped. "This time, we're talking about *you*."

"No one feels sorry for the little girl who has the best of everything," she said. "Amazing house. The opportunity to attend the best private schools, university and law school. A political family and the chance to follow in their footsteps without breaking a sweat."

"And parents who embarrassed you again and again, expected you to willingly be a part of their Stepford family, and had and still have zero interest in ever really knowing you."

Deirdre blinked, the leaves above her moving in and out of focus. "I never said all that."

"No, but I'm not that far off, am I?"

He wasn't, and she didn't know what to make of it that he'd come so close to the truth. "I must not have thought it was that bad. I married a guy just like my dad."

As soon as the words were out of her mouth, she regretted them. Why did she keep volunteering information to this man, telling him things he had no business knowing? She was like a suspect, who was stopped for a broken taillight and ended up confessing to murder. She had a right to remain silent and should use it. For some reason, though, she just couldn't help herself. Had a near stranger touched on feelings she'd pretended didn't exist and betrayals she'd never before admitted out loud?

"You know, that's the least surprising thing you've said to me," Micah said.

She popped up from her reclining position. "How can that even be?"

"The same reason that children of drug addicts become involved with drug addicts. You do what you know."

His words made sense, but she couldn't accept the easy excuse he offered.

"Well, I should have known better. Brandon and I were both political staffers. My dad was his hero, and I ridiculously thought it had to do with his actual office activities. Not extracurriculars." She shook her head, shame she'd thought she could no longer feel settling heavily on her chest.

"He knew what I would be willing to put up with. The worst part? He was right."

"That sounds terrible. How long were you married to him?"

"Three years. The whole time Brandon had a conga line of lovers trampling all over the marriage."

He rubbed his eyes. "That's a vivid image. But, hey, your marriage was *twice* as long as mine."

"That's not a fair comparison, and you know it. Yours didn't end voluntarily. It was an accident."

Micah straightened and then turned on the blanket, suddenly interested in the goat enclosure about two hundred feet away from them. "Whoever said life was supposed be fair?"

At Micah's solemn words, Deirdre's chest squeezed. His pain became hers, his loss an open sore on her heart. She glanced at his hand, so tempted to reach for it again that she had to lace her fingers over her abdomen to resist. She'd stepped back, and she needed to stay back.

"Want to hear a really sad one?" She paused, waiting for him to turn back to her. He didn't, but she continued telling her story anyway, needing to share her shame. "*He* left me. All those affairs he had, and if he asked me to, I *still* would have stayed."

Now Micah swiveled back to her, a stark look in his eyes. "I'm sorry he did that to you."

She needed to stop, but she couldn't. The words kept coming and would keep coming until she had nothing left to say.

"Brandon probably thought I was like my mother, who built herself a life filled with the good things and wouldn't let something insignificant like more infidelity mess that up for her. He was wrong about me, though." She shook her head to emphasize that point. "I would have stayed because I believed in marriage. And I'd promised I would."

"Your determination is admirable," he said. "Not everyone would have been able to stick it out. But he didn't deserve your loyalty."

"I know that now. Believe me, I know it."

"Maybe there's honor in staying. Maybe not. But you have to be grateful that he saved you from having to make that choice."

"Are you serious? You want me to be grateful to *him*?" That word caught in her throat. "After everything I've said—"

Micah shook his head to interrupt her. "Not *to* him. Just that he chose to leave. He didn't make the decision for you. He did it for himself. Some people can't think beyond their own wingspan, and there's nothing the rest of us can do to change that."

Deirdre squinted at him, his words strange. Though his description of Brandon wasn't so far off, Micah had never met the man. He didn't seem to be talking about her loser of an ex-husband at all. *Nothing the rest of us can do to change that?* Why did he include himself in her sad story?

"How do you know—"

"They don't care who they hurt," he said, interrupting her. He looked away. "Or who they leave behind."

Her suspicion deepened, but before she had a chance to ask Micah more, the child next to her wiggled and then roused. The toddler came up on his hands and knees and rocked back and forth, his face pinched.

"No nap," he whined.

"Naptime's done, kiddo," Micah said.

The child whined again, his lips forming a pout.

"Better get him back to the house," Micah said.

He dumped the rest of the plates and trash into the cooler and checked around for any litter. Then, lifting the cooler by its handle, he bent to pull his son onto his hip.

"Could you bring the quilt?"

At her nod, he started away, walking quickly up the drive toward the house. She grabbed the blanket, looped it over her arm and hurried after him. She caught up with him just outside the slider.

"What aren't you telling me?"

"What do you mean?"

But his tight expression suggested he knew more than he was willing to say.

"You said, 'they don't care who they leave behind'? Is this about Maeve? Did you remember something else about her?"

Micah rolled his eyes as he opened the door. He stepped inside and toed off his boots, waiting for Deirdre to follow him.

"This might come as a surprise to you, but not everything is about Maeve O'Leary."

He turned and strode off with Derek. She let him go as what she suspected was the true meaning of his words sank in. This wasn't about her case. Or even his. He was hiding something about his wife, and when he was ready, she would convince him to tell her the truth.

Chapter Ten

Deirdre took the chair in the corner of Sheriff Guetta's office two days later, the space so tight that her knees hit the desk when she sat. The sheriff glanced at her from over his desk, stacked high with case files and who knew what else, and shrugged.

"I don't usually do suspect interviews in here, and we needed to squeeze in another chair." He pointed to the empty one. "We usually conduct those in the interview room down the hall."

"But you agreed we should speak with her here since this is just a casual, voluntary conversation," she reminded him. "Just to rule her out."

He laughed. "Did you make sure the security cameras outside didn't get any footage of you visiting my office as well? Wouldn't want anyone in DC to know what you were doing on your spring vacation out West."

"Are you going to spend the whole time making fun of me, or do you want to get this thing over with?"

She tried to cross her legs in the same pair of jeans she'd already worn for too many hours this week, but she couldn't accomplish it. If she had to conduct more potential suspect interviews, she would need a second shopping trip. And hopefully not another visit to Gary's.

"Did you tell Micah that in addition to picking up records, you asked me to call Kara in?"

She shook her head. "It's not *his* investigation, but no, I didn't. And we have to start somewhere." Not that they'd had any real conversations since yesterday when it had been too easy to share with him. Now she felt far too vulnerable that she had.

"Has anyone already interviewed her?"

"I have to say no," he said with a grin.

"Then let's see if we can mark someone off the list."

Richard reached for his desk phone and pushed a few buttons. "Liz, could you send her in, please?"

About thirty seconds later, someone knocked at the door.

"Come in, Mrs. Jackson."

"Mrs. Jackson?" A petite brunette opened the door slightly, a quizzical look in her striking blue eyes.

Clearly, she'd been on a first-name basis with the sheriff before that morning. She pushed the door wide and squeezed inside, lugging a handled infant car seat. She balanced the carrier precariously as she pushed the door closed with her hip.

Deirdre immediately wanted to abort the whole interview, not just because the room didn't feel big enough to share with a woman Micah Perry had dated and kissed and with whom he'd possibly even been intimate. Not because she was jealous of the woman or any of those other things, either. With a fine-boned frame like that and those manicured hands, Kara Sullivan Jackson was about as likely a suspect to have completed those strenuous acts of sabotage as Micah himself.

"Here. Let me help with that." Deirdre leaped up from her seat but found no way to maneuver over to assist the woman.

"I've got it," Kara said through teeth grinding with effort, as she wrangled the seat into the one bit of open space between the door and the desk. The baby inside, probably a girl, given the abundance of pink ruffles on the carrier and clothes, somehow slept through the whole ordeal, a blanket tucked up under her chin.

Task completed, Kara dropped into the chair next to Deirdre. "I'm stronger than I look."

Not that strong. She still couldn't picture the woman pulling over an enormous wood cabinet or cutting through huge sections of cattle fencing. At least not without help.

She looked back and forth between the two law-enforcement officers. "My husband said you wanted to see me."

"Thank you for coming, Kara." The sheriff stood up behind his desk. "I'd like you to meet FBI special agent Deirdre Colton.

"Special Agent Colton, this is Kara Jackson."

As the two women shook hands, Guetta sat again.

"You have a beautiful baby." Deirdre paused to admire the sleeping child.

"I do, don't I?" Kara stared down at her child and then looked back at the sheriff expectantly. "Jerry said you needed help with a case. Happy to do what I can, but I can't stay long. Babysitter's with my two stepkids, so I'm on the clock."

"Special Agent Colton is helping investigate the series of suspicious incidents at Harmony Fields Ranch," the sheriff told her.

The woman's head jerked, and her jaw tightened. "What are you talking to me for?"

"Now, Kara, relax," Guetta said, gesturing downward with his hands. "We're not accusing you of anything. There's just been quite a few cases of malicious destruction of property on the ranch, and we're having a chat with a few individuals on a list of those who might have had a problem with Micah in the past."

"And you're talking to *me*? I don't have a problem with

Micah Perry. I had my stepkids over at his petting zoo two weeks ago."

Deirdre leaned forward to take control of the interview, shifting the notebook in her lap. "Mr. Perry mentioned that you dated at one point."

"*He's* the one that put me on that list? That son-of-a—"

Kara managed to stop herself, but not before the sheriff and Deirdre exchanged a look. Micah's onetime girlfriend was a hothead, all right.

Deirdre twirled her pen in her fingers. "Do you remember a comment you made about his infant son?"

"He told you that? That's just ridiculous. He had no busi- ness—" Again, she stopped. This time, her gaze narrowed. "Do I need to have my lawyer here?"

The sheriff shook his head. "I don't think so."

"Look, I was angry, and I said some awful things," Kara said, folding her hands in her lap. "But I haven't done any- thing at Harmony Fields."

Deirdre nodded. "And whatever was between you two is in the past, right?"

"Oh. Absolutely. I'm a married woman." She gestured to her wedding band and then to the baby in the carrier next to her.

Deirdre stood then, resting her hands on the desktop. "That's all we'll need. Thank you so much for coming in."

She shook the woman's hand and waited as she wrestled the car seat out of the room. Once Kara stepped down the hall, Deirdre closed the door.

The shocked look that Guetta gave her probably matched the one on her own face.

"Hell hath no fury like a woman scorned," he said.

"Micah was right to say she hates him, but do you think she should still be considered a possible suspect regarding any of the sabotage damage?"

He shook his head. "I'm pretty sure that was all bluster."

"Yeah. Me, too."

"Still, if I were Micah, I would avoid meeting that one in a dark alley."

Though she recognized that the jocular sheriff was only kidding, she still couldn't laugh. Maybe this potential suspect wasn't threatening Micah and Derek, but someone still was. Even if she could find the answers for her own investigation, suddenly the idea of leaving Wyoming before stopping whoever was targeting them sent a chill up her spine. How could she walk away without knowing they would be safe?

THE DARKNESS NO longer seemed so suffocating, Deirdre decided with surprise, as she and Micah tromped toward the petting zoo later that night, their two flashlights providing twin cones of illumination on the dirt road before them. She appreciated the night sky's generosity in providing hundreds of brilliant pinpoints on its canvas, but she suspected that a person could get used to even the nights where cloud cover veiled all the stars, if she chose to. And if she were in the right company.

She tucked her hand in her jacket pocket, her fingers coming into contact with her holster. Though she'd changed back into ranch gear after returning from the sheriff's office, she'd kept her weapon with her. Even if there'd been no evidence of new vandalism on the ranch since she'd been there, after meeting with Micah's unusual ex, she was convinced that they would all be safer if she remained armed.

"Do you think the animals will mind having nighttime visitors?" With the flashlight in her other hand, she pointed in the direction of their destination. "They have to know it's not regular zoo time, and they might demand overtime pay for having to entertain during off-hours."

"I'm sure they'll cut us a deal if we give them snacks."

"Always works with me."

"I'll remember that." He patted his pocket, and the crinkling sound of cellophane filtered over to her. "I've been known to carry candy sometimes."

"I've been known to *eat* candy."

"Those two things just might go together," he said.

He was flirting with her. She should have avoided it, or at least tried not to play along, but she'd spent the past few days telling herself all the reasons she should keep her distance from Micah and his son, and she was tired. Tonight she just wanted to relax with him and take a break from searching for answers that had been harder to come by than she'd expected when she'd planned her little Wyoming getaway.

"So what shows do you think the animals will put on for us tonight? I'm on vacation. I need entertainment."

"You do realize these are animals, don't you?" He pointed the flashlight at her face. "You might get a little more than you're bargaining for with their nocturnal activities. Not that they always wait until nighttime."

"Right." She cleared her throat, her cheeks warm despite the drop in temperature after sundown. Were they really talking about animal mating habits while they walked, just the two of them, under a starry sky? She appreciated the darkness even more.

He redirected his flashlight to the road ahead, and they silently waved their lights back and forth to check for tripping hazards now that words were more difficult to come by.

"But not bunnies, though," Deirdre said to break the silence. "Unless they've dismantled your gender-segregation plan."

"I wouldn't put it past them. They don't care anything about population control."

As they drew closer to the goat barn, with bleating sounds breaking the silence, Micah slowed and used his flashlight to scan the building's exterior. "I thought Derek was never going to go to sleep tonight. 'One more book, puleeze.' Bet it's just because *you* were reading."

"That's a solid toddler imitation," she said, trying not to be flattered.

"I get a lot of practice."

He probably didn't have a lot of adult conversation with just him and Derek living together on the ranch, but Deirdre resisted the urge to ask if he was lonely there. They were finally comfortable with each other again, and she didn't want to mess that up.

"I thought his begging was cute," she said instead, reaching back to his earlier comment. A safer one.

"Parent manipulation 101. How to avoid bedtime."

"I know." She tried to ignore the gooseflesh that peppered her arms over his reference to "parents." He could have said "adults" or "grown-ups," but he'd used the one word that described the role that until now she never knew she wanted.

"But he was trying so hard to stay awake. Those poor little eyelids. So heavy." She smiled into the darkness, remembering.

"As I said before, they have a way of winning your heart, don't they?"

She sensed him watching her, but she didn't dare turn her flashlight on him. She wasn't sure she could trust her response if she caught him staring.

"Bet Derek never had to win you to his side," she couldn't help saying anyway.

"Nope. He made his loud, messy appearance, and just like that—" he paused to snap his fingers "—I was a goner. He became the center of my world."

Emotion swelled in her throat then. Had her own father ever once seen her as the most important person in his life? Or even the top five? Had she ever been more than "the family" for the political flyer or a list of academic accomplishments to brag about at cocktail parties?

Her flashlight caught on Micah as he reached for the baby monitor attached to his belt and peeked at the little screen.

"Is he doing okay?" She hoped that at least one of them was.

"Sleeping like a baby."

They chuckled over his corny joke. She, for one, really needed a laugh. Maybe that would relieve some of the electricity in the air around them and pulsating from her earlobes to her baby toes. Good thing no rain was in the forecast, since one lightning bolt would turn her into a pile of smoldering ash.

She steadied her legs and followed Micah through the staff entrance into the pygmy goat enclosure. But a single brush of his fingers over her jacket-covered arm as he guided her inside sent another round of tingles up to her shoulder and reinforced her warning to stay out of the rain. She drowned out her other suspicion that spending time with Micah in the dark would be a mistake.

Micah latched the door and then flipped a switch. Immediately, the goat barn and the enclosed yard surrounding it were awash with a warm glow from twinkling string lights. If the darkness had seemed dangerous, this magical shimmer doubled down on the risk.

"This is amazing," she breathed anyway because it was. How she hadn't noticed all those lights when they'd visited earlier, she couldn't imagine. "Doesn't exactly look farmlike."

"It's not supposed to, because it's a—"

"Zoo," she finished for him. "But the kids aren't here at night. They'll never get to enjoy all these lights."

"They're part of an idea I cooked up for parents. Maybe

a chance for them to leave the kids with a sitter and spend a little time as a couple."

"Date night at the zoo. It has a nice ring to it." Too nice, in her opinion, based on present circumstances and company. The setting was also far too romantic for a place scented with hay, goat and muck.

She crossed her arms and gripped her sleeves, suddenly needing to hold on to something. "You never said why you wanted me to come out here with you now."

If he said, "for a date," she wasn't sure what she would say. Or if there would be any way she could stop herself from tramping across the play yard to throw herself at him.

"I have a job for you to do."

She sighed, her hormones taking a well-deserved beatdown. "Should have known. More free labor."

"I think you're going to like this one." He held up his forefinger in a signal for her to wait and stepped past a stack of hay bales in a protected extension of the building with a gabled roof but open on both ends. When he returned, he carried a black-and-white-spotted baby goat, small enough to fit comfortably in his arms.

"A new baby?" She approached slowly to avoid startling the animal that seemed perfectly content with Micah holding her.

"A *kid*. Or, more specifically in her case, a *doeling*. Our first this season. Since the petting zoo is so new, it's only our second full season. The other does have a few more weeks to go before kidding." He nodded at her strange look. "Yeah, that's what it's called when a goat gives birth. Want to hold her?"

He extended his arms to hand the doeling out to her. Without hesitation, she accepted the transfer. She brushed her fingers over the animal's coat, coarse on top but downy closer to its skin. The tiny goat cuddled against her, seeming to enjoy the attention.

"She's sweet." Deirdre touched the animal's snout, and it nibbled her finger.

"Only a few days old." Micah petted the doeling's head. "In their first few weeks, it's important to get out here and cuddle them several times a day. That way they'll be comfortable around people."

"It's a tough job, but somebody has to do it." She grinned, hugging the goat close so its snout rested just beneath her chin.

"Told you you'd like it. You seem pretty comfortable holding her."

She glanced up, still brushing her fingers through the doeling's coat. "Didn't want you questioning my bravery again."

"Believe me, I would never do that. Richard told me you insisted on having a chat with Kara." He shivered visibly. "She's scary."

"He wasn't supposed to tell you."

Micah answered with a shrug.

"What did you do to her, anyway?" she asked before she could stop herself.

"As a gentleman cowboy, I shouldn't say."

"If it has any bearing on the case, you should."

He met her gaze levelly. "It doesn't, but since you won't believe me, I'll just tell you that in addition to pushing for a wedding ring, she offered me her kindness—uh, all of it. Since I couldn't see us having a more long-term thing, I politely declined."

"Ouch!"

"I know." He stared at his hands.

"And *kindness*? That's what the kids are calling it these days?" Even she could hear the embarrassment in her laugh.

Now, in addition to animal breeding, they were discussing human sex as well.

"I have nothing more to say about that."

He rolled his lips inward, looking more than a little uncomfortable himself. Deirdre found it surprising that he'd said as much as he had. Maybe he'd just been trying to defend his actions, as Brandon would have done, but she sensed there was more to it. Micah seemed to want her to know that he hadn't slept with Kara when he could have had a casual thing with her. That only gave Deirdre more questions. Like why he'd thought she should know and, more importantly, why she cared.

The goat wiggled in her arms. She lowered it to the hay-strewn ground. As the animal took off, probably in search of its mother to feed, Deirdre leaned against the fence, on the opposite side of where she'd stood with Derek just that afternoon.

"Hey, you haven't told me her name."

Micah leaned against the fence next to her and crossed his arms. "I thought you might like to name her."

"Are you serious? Are you sure you don't want to do it? Or Derek? You really want to trust me with that responsibility?"

Micah grinned, getting a kick out of her babbling excitement tinged with insecurity.

"It's just a name." He chuckled and then pushed back his shoulders, pursed his lips and spoke in a low voice. "The mission is yours, should you choose to accept it."

"I don't know." She searched around the pen again for the baby goat that had already located its mother and latched on to a teat. "It's *so* much pressure."

More than that, it felt like a gift. He'd asked her to leave a mark on Harmony Fields, one that would linger there with him and Derek for years after she'd returned to Washington and moved to more high-profile cases than even Maeve

O'Leary and her trail of dead husbands. Something to spark their memory of her when she already knew she would never forget *them*.

"Just think for a minute and go with your gut."

"What happens if I come up with something ridiculous?"

"Then Abraham and Mary from over in the rabbit enclosure will be in good company."

"Good point." She watched the animal, drinking greedily, and the long-suffering mother, readjusting its stance every few seconds to maintain its balance. "How about Eleanor Roosevelt?"

He watched the hungry goat for a few seconds and then nodded. "Independent. Outspoken. Eleanor it is."

"Hope you won't expect too much of her," she said. "Those are awfully big shoes to fill."

"She'd eat those shoes, anyway. It'll just be nice having Eleanor here as a reminder—"

As Micah cut off his words, Deirdre couldn't help but to glance over at him, and once she'd met his steady gray gaze, she couldn't look away. She didn't even want to. He must have leaned toward her, as he suddenly felt close. Intimately close. The tip of his tongue darted out to dampen the corner of his mouth, his gaze lowering to her lips. It lingered so long there that her skin tingled.

He was going to kiss her. She could tell herself that she didn't want him to, that it would be an awful idea and a complication to a case with more than enough of those already stuffed in its file, but her thundering heart and sweaty palms revealed that her body and maybe even her heart were completely on board.

Micah leaned forward. Or was it her? But now he was so close that his warm breath tickled her ear, and her heart pounded hard enough to unzip her jacket. Maybe she'd done that, at least in her thoughts, too.

But just when their lips were near enough that their tongues could touch with barely a reach, he stopped his slow lean, his eyes wide, his mouth forming a soft O. "Maybe we shouldn't—"

A sound escaping her throat that she could only define as *desperation* cut off his words, but it was her lips that prevented him from completing whatever he'd been about to say. She pressed her mouth to his, not in one of those delicate kisses like those sweet maidens from the movies she loved but with a hunger that mirrored that of the famished baby goat. Whatever his reticence before, Micah returned her kiss, equally greedy and desperate and wanting.

Deirdre didn't wait for him to dab her lip for permission and instead glided her tongue over the seam of his until he opened for *her*, their mouths mating in a simulation tantalizing enough to make the goats blush. His mustache and beard tickled her skin as he dazzled her mouth and then neck from earlobe to collarbone. He splayed his hands over her back, their reach beginning at her bra strap, then following the curve of her waist and finally straying to the pockets of her jeans. She wanted more. Needed more.

With an urgency that surprised her, she slid her arms over his shoulders, the muscles she'd only been able to admire before flexing beneath her touch, tendons stretching and ligaments working. Every bit of it was driving her out of her mind.

Even when Micah broke off the kiss to gasp for breath, another of those humiliating sounds of protest escaped her. He smiled against her lips and, turning with her in his arms, leaned her backside against the fence. Then, on an exceptionally deep and delirious kiss, he settled himself against her. All of him.

Her eyes, already heavy with desire, shot open then. An

equally shocked Micah stared backat her. They both jumped back as if caught by a monitor in the hall of any high school.

"Sorry," he said before she could form the words.

"No. I'm sorry." She'd definitely started it, but he hadn't exactly fought her off with a shovel, either.

"I don't know what that was," he said, still shaking his head.

Despite her humiliation, she had to turn away so he wouldn't see her smile. If Micah really didn't know what *that* was, there were plenty of animals on the ranch that could explain it to him. He'd been close enough for Deirdre to be intimately aware of his willingness to take that undefinable thing to a satisfying conclusion, but what she couldn't explain was why she hadn't stopped it before it even started.

He cleared his throat, stepping back and giving her a wide berth. "We'd better get back to the house."

"Yeah, we should."

She turned her head, focusing on a pair of goats, already wrestling with their newly emerged horn buds. What were they supposed to do now? Micah seemed to be able to turn off his hormones as quickly as he had the faucet for the goat trough. If only she could shut hers down as easily when her whole body had awakened from its hibernation and had no interest in taking another nap.

They stepped outside the enclosure, and Micah shut off the lights. But just as the space descended back into near darkness, with the only illumination from a few remaining safety lights, a chill tripped up Deirdre's spine. Was it a sound, or were her senses just out of whack after a kiss that made her knees weak? She wasn't sure. But something told her they were not alone.

Micah shifted closer to her, his flashlight's beam directed to the ground. "Did you hear that?"

She touched his jacket sleeve to ask him to be quiet. Like

her, he pressed his back to the side of the building, and other than his breathing, he didn't make a sound.

They waited. And listened.

No footsteps. No sounds beyond the bleats from the goats and what could only be the rumble of cattle in the distance. She'd almost convinced herself that she'd imagined it, but as her gaze slid to Micah, her breath caught again. He knew someone was there, too.

He leaned close and whispered again. "By the alpacas."

"Oh, hell, no." Her words came in a stage whisper at best, but she couldn't help herself. Just as she'd refused to let whoever this was get to Micah or Derek, she wouldn't let them frighten or endanger more of the animals.

She zipped her flashlight in her pocket and withdrew her weapon from the holster. But as Deirdre started to pull away from the wall, Micah reached out an arm like the reflex of a driver shielding a passenger upon impact.

"You can't go out there," he whispered.

"I've got this." She shifted out of his reach as she said it.

"Not alone."

This time she rested a hand on his shoulder. "I'm armed. You're not. You don't know if *he* is."

He shook his head. "You can't—"

"Think of Derek."

Deirdre knew the moment she got through to Micah as he tipped his chin up and leaned his head against the side of the building.

"Trust me. Please," she whispered and then pushed away from the wall.

Praying Micah wouldn't follow, she rushed from one bit of cover to the next. She rounded the rabbit enclosure, barely registering that the animals were skittering about, either hearing or sensing her presence.

Deirdre pressed forward, aware of the danger in looking

back. Still, opposing needs pulled her in two directions—backward to ensure she hadn't left Micah exposed to attack and forward so the suspect she believed was there couldn't escape. She'd lost her edge, and there didn't seem to be any way to get it back.

Then, in the open pasture on the far side of the alpaca enclosure, under what had to be the worst lighting of anywhere on the ranch, someone in a dark hoodie appeared to be running with the animals. Or chasing them. They were trying to get away from him, all right, in a bleating chorus of kazoos and panicked circles, their long necks swaying like those of giraffes. Then, one by one, they recognized the missing section of fencing on the southeast side of the enclosure and escaped through it.

"Stop! FBI!" she called out to the only one who would understand.

The suspect looked over, face obscured in shadows and the hood of the jacket. In a movement that could have been a reach for a weapon or an attempt to surrender, the individual covered his or her mouth. A shrill mechanical whistle eclipsed the sounds of even the terrified animals before the one who'd produced the sound sprinted to the mangled section of fencing.

Deirdre raced around the enclosure's perimeter toward the same opening, as though she could halt both the suspect and the stampede. She couldn't get there fast enough. The suspect had too much of a head start. Refusing to concede, she remained in pursuit and followed the suspect into a bank of trees, where branches tore at her sleeves and brambles brought her to her knees. She had to take the risk of holstering her weapon and using the flashlight from her pocket just to get past the brush.

As she finally emerged on the other side, an engine roared to life in the distance. With its lights off, the vehicle—probably a truck—raced down the drive and off the property. Defeated, she returned through the line of trees—and found Micah on the other side, already chasing down the terrified animals.

Though she didn't meet his gaze as she approached, she sensed his disappointment anyway. She'd had the chance to take down the suspect who'd terrified Micah and put his son in danger. But she'd been too busy making out with a witness and forgetting about her responsibility, and, like with everything else lately, she'd failed.

Chapter Eleven

Micah dropped onto the sofa two hours and a shower later, a mix of frenzied energy and collapse pressing him into the cool leather. Even though his hands were raw from repairing fence wires, and his muscles ached, he should have been more grateful. None of the alpacas had been injured beyond an intense cardiac workout from the ordeal, the newest crime had been photographed and recorded, and the temporary fencing that he and Deirdre had put in place would hold until he could figure out a more permanent solution.

They'd been incredibly lucky. Again. That was the problem. These attacks would never stop until somebody got hurt. Maybe Derek. Maybe him. Or, now, Deirdre.

The woman who'd scared the hell out of him earlier dropped her phone on the coffee table and collapsed on the other end of the sofa. Like him, just back from a shower and dressed in a T-shirt and cotton athletic shorts, Deirdre sat with her damp hair spread across the backrest and closed her eyes, lacing her fingers behind her head. He tried not to notice how amazing she smelled or how soft the skin on her bare legs looked in those athletic shorts or to think about how amazing she'd tasted and felt against his body earlier.

"What a crazy night," she said without moving or opening her eyes.

He had to agree with that. Neither of them could have predicted this evening would include both a kiss in a goat barn that had them walking on eggshells around each other *and* chases of the suspect who'd targeted his family and loping creatures set free to fend for themselves.

Good thing they'd both put a *whoa* on that kiss that would have had him laying her back in the hay with the smallest encouragement. He knew what a bad idea it would be to get involved with the special agent, too. So why were his hands still prickling with a ridiculous need to touch her even now? Why was his body still aching to finish what they'd started? Maybe his moment of panic when he couldn't find Deirdre anywhere, when he'd failed to protect her, too, had messed with his head more than he'd realized.

"Wait." Her eyes opening, she immediately shot a look at the front door. "You checked all the locks, right?"

She pushed off the sofa and started that way herself.

"Hey, stop. We already checked them together."

Finally, she stopped and turned back to him. "We did, didn't we?"

"Twice." Before she had a chance to mention them again, he added, "As for the shotguns, both are positioned near the doors and ready, ammunition responsibly stored nearby."

"Sounds like everything's fine."

She returned to the sofa but crossed her arms as she sat. Clearly, she wasn't fine—hadn't been since they returned from the petting zoo.

"Are you cold? Want me to make some hot chocolate?"

She shook her head.

"How about a fire?"

She glanced at the fireplace, considering. "Sounds nice, but I don't want to put you to any more trouble tonight."

He shot a glance her way, wondering which part of the evening she'd considered problematic for him, but she avoided looking at him.

"No trouble." At least not this time. He grabbed the remote off the mantel and hit the button, a crackling fire immediately lighting on the grate in the gas fireplace.

Deirdre did look up this time. "You don't have a wood fireplace? Out here on a ranch?"

"I make plenty of fires outside," he said with a shrug. "When I get home, I just want to relax and enjoy a fire."

"It does feel nice."

She sank back again and closed her eyes, but almost immediately, she jerked and sat forward, as if chased from any thought of relaxation. "I still can't get over how fast the alpacas could move," Deirdre said. "Poor things. They were so scared."

They weren't the only ones. As memories of the not knowing and then the chaos replayed in his mind, Micah shivered. He sneaked a peek at her, relieved to find her watching the fire instead of him.

"I'm just glad we were able to get all ten of them back inside the fence," he said. "I don't know what we would have done if they'd escaped to the other pastures or the road."

She turned to face him then, resting her elbow on top of the sofa and pressing her cheek against her fist, her expression serious. "Well, I know exactly what we would have done. We would still be out there hunting. Until we found every one of them."

He believed her, too. She would have helped him all night. As much as she played the tough FBI agent, she had a soft spot for animals. And for children like his son.

But he couldn't shake the worries and the sense of helplessness that had filled him as she'd left to pursue the suspect and expected him to stay behind.

"If we hadn't gone down to the petting zoo tonight…or

if the alpacas had been out all night—" He stopped himself, the what-ifs too frightening to consider.

"But we *did* go. And they weren't stuck out all night."

"How do we know we'll be there next time?"

She held out her right hand, palm up, and then lowered it. "We can't know that. Just as we won't know if the suspect will be armed next time. Or even if a weapon was present tonight but the suspect chose to flee rather than engage. That's why you should have listened to me when I told you to stay back."

This wasn't the first time she'd mentioned it, so he tried to explain.

"Don't you get it? I couldn't just stand there like a coward while you put yourself in danger. What kind of—" He stopped, rethinking since he'd almost said, "man."

"What kind of *person* would I be?"

Her gaze narrowed. "Can we set aside your fragile male ego for a moment? Like I said before, you were unarmed. And only one of us is a trained FBI agent. It's my *job* to pursue suspects."

"My male ego isn't—" After considering those words, he frowned, his whole argument contradicting the claim he'd been about to make. He tried again to explain instead. "And it's my job—my *responsibility*—to protect everything on Harmony Fields."

That Deirdre automatically glanced to the stairs leading to Derek's nursery signaled she still didn't understand that his instinct to shield would extend to her. Or even why it should.

"He's still doing okay?" she asked.

Micah nodded, grateful she'd decided to let the subject go. They would never agree on it, anyway. "Just checked on him. Still sound asleep. I worried he would wake up while we were still out working on the fence."

"That's one good thing."

Leaning forward, he gripped opposite elbows and braced them against his knees. "I only wish I could have gotten a look at the suspect."

"And I wish I'd gotten a *better* look."

He would second that wish. Especially since this suspect had escaped capture. Again.

"But you witnessed him in the act," Micah reminded her. "That's more than any of the other investigators have accomplished so far."

"Fat lot of good it did me." She crossed her arms, sinking deeper into the sofa cushions. "We still don't even know what he wants. And he got away."

"You're saying 'he' now. Are you convinced the suspect is a guy?" He watched her closely, her answer more critical than he was ready to share.

"My vantage point and the lighting were so bad that I can't be certain of much." She pressed her lips into a flat line. "Well, except that the suspect was tall and lanky. You can't shield that behind a darn hoodie like you can hair and skin color."

"So, we're looking for a tall and thin man—or woman— with no specific hair or skin color? Someone who happens to own a sweatshirt."

She gave him a mean look and then shook her head. "So many times I've pressed witnesses to give me more detailed descriptions of suspects. Now I know how hard it is when you really didn't see anything useful. I hate to have to put this description at all in the report to the sheriff."

"At least we can rule out Kara Jackson. No one would ever call her tall and lanky."

He couldn't say the same about Maeve O'Leary, who'd been a Pilates devotee before it ever became a national fitness craze. His rationale for not sharing his ridiculous suspicion was becoming less justifiable by the minute. If the suspect turned out to be Maeve, and something happened to Derek or Deirdre, he would never forgive himself.

"Kara couldn't have run that fast, either."

She sent him a skeptical look. "You still weren't ready to rule her out?"

"I was even before you interviewed her." As for another woman, not so much. "What about the voice? Did the suspect call out to the alpacas?"

Deirdre shook her head. "Not that I heard. Just the whistle. It was so loud that you could probably hear it clear back in Casper."

"I heard it." He swallowed, forcing himself not to shiver again as she was watching him this time. "At first, I thought it was one of the rabbits."

"Rabbits whistle?"

"No, they *scream*. Like a child. But only when they're terrified."

"That's what you thought you heard. And that's why you followed me."

They exchanged a look that said more than words could. "Yeah."

Deirdre appeared to file away that information as though she could understand, just a little, why he'd come after her.

"I just wish I could have made an arrest tonight." Leaning forward, she propped her elbows on her knees and rested her hands in her palms, sighing. "We could have put an end to all of this. But I dropped the ball."

"You did everything you could."

"Not everything." She met his gaze, her eyes sad. "He, or *she*, is still out there."

"This isn't exactly the life I'd planned to provide for my son, either. One where we're always looking over our shoulders. I'm supposed to make him feel safe."

She smiled then—not the delighted, impish smile he'd

come to enjoy a little too much these past few days, but it was something.

"You make your son feel safe and loved every day. Not every child can say that. You'll also protect him from this vandal or anyone else. If he doesn't already know that, he'll figure it out in a few years."

"You sound like you're filling out my application for Father of the Year." Micah settled back into the sofa cushions, relaxing for the first time since they'd heard sounds outside the goat enclosure.

"I'd better get a pen. You might have a good shot at winning. Can you name any other father who built a petting zoo just so his child and those of his neighbors could spend time with some interesting animals?"

"Hey, I would vote for that guy," he said, chuckling.

Her smile was warm enough to make him shift in his seat. "Me, too."

Deirdre turned in her seat as she had earlier, settling into the listening position with her elbow propped on the back of the couch.

"You know, in all the information you've given me about Harmony Fields and about your life back in New York, you've never told me how you became a cowboy. And how you ended up with all this." She gestured with her free arm to indicate the great room around her.

"I can tell you, but it's not some *Young Guns*–type story. Not Hollywood at all."

She lifted her chin and made a serious face. "I'm prepared to be disappointed but tell me anyway. I really need to hear a boring story. I'm all keyed up after everything tonight. Maybe it will help me get to sleep."

"I'll do my best to be a good sleep aid."

Deirdre shifted on the seat, tucking her bare feet under her, and waited.

"After Dad…you know, I wasn't sure what to do. I only had a few hundred dollars in my savings account that Maeve somehow missed and a few hundred more that I'd just received as birthday presents. Since I could be penniless anywhere, not just in New York, and it was too hard being in a city where everything reminded me of my dad, I bought a bus ticket to Wyoming. I chose it because it was the Cowboy State."

"That's a pretty brave thing for an eighteen-year-old kid to do."

He waved his index finger at her. "Now, don't go calling me brave and messing up my boring story."

"Oh. Of course." She gestured with a flourish for him to continue.

"I know it sounds hokey, but ever since I was a kid, I'd dreamed of being a cowboy. Probably a strange career goal for a kid from the Upper East Side, with an equity fund–manager dad. I didn't even know the difference between Western boots and ropers." He grinned at her then, pleased when she dipped her chin and glanced up at him bashfully over her own boot education.

"Where did you even get a career goal like that?"

"Where else? Westerns. Loved 'em."

Deirdre covered her face with her hands and started coughing.

"You okay?"

"Yeah. Fine." She coughed again. "Go ahead."

"You know, John Wayne, Gary Cooper and, of course, Clint Eastwood."

He narrowed his gaze at her as she cleared her throat again. "You sure you're okay?"

She waved him on.

"So, yes, I wanted to be a cowboy, but I didn't have any idea what one actually did besides ride horses, chase outlaws, impress women. I showed up in Laramie and tried to get a job as a ranch hand."

"I take it you weren't much in demand."

"Not a top candidate. But Doug Blevins, an old rancher who lived not far from here, was looking for some help and didn't mind training a greenhorn from New York City. Even so, it took everyone a while to understand my accent."

"You don't have an accent, as far as I can tell."

"Fifteen years will do that." He tilted his head, studying her. "Getting drowsy yet?"

"Working on it. Would you just tell the story so I can get to my nap?"

"I slept in the bunkhouse at Doug and Marie's place and helped work their land for the next three years, saving money while Doug taught me everything he knew about running a ranch. Then I bought my first piece of property and started my own small operation."

"The ranch that was foreclosed on? How long before you were no longer considered an outsider?"

"I'll let you know when that happens." He chuckled at his own joke. "But seriously, around here, there are some people you will never win over if you weren't born in a ten-mile radius of where they're standing. Good thing there are plenty of others. Once they realized I wasn't going anywhere, they welcomed me like one of their own."

"I can't even imagine what that's like."

"It's nice."

"I bet. Were that rancher and his wife some of the people who welcomed you?" She waited for his nod before continuing. "Do you still get to see them much?"

"Quite a bit, actually. Remember the cook I mentioned?" He waited for her nod before continuing. "That's Marie. And the neighbors who watch Derek sometimes? Doug and

Marie. And the neighbor who made the quilt you thought I was destroying?"

"Let me guess. Marie?"

"You're good at this game."

Deirdre stood up from the sofa and stepped closer to the wall of windows. "I can see how you started now, but I still don't understand how you were able to move from broke cowboy to rancher to über-successful rancher, all in just fifteen years."

"First, fifteen years is a long time. The second part dealt with determination. I kept my head low, worked my tail off and reinvested profits from livestock sales back into the ranch."

"And the house, of course." She leaned her head back and stared at the woodworking on the great room's ceiling.

"That was mostly Leah's project. I was still living in the old house, located right here, when I met her."

"I wondered how she fit into all of this."

He shook his head, recalling the memory of color swatches and chaos over signs of success that hadn't mattered much to him. "Don't get me wrong—I love this house. It's amazing. But I really liked the old house, too. I would probably have stayed in it another ten years if she hadn't suggested that we needed a bigger place to make Harmony Fields look like a *real ranch*."

"As opposed to the *pretend* one you were living on before."

"I thought the same thing," he said, rolling his eyes.

"I wondered if you got to make many of the decorating decisions for this place. Some of it, well, just doesn't seem like you."

Micah slid a glance her way. Deirdre had only been here a few days. She couldn't know him that well, and yet she seemed to see him more clearly than Leah ever had.

"I got to have an opinion on some of it." He shrugged, smiling. "Okay. Not much."

"Like the guest room?"

He shook his head. "Or the paint colors for the master bedroom and the nursery. The architect, the builder, Leah and the interior decorator she insisted on did most of it."

"And did a great job mostly."

He glanced around. Some choices he should have expressed stronger opinions about, and some, like that ridiculous pecan range hood cover, he should have nixed for the showy extravagances they were.

"Wait." He pointed to the fireplace and the sofas and the accent chairs by turns. "I chose those stones for that wall myself. And I picked out all of this furniture."

"My two favorite things in the whole house."

Micah would have wondered if she was joking if she weren't stroking the sofa arm like she would a cat. Or him, his thoughts added without permission.

"Mine, too." But he didn't look at her as he said it, worried he'd be too tempted to touch her the way she had the soft leather.

"Do you have any photos of the original house? I bet it was nice."

"Well, 'nice' might be a stretch, but it was comfortable. Homey."

"A nice place to raise a family," she said before he had the chance.

"Yeah." The bookshelf in the corner drew his attention. Some of the photo albums, including his wedding album, had been destroyed by the vandals, but he'd filled the new shelves with some that had been relegated to a back bedroom before.

"You know, I might have photos of the old house in one of those books. You sure you want to see them?"

"Only if they'll make my bedtime story even more sleep-inducing."

"I'll do my best." He crossed the room to the bookshelf and pulled out a couple of albums, including one filled with Derek's baby pictures. Then, as an afterthought, he grabbed the single scrapbook that included photos of his life back in New York. He carried them all back to the sofa and piled them on the coffee table.

"What are all these?"

"I'm not sure which book they're in." He gathered the first and started flipping through pages.

As if she recognized this delicate invitation into his past, Deirdre sat back, folding her hands and waiting instead of reaching for a book.

One of the books contained only construction photos for the house, as his late wife had documented every step from demolition to framing to closing in to near completion.

Deirdre scooted closer to him so she could get a better look at the photos.

"If she recorded the whole process, why are there no pictures of the house before they tore it down?"

"I asked her that," he admitted. "I also wanted to know why she'd print out all these photos that she took on her phone. She wasted a ton of printer ink to make this album."

"Maybe she was just excited to build her dream house and wanted to record every step in the process."

"Maybe."

Leah hadn't been nearly as enthusiastic about recording the milestones in her pregnancy, he realized now. She'd refused to let him take photos of her, saying she didn't want any record of her looking so fat. In retrospect, that truth offered a prediction of what would take place later.

"Not a single photo of the old house?" Deirdre asked as Micah closed the first album and set it aside.

"Nothing yet, but I'm sure there has to be at least one somewhere."

Despite that he probably wouldn't find it there, he couldn't resist selecting a newer book next.

"Are those Derek's baby pictures? Let me see." Deirdre scooted closer again, this time so close that their legs nearly touched, as she took hold of one side of the album.

This book recorded his son's life from those first messy moments while the obstetrics nurse cleaned up his tiny red body. There was even a photo of Micah holding the baby next to Leah in the hospital bed—after she'd applied her makeup and fixed her hair, of course.

"You have a beautiful family," Deirdre said automatically and then shifted on the cushion next to him. "I mean, Leah was pretty."

"Yes, she was," he managed in what he hoped was a normal voice. No matter what had happened after that, the statement was no less true.

He continued turning pages, with most images featuring Derek alone, lying on a play mat looking cute, sitting in a highchair, his face painted with birthday cake, being coaxed to touch one of the first arrivals at the petting zoo. Micah could be found in some of the photos. Leah was in far fewer, but he'd printed all of those, since they would be the only things his son would have to remember his mother.

Deirdre had a sweet comment to make about each one, excited as though she'd never seen a baby picture before. Her words touched him in the way that all parents love to hear that others think their babies are beautiful, but there was something more to it. Something tender.

"Oh my gosh, that boy is so cute. How could you ever be upset with this sweet little guy?" She pointed to a photo of

Derek with a bowl of mac and cheese that he'd dumped on his head.

"I believe we've discussed the baby-puke moments." But he couldn't help grinning. "Anyway, you said you couldn't coo."

"I wasn't cooing."

"That was definitely cooing."

Deirdre crossed her arms and pushed out her bottom lip in a pretend pout. "And if it was, he's not here to hear me, so it doesn't count."

"Whatever you say." He set the book aside and reached for the third album.

"What's in this one?"

"Just some old photos," he said vaguely. "If the old house isn't in this one, I don't know where the pictures would be. And they're not on my phone anymore."

But a few slipped out the moment he opened the cover. "Here they are."

He shuffled through the small stack, showing Deirdre the interior and exterior of the three-bedroom bungalow that had only had room for two.

"These are the photos that Marie took and gave to me. She's all about still using a traditional camera and film." After closing on the property, he'd been so proud that he'd brought Doug and Marie by for a tour.

"It's really nice." Deirdre pointed to the photo of the tiny living room with a big picture window. "And you're right. It does look homey."

He didn't know why it made him so happy that she could see that, but it did. After setting the stack on the table, he flipped to the next page of the book.

"The rest of these pictures are of my life back in New York."

Deirdre met his gaze then and dampened her lips. "But I thought you said there aren't any—"

"There aren't," he assured her. "Truth is, I'm lucky to have any photos at all."

Micah flipped through the pages in what felt like a crowbar pulling open a sepulcher.

"This is my mom, Tonya," he managed, despite the thickness in his throat.

"She was beautiful. You look like her."

He blinked several times, trying to hold back emotion, but Deirdre's gaze felt warm on his profile.

"Are you saying you think *I'm* beautiful?" He'd meant it as a joke, but when he glanced her way, Deirdre's cheeks pinkened prettily. Her reaction pleased him more that it should have, and if he were honest with himself, he would admit that he thought the same about her. "If you think I look like her. You need to see a photo of my dad."

They exchanged an awkward look since she'd probably already seen pictures of murder victim Len Perry. But he continued flipping through pages anyway, surprised to find that, like in Derek's album, most of the photos were of him alone, not with his parents. Finally, he came across a shot of him and his father near Castle Garden in Battery Park. From his age and their forced smiles, he could only guess that his mother had taken it.

He pulled back the plastic covering, peeled the photo from the sticky adhesive and handed her the print.

"You're right. You do look like him. Much more here than in the photos we already had of him."

He forced himself not to think about what pictures they did have, since one of them was probably postmortem. "You're saying that because we're photographed together."

She studied it through squinting eyes and then shook her head. "I think it's more you both look so sad in it."

"But we were smiling." It unsettled him that she'd picked up on the truth that most would have missed. She'd never known his father beyond a weathered case file. But she knew him, he realized, his legs feeling so unsteady that he was glad they were seated.

He accepted the photo back from her and stared at those long-ago faces.

"We both know that anyone can smile in a photo, but it doesn't always mean the people in them were *happy*."

"Guess you were right about that one. Mom took it from her wheelchair. You can tell by the odd angle. Dad and I put on our brave faces, but we must not have been all that convincing. That was the last outing we had as a family before she died."

"I'm sorry."

She wore a solemn expression, as though she regretted being right.

"I'm not. It was a good day." Though his throat filled again, he added, "I'm glad we got to spend it together."

"I'm glad, too."

He turned the pages silently, hoping to find more that Deirdre would want to see but pretty sure he wouldn't. His father had never been a fan of being in front of a camera, even on good days. Neither remarked on the awkward middle school pictures, the team photo from JV basketball and the random selfie that offered no explanation why his thirteen-year-old self had thought that printing it out was a good idea.

On the pair of photos of him with a birthday cake, Micah stopped, his breath catching.

"That's my eighteenth birthday party. I'm there." He pointed to himself next to the cake, looking as uncomfortable as he always had around Maeve. "And Dad's over there."

He indicated a slightly out-of-focus image of his father applauding, his elbows lifted at shoulder level.

"What about her? Can you see her?" Deirdre leaned over

him, partially blocking his view of the photo. "She didn't take the picture, did she?"

He bent closer, examining it, and then shook his head. "No, but she's not in it, either. Well, she is, but…" He pointed to the hand in the corner of the image, cutting the cake.

"Of course, she would be the one with no face in the picture but holding the knife. She probably tried to avoid the camera."

Micah couldn't stop shivering. He didn't even try to tell himself Deirdre hadn't noticed as she pulled back from the photo album, her gaze narrowed. Though he turned the page and tried to act natural as he peeled apart two pages stuck together with that photo-destroying adhesive, he braced himself for her barrage of questions. He was still hiding something, and if she didn't already know it, she at least suspected. Finally, he pulled the two pages apart.

"Is there something about—" Deirdre gasped and pointed to the book.

He followed her finger to the photo album lying open on the page that had been between the two glued together. His breath froze in his throat.

His father and the woman who would murder him stared back at them from a souvenir wedding chapel photo, complete with an Elvis impersonator and a heading that read, We Got Hitched in Vegas.

Chapter Twelve

"Well, *Viva Las Vegas*."

Deirdre managed to avoid clenching her teeth when she said it but couldn't keep it up afterward. "I thought you said you didn't have any pictures."

After all the things they'd shared in the last couple of days, including that kiss that still hung over them like a pair of huge, puckered lips in the corner of the room, he'd been lying to her all along. He'd just humored her to get help finding who'd been targeting his family. But if he ever aspired to try a career off the ranch, she would suggest acting. He feigned shock really well. For the longest time, he didn't even close his mouth. When he did, he swallowed visibly and then lifted his gaze from the photo album, looking like he'd seen a ghost. *Bravo!*

"I *didn't* have any."

His voice sounded strange, as though his own words didn't make sense to him, but she refused to buy what he was selling.

"It's not a good idea to lie while the evidence is staring us right in the face."

He had the nerve to glare at *her*.

"Believe what you want, but I can tell you that until this

moment, I didn't know this photo existed. I wasn't even at the wedding. I'd hoped no photos existed from that day."

Strange how she wanted to give him the benefit of a doubt, wanted this to be an accident and not a lie. Had her father and ex-husband taught her nothing about the risk in trusting men?

"Then how do you explain how it got in your photo album?"

Micah raised both hands and lowered them. "Your guess is as good as mine."

Then, lifting a brow, he flipped back to the birthday-party photos. "You know, I've never seen those pictures before, either."

"You didn't put them in the book?" The tiny hairs on the back of her neck lifted as she realized he might be telling the truth.

"Would have been hard to do, since I didn't know about them."

He met her gaze as though daring her to accuse him of lying again. Then he shook his head, his expression pinched.

"You don't think…?"

"That Maeve would have put them there? Doubtful." She'd considered it herself but immediately dismissed it. "She doesn't seem like the sentimental type. And since she probably planned to have a different identity not long after that wedding day, she wouldn't have wanted photos of those nuptials floating around."

"I don't mean her." In the party photo, Micah brushed the tip of his forefinger over the image of his father, the plastic covering separating it from his touch. "I mean *him*."

"I can see the party pictures, but why would he put his wedding photo in *your* album?"

Micah wasn't listening. Nor was he focused on the photo that most interested her. Instead, he pulled back the plastic film over his birthday photos and slid his finger under each of them as though performing delicate surgery. When both shots were free, their four corners curling toward their centers, he flipped the first one over. He appeared disappointed with the adhesive residue he found on the other side.

"What were you expecting? The date stamp?" That made sense since photo shops used to print the month and year on the back of developed pictures.

"It's probably nothing."

But his breath hitched as he turned over the second image. Deirdre leaned closer, trying to get a better look. Someone had written in script on the back of it.

"What does it say?"

He handed her the photo and let her read it for herself.

You see, your party was as wonderful as I told you it would be. Ariel does love you. Pretty soon you'll love her as much as I do. Love, Dad

"Wow. I'm sorry."

He accepted the photo back from her and lowered it facedown on top of the book.

"Why did you think to look there?"

"It was just something Dad did. After Mom died, he started leaving notes for me. In my backpack. Inside the refrigerator. Under my pillow. He must have found it easier than talking about feelings, and he wanted me to know he was there for me."

"That's sweet. It probably helped during that shaky time after he met Maeve."

As she waited for an answer that didn't come, her stomach felt queasy. "Don't tell me he stopped writing the notes after he started dating her."

He cleared his throat. "Okay, I won't tell you."

"I'm really sorry, Micah."

"I never received any sort of note from him after that. Until now." He pointed to his father's clear handwriting. "I hate that I'm a thirty-three-year-old man with a kid of my own, and it still matters. This was his last message to me—ever—and it was still about *her*."

He spat the last word, and his shoulders curled forward as though he were eighteen again, feeling all the pain and betrayal for the first time.

"I'm so sorry."

Micah gave her a side glance. "You're going to have to stop apologizing. Even about losing the suspect. And the other thing. You didn't do anything wrong."

"You know I did. In addition to everything else, I came here and forced you to dig up a past you wanted to forget."

Her gaze lowered to the photo again. They'd finally located a decent image of Maeve O'Leary—this time purporting to be Ariel Porter Perry—and though the photo would be great for use with facial-recognition software, she couldn't bring herself to even ask him for it. Because of her, he'd found the note that had to be like losing his father all over again.

"I'm really—"

He lifted a hand to stop her from apologizing again. "Don't be. I never looked at those albums. If you hadn't urged me to look back, I might not have found this stuff for *another* fifteen years."

"Your dad's promise that you would one day love his murderous wife?"

Deirdre winced over her harsh words even though resentment against the senior Perry lingered like a hard rock in her stomach. Micah only offered a sad, closed-lipped smile.

"Not that. I could have waited a few more decades before seeing that message. I'm talking about this."

He turned to the page with the wedding photo, peeled back the plastic and loosened it from the adhesive. Though he flipped it over to check the back, this time he found only residue.

"You wanted *that*?"

"No, but you do." He handed it to her. "And I needed it as a reminder of Las Vegas."

"Because your dad thought you would one day want memories of his wedding?" Deirdre stared down at the smiles of the deceitful bride and the vulnerable widower she'd targeted.

"The picture reminded me how much Maeve loved Vegas. Remember? You wanted to know about her favorite places. And whether my dad planned to or not, he just helped in maybe locating his murderer."

"So she liked Las Vegas," Deirdre said evenly.

He nodded as though he'd just given her the address of Maeve O'Leary's hiding place.

"She talked about Vegas all the time, like it was heaven or something. There would be plenty of places to hide there, don't you think?"

"Thousands. But it's something." Though she'd tried to sound upbeat, his frown told her she'd failed.

"That's not helpful at all, is it?"

She shrugged. "From what I've read, about thirty million tourists visit that city every year. I bet a lot of people go there to disappear."

"So, it wasn't helpful." He tapped his fingers to his forehead several times in quick succession, as though trying to shake information loose. Then he pushed back his shoulders. "But this will be. The other place that Maeve loved was Greenwich Village. I don't know why I didn't think of it before. She visited there constantly. The population has to be smaller than thirty million, right?"

Deirdre lunged for her phone and did a quick search. "Just twenty-two thousand."

"Do you think she could be hiding somewhere in the Village?"

"Maybe." She stared down at her phone, regretting what she would have to say next. "It's something, anyway. Enough that I need to check back in with the team."

Micah glanced down at his watch. "You're going to call them this late? If it's nearly eleven o'clock here, then in New York it's—"

"Almost one." She clicked through her series of contacts until she found a listing for Sean Colton.

"If you call your cousin now, you'll just wake him up and make sure someone else has trouble sleeping tonight."

"You're right." She set her phone aside. "But first thing in the morning, I need to give the team an update. This is the best lead we've had in a while."

"Since learning about my dad? And me?"

When Deirdre shrugged, Micah grinned. "Well, it's about time for that hot chocolate. Want some?"

She nodded. It wasn't as if she would be able to sleep anyway now that she had both a photo and at least one solid clue about where to locate Maeve O'Leary.

Once Micah had crossed to the kitchen, she reached for her phone again and stared down at Sean's contact information. Sean probably wouldn't mind being awakened in the middle of the night if she'd arrested Maeve and located Humphrey Kelly, but this information didn't come close to that.

Deirdre crossed and uncrossed her legs as a thought that had been niggling since they'd discovered the photo settled bluntly in front of her. Once she reported in with the information she'd located in Wyoming, the team would rightly expect her to be on the next plane to LaGuardia to join their search of Greenwich Village. Micah probably expected her to go, too, now that she had the information she'd come for, whether she'd fulfilled her end of the bargain or not. She still had to prove herself to the FBI, after all.

How was she supposed explain to any of them her need to stay at Harmony Fields a little longer? Well, she didn't care what she had to say to them. Someone was still out there targeting Micah and Derek. She had to convince the team to let her stayuntil the suspect could be stopped.

MICAH SHOULDN'T HAVE been surprised to catch Deirdre searching the wedding photo for more answers when he returned with the hot chocolate, so it shouldn't have bothered him that he did. He'd bargained for her help with the investigation on the ranch while he'd still believed he could offer her no valuable information. Now they were even. She'd come to Harmony Fields searching for pictures and other details, and nothing could keep her here now that she had them.

He shook away his annoyance as he set the mugs on the table, reminding himself that he didn't want her to stay. Deirdre blinked and looked up as if only then realizing he'd returned.

"Thanks." She pointed to the chocolate concoction with whipped cream on top and then glanced down at the photo again. "Maeve O'Leary is a beautiful woman. Just like you said. They both look so happy and in love." She paused to set aside the photo and collect the mug instead. "It was a lie."

"Only one of them was lying," he said.

She nodded, her eyes wet. Something squeezed inside his gut. Like him, Deirdre understood intimately the pain of betrayal, but her empathy for his father touched his heart, surprising him.

He took a sip of his drink and returned it to the table. "I

wonder how many other photos Maeve owns that look just like that one. Only with different grooms."

"None is my guess," she said. "If she planned to marry and murder more husbands, she wouldn't want any photographic evidence around for police to track her."

"You mean, if police were even smart enough to recognize that the guys' deaths weren't accidental."

"Good point." She lifted her mug to her lips and took a sip. "Even so, if not for your dad tucking that photo into your album, which just happened to have cheap, sticky pages that stuck together and hid it from Maeve, we wouldn't have any evidence at all."

"So, you're saying I'm *lucky*?" Even the word tasted acidic. Nothing about this whole situation could be called that.

Deirdre set her mug aside and then turned on the sofa to face him.

"I would never say that about your life then. What happened to you was tragic. But now?" She paused and gestured to the balcony upstairs, through which his son's closed bedroom door was visible. "You have to admit you are downright blessed."

"Sometimes your bad luck follows you no matter where you go."

As soon as the words were out of his mouth, Micah regretted them. Did he want her to ask questions? Did he need her to know the one thing he'd spent so much time and effort hiding from all his friends here?

He stared at his hands, gripped tight, but he couldn't seem to loosen them. Though she didn't speak, he could feel her gaze on him. Intense. Unwavering. And seeing right through the decorative wall he'd built around the ugly truth of his life.

"When are you going to tell me?"

Looking up, he found her watching him just as he'd predicted. "What are you talking about?"

She leaned toward the coffee table and flipped the photo of his father and stepmother facedown. Then she turned back to him. "What really happened with your wife?"

His throat tightened, the distance between wanting to tell her and really forming the words long and expanding.

"I've already told you all about her."

"There are a few things you didn't explain. Like why you got rid of her clothes so quickly. Why there are no photos of her in this house, except for one album. And why you throw your wedding quilt on the ground for picnics."

He shook his head to make her stop, but she only peppered him with more questions.

"Why did you mention to me about people who think only of themselves? People who don't care who they leave behind." She paused, pressing her lips together. "And why aren't you constantly telling your son about his mother, so he grows up knowing that she loved her family?"

"Because she didn't!"

His words were loud and felt as if someone had ripped them from his throat. Deirdre stared back at him with wide eyes, her mouth slack.

"You wanted to know." Leaping up, Micah stepped to the fire to warm his hands. He spoke to the flames rather than to face her judgment or, worse, her pity.

"Now do you see why I haven't spoken about it? It doesn't help anyone to agonize over things no one can change."

"Talking about it might help *you*."

"What are you, my counselor or something? I was doing fine before you came here, asking questions and opening old wounds." He glanced over his shoulder, confirming the pity, and something else. Something he couldn't define.

"Were you really? Fine, that is? Don't you think it's finally time that you told someone?"

He considered her words as he stared into the flames,

which were far more under control than his life lately. Then, with a sigh, he returned to his seat.

"Leah was already planning to leave when she died," he said before Deirdre could pose another question.

"I'm so sorry."

He shook his head, not wanting to hear her platitudes or allow them to stop him now that he'd started.

"It didn't matter that she had a six-week-old baby. She was already packed. The accident happened when she'd gone into town to pick up a rental truck for her stuff. She lost control of her car and hit a tree."

Deirdre looked stricken, just like all those mourners at the funeral home who'd come to offer their condolences. Only, she knew the truth.

"It was what it was." He focused on his hands in his lap. If he planned to get through this discussion, he had to avoid looking at her again.

"Did her choice to leave come as a surprise to you?"

Despite his plan, he shot a look her way. "Why are you asking—"

"Was it?"

He shook his head.

"Did you love her?"

"I thought so. She was my wife." He waited for her to ask another question, but when she didn't, he finally answered. "Yeah."

His throat tightened as anger and hurt wound together, as they always did when he allowed himself to really remember Leah.

"I thought we shared this vision," he explained. "We would build Harmony Fields together, raise a family and make a difference in our community. It turned out she just liked the idea of being a successful rancher's wife. The land. The house. Kind of ironic that she hated living here."

"It's not for everyone."

He narrowed his gaze at her. "You should know."

"Did it get better after she got pregnant with Derek?"

"If anything, it got worse. It wasn't what she'd signed up for." He blinked away the memories, many of which had charitably passed in a fog. "And then the house was suddenly filled with the stress of a newborn, and she wanted out."

"You hid all this from your neighbors?"

"Leah was already gone. What good would it have done for me to malign her character at that point? We were already in mourning and had enough to deal with. She hadn't filed for divorce yet, and no staff were working at the house at the time, so I tucked the boxes away until after the funeral. Then, when I did donate her stuff, I drove to Cheyenne."

"Why go through all that trouble? You crafted this alternate story because your wife left you?"

"No." He shook his head. "You don't understand. I didn't do it because she wanted to leave me. It was because she left *him.*"

"And she planned to divorce *you.*"

"Yes, she did. She also said she wouldn't be leaving empty-handed."

"No prenup?"

"You'd think I would have learned from my father's experience. But no. I would have lost the ranch if we'd divorced and been forced to split everything."

"She didn't say anything about child custody?"

Her wary expression told him she already knew the answer.

"In all her threats, she never once suggested that she wanted custody of her son. What kind of person leaves her own child?"

"Apparently, a lot of people do."

Micah held his hands wide. "Now do you see why I kept

this information to myself? I didn't want anyone to know. I didn't want *my son* to know."

"So the idea of abandoning a kid didn't catch on with all your neighbors and upset the delicate social order in all of southeastern Wyoming?"

He shook his head, scrunching his face and mouthing the word *what*. "No one needed to know that Derek's dad was ridiculous, just like his grandfather."

"What are you talking about?"

"Are you trying to say you don't see the similarities between the two stories? They're exactly alike."

"No, Micah. They're not." She shook her head hard for emphasis. "The circumstances are completely different."

"My father and I both married women who made fools of us. I don't want Derek to be ashamed of me like I was—" His words broke then, but the truth lay open in the air between them.

"Of him," Deirdre finished for Micah, shaking her head. "Your father was taken in by a black widow. And you were unlucky enough to have a wife who realized too late that marriage and motherhood weren't for her. The situations weren't the same."

"But I *knew* better," he insisted. "I'd watched Maeve sink her manicured nails into my father and then twist and turn them until she got her way. Still, I came across a woman just like her—one who found my bank account more attractive than me—and I let her do the same thing to me."

"You're conflating two situations that have nothing to do with each other. Whether Maeve took advantage of him or not, your dad was a grown man. He was responsible for his own decisions, and, unfortunately he *chose* a woman over his son.

"You're *nothing* like your father." Deirdre leaped up from the couch and whirled to face him.

Micah stood as well, Deirdre's words feeling like an easy way out, an escape he didn't deserve. "You didn't even know my father."

"But I know *you*." She crossed her arms, lifting her chin, daring him to argue. "I know you put your child first every time. When Derek grows up, he'll only be proud to be your son."

"You think you know me…"

"I know you," she repeated, her gaze never leaving his. "And if your wife didn't know how infinitely lucky she was to have you in her life—"

Deirdre never had the chance to finish what she'd been about to say, as Micah shot forward and pulled her to him, firm strength against an equal match, hearts pounding with the same frenzied pace. At first, she stared up at him in shock, but then the corners of her mouth softened in welcome, and he crushed his lips to hers.

Chapter Thirteen

Deirdre braced herself against an incoming tide as she absorbed Micah's kiss that tasted of desperation and, maybe, relief. She recognized that he was probably just grateful for the things she'd said about him, but his arms felt so good around her, his body so tempting pressed against hers. She couldn't help but to join him in the frenzy.

Her hesitation earlier now feeling like someone else's life, in some distant reality, she claimed his mouth, reveling in the pressure and texture of his lips. She brushed hers over his once, twice and then a third time before settling in deep. Quickly, she discovered she wanted more, craved it with a breathlessness and heat that eclipsed the flames still dancing in the fireplace. Tonight, even just kissing Micah Perry would not be enough.

A fleeting appeal for caution stole through her thoughts, but she hurled it aside. She didn't want to be careful this time, chose to ignore the clash between what she wanted and what she deserved. On this one magical night, she would show him how amazing he was and how much she wished they were different people. Ones who stood a chance of winning the lottery and ending up together.

She slid her hands up his arms and over his shoulders, reveling in the flex of his muscles beneath her touch. Once her fingers reached their destination at his nape, she fitted herself to him, convex to concave, demanding strength to welcoming softness. Micah pressed her to him as well, his effort and the ineffective masks of their cotton shorts leaving no questions about the depth of his desire.

They kissed with the urgency of the last dance at a bar closing forever, each touch a gift, each taste a memory. Though she grew light-headed, she still protested with a groan when Micah slid his mouth away from hers, and they both gasped for breath.

"I love your sounds," he breathed against her neck and then moved on to adore her earlobe.

"That's a compliment I've never received before." Her desire-roughened voice might have embarrassed her another day. Now she didn't care.

As Deirdre initiated another fevered kiss, she pressed her thigh to his and walked him backward the few steps to the couch. Micah stretched out on the leather, his head on a throw pillow, and reached out to her. With a wicked smile, she braced herself over the length of his frame and lowered to him in slow, halting steps.

Impatient, he reached up and jolted her elbows, causing her to land with her full weight on top of him. She buried her face, laughing against his cheek.

"Oof." He winced and then chuckled. "That was supposed to be a smooth move."

"It was. Really." She propped herself up on her elbows again.

"Thanks for protecting my fragile male ego."

"Thought you didn't have one of those. Don't worry. I've got your back." She glanced over her shoulder and down the length of their perfectly stacked bodies. "Or front."

"Front is good."

He gave her one of those smiles that made her heart pound

and her body warm in all its secret places. Then, when Micah's expression became serious again, ice poured uncomfortably over those same spots.

"Is this a good idea?" he asked.

"Probably not."

"Only probably?"

She leaned her forehead against his. "*Absolutely* not."

He cleared his throat. "But do you still want to…?"

For a few seconds, she pretended not to understand what he was asking. Then she grinned. "Oh, hell, yeah."

"You took the words right out of my mouth."

He found another way to keep those lips busy, lifting up and pressing his mouth to hers. She followed him back to the pillow and returned his kiss as if it were her first but one she was determined to perfect. She strained against him. Wanting. Needing. Demanding.

She gulped air when she reluctantly lifted her head. "Do you, uh, have…something? I mean, I'm on the pill, but, you know, nowadays I can't afford to take any sort of risk."

Deirdre frowned. She sounded as nervous as a teenager who'd never been in this position before. The nervous part, that was real.

"Kitchen."

Kitchen? She lifted off him, and he sat up, brushing back his hair that already stood every which way. When he was finished, he hurried from the room.

After several seconds of rustling and drawer slamming, he returned to the great room, carrying a small box of condoms.

She watched him over the back of the couch. "Did you just pull those out of your junk drawer?"

He shrugged, grinning. "Lucky they were there, too. Right beneath some AA batteries, a box of broken crayons and a package of pacifiers with just one left in it."

"Sexy."

"What can I say? I'm a responsible single dad. Not a saint. The junk drawer has a baby lock on it, too, so I guess we can call this *supersafe* sex." As he rounded the end of the sofa, he hesitated. "I mean, if we're still going to do this."

"You never know." She cleared her throat and then managed to add, "I might lose interest if you keep dawdling."

"Can't let that happen."

He hit the wall switch as he passed, leaving only the fireplace and a small lamp in the corner to cast light and shadow about the room. When he sat next to her, he immediately started tracing a line of kisses along her throat. As he dipped his thumb and forefinger just beneath her T-shirt collar and traced mesmerizing lines along both her collarbones, Deirdre closed her eyes and all but swooned.

"There's a four-poster bed in that room if you'd like to relocate." He pointed to the closed door that led to the main-floor master suite. "Great new mattress."

"And leave one of your favorite pieces of furniture?" Trying to look more confident than she felt, she smiled and brushed her hand slowly over the leather.

"It's about to become my all-time favorite," he said.

He took her mouth again in an exquisite kiss that reignited her passion until she squirmed next to him, trying to move closer. When he reached for the hem of her T-shirt, she yanked it over her head herself, but then she glanced down and covered her plain sports bra with crossed arms.

"Let's just pretend that's something lacy and feminine."

"Why would we need to do that?" He gently peeled her hands away from her chest and then tried to slide one of the bra straps over her shoulder. "Everything I'm dying to see is right here."

"You'll never see anything if you try it that way." She chuckled, took a deep breath and pulled the viselike contraption over her head.

Micah didn't even touch her. He followed the lines of the newly exposed skin down the slope of her neck, over the curves of her breasts to the dip of her waist with only his gaze, and yet her skin tingled and warmed as though he'd touched her everywhere. Loved her everywhere. If he didn't do just that, and soon, she would ignite like the log in that gas fireplace.

"I knew you'd be perfect."

He breathed the words, close to her neck but still without the contact she craved.

"I'm not—"

"You are to me."

His words were like magic, setting free something inside her, opening locks and smashing shackles. She pressed herself to his chest and claimed his mouth, drawing in his gasp and then following his movement as he smiled against her lips.

She bunched up his T-shirt and slowly exposed the chest and taut belly that even his tight work shirts had failed to properly predict. He reached back with both hands and ripped it over his head. Unable to hold back any longer, she splayed her hands over his chest. Micah chose that moment to touch as well, first with gentle, exploring fingers and then with purposeful hands, capable of breathtaking finesse.

Her hands found a mission of their own, working at the waistband of his shorts until Micah stopped what he was doing, stood and stepped out of them along with his briefs. Another of her sounds must have escaped as her gaze followed his lines of work-earned strength and masculine virility. Of broad shoulders, tapered waist and powerful thighs. All backlit by lapping flames. He grinned back at her knowingly. Then he drew her to her feet and peeled away the last of her clothing.

When they both stood fully naked, Micah drew her against

him and kissed her slowly, luxuriously, in no hurry despite the obvious insistence of his body. He backed her to the sofa and waited as she stretched out, but when she reached up to draw him to her, he held up a forefinger, asking for a delay.

He made the wait worth her while, bending first to press an openmouthed kiss to the inside of her ankle. Then he started a journey northward, sharing delicious attention in some spots along the way and ignoring the pleas of others until she wiggled and squirmed. Finally, he edged Deirdre onto her side and stretched alongside her, giving her access to him as well. Her passion building with each sigh, each shiver, Deirdre joined him in fervent exploration, first with hands, then lips and tongue. She wanted more. She needed all.

"Please!"

"Well, you did ask nicely." Micah grinned as he sat up and made quick work of putting on a condom.

He glanced back at her over his shoulder. "You're sure about this?"

"You're still asking?" She gestured, indicating all that had already taken place on the sofa. But at his serious expression, she nodded. "Yes, I'm sure."

He shifted then and braced himself above her, waiting. "You said you couldn't take a risk. But everything about what we're doing here is one of those. The biggest risk of all."

She knew he was talking about more than sex. More than two consenting adults borrowing each other's bodies and seeking momentary relief. He referred to complications when everything about their fledgling relationship was so blanketed with them that there should have been caution signs posted all around them.

She couldn't think about that now. Not if she planned to be in the moment. To experience all of it, even if it would be just this once. After another nod from her, Micah brought them together in one slow shift. They began to move, first slowly, then with intention, then with desperation. Deirdre fell first, her release both blissful and bittersweet. Micah followed soon after and buried his whiskered face against her neck.

For a long time, the only sound beyond their labored breaths was the crackle and pop of the fire. But as Micah shifted away and slid on his shorts to dispose of the condom, the thoughts that Deirdre had been pushing aside gathered inside her, determined to be heard now.

Micah was wrong. Sex wasn't the biggest risk between them, beyond the crapshoot physical relationships always presented. The gamble was that one of them would let it go too far, let a search for pleasure and relief become something more. Would make the mistake of falling in love. If that was the biggest risk, she worried that for her, it might already be too late.

AS MICAH PULLED his T-shirt over his head and started for the stairs, he had to remind himself not to run. That was ridiculous. He'd never been one of those awkward-morning-after guys, who tiptoed out before their intimate partners had barely made it through the afterglow. But something about what had just taken place between Deirdre and him felt different.

He should have known it would be a mistake to go to bed with Deirdre, even if technically they'd never made it close to anything with a mattress or sheets. Just kissing her should have been enough of a warning. Even then, all he'd been able to think about was finding another chance to taste those lips. But more than that, he should have known that having sex with Deirdre Colton would rock his world and make him desperate to repeat that act anytime and anywhere she liked.

Just the possibility that she could have the kind of control over him that Maeve had had over his father scared the hell out of him. Why had he even started something with her, knowing there was no possible future in it? She belonged in Washington, and Wyoming was his home. Nothing could erase those seventeen hundred miles between them. Until now, that had been just fine by him.

When he reached the landing, he couldn't resist looking back at her, though he'd promised himself he wouldn't. Though her back was to him, she still appeared dejected, her shoulders dropping, her head hanging, as she pulled her T-shirt back over her head. She had to assume that he was rejecting her right after making love with her, but why wouldn't she believe that? He'd practically leaped off the sofa the moment their breathing returned to normal, and his excuse about checking on Derek sounded as weak then as now.

His mouth went dry as she pulled the shirt down so far that it nearly covered her shorts. He hated that she felt the need to hide now, after he'd already seen and sampled all her beauty beneath those layers of cotton, but he couldn't tell her how those images were burned in his memory. Or how he'd run because he was scared, not that he didn't want her. Hell, from now on, he would probably be turned on every time he saw a sports bra at the store, since it would remember him of her creamy skin beneath hers.

He shook his head to dispel the images but couldn't help sneaking another peek at her. Though he caught her watching him, she shifted her gaze to the fire and then grabbed the remote to shut it off.

"Is Derek okay?" She made a show of crossing to put the remote on the mantel instead of looking over at him again.

"I haven't checked yet. I'm going now."

"Oh. Right."

Deirdre shook her head, signaling he wasn't the only one who felt discombobulated after what had just take place between them.

"I just wanted to make sure he's all right," he said.

She nodded, but her gaze flicked to the video baby monitor he'd left on the coffee table. He could easily have checked on his son that way, and they both knew it. At least she didn't point it out.

He continued up the stairs and down the hallway, needing to put a little distance between them. From the stark look on her face, he could only guess that she needed it, too. Beyond that she thought he was rejecting her, Deirdre had to wonder what she would tell her team when she called them in a few hours. He might have been a rancher who'd slept with an investigator, but she was an FBI special agent who'd had sex with a witness.

If only his feelings about what had happened between them were as easily definable. He'd known that Deirdre was only in Wyoming temporarily. She hadn't even planned to spend one night when she'd first arrived. She hated everything about this part of the country and the ranch, and yet he'd let himself become involved with her anyway. Worse even than his history with Leah had taught him nothing, but he'd let her get close to his son, too.

Outside Derek's room, Micah paused, rubbing his forehead. Derek would forget about her. Kids were resilient that way. But Micah wouldn't forget. He wouldn't even be able to cuddle Eleanor Roosevelt in the goat enclosure without thinking of her. As for that couch, he would never be able to sit on it again without seeing Deirdre lying there.

He carefully turned the knob and opened the door and stared into the darkened room. With the only light coming from the hallway, he could barely make out Derek's bed, the toy shelves, the dresser and the rocking chair. Glad he'd remembered to pick up his phone, he pulled it from his shorts pocket and clicked on the flashlight app.

He didn't want to awaken Derek, but he had to get a peek at him, maybe sneak an extra good-night kiss. After everything that had happened since they'd put Derek to bed—first the trespasser and then everything with Deirdre—Micah just needed to watch his little boy sleep. He hated that he was there for his own needs, not his son's. Deirdre was wrong about him: he didn't put Derek first.

Still, he was already there, so he crossed the room to Derek's bed, holding the light low so it didn't shine on the boy's face. Derek looked so sweet, sleeping as he always did on his back with his fisted hands above his head. Micah brushed the little boy's hair back from his face. After Deirdre left in a few hours, it would be just the two of them again. Maybe it would be hard for him to return to that, but he could be more focused on protecting Derek from the suspect targeting them.

As he bent down to drop a kiss on the child's head, his gaze caught on something that looked white against the dark headboard of Derek's big-boy bed. Micah redirected his light on what turned out to be a piece of paper taped to the headboard. He ripped it off the wood and brought it closer, aiming the flashlight app at it. He stiffened as he read the words, blood freezing in his veins.

Leave Wyoming or the kid is next.

Chapter Fourteen

Deirdre stood at the bar in the kitchen, taking her first sip of the chamomile tea she'd spent fifteen minutes trying to locate, when she heard Micah tromping down the stairs. She barely had time to brace herself before he rushed into the kitchen.

"Good. You haven't gone to bed," he said.

She set down her mug to avoid spilling it and raised her right hand to signal for him to stop whatever he'd been about to say. "Look, I'm tired. Can we just skip the postmortem for now? It's been a really long night, and I get that everything was a big mistake, but I'm not ready to discuss it."

Rather than to look away as she'd expected him to do under these awkward circumstances, he pinned her with a look she couldn't quite define.

"That's not what I want to talk about."

Deirdre wrapped her hands around her mug. "I'm not in a good place to talk about anything else, either. I'm just going to drink this tea and—"

"Well, you'd better get in a good place. And fast."

He produced a piece of paper. Holding it by the corner, he set it on the counter next to her.

"What's this?" Something telling her not to touch it, she leaned closer to it and read. Her chest tightened as though she'd been the one running from upstairs. "Where did you find this?"

"Taped to the headboard of Derek's bed."

She shot a look to the stairs and then back to Micah. "He's been in this house?"

He didn't have to answer. His ashen coloring and overly bright eyes did it for him.

"Any idea when?" She started working out the timeline in her head.

"Well, *that* wasn't in his room when we put him to bed."

"So, sometime between seven thirty and—" she paused to glance at her watch "—just after 1:00 a.m." Hours that had included a sweet interlude in the petting zoo, the chase of a vandalism suspect, an alpaca roundup and whatever they could call what had happened between them on Micah's sofa. Her gaze drifted into the great room all on its own, but when she jerked it back, she caught him watching her, his eyes cold.

"Yeah, someone got *to my son* when I wasn't paying attention."

She squeezed her eyes shut and opened them again, her stomach feeling like a rock. While her thoughts were flitting to all the unimportant matters, he'd stated the succinct and critical truth. This was about Derek. Nothing else mattered, and if she hadn't been off her game from the moment she'd arrived at Harmony Fields, she would have recognized that.

"He isn't hurt, is he?" She started away from the counter to go check for herself.

"Wait." He didn't say more until she stopped and turned back. "He's fine. He's sleeping."

Then he gripped the edge of the counter, his knuckles white, and tucked his chin, closing his eyes.

"He's okay," she blurted. "You just said it yourself. No one hurt him."

"But they could have."

"The baby monitor." She pointed to the great room, where the device still rested on the coffee table. "You had it with you the whole time."

The look he gave her made her squirm, and not in a good way.

"I wasn't watching it all the time." His gaze flitted to hers and away. "As long as the suspect was quiet and didn't wake up Derek, I would have had to get lucky to check the monitor in time to catch the intruder."

"We weren't that lucky." She included herself in that responsibility because she shared it now. Micah might have felt guilty for failing to shield his son, but she'd been with both of them on the ranch, and the invader had gotten past her as well.

"We know it wasn't at eight thirty." Micah watched the moving hands of the ornate, analog clock on the wall that separated the kitchen from the great room. "The suspect was too busy chasing alpacas to be up here at the house."

Deirdre shook her head. "We don't know that for sure. We still haven't determined if we're looking for just one suspect."

He paced to the sofa and back to the bar. "Another one could have been here at the same time."

"And though I heard a vehicle drive off, that doesn't mean he or she couldn't have parked just down the road and backtracked to the house."

"While we were busy tracking down a bunch of terrified alpacas." He tilted his head back, his jaw clenched, and jerked both hands out, fingers splayed. "He was in here with my *son*!"

"I know, but we have to try to stay calm. We have to think this through." She didn't even mention that the suspect could also have been in the house during the time that they'd been preoccupied in the great room. That would have been too much for him to bear. Or her.

"How do you expect me to stay calm?" He continued to pace, his words coming in that same staccato clip. "I've done everything I was supposed to do. I've reported every incident to local police. I've even traded everything I know about my stepmother for your help, but we're no closer to finding answers than we were before."

"We can't let him win." She tried to look calm, but her skin was the only thing keeping her from flying apart, just as he was.

Micah stopped then, turning his whole body to face the counter, where she still stood, trying to appear in control. Finally, he gripped his forehead.

"You're right." He took several deep breaths and returned to the bar stools. "What do we do now?"

"First, we call the sheriff's office." She pointed to the note. "How much have you touched that thing?"

"Just by the edges."

"That's good." She pulled out her cell phone and dialed the direct line for the sheriff's office, though at this time of night the dispatcher would answer it just like the emergency line.

"They can still dust for fingerprints," she said while she waited for it to ring. "They might find something."

"Unless whoever wrote it did the same thing you did or wore gloves, like in all the other incidents."

Deirdre scowled at the phone until she heard the click as the call became active.

"Albany County Sheriff's Office, what is your emergency?"

She paced into the great room and filled the dispatcher in on the basic details, noting she didn't believe the suspect remained on the premises.

"A deputy is on his way to take the report," she told Micah when she returned to the kitchen.

She reached up to touch her hair, which had to be a nightmare by now. Crossing to the sink, she wetted her hand and brushed her fingers through it. Then she finger-combed it into semblance of order and tied it in a ponytail, using the band she kept on her wrist. Micah must have gotten the idea, too, as he stepped to the sink and used some water to wet down his hair as well.

Deirdre took a few steps back, giving him a wide berth. "One thing the deputy will want to determine is how the suspect gained access to the house."

He sighed. "The alarm system I'm supposed to have installed is on backorder. If it had already been installed, we would have heard it all the way from the petting zoo and maybe farther."

"Only if you set it. A lot of homeowners have a system and then forget to arm it."

"I'll never forget to do it," he said as seriously, as if he were taking an oath.

She believed him, too. He'd put up with more than anyone should have to from the trespasser on his property.

"I still don't understand how the intruder got in *again*," he said. "We replaced the locks after last time."

"I have a theory on that one." She led him through the kitchen and down the stairs to the lower level, stopping at the slider. Sure enough, the operational side of the door appeared closed but had only been propped over the open space. "One of the oldest tricks in the book."

"But it had a broom handle in it." He pointed to the piece of wood, exactly where it should have been.

"That trick is a myth, unfortunately. At least for some sliders, where it only takes a simple screwdriver to pop it off the track."

He blew out a frustrated breath. "I'll remember that for the next time someone breaks into my house."

She met his gaze directly then. "Let's hope this is the last time."

He did his best to put the door back in the track and then tromped back up the steps after her. She moved back to the bar and sat on a stool.

Micah stood on the other end but didn't sit. "Wait. You said *first* before. What else do you recommend I do?"

Deirdre pointed to the closed door of the bedroom where he'd invited her to join him just an hour before. "Then you start packing."

"What are you talking about?"

She pointed to the letter, still on the counter, the piece of tape at the top holding it in place. "I think you should do what it says."

"What do you mean?"

She nodded. "Whoever wrote that wants you to leave the state. I think you should do just that. Get out of Dodge."

"Then what was all that earlier about not letting him win?" He planted his elbows on the counter and rested his angry face atop his fists. "I am not leaving Harmony Fields. No one is going to drive us from our home. Harmony Fields is my legacy for my son."

"Nobody's forfeiting a legacy here. It's just a few days away to give law enforcement a chance to do their job." Since he was still shaking his head, she pulled out her trump card. "You'll also be removing Derek from what has become a dangerous situation, and I know you'd do anything to keep him safe."

He glared at her, but he pushed back from the counter and crossed his arms. "In this grand plan of yours, who's supposed to take care of the livestock and the petting zoo? And, for that matter, where exactly are Derek and I supposed to go?"

Deirdre lifted a brow.

Micah pointed at her and started backing away. "Oh, no. We are not going with you to New York. That's an awfully convenient solution for you, anyway. Almost like you planned it."

This time Deirdre crossed her arms. "You really think I created a hoax threat to Derek just to make you fly to the East Coast with me?"

He sighed and shook his head.

At the clang of the doorbell and the sound of pounding to go along with it, Micah crossed to the door. "That didn't take long."

But instead of the deputy, Sheriff Guetta stood on the decking outside the front door, his frown deeper than Micah's.

"What are you doing here?" Micah stepped back and let the sheriff inside.

Dressed in a nylon sweat suit, its jacket zipped over what appeared to be a pajama shirt, Richard stomped through the house to the bar where Deirdre still sat.

"My dispatcher thought I might be interested in this one myself," he groused. "I assure you, I wasn't."

Micah rolled his eyes. "And yet you're here."

Richard sat on one of the bar stools and drummed the countertop. "It's looking like déjà vu, too. So, give me an overview here. I didn't love getting pulled out of my beauty sleep."

Micah and Deirdre took turns filling him on the details— at least the ones he needed to know. The sheriff listened, asking an occasional question and sometimes jotting down something in the tiny notebook he produced from his zippered pocket.

"Now Special Agent Colton believes that Derek and I should go with her to New York to follow up on a lead for *her* case."

"It's the most reasonable idea." She frowned at Micah before focusing on the sheriff. "Just for the weekend. The ranch hands can take care of the livestock and the petting zoo. Your department could keep watch over Harmony Fields, maybe even sending a deputy to patrol the property a few times a day.

"Then, in New York, I'd like to take Micah to Greenwich Village just to see if there's a place that sparks some memories. Maybe a specific place that Maeve O'Leary might have mentioned."

"You see?" Micah said, gesturing to her. "It sounds like a crazy idea. Not to mention self-serving."

Richard spun in his chair to face him. "You know, I'm inclined to agree with her."

Micah's eyes widened. "You're what?"

"It's a reasonable plan, Micah. One that will keep your son—and you—safe. I'll put Sheriff's Deputy Greg Martin on the assignment."

"Greg's a good guy, but—"

"Micah," he interrupted, "it's time for us to take care of this, once and for all." He brushed his hands as though the matter were settled. "I don't know if taking down a serial killer could be considered self-serving, either."

"Since you've decided to gang up on me, fine. I'll go. At least we can get Derek out of danger." He focused on Richard alone. "You're right. We need to get this over with. It has to stop."

Micah dug through his junk drawer and handed Richard a spare key. "Here. For the deputy."

"What about this?" Richards pointed to the note on the counter. "Who has touched this?"

"Just me. And just the corners," Micah told him. At the sheriff's direction, he produced a paper lunch bag from the pantry to put it in.

"Great." Richard clapped his hands once. "I'll text you Greg's contact information, so you can stay in touch over the weekend. Now, I don't know about you, but I have a bed calling my name."

"Thanks, Sheriff Guetta," Deirdre said. "I'll be checking in with my team, and we'll be on the first flight we can book tomorrow."

When the sheriff waved away her comment with a brush of his hand, she braced herself for whatever he would say next. Maybe he wouldn't be her ally on this, after all.

"You can call me Richard," he said after a few seconds.

"Thanks."

As he stood up from his stool, the sheriff leaned his head back and chuckled. "I sure would like to be a fly on the wall for this little trip of yours. You two are a hoot."

"Thanks, Richard." Micah patted the lawman's back harder than was necessary and then led him to the door.

Richard glanced back just as Micah reached for the latch. "Oh. I need to have a few words with the special agent. Just police stuff."

His gaze narrowed, Micah gestured for Deirdre to take his place. "I'll just be in my room. Packing."

He crossed to his bedroom, went inside and closed the door.

Despite her trepidation, Deirdre stepped to the door and waited. "Yes?"

"Just wanted to wish you luck that you find some great leads on your trip."

"Thank you." She tilted her head and narrowed her gaze.

Richard grinned and lowered his voice. "Also wanted to give you the heads-up that your T-shirt is inside out."

"Oh." She glanced down, her cheeks burning, and then cleared her throat. "I wear it like that sometimes."

"I bet you do. Cheers." He grinned as he opened the door, stepped outside and closed it.

Deirdre glanced over her shoulder to ensure that Micah was still in his room, then yanked off her shirt and righted it.

If even a stranger had been able to pick up on the fact that something had happened between Micah and her, how would they be able to keep it from a whole team of investigators in New York? Particularly a whole team of Coltons.

CROUCHED BEHIND ONE of those excessive outbuildings, the spectator nearly cheered as the rental car carried the rancher, the kid and their guest from Harmony Fields. But despite the change in circumstance, it remained important to stay low and stick to the plan. Still, it was a moment for celebration. Micah Perry was finally running scared.

After all the little events taking place around the ranch— so much work for so little reward when damage could be repaired in a matter of days—who knew that it would only take a note placed close to a sniveling two-year-old to make the cowboy run for the hills? It was just a threat, mostly. Placed during that perfect time while the rancher and the lady chased alpacas in that ridiculous petting zoo. The kid wasn't the target—at least not the original one. Collateral damage was always a problem.

The rancher had needed a wake-up call, anyway, since he'd been spending too much time trying to get *into* the pretty investigator and not enough time planning to get his ass *off* the ranch.

Now that the rancher had abandoned ship, it would be important to observe his next steps. The spectator couldn't begin to tell him what a mistake it would be to return to this place that wasn't his. If they could stay gone, they would get to continue to enjoy breathing in and out and the steady thump of their heartbeats. But if he'd only gone for reinforcements, some promises would just have to be kept. The kid would be the first to go.

Chapter Fifteen

Micah followed Deirdre into the low-lit New York hotel restaurant the next evening, as out of place as she must have felt when pulling her rental car onto his ranch several days before. He'd paired his dress boots with khaki trousers and a fitted navy dress shirt and left his hat at home, but he still couldn't shake the feeling that everyone was watching him and wondering about the cowboy who'd strayed too far from the ranch.

He shouldn't have worried about standing out, though, when the most beautiful woman in the room carried his son through its center, drawing every eye as she passed. Including his. She wore the same incredible jeans as the day he'd met her. Same boots, too, though tonight she appeared as though she belonged in them. The creamy blouse with the strappy thing under it could make any guy long to see what was beneath those layers, but now that he knew all that promise, he was in a worse position. He could think of nothing else.

Micah shoved away his hazardous thoughts as he'd been forced to so many times during their drive to Casper and then on their flight to LaGuardia. On his first trip back to New York City since he'd buried his father, and with an even more perilous situation unfolding back home, he couldn't spend the whole weekend only thinking about her. Wanting her. Wishing things could be different. The little boy cuddled against her shoulder served as a neon sign, a reminder that he wasn't the only one who could be hurt if he got that wrong.

The waitress took one look from them to Derek and then led them to a booth in the back of the restaurant. Discrimination against child patrons aside, she couldn't have chosen a worse place for them with its privacy offering an automatic intimacy that he, for one, didn't need, and the battery-powered candle reminding him of the blaze in the fireplace the night before.

Deirdre shot a look at the same candle and then busied herself, sliding Derek into the wooden highchair that the waitress had positioned at the end of the booth.

"You're good at that," Micah told him once she had latched the buckle.

"He's just taking pity on me and making it easier."

She sat and immediately used her phone to scan the QR code for the menu, signaling that he wasn't the only nervous one.

"Sorry that he insisted on you carrying him."

Derek had thrown his head back the moment Deirdre stopped by their hotel room to collect them for dinner, insisting that "Dee-Dee carry me." Micah hated that he'd given in *again*, but an impossibly extended travel day could have stretched even longer.

"You kidding? He's been a trouper all day. From rental cars to airplanes. Even on that scary taxi ride from the airport. He didn't scream once on the plane, which I thought was a requirement for anyone under three. So if he's a little grumpy now, I'll cut him some slack."

She set a napkin in front of Derek, reached in her purse and poured a few oyster crackers onto his tray from the little bag that had been a lifesaver all day.

"I don't remember seeing that shirt back at the ranch." Micah winced. Now she knew he'd noticed.

Deirdre crossed her arms as if to cover her top. "I didn't have many choices in my suitcase that would work here, since I didn't get a chance to make a stop in DC. Heck, I don't even *have* a suitcase. Just that duffel from Gary's."

"Told you it would come in handy."

She rubbed her hands up and down the see-through material that covered her arms. "I paid entirely too much for this in the hotel gift shop. It was the only one I could find, though. I'll have to pick up a few things tomorrow."

"It looks great... I mean...fine. Not much call for muck boots and Henleys in your job here, I would imagine."

"Or flannel," she agreed. "You're not wearing any tonight, either."

He shifted on the wood bench. "Thought we would be meeting your team here."

She set her phone aside. "I told you what Sean said when I called him with updates about Las Vegas and Greenwich Village. It wasn't stuff I needed to tell him in person."

"Oh, I remember. But what about the photo?"

"I just took a picture of it with my phone and then texted it to the team."

"Right. Technology." He couldn't have sounded more ridiculous and apparently hoped for a world record for moronic comebacks. For an escape, he pulled up the QR code and pretended to read the menu.

"Depending on what we find in Greenwich Village tomorrow, maybe we'll meet with them after that," she said. "He was a little curious why I would bring a witness with me to New York, so I had to explain about the situation on the ranch."

"You didn't tell him about Richard coercing you to help with the investigation, did you?"

She lifted a brow. "I told you that the whole team is in law enforcement, right? So, I presented all information on a need-to-know basis."

They exchanged a look that hinted on additional details the team had no business learning about, and then she went back to studying the menu on her phone. In the low light, he couldn't tell if she was blushing, but his cheeks and neck had to be the color of the ketchup bottle.

Then she looked up. "Wait. You got dressed up just to meet my team?"

He blinked over her quick return to the earlier subject and glanced down at his shirt and khakis.

"Possibly." He could have argued that the team also happened to consist of her cousins and brother, and he felt the pressure to impress them, but he'd dressed tonight for one person alone. It irked him that both of them knew it.

He considered pointing out that she'd gussied up, too, even purchasing a new shirt for dinner, but that just could have been because she wanted to look presentable in the city. Even if he knew some intimate details about her past and had had a decent introduction to her body, the truth was that he knew little about Deirdre's life on the East Coast. At a minimum, it had to be far more glamorous than the one he led on the ranch.

Though he continued to pretend to study the menu, when the waitress returned, he hadn't read anything beyond the words *appetizers* and *main courses*. He took a risk, based on the condiments on the table, and ordered a hamburger and fries and an IPA for himself and a grilled cheese and milk for Derek. With his luck, the restaurant would be vegan. Deirdre added a burger and a beer to the order, confirming his gamble.

When the food came, they ate as though someone had set a timer for them to clear their plates. Micah hadn't even realized how hungry he was until the food arrived, and he had to force himself to take breaths between bites. Even Derek got over his grouchiness long enough to shove the triangles of sandwich that Micah cut for him in his mouth.

"It's probably strange for you being back here after all these years," Deirdre said, finally taking a break and wiping her lips with a napkin.

"It does feel like all the people are headed to different places, and they all expect to get there this instant, no matter who they have to step on or drive over to make that happen."

She chuckled at that, sitting back and appearing to relax for the first time since the waitress had put them in the corner. "Remind me not to take you to Times Square while we're here."

"You forget that I was born here," he said and then shivered as he imagined all that humanity squeezed into that square between Broadway, Seventh Avenue and Forty-Second and Forty-Seventh Streets. He shook his head. "Funny how that never bothered me when I was a kid. It was home then, I guess."

"I'm sure it was different."

He shrugged. "I'm just not used to *so many* people anymore."

"You mean because there are eight million across the five boroughs and closer to two million in Manhattan alone?"

"Doing random info searches again?" At her nod, he added, "Did you know there aren't quite six hundred thousand in the whole state of Wyoming?"

"I looked that up, too," she said with a smile.

He handed Derek a fry and then watched as his son jammed the whole thing in his mouth.

"On the ranch, if you choose to, you can spend a few days without seeing a single other human being." It could also get awfully lonely there, but he didn't tell her that, since Harmony Fields would be emptier when he and his son returned there without her.

"Feeling a little homesick?"

Something, anyway. "I guess so."

"Well, you won't have to deal with that for too long. You've already got a return flight on Sunday night. I'm not sure how long I'll have to stay in the city before returning to DC."

"Don't you mean *home*?" He squinted, trying to remember if she'd ever referred to the place where she lived that way.

She straightened. "Of course, home. What did you think I meant?"

Though he didn't answer, she shifted again. "Living in the city—here or Washington—isn't better or worse than the rural Northwest. You have to know that, since you've experienced both. They're just different ways of life."

He couldn't help but to grin at that. "You sure seemed to think the East Coast was superior when you first arrived at Harmony Fields."

"I apologize for whatever I said that day. I was a stressed-out traveler, and you weren't exactly the most cooperative witness."

"Guilty."

They'd both had preconceived notions about each other. They nibbled fries and finished their beers, probably remembering their first meeting far differently.

He watched her for several seconds and then dived into the subject they really needed to discuss. The one they'd tiptoed around all day, careful to add extra space and avoid a misstep.

"You know, at some point we need to talk about what happened between us back in Wyoming."

She crossed her arms and tilted her head. "Must we?" Then her shoulders drooped. "I know we should. And we will when the time is right. Is it okay if that isn't tonight, while we still have so much to deal with over the two investigations?"

He nodded, though he doubted that she would find a right time to discuss it.

"Did you get a chance to talk to Deputy Martin?" she asked, quickly changing the subject.

"Just three times," he admitted. "I talked to Rob and Kevin, too. All the ranch hands assured me that the cattle and the petting zoo animals got their dinners just fine, no one has burned the place down yet, and there have been no escapees."

"So, a pleasant day on the ranch, then. I take it you've never taken a vacation away from Harmony Fields before."

"Ranchers don't get vacations. At least not spontaneous ones and not without a huge support system." He set the last bite of his burger back on the plate instead of eating it. "This isn't a vacation, either."

How many times would he need to remind himself of that?

"Guess not." She sipped her beer and set it aside. "You never told me what the deputy said."

Stop calling me so often. Well, maybe he wouldn't share that. "No signs of trespassing or damage yet," he said instead.

"Did he check inside the house or just the perimeter?"

"Both, as well as all the outbuildings. He used the key I left with Richard and said he'd walked through all three levels each time and hadn't seen anything out of the ordinary."

"How would he know what was ordinary?" She pointed at him with a French fry.

"I asked him that, too. But he only kidded me about the note I left on the table in case there were any visitors while we were gone."

"You left a note? You didn't tell me that."

He stared down at his plate, swishing his own fry through the leftover ketchup. "We were so busy packing the bags and the car seat and the rest of the stuff for Derek that I didn't get the chance to mention it."

She gave him a dubious look and waited.

He shrugged. "I just told them to take whatever it was that they were looking for and to leave us the hell alone."

"What if what the person wants is the ranch?"

"I don't know what I'll do. I just know that it has to stop before someone really gets hurt. Or worse."

As if they'd timed it, they both shot a look to the highchair. The child he'd sworn to protect sat with his chin tucked to his chest, his head bobbing in sleep, a chunk of grilled cheese still grasped in his hand.

"I won't let anything happen to him."

At Deirdre's promise—which she shouldn't have made, since she wasn't even working on his case anymore—Micah turned back to her. She tilted her chin, and something fierce and determined flashed in her too-shiny eyes. A surety filled him that hadn't been there even a minute before.

Whatever else he didn't know about Deirdre Colton and how many questions still lay between then, on this commitment she'd made, he absolutely believed her.

DEIRDRE STOPPED JUST past noon the next day and bent her head back to stare up at the pattern of square carvings inside the opening of the massive marble Washington Arch. Now at the north gateway to Washington Square Park, just past the two statues of George Washington on the arch's piers, she and Micah took a moment to breathe. Even after traipsing around Greenwich Village all morning, past cute brownstones and mom-and-pop pizza joints, they still hadn't seen anything that reminded him of Maeve O'Leary. Her neck and back hurt, and she wasn't even carrying Derek in the backpack the way that Micah was.

"Don't tilt too far back or you'll fall over," he said.

Next to her, Micah somehow still stood upright with Derek and the backpack pressing down on his shoulders. At least he'd had a break an hour earlier when she'd helped him slide off the flannel he now wore knotted around the carrier's waist strap. The sun and low-seventies temperatures in Manhattan felt much warmer without the Wyoming wind.

"And don't you look up at all, or you'll fall over and squish him."

"Sound advice."

Since father and son should have been wearing matching Yankees baseball caps, and only Micah had his, she searched the ground for the smaller hat in the pickup game they'd been playing for the past two hours. She plunked it on the child's head, but he immediately pulled it off again by the bill.

"Why don't you just put in that pocket on the bottom."

After she'd done as he asked, Micah pointed through the arch to the plaza, with dozens of New Yorkers surrounding the fountain at its center.

"Are we going in?"

"Might as well," she said. "You probably need a break, anyway."

"Is that you volunteering to carry the backpack for a while?" He grinned over her and waggled his eyebrows, causing the cap to lift and lower on his forehead. "I know how much fun you had last time."

"Not a chance."

He shrugged. "Had to give it a shot."

"I won't fall for that again."

As they stepped into the wide circular plaza area, Micah slowed and looked around, appearing as if he were mining his memories at the same time. "I remember coming here as a kid."

"With Maeve?" she said hopefully.

He shook his head. "With my parents. And then with Dad after Mom died. That was still pretty new the last time I was here."

He pointed to One World Trade Center, with its mirrored exterior and towering spire, visible from the park.

Despite the spectacular and poignant view of the building with the memorial, constructed after the tragedy of September 11, she sighed.

"I suppose it was expecting a lot for me to think we could just walk around town and you would suddenly see a place that sparked a memory with Maeve in it."

"We had to give it a shot," he said.

With slumped shoulders, she led him deeper into the park, away from the fountain, which would be a draw for Derek. At one of the benches positioned along the path, she helped Micah remove the backpack and freed the toddler from the harness. After a quick diaper change, she lowered the child and started a game of chase, giving his dad the chance to stretch his neck.

Just as Deirdre caught Derek for the third time and swung him in a circle, her arms crossed over his chest and tiny feet swinging out like a propeller and squeals of delight filling the air, her phone buzzed in her pocket. She rested Derek's feet on the ground, the child immediately taking off again, and pulled out the phone.

When she read the words on the screen, she froze.

"What is it?"

Micah was suddenly next to her, the boy he'd caught on his way to her giggling and bent over his arm.

"It's from my cousin Eva to the team group text thread." She flashed screen to him and then read it again herself. "She wanted to let us know that someone tried to kill Ciara Kelly today."

"That's terrible." After a few seconds, he added, "Now who's Ciara Kelly?"

Deirdre had been typing a return message, asking for more details, but at his question, she jerked her head up, blinking.

Of course he wouldn't know that part of the story. He knew little of it, and yet he was still there helping.

"Ciara is Humphrey Kelly's wife. Originally, she was questioned in the case since they'd only been married six months when he disappeared."

He tilted his head. "Another black widow?"

"Not this time. It's pretty complicated, but she's no longer considered a suspect. Their marriage turned out to be one of convenience so that Ciara could inherit the money from her grandmother's will and use it to pay for her own mother's cancer treatment. It looks like Maeve has somehow convinced Humphrey to go along with her plans."

Deirdre didn't realize that her words were coming faster and faster until Micah shook his head, his eyes wide.

"I said it before," he said as he carried his son back to the bench, where he'd left the backpack, "but—"

"The truth is better than fiction," she finished for him. "Yeah, I know. And, again, you have no popcorn."

She waited for him to make a joke, but he only stared back at her, straight-faced.

"Now this Ciara is a victim, too? What happened?"

As she returned to the bench to help him with the backpack, she glanced down at her phone again, waiting for it to buzz and provide her with more answers. When it sat frustratingly silent, she had to resist the temptation to shake it. Finally, she looked up at him.

"Apparently, I won't be receiving any more details right now. All I know so far is that sometime today, a driver in a small, dark car tried to run Ciara down. My brother has been assigned to watch over her until Humphrey and Maeve are apprehended."

Micah had just snapped the backpack harness over his son's shoulders and turned away so Deirdre could lift it onto his back, but at her words, he whirled to face her again.

"Couldn't that be a long time? Do you really think you're that close to catching Maeve?"

"Well, it would be awfully coincidental if someone other than Maeve or Humphrey or at least one of their accomplices made an attempt on Ciara Kelly's life today."

"You said before that you don't believe in coincidences."

"I still don't." She let that sink in as she lifted the pack onto his shoulders. "We believe that Maeve and Humphrey are somewhere in this city right now."

"Then we'd better get back." Micah snapped the buckle and walked several steps. "Are you coming?"

"But we still haven't found any place Maeve would have frequented."

"I'm doubting that whatever I would have to say would have any impact right now."

He kept walking, so she fell into step beside him as he hurried toward the arch and the park's exit.

"You're probably right." She didn't try to hide her disappointment. Even if she knew she was being selfish, she still needed for her lead to be the one leading to Maeve's whereabouts and arrest. Otherwise, after everything, she still would have nothing to take back to the bureau at the end of her *vacation*.

"Your team probably needs to get together to strategize, too."

This time, she simply nodded but glanced over and caught him watching.

"I know you hoped to close this case yourself, but you might have to settle for just being part of the *team* that finds this missing psychiatrist and brings down a serial killer."

"That has to sound ridiculous to you."

He shook his head but walked even faster, forcing her to jog to keep up, even with the extra thirty pounds on his back.

"We all have our motivations for what we do. For me, I've

been waiting fifteen years for Ariel Porter Perry—or Maeve O'Leary or whatever name she's going by today—to face any sort of justice for murdering my dad."

Deirdre shook her head, her stomach queasy with the truth of her self-centered mission. "I'm sorry. That was so insensitive of me to—"

He shook his head until she stopped talking so he could finish.

"If there's anything I can do to speed up that process that will put her in prison for the rest of her life," he said, "I'm ready to do it."

Chapter Sixteen

Micah wasn't sure why he'd even suggested that they take one more look around Greenwich Village, attempting to find spots they hadn't crossed the first time, before hitting the West Fourth Street–Washington Square subway station. He couldn't remember seeing Maeve anywhere in that area, anyway, and even if something had sparked a memory, he didn't really want to help Deirdre right now.

Had he ever met a more selfish person? Someone who had less trust in others? Even when they were this close to catching his stepmother, Deirdre really believed that saving her FBI career by being able to take credit for stopping a serial killer was more important than actually putting one behind bars.

He tightened his jaw, but that only reminded him that his neck hurt after carrying Derek all day. His shoulders hurt. And his back hurt. In fact, it would be easier just to say that every part of him felt as if he'd been run over by a truck and save himself time in describing it.

On his back, his son only added to the tension by choosing this moment to sing his new favorite song, which sounded something like, "Dee-Dee, Dee-Dee, Dee-Dee, Dee-Dee," forever and amen.

"You don't have to keep looking," she said. "We can just

go back to the hotel. The team's already trying to set up a meeting."

Micah didn't answer. The least she could do was be honest with him—this was about her. It had always been about her. He'd thought behind the walls she'd built to protect herself from those who'd hurt her, there was a tender, kind and giving person inside, but he'd been wrong. The other day he'd told her that some people couldn't think beyond the length of their own wingspan. He just hadn't realized that he was talking about *her*.

"Just a little longer," he said finally.

He couldn't hold out too long, or Derek would miss his nap, and it would be a really long night.

"I'm sorry."

"So you've said." He continued scanning the area as they passed, redbrick brownstones with fenced patios, walk-ups with probably incredible views, cast-iron lampposts and trees planted right into the sidewalk.

"I mean it."

"Good to know."

"You can't forgive me for needing to be the one to make this arrest?"

He could. That was the crux of it. He could, and he wanted to, and she didn't damn deserve it. If he needed a reminder that he was just like his father, she walked next to him, the best and worst thing that had happened in his life in years.

"Okay. I give up."

He'd meant the search, not giving in to her plea for forgiveness, but even as he said it, something farther up the street caught his attention. Though he'd been sweating all day while carrying an extra thirty pounds on his back, a chill skittered up his spine. The shiver started inside him and worked its way out.

"What is it?" Deirdre asked, her eyes wide.

Without answering her, he rushed up the street and stood in front of the eight-story Art Deco–style building with metallic-gold reliefs that looked like the scales of justice. The place dripped of money and class—the first, the thing Maeve always craved, the second, something she'd never had.

"This is it! I remember now."

"The Village Historical Hotel?" she asked, reading the sign.

"Maeve loved this place." He tipped his head up slightly to get a better look at the more pronounced penthouse floor with a balcony. "What's not to like? A five-star hotel. The priciest in the whole city. I never saw her here, but I remember her talking about it in this dreamy voice. She said she would live here if she could."

Deirdre leaned close and spoke in a low voice. "She wanted to *live* here?"

He nodded.

"We've got to go," she whispered. "Now." She linked her arm through his and rushed him down the street.

"What's going on?" He spun around and pointed back to the building. "Why are you doing—"

Realization dawning, he stopped and looked from Deirdre to the hotel and back. "You don't think—"

She shrugged. "I don't know. But if she is there, she can't see you standing on the sidewalk in front of the place."

"You're right. We need to get out of here. You have to get back to your team."

Micah hurried to the corner and turned north in the direction of the subway station. He was still reluctant to help Deirdre, but that didn't seem to matter anymore. After all this time, after all the things she'd done or might even still be doing, he might be able to help take down Maeve O'Leary.

DEIRDRE TOOK A deep breath later that afternoon and pulled open the door to the A Grind Above coffee shop on the Upper

West Side. As nervous as it made her to meet in person with the team for the first time, the fact that she would have given anything to have Micah there with her bothered her even more.

How was she supposed to pull back from him when she couldn't do anything these past few days without wondering what he would think about it or wishing she could share it with him? The worst part was that this time Micah truly deserved to be there. Even if he was clearly frustrated with her, without his help that day, she would have nothing new to report to the team.

The place was as busy and loud as Eva had predicted it would be in the group chat, but Deirdre still found her four cousins squeezed around a table in the corner, compostable coffee cups in front of them. Although they had some general resemblance, their varying hair colors from Cormac's dark brown and Liam's dirty blond to Eva's dark red, plus a full range of eye colors, made it tough to pinpoint. Had Deirdre not already known that they were siblings, she wouldn't have guessed it. Still, compared to her and Aidan, they were all practically identical.

Sean, both the team leader and the oldest brother on that branch of the Colton family tree, noticed her first and waved her over.

"Sorry I'm late," she said, resting her hands on the back of the one empty chair. "I had a hard time figuring out the subway map."

"You're lucky to have a place to sit. We had to fight off a bunch of poachers," Liam, the ex-con–turned–NYPD informant, said with a grin.

Sean, the detective from the NYPD's Ninety-Eighth Precinct, rounded the table to greet her with his hand outstretched. "I keep forgetting that you're not from New York."

He must have thought better of shaking her hand, as he

pulled back and then gave her the awkward hug of a distant cousin. Deirdre forced herself to keep a straight face. Working with relatives was difficult enough without family being little more than strangers.

Eva, the rookie cop and the youngest of the four, pushed a paper cup to the spot they'd left for her. "Hey, Deirdre. I got you a latte. Hope that's okay."

"It's great. Thanks." It gave her something to do with her hands besides wring them.

She appreciated that Eva and the twins, Cormac and Liam, waved instead of standing for another round of uncomfortable greetings.

"Well, let's get started." Sean rested a manila folder on the table and leaned his elbows on it rather than open it. Despite all the conversations taking place in the coffee shop, he glanced around to see if they would be overheard and kept his voice low. "I really appreciate all of you coming together so quickly. I'd expected to schedule a meeting while Deirdre was in town, but because of these new developments involving the attempt on Ciara Kelly's life, we need to change our timing and format a little."

He pulled his phone from his pocket and propped it against the decorative canning jar filled with coffee beans at the table's center. "Because his role has changed, Aidan will now be joining us by video call."

Sean clicked the call button, and her brother's face appeared on the screen.

"Hi, everyone," Aidan said. "Checking in from the Kelly home. All is well. The victim received no injuries and is resting comfortably. Because Maeve O'Leary has been named as a person of interest in today's incident, and she remains at large, I will stay with Mrs. Kelly, pending further instructions from the team."

"Thank you, Aidan," Sean said. "Now, let's have Deir-

dre fill us in about the discovery she made today in Greenwich Village."

Deirdre cleared her throat, suddenly more nervous than
she'd ever been for any report in the DC field office. "In
addition to providing us with a photo of our suspect that
I shared with you for identification and facial-recognition
purposes, witness Micah Perry has offered other critical information about Maeve O'Leary, a woman he knew under
the alias Ariel Porter Perry. Maeve, who was Micah's stepmother, is wanted for questioning in the suspicious death of
his father, Len Perry."

Sean gestured in a circular motion. "And today you discovered…?"

She crossed and uncrossed her legs. "Micah had suggested
that Maeve spent a lot of time in Greenwich Village, so he
and his toddler son accompanied me to New York with the
hope that he could identify places where Maeve enjoyed
spending time in the Village. Places where she would possibly hide."

"And you found a good lead, right?" asked Cormac, the
private investigator who regularly worked with the NYPD
and the DA's office.

"We did. The Village Historical Hotel seems to be a solid
path for us to follow. Micah was able to recall that Maeve
loved the hotel. She once even said she would live there if
she could."

"Well, that's something," Aidan called out from the phone.

Deirdre shifted in her seat but covered it by taking a sip
of her latte. She didn't need any feedback from her sibling
with far more experience in law enforcement than she had.

Liam leaned closer to the rest of the team. "Do you think
that this whole time we've been searching for Humphrey and
Maeve, they've been living high on the hog at the Village
Historical Hotel?"

"Maybe," Deirdre said.

"If he's still alive, that is," Eva chimed.

"There is that," Liam agreed.

Sean frowned at his sister and brother by turns. "It's a solid premise. One I think we should definitely check out."

"Best we've had so far," Cormac noted.

Sean held his hands up, taking control again. "I think we should set up some careful surveillance of the property, both inside and at the perimeter."

Eva raised her hand. "I volunteer for inside. Carmine and I could use a night out, and from what I've heard, the Village Hotel has an amazing restaurant—its bar has all this rich, dark wood and even tin ceiling tiles."

"Sure you and your detective boyfriend will be able to focus on something besides the romantic decor?" Cormac asked, earning a mean look from his sister.

"You're not going to get to expense this dinner, either." Liam, who since his release from prison ran a juvenile awareness program with the Ninety-Eighth Precinct, pointed to their older brother. "Tell her, Sean. You don't have the budget for that, do you?"

"Thanks for the input, Mr. Always Play by the Rules, but I wasn't going to ask to expense it," Eva said.

As much as Deirdre appreciated knowing that hers wasn't the only family where sibling rivalry played a part, she didn't have time for it now.

"Aren't we talking about stopping a black widow here?" she said in a low voice. Then, when she had everyone's attention, she added, "Micah and I should be there, too. He's the only one of us who's ever seen Maeve in real life. The one most likely to be able to pick her out, even if she's in disguise."

Deirdre's chest tightened, and her palms started sweating as she waited for them to respond. Could they see straight through her to know that she and Micah had been far more involved than any special agent and witness should be?

"He's also the only one Maeve could recognize," Liam pointed out. "He's not in law enforcement, either."

"Don't you think that's a good thing?" Deirdre said. "We all don't want to look like we're on a stakeout, do we? Micah's a really smart guy. He won't mess it up. I would think that any of you who participate would need to be in disguise, anyway. Didn't you say Humphrey knew your family well? I'm the only one that *he* wouldn't recognize."

"What will you and Mr. Perry dress up as?" Aidan called out from the phone. "A couple on a date? A married couple? Maybe one with a kid?"

Deirdre straightened in her chair. What was her brother's problem? Was she more upset that he was making those comments to question her professionalism or that he had come awfully close to the truth?

"We would never involve his son in the matter, Aidan. That's out of the question. But don't you think pretending to be a couple is better than, I don't know, declaring, 'Hey, I'm an FBI special agent staking out the place'?"

Her cheeks and neck burned. She didn't bother fooling herself into believing the other members of the team didn't notice. Hopefully, they thought it was indignation over her brother's words and not her inappropriate relationship with the witness himself.

"She's got you there, buddy," Liam said with a laugh. "Sounds like they're doing some great training down there at Quantico."

Eva crossed her arms and studied her cousin. "Why didn't you bring Mr. Perry with you tonight? Especially after he's been so helpful to you, providing information for the case."

"Like Liam pointed out, he's not in law enforcement."

"But haven't you already involved him in the case?"

It felt as if she were a hostile witness in a criminal case. Only instead of one attorney or legal team, five different investigators were pelting her with questions, plenty of which it might not be in her best interest to answer. But since this one was more benign that most, she decided to answer it in an abbreviated fashion. If anyone asked her to take a polygraph test, she would fail with flying colors, focusing so hard on telling as little as possible of the truth.

"Yes, he's been helping me, in exchange for my assistance looking into a series of crimes on his property, Harmony Fields Ranch. Someone has been targeting his property, his animals and now him and his son."

Cormac tilted his head. "Do you think it's possible that those crimes could have some connection to those we're investigating here?"

She'd never considered it before, but she immediately shook her head. "Of course not."

"Even though Maeve is a suspect in his dad's death?" Cormac pressed.

She shook her head again. "The only connection is that Micah was dealing with the fallout from the escalating series of vandalism incidents and, now, personal threats when I arrived to interview him about Maeve O'Leary."

"Awfully nice of you to help him out with his case," Aidan called out from the cell-phone peanut gallery.

Deirdre lowered her gaze to the phone. If she could get by with *accidentally* dropping the call, she would do it instantly. "Anyway, Micah agreed to come with me to New York because of a direct threat to his son there. He's probably back in his hotel room dealing with the sheriff's office right now."

Sean gripped the edge of the table and waited for the team to turn back to him. "Enough chatter. We need to take Humphrey and Maeve O'Leary into custody, and this is the best lead we've had so far. Deirdre's right. Perry has the best chance of being able to identify Maeve, particularly if she and Humphrey aren't together."

"So, you want me to make a reservation?" Eva asked.

Sean nodded. "For two." He turned back to Deirdre. "You can make a second one for you and Perry."

Cormac gestured from himself to his twin. "What are we supposed to do?"

"Glad you asked." Sean pointed at Cormac. "You'll be part of my surveillance team, posing as a package-delivery driver." He turned to Liam. "And you're a jogger, running through the neighborhood and checking out behind all the buildings."

"How come I always get the dirty jobs?" Liam asked.

This time Sean smiled. "Got to keep you in shape, to keep up with the kids in the juvenile program."

"What about Derek?" Deirdre asked.

Eight pairs of eyes stared back at her with confusion. Even Aidan was quiet for once.

"You know. Micah's son. We can't leave him back a the hotel with a bottle of soda and the remote."

Sean nodded. "I'll get one of the officers at the Ninety-Eighth Precinct to give him a tour and encourage him to choose a career in law enforcement."

"What if he wants to be a rancher like his dad?"

"Just giving him options." The team leader grinned. "So, we're set, right?"

Sean's siblings all made affirmative sounds and cleaned up their coffee cups and napkins to prepare to leave. Deirdre made the same sounds, but she wasn't close to set. She might have volunteered Micah's services in participating in what amounted to a sting, but she hadn't asked him if he was willing to do it.

This would be more than just asking him to stir up old ghosts by walking up and down the streets of Greenwich

Village, looking for something that sparked a memory. Now she had to convince him to not only pretend to be on a date with her—which he probably wouldn't be too happy about after the way she'd left things earlier—but also risk seeing the devil who'd murdered his father face-to-face.

THE UNUSUAL RING of a video call interrupted Deirdre two hours later as she bent close to the hotel bathroom mirror to apply mascara. Her already-unsteady hand jerked, creating imaginary lashes up the side of her eyelid. Grabbing a makeup-remover cloth, she marched out to the hotel room desk, where she'd plugged in her phone.

When Aidan's name flashed on the screen, she considered not answering. He'd rarely called her before, never by video, and this wasn't a good day for him to start. Only with her luck, he would probably call Dad and give him another reason to be disappointed in her.

She tapped the button, and Aidan stared back at her, his black eyes narrowing.

"What is it? I'm kind of busy." She brushed at the makeup smeared on her eyelid.

"I can see that. What's all over your eye?"

She stopped wiping long enough to give him a dirty look. "What do you need? I have to be ready in twenty minutes."

"For your big date with the cowboy?"

"You know it's not a date." She frowned at the screen.

"Of course I know it's not. The question is, do you?"

"I don't know what you're talking about."

But because she did, and he didn't appear to be ready to let her off the phone, she carried it back into the bathroom, where she'd spread cosmetics all over the counter. The wig and the glasses she would need to wear rested next to the sink. She propped the phone against the backsplash and grabbed her tube of mascara.

"Say whatever you need to and be done with it so I can get off the phone."

"You should be careful, big sister. It's all kinds of unprofessional for you to get too close to a witness. And you're already in enough trouble with the bureau."

She bristled over his accurate review of the situation, but that didn't stop her from shooting back. "I get it that you're this law enforcement expert after nearly a decade with the US Marshals Service, but I'm not 'too close' to Micah Perry."

She kept her gaze on the mirror as she lied, her hand shaking more than it had earlier.

"I heard how you spoke about him during the meeting. I *know* you. I'm your brother."

"Clearly, you don't know me that well, and you're my *half* brother." As soon as the words were out of her mouth, she regretted them. She was becoming defensive and mean.

After a long pause, he spoke again.

"Okay, then, I *half* know that you're lying and have become involved with a witness. To what degree, I'm not sure. And I *half* know that you could be messing up your career."

She didn't bother trying to argue with him. "Don't you think you should be focusing on taking care of our witness?"

"*Mrs.* Kelly is safe. She's in her kitchen, cooking dinner. I'm doing *my job* just fine."

Deirdre picked up the phone from the counter and stared at his face. "Good to know. I have to go now."

But before she could cut off the call, her brother got in a parting shot.

"I just hope you know what you're doing if you're *taking care of* Micah Perry."

Chapter Seventeen

Eva sighed as she stared at the man sitting across the table from her at the magnificent bar inside the Village Historical Hotel the next evening, even if he couldn't keep a straight face when he looked back at her and had avoided it for the past few minutes. So much for combining a romantic dinner with Carmine DiRico with a little police surveillance.

A least Carmine didn't have to wear a disguise since, as far as they could figure, Maeve O'Leary had no way to know him, and Humphrey Kelly had never crossed him while serving as an expert witness in court. He looked like the same dark, beautiful NYPD detective who'd been her partner for a brief time and her pretend husband for a few days in an undercover operation and now had promised to be her love for life.

She, on the other hand, had to look like an escapee Morticia Addams with that ridiculous black wig against her pale skin. How was she supposed to blend in when even the man who loved her most couldn't look at her without laughing?

Across the room, Deirdre sat alone at a table, waiting for her "date" to arrive. She had a spinster-librarian thing going on with her hair tucked in a light brown wig, arranged in a bun, reading glasses riding low on her nose. The combination was designed to help cover the wireless earpiece/microphone that kept her in contact with the team members in the surveillance van outside. Deirdre didn't really have to be in disguise, since neither suspect would recognize her, so Eva had to give her cousin credit for being a team player. Someone might ask her about the Dewey Decimal System, but at least she wouldn't have to deal with someone inquiring about her kids, Wednesday and Pugsley.

After taking a sip of her Shirley Temple, she patted her hair again and settled her purse where she held her weapon in her lap.

Carmine turned back to her, his smile practiced and benign. "Please stop playing with your hair. It doesn't look too bad."

She returned his loving look. "This should serve as your reminder never to lie to me in our marriage. You're a lousy liar."

"Noted. Now, how come you got the best seat? I wanted the door-facing seat."

He didn't have to mention that there wasn't a police officer alive who felt comfortable with his back exposed to anyone entering a room or building.

From her seat, she could see not long the heavy wood-and-glass doors that separated the bar from the lobby, the whole bank of elevators and more beautiful doors that led to the outside. "Because this time, Detective, I get to pull rank on you. I'm the member of this investigative team. You're my arm candy."

"I'll try to remember my place."

She winked at him, knowing she would have his support and firepower, if necessary, from the weapon tucked in his ankle holster, should she need it.

"I'm thinking this whole plan might be a wash," she whispered, reaching out to touch his fingers on top of the table.

"Did anyone on the early surveillance team catch even a glance of either of the suspects?"

Eva shook her head. "We still don't know if they're even staying here, and as much as Deirdre talked up her super-witness, Micah, he hasn't even shown up."

She focused as the exterior door opened, and Micah, with spiky bleach-blond hair and a close-trimmed dark beard, sunglasses covering his eyes, strode inside. And she'd thought her getup was bad. He would probably have to shave his head to get rid of that style.

"One superwitness, present and accounted for," she said.

Sure enough, the visitor crossed to the table where Deirdre sat and took the seat next to her for the better vantage point, immediately tracing kisses down her cheek to justify the cozy seating arrangement.

Deirdre stiffened as she caught Eva watching the display, her hands gripped in front of her, eyes blinking too much.

"Mark my words," she whispered to her future husband. "There's something more to that story than playacting."

"Ah, you're just happily coupled, and now you want everyone else to be the same." He reached over the table to caress the back of her hand.

"Maybe. But mark my words anyway."

She glanced from the lobby to the exterior door and then back just as the elevator doors opened. A couple stepped out and crossed into the bar, heading to a table away from the windows. Her breath caught in her throat.

Humphrey. The height and weight were the same. He obviously wore a disguise—a prosthetic nose, strong-framed glasses and a wig as bad as hers—but she would have bet her life and those of all three of her brothers that the man heading to that table was the same one who'd supported them after their father's death.

"That's Humphrey. I know it," she whispered to Carmine, who had to nod and continue to face her since he couldn't afford to take the chance of turning to look. "He's in disguise, but I'll never forget his kind eyes."

He did reach down to scratch his calf, just in case.

Eva was tempted to rush, to demand to know why Humphrey, who'd once seemed like such a good man, someone she and her brothers had relied on, had turned out to be just another criminal. One who'd manipulated her and her brothers to suit his own needs.

She took the signal from Carmine to watch and wait. They'd taken this long to track down Humphrey, believing that he was a victim. Now they just needed to wait for the perfect time to take him down.

MICAH'S INSIDES SHOOK as he sat so close to Deirdre, touching her as he'd longed to so many times in the past two days. Kissing her neck and watching her pulse beat in her throat. Hearing her breath hitch. Feeling her nervousness, even before her tongue darted out to dampen her lips.

All of it was for show.

He had to be in this spot to be able to see guests entering the bar, and the only way he could justify that cutesy seating arrangement was to pretend he couldn't keep his hands off her. Whether invention or truth. He tried to fight it, to make it just as much a work of fiction as their days on the ranch had apparently been. Perfect yet finite. A long drive that led only to a brick wall.

So, why even at this awful, inopportune time, did her pull remain so strong? At first, he'd said no to this theater performance. He'd even asked her why she needed him now when she'd insisted on pursuing the vandal alone the other night. But she'd said this time was different. That he was the only one who'd seen Maeve close enough to still identify her in disguise. It was just like the other night, when he'd wanted to talk about what had happened between them. To make sense of something he couldn't let go of no matter how much he hyperextended his hands. Like with everything else, she'd made it on her terms. When the time was right. *Her time.*

Still, when she'd come to him for help, he couldn't deny her, even knowing she only wanted it for herself. He'd given in. Just as he suspected he always would with her.

He was just like his dad, after all.

Deirdre cleared her throat and whispered, "Please."

She didn't even say what she was begging for. That he would touch her more? Or never again? His body and maybe even his soul longed for the former, but he suspected she'd requested the latter. She touched her ear to indicate the earpiece/microphone and watched him out of her side vision. Even if she wanted to, she couldn't answer him now.

But he was tired of asking. He would give her that space she craved soon. And then he would walk away. Or drive, really. Then fly. Back home, he would have the chance to lick his wounds, heal and thank God that Derek was too young to remember what Micah could never forget.

"Do you see Eva?" she whispered and then gestured with a tilt of her head to the table across the room.

Micah caught sight of the black-wigged woman that he assumed was her cousin, but the couple that Eva watched at one of the tables drew his attention. Though both of them were in disguise, just like he was, he ignored the guy completely. Only the woman mattered. Micah tried not to stare, but a roaring sound filled his ears and heat welled in his chest, stretching and spreading, until it was all he could do to remain seated and not leap up and throw the jacket that Deirdre had borrowed for him to the floor.

It was Maeve O'Leary.

This was the same woman, the one who'd waltzed into his family and stole first his father's good sense and then his life and then moved on with impunity to destroy other families.

Did she really think she could hide behind that ridiculous, short-blond wig with all those bangs across her forehead? She'd made the mistake of not covering her eyes. Those despicable, frigid eyes. He would never forget them for as long as he lived.

He glanced over at Deirdre and nodded, signaling both his positive identification of his stepmother and that the time had come for her to signal those in the unmarked police van outside, Liam, Cormac and Sean among them.

Suddenly, the air in the room changed. Maeve and the man, who he could only assume was Humphrey Kelly, stood and started toward the door.

"Signal," he whispered to Deirdre.

But her head was already turned. "H and M, on the move," she said in a low voice to her microphone.

In Micah's peripheral vision, Carmine and Eva came to their feet. As she turned back from passing along the message, Deirdre stood as well, her gaze moving from the perimeter of the room to the exit, and he followed her lead.

As Maeve and Humphrey continued toward the door, Humphrey darted nervous glances at Eva. The man recognized her, too.

The rest happened so quickly that Micah wasn't certain what took place first.

"Stop! Police!" Eva called out, her firearm aimed at the couple.

At what felt like the exact same time, Maeve yanked a girl of maybe six from a table where she sat with her family, positioned the terrified child in front of herself and held a gun to the little blonde head. The low murmur of voices around them became shrieks and cries as guests dived under the shiny wood tables.

At Maeve's signal, Humphrey sidled next to her, at least

having the decency to appear anguished at the events taking place around him.

"Drop your guns or the kid dies," Maeve called out.

Guns, plural? His ears reverberating with the sound of that shrill voice that he hadn't been forced to hear for fifteen years, Micah shifted his gaze from side to side. Carmine and Deirdre had their weapons trained on Humphrey and Maeve as well, but, like Eva, they bent to lower them to the ground.

Instantly, Maeve backed out of the restaurant, using the child as a shield, Humphrey at her side. They darted through the lobby and out the door, where they faced off with police and the rest of the team. Carmine and Eva grabbed their firearms and raced after them, Micah and Deirdre right behind them.

Just as they reached the sidewalk, Maeve forced a driver from a running black four-door and leaped inside, Humphrey sliding into the back seat. Then she pushed the little girl to the sidewalk, slammed the door and pulled into traffic. As one police officer rushed to grab the child and return her to her family, the others climbed back into the van. Carmine and Eva squeezed in with them, but there didn't appear to be any more space.

Deirdre shot a frustrated look back to Micah. He looked back and forth for options.

"Micah, Deirdre, over here." Sean stood inside the open door to his unmarked patrol car.

They ran over to him. Deirdre leaped in the passenger seat, while Micah slid in back. Sean peeled out after the van and flipped on his lights and siren.

Micah pressed his face to the center section of the window partition that separated the front seat from the back and spoke through the little square holes. "Can't you go faster?"

"Are you and I seeing the same traffic here?" Sean asked,

keeping his focus on the road. "Could you do me a favor and put on a safety belt? I'm Sean, by the way."

"Oh. Right." He scooted over to the door and clicked the belt. "I'm Micah. But could you—"

"He's going as fast as he can," Deirdre said.

But she seemed to be rocking in the seat, as anxious as he was. Micah closed his eyes, nausea and hopelessness welling in his throat. It was their one chance to stop Maeve O'Leary, and they were letting her get away.

THEY WOUND THROUGH the city, chasing the van that pursued the stolen vehicle. Soon they were out of Manhattan on Interstate 87. Then the interstate became county routes, and the busy city streets transformed to open expanses, rolling hills and then jutting mountain peaks, all of it eventually becoming hidden behind a mask of night.

"Why haven't they stopped them?" Deirdre pointed to the police van ahead of them on the two-lane road, the car already having vanished over the hill ahead. "Why haven't they—"

"I don't know," Sean said with a sigh. He shook his head. "I have no idea what's happening up there."

Deirdre couldn't blame him for being frustrated. She'd probably asked some variation of that question each fifteen minutes of the past ninety, and Micah had slid a few similar queries in between hers, interspersed with his own through long bouts of silence. But Sean had to know that they were as frustrated as he was. They'd been so close to arresting Maeve, to finally getting justice for Micah and for the Maeve's other victims, and now every mile they drove seemed to make that less and less likely to happen.

She pulled the earpiece she'd worn earlier and held it out where her cousin should have been able to see it in his peripheral vision. "I can try to contact—"

Sean shook his head. "You can't even get a decent cell signal out here. I wouldn't count on Bluetooth."

"Wait."

Micah stuck his head against the partition again. "What's going on?"

"Something's happening now." Sean leaned his head as if that would help him to see around the van with its flashers on. "They shot out the tires."

"They waited all this time to do that?" Micah said.

Sean didn't answer, but Deirdre was with Micah on that one. They could have taken that action several counties ago.

Their driver pulled to the side of the road, opened the door and drew his weapon. "Stay here."

"I'm not staying here," she said, but he was already gone. Deirdre opened the door and pulled her pistol from the holster. She glanced at the man in the back, where arrest suspects usually sat, memories of a different night and a different risk making her chest tight.

"You stay here."

She didn't wait for his answer—she closed the door and rushed to catch up with the others.

The disabled car now rested abandoned on the side of the road, and police were using rechargeable searchlights to scan the area for the suspects. They didn't have to look far. No more than one hundred feet from the road, Maeve stood with her weapon pointed directly at Eva. Humphrey shifted next to her, appearing nervous and upset.

Deirdre stepped over to Liam. "How did this happen?"

"Eva had it under control, but Maeve threatened to shoot Humphrey if she didn't put down her gun."

"You mean shoot her next meal ticket?"

"Never said she was thinking rationally," Liam said.

Out of the corner of her eye, Deirdre caught Micah joining the group gathered by the van.

She slipped over to him. "What are you doing here? I told you—"

"No way I'm staying in the car and letting you—I mean *any of you*—handle this alone."

Her throat tightened with just the idea that she'd let Micah put himself in danger to identify Maeve earlier, and now she was doing it again. But arguing with him didn't seem to make a difference. "Could you at least stay behind the folks with the weapons?"

"Will do."

She could relate to Carmine's fear when he jumped out of the van, carrying a bullhorn to reason with the suspect holding the woman he loved, but Cormac wrestled it away from him before he had the chance to speak.

"You don't want to do this, Maeve," Cormac called into the bullhorn. "There's no way out. You don't want to hurt someone Humphrey cares about, do you?"

Eva stood with her hands up, bravely facing the woman holding the gun on her. But Humphrey appeared nervous, shifting from one foot to the other.

"Maeve, honey, please don't do this," Humphrey said, needing no bullhorn to be heard.

"Shut up, you ridiculous, weak man!" She'd glanced over at him but jerked her head back as Eva lunged, trying to reclaim her weapon. "Get your hands back. You know I'll shoot."

Maybe it was because they all knew she could—and probably would—that Sean rushed in that moment, weapon in hand. He placed himself between his little sister and the woman threatening to kill her.

"Laying down your life for a friend seems pretty cool until you really have to do it." With a laugh, Maeve aimed and fired.

Only she'd missed Humphrey's movement before. He

leaped out, putting himself between Sean and the gun. The bullet struck him right in the throat.

"You idiot!" Maeve shouted at him as he bled out on the ground.

With tears in his eyes, Sean sat on the ground with his mentor, holding his head in his lap. "You lost your way, but I always knew there was good in you."

Humphrey gasped and attempted to speak, but he only gurgled, the air streaming from his lungs for the last time.

Chapter Eighteen

As the others crowded around Humphrey, delivering first aid that would relieve no pain and waiting for the ambulance that would serve as a hearse, Micah scooted through the group to the target that drew him far more—Maeve. Yes, he felt bad that she'd had the chance to take another life, but the time had come for her to account for one earlier on her hit list. The chaos had to be to blame for the fact that though she was no longer accessorizing with a .22 pistol, she didn't yet have a pair of matching bracelets on her wrists, and she hadn't been secured in the back of Sean Colton's patrol car.

That lucky truth didn't appear to be lost on Maeve, either. Now outside the beam of the spotlight, she inched closer to an area where it would be easier for her to make a break for the woods. Good thing that darkness benefited him, too, even if he shivered with revulsion just stepping this close to her again.

"Well, if it isn't Mommie Dearest."

Maeve jerked her head to look over at him, though she wouldn't be able to see his face. He fixed that problem by awakening his phone and turning that soft light on himself.

"Micah?"

"Are you seeing a ghost, *Maeve*? Or would you still prefer me to call you Ariel?"

She chuckled into the darkness, having recovered from the surprise. "It was a pretty name, wasn't it? Len Perry's son, all grown up. How long has it been? Twelve years?"

"Fifteen. Seems as if you'd have more vivid memories of your murders. Becoming too many to recall?"

"You always did have such an imagination."

He flicked on his flashlight app and flashed it over to all the law-enforcement personnel still gathered around the most recent victim.

"You saw that yourself. It was an *accident*."

"Tell that to the judge."

"Guess I'll have to."

She sounded sad, but if that emotion was authentic—he didn't hold his breath on that—she regretted only her potential loss of freedom.

"I have one question for you, and the way I see it, you owe me one."

"I don't owe you anything, but I'll give you a gift, since I never really gave you one at your party."

"I want to know *why*." To his shame, his voice broke on the last word.

"Why did I marry your father?"

He gritted his teeth that she'd purposely misunderstood his question, but her answer made him shiver anyway.

"A lady needs things. Pretty things. It was just wonderful that your father wanted to provide so well for me."

"Then wherever he is, I'm sure he's happy knowing that his son wanted to give you something, too—a new address, where you'll live for a long, long time."

The sound of approaching sirens drew everyone's attention and gave Maeve a chance to make her break for the woods. In the hours that followed, the team and other officers combed the woods, but without the help of tracking dogs, they couldn't locate her. She was gone.

DEIRDRE COULD BARELY keep her eyes open by the time Sean dropped Micah, Derek and her back at their hotel at well past midnight. The extra stop at the Ninety-Eighth Precinct to pick up Micah's son made it even later. At least the child had been in good care there, as they'd found him fed and asleep on the sofa in the captain's office, with an officer nearby, when Micah had gone in to collect him.

Besides his thank-you to that officer and to Sean when he left them, Micah had barely spoken during the whole trip back from rural New York.

She glanced over at him as he carried Derek down the hall to his hotel room, his expression showing the wear of a long, exhausting night.

"Do you want to talk about the conversation you had with Maeve?"

He shook his head as he used the key card to open the door. "I don't want to talk about *anything* tonight."

"Just tonight?"

Micah shrugged, confirming her suspicion that he might never want to share anything his stepmother had said before she'd escaped, though she suspected the team would want to interview him about it. She hated that he would be forced to discuss it, since it was obvious that whatever he'd learned had done nothing to salve his pain.

"Are you ready to fly out tomorrow?" She glanced at her watch. "I mean, later this morning."

This time he answered with a shrug, but he didn't protest when she followed him into the room. Other than the portable crib stationed in the corner, his room looked just like hers.

Micah laid Derek on the spare bed, changed his diaper and put on his pajamas, saving the bath for the morning. The toddler whined when his father brushed his teeth, but he snuggled right into the crib the moment Micah lifted him inside.

"Well, I guess this is goodbye," he said when he looked up at her again.

A rock immediately settled in her belly, and her eyes and nose burned. "Maybe we can meet for coffee downstairs before you leave."

He shook his head. "There won't be time. I thought Derek and I would grab breakfast at LaGuardia before our flight takes off."

She swallowed against the lump forming in her throat. "Sounds smart."

Micah grabbed two bottles of water from the minifridge and handed one to her before opening the second. He sat on the end of the extra bed.

"I'm sorry Maeve got away. I know how important it was to you that you would get credit for arresting her."

"That's not—" she began and shrugged, lowering to sit next to him on the bed. He was right about her selfish agenda, but that didn't matter anymore. It hadn't worked out how anyone on the team had planned it. Maeve had escaped, and Humphrey was dead. They'd tried to stop a black widow from killing again, and they'd failed.

"Whatever happened, I'm still grateful to you for helping us to locate Maeve and Humphrey. So thank you. Maeve will try to go underground to avoid capture now, but the team is even more determined to bring her to justice."

"You're welcome," he said. "It's too bad that your cousins lost their friend, but maybe Humphrey's act at the end helped to restore their faith in humanity. They're lucky that way."

She narrowed her gaze at him, his words confusing. Was he hinting that she'd contributed to his loss of belief in others?

"It will be good that you can finally get back home, where you can focus exclusively on your own situation so you can figure out once and for all who's been targeting the ranch."

She paused to open the water bottle and take a long drink, her throat suddenly dry.

"Until this weekend, I thought it might be Maeve."

Deirdre had just lifted the bottle to her lips, but at his confession, she drew in a sharp breath and choked on the water. She coughed into her elbow several times, eyes watering. "Maeve?" she managed.

Suddenly, a few things made sense. "That's why you kept asking if I thought the suspect could be female, isn't it? That's what you were hiding, too. But you didn't put her name on the list of possible suspects. Why?"

"It felt like a ridiculous theory, so I didn't want to tell you. That my stepmother could have gotten low on funds from her most recent husband, somehow learned that I'd become successful with the ranch and then come to take everything from me again." He shook his head, smiling. "It sounds outlandish now, but I just couldn't shake it."

"Do you still believe it?"

He shook his head. "I don't think so."

"I wish you would have told me then. If you had, I would have helped you to see that she was an unlikely suspect—for the crimes on the ranch, at least."

"Why do you say that?"

"She's a black widow. She uses sex and the promise of love to control the men she targets and make them not question while she gains control over their assets. To come after you—a stepson who already suspected her—wouldn't be her modus operandi at all. You wouldn't have your blinders on around her.

"More than that—" she paused, gesturing with the closed water bottle "—you wouldn't have been a good mark for her, because your assets are tied up in the ranch. In the land. The equipment. The livestock. Even the petting zoo. All of that would have to be liquidated, which takes time, and Maeve likes to cash out and vanish right after her victims die."

He nodded, lowering his head. "You're right. I should have told you. Then I could have let it go, so I could focus on more plausible theories."

"I think the answer is far less complicated than you first thought. Probably someone closer to home. Some who wants the ranch itself and not the money from selling it off."

Micah sat quietly, appearing to consider her words. "I bet you're really good at your job," he said finally.

She scoffed at that. "Tell that to the special agent in charge in DC." But warmth spread in her chest at his little offer of praise. "Did you hear any more from Sheriff Guetta or Deputy Martin today?"

"That's the thing. I really haven't. I've been trying not to call Richard since he put Deputy Martin in charge, and Greg has stopped getting back to me. I haven't heard from him at all since Friday night."

"Is it possible that you were bugging him too much with all the texts?" The way the hairs on the back of her neck lifted suggested there might be more to it than that, but she didn't want to overreact when Micah was already worried.

"I don't know. Maybe."

She glanced at her watch and then calculated the hour, even in the Mountain Time Zone. "It's a little late to call Richard tonight, but if you don't hear from the deputy by morning, you could call the sheriff before your flight."

"That sounds like a good idea. I'm sure everything's fine, anyway. The ranch hands have checked in. Cattle are doing great. Kevin even texted me photos of Harriet Tubman and Booker T. just so I would know that the petting zoo crew is getting the best care."

"Not Eleanor?"

She expected him to smile like she still did when she thought of the doeling. He didn't.

"There haven't been any incidents since we've been gone," he said. "None. So, I'm sure everything's fine." Then he nervously scratched his neck.

Of course he was worried. He'd spent the weekend helping her to chase a vampire in New York City while pretending that his own problems wouldn't still be waiting for him when they returned home. And the last thing he'd seen before they'd left the ranch was a threat against his only child.

Leave Wyoming or the kid is next.

Cold fingers of dread traveled up her arms as she recalled the note, leaving a trail of gooseflesh. She couldn't send them back to Harmony Fields without her.

"You know, I still have a few days left before I'm expected back at the DC field office."

His gaze narrowed. "What are you saying?"

"I think I should come back with you."

Immediately, he shook his head. "It's not your responsibility."

"I promised I would help you figure out who was targeting the ranch, and I haven't upheld my end of the bargain."

"We both know it wasn't really a bargain," he said. "But thanks anyway."

"Well, after everything you've done here, I still owe you."

"You've helped a lot already. You spent hours running around the ranch, looking for clues. You even interviewed my not-quite-stable ex."

"Really—"

"You don't owe me anything."

Her knees felt weak as Micah ushered her toward the door. Her heartbeat raced. He was dismissing her, and she couldn't let him do it.

"Micah, please."

Instead of responding this time, he watched her, waiting.

"This is about Derek. If something happens to him—or you—and I could have done something about it, I will never forgive myself."

He appeared to consider for a few seconds and then nodded.

"What does that nod mean?"

"Guess you need to get online and book your ticket. Get ready for another vacation out West."

SOMETHING ABOUT THE quiet on the ranch struck Micah as odd the moment that Deirdre pulled the new rental car up the drive the next afternoon, past the barn and the outbuildings to the house. The vehicle's windows were closed, so it wasn't really a sound. More a heaviness in the air, pregnant with foreboding. It didn't make sense. Nothing was out of place. The cattle still grazed on the fields in the distance. The doors on all the supplemental structures appeared to be closed, if not locked.

Not for the first time, he was relieved that Deirdre had decided to return with him to Wyoming, but there was no way he would tell her that. He was still trying to figure out what had been in that decision for her, and though he hadn't figured it out yet, he was certain there would be something.

"We're probably overreacting," he said, trying to convince himself of that fact. He hadn't been away from the ranch in years. Maybe other people felt the same type of uneasiness when they returned home from a trip.

Deirdre shut off the ignition, and as she looked through the windshield and side and rear windows at the same scenery, her gaze narrowed.

"We don't know that. We still haven't heard back from Deputy Martin. When I texted Sheriff Guetta, he agreed with me that it was a bad sign. He said he would send some-one else to check on the place."

"I don't like the idea that Deputy Martin is out of contact, either, but Richard could already have sent another deputy by. We won't be receiving a report card showing all the places they checked."

She frowned down at her phone. "But a text telling us they've finished would be nice."

"Maybe Richard just hasn't gotten around to sending it yet."

"You're probably right." She looked around once more, then opened the car door. "Let me take a quick look around at the outbuildings, and then I'll come back and check the house. You two stay here for a few minutes. By the time I get back, we'll probably have the all clear from Richard. I'll let you know when I receive it."

"Sounds good."

He separated the spare set of farm keys from his house keys and handed it to her. She gave him the key fob for the rental so he could crack open the windows.

Micah waited, trying not to worry as Deirdre headed into the first building, her weapon drawn. She was trained for this work, he reminded himself. Competent.

"Want out," Derek called from the back seat.

"I want out, too, buddy. But we have to wait for Miss Deirdre."

Derek kicked his feet. "I go with Dee-Dee."

"You get to go with *me*, but we have to wait just a few more minutes."

Deirdre emerged from the first building about a minute later and continued on into the second, about twenty-five yards from it. She didn't stay there long, either, but when she reappeared again, she gave him a thumbs-up with her free hand.

"Good news, my man. She received the text from Richard. Now you and I can go in the house."

While Deirdre continued farther down the drive to the last of the outbuildings before the main barn, Micah climbed out of the car and opened the back door to unbuckle Derek's car seat. Figuring he could bring in the luggage later, he started up to the house with son riding piggyback. He chose the first-level slider rather than the front door upstairs, so he would get a look at the amount of work necessary to fully repair that entrance. He would put it on his to-do list for the week to make an appointment with a door company. Then he would check back in with the alarm company to finally get an installation date.

Switching his son from his back to his hip, he inserted the key into the sliding door lock and opened it. From his first step inside, he sensed that something was different. With another look from the bar to the entertainment room, Micah flipped on the stairway light and started up the stairs.

"You're going to love getting to take your nap back in your big-boy bed today."

Derek shook his head. "No nap."

"Yeah, you slept a little on the airplane, didn't you?"

"Airplane. No nap."

"How about we talk about this after lunch?"

At the top of the stairway that led into the kitchen, Micah froze behind the closed door and listened to the difference he'd sensed downstairs becoming clear. It was the sound. Like voices, or music or something. Had he forgotten to turn off a Bluetooth speaker when they'd left for New York? Would the speaker even work when he'd taken his phone with him on the trip?

He reached for the doorknob and turned. A house that didn't look anything like the one he'd left greeted him on the other side. A sink filled with dishes. Wadded paper towels, frozen-pizza boxes and an open peanut butter jar with a butter knife still protruding from its center covered the counters.

"What the…" He closed his mouth and then held a finger to his lips to signal for Derek to stay quiet.

Micah stepped through the doorway and glanced back and forth, relieved to find no one in the kitchen. Had someone been squatting in his house while they were out of town? Could it have been the deputy, who had a key? Had he stopped communicating with him in favor of spending a weekend in a free vacation house, complete with a stocked refrigerator?

Cautiously, he rounded the corner and stepped into the great room. More of the same greeted him in that massive room—garbage and empty food containers littered the coffee table, and laundry and discarded shoes had been strewn on the floor. The source of the sound, Micah's seventy-two-inch flat screen, sat with its power still on, some reality TV show with bikinis and tropical sunsets covering the screen.

Micah's scalp prickled. His gaze lowered to the cherubic little boy in his arms, the child he was supposed to protect. He started backing out of the great room. Whoever the squatter was, he could still be in the house, and he might not be willing to give up this prime getaway location without a fight.

What had he been thinking, bringing Derek back into the house without at least having Deirdre check it first? Had the signal she'd given him from the driveway even meant that she'd heard back from Richard, or had she only been indicating that the outbuilding was clear?

He moved quietly, watching for movement around him. They needed to reach the lower level, and then he would find Deirdre outside. Just as they'd joined together to locate Maeve in New York, they could face this intruder together as well.

As Micah spun around at the bar, the basement door in sight, a man that he could only describe as a human grizzly bear stepped into his path. With linebacker shoulders and eyes as wild as his beard and mane of hair, neither of which had seen a barber or a bottle of shampoo in weeks, the man planted himself between Micah and the door to the basement.

But nothing about the guy was as terrifying as the shotgun he had aimed right at Micah and his son.

Chapter Nineteen

Deirdre closed her eyes and lowered her chin to her chest after closing and locking the third outbuilding, where everything appeared perfectly in order. Just the barn and a quick look around the house and then she could collapse inside, knowing she'd kept Micah and Derek safe. At least someone was thinking of them, since it was clear that local law enforcement had fallen down on the job. She lifted her head, holstered her weapon and pulled her phone from her pocket to check the screen in case she'd missed the vibration from a text.

No missed calls. No texts. She sighed. First Deputy Martin, and now Sheriff Guetta was MIA as well.

"Some kind of friend you are." She scrolled through her contacts to the listing for Richard, ready to tell him just what she thought of him. Then she reconsidered. Micah was as exhausted as she was and probably dying to get the all clear to bring his son into the house. It wasn't fair for her to make him wait any longer than necessary.

She tucked her phone away and withdrew her weapon again. With a quick glance back at the rental car, she pulled open the heavy barn door.

The putrid, unmistakable smell of death hit her before she took a step inside. She gasped, squeezing her eyes shut and pressed her lips together to fight back the overwhelming need to retch. They'd wondered what had happened to the deputy. Now she knew. Her dominant hand shook so badly that even her support hand probably wouldn't be enough to steady it if she needed to fire, but she had to do this. Micah and Derek were counting on her. She couldn't let them down.

Pulling her long-sleeve T-shirt's collar up over her nose and mouth, she stepped inside the barn and flipped on the LED bay lights. Like Micah had told her, most of the stalls were empty, since the horses spent most of their time out in the pasture, but she still had to open each door and peer inside. A man she assumed was Deputy Martin, from his black uniform, lay slumped in the stall at the far end of the barn, a gaping hole in his chest, a crimson puddle of dried blood spread on the hay all around him. From the look and the smell, he'd been there awhile.

Deirdre started toward the door. She needed to reach the car and get Micah and Derek off the property immediately. But as she passed the tack room, she couldn't help but peek inside. Another deputy, probably the one she'd asked Sheriff Guetta to send, had collapsed against a saddle rack, still sitting up, his head slumped forward. As a cry escaped her lungs, she rushed over and checked for a pulse. When she found nothing, she swallowed. The blood and the condition of the body told her he hadn't been there long.

This time she rushed all the way out, wiping blood on her pant leg as she went. She ran faster, second-guessing herself with every step. Should she have taken them to safety the moment she'd entered the barn? Should she have refused to take them to the ranch at all until the threat was eliminated?

Her lungs ached from the exertion by the time she reached the car. She pulled open the door. "We've got to get out of here."

A sharp cry escaped her as she realized she was alone.

The massive house ahead of her, the one she'd found so beautiful only days before, looked like a trap now. But Micah and Derek were inside. She knew it. And they weren't alone. For her, it might be suicide to rush in, but she had no choice. The man and the child she loved needed her. Now more than ever.

After dialing 911 to report the murders and making a promise she intended to break, saying she would wait for backup, she rushed over to the house. As she moved from slider to slider on the lower level, hoping to find one that was unlocked, heavy footsteps pounded on the decking above her.

"Oh, officer," an unfamiliar voice called out. "We're up here."

More stomping continued until Micah came into view on the deck stairs, Derek in his arms. A burly-looking man walking closely behind them held a shotgun to Micah's head.

At the bottom of the steps, the man turned Micah to face her. The rancher had a tight expression, but he held his son tight, as though he could protect him from gunfire with his own body. Her pulse hammering, her breath coming in short gasps, Deirdre positioned her weapon between her dominant hand and her support hand and aimed.

"I wouldn't do that if I were you," the man said, chortling. "It'll get so messy when I have to shoot them both. Do you know how big a hole a shotgun can make at short range?"

Because she did, she lowered her weapon.

"Now, that's a good girl," he said. "Why don't you go ahead and drop that on the ground?"

She did as she was told, keeping her hands away from her body.

"That's much better. Now, you're law enforcement, too, right? I heard FBI."

She nodded.

"Well, I would like to report these trespassers. They

broke into my house, and I think they should have to pay for doing that."

"*Your* house?" Even with a gun to his head, Micah tried to look back at the other man. "It isn't your—"

When Micah stopped himself, the man chuckled again.

"You're the Beckett boy, aren't you?" Micah said. "You're Willie Beckett's son."

The hairy guy grinned. "Took you long enough to figure it out. But I'm not a boy anymore." He shifted his gaze to Deirdre. "We haven't been introduced. I'm Josh. This squatter has been living on my ranch and in my house. That doesn't seem fair, does it?"

Deirdre studied him, recalling the story Micah had told her when he was coming up with a suspects list. "Didn't your dad lose the place to—"

"Foreclosure?" Josh said. "That's what the bank called it, but it's really stealing a man's land and his dignity. My dad had a heart attack over it when the bank took it."

He used the shotgun to hit the side of Micah's head. "Then this guy stole the place right out from under my dad."

"I'm sorry your dad lost the land, but that parcel was only ten acres. I've bought hundreds since then. Harmony Fields isn't the same ranch at all."

"My house was right here." Josh gestured to the new structure.

"It was, but this house is five times as big as the original one," Micah said.

Deirdre shook her head at Micah. He needed to stop arguing with Josh. A man who had nothing to lose was the worst opponent.

"I don't care what you did to dress it up. This is *my* house and *my* ranch, and I'm not leaving," Josh said.

"Do you plan to kill us to keep it?" Micah asked him.

Josh laughed again. "You act like that's hard to do. Ask

your friend Deirdre what happened to the deputies who were nosing around in my business while you were gone."

Micah looked pale. "*Deputies?*"

Deirdre held up two fingers. Micah shivered visibly.

"It's too bad, really," Josh said, shaking his head. "You could have made it easier on yourselves. I gave you so many warnings. So many opportunities to walk away with your lives. Now you won't get to go at all."

He flicked off the safety on his pump-action shotgun and racked it. "I need you to give me all your weapons and your cell phones. Or this poor little guy...well, you know."

Deirdre tossed her phone his way and then took a few steps forward and kicked her weapon in his direction. Micah gave him his phone as well, but as he turned, Josh ripped Derek away from him anyway.

Immediately, Derek shrieked.

"No. You can't take my son."

The other man smiled. "I can do whatever I want to do. I'm the one with the gun."

Deirdre took a few slow steps forward, her hands steepled as if in prayer. "Please, Josh. It doesn't have to be this way. I know you'd never want to hurt a child."

"Of course I don't. I'm not an animal."

"I know you're not." She took a few more steps. "Just let us go. We'll disappear. You'll never have to see us again."

He shook his head then. "You make it sound so easy."

"It can be. Really."

When he glanced down at the toddler, Deirdre lunged for him. His reflexes quick, Josh squeezed the trigger. Fire immediately burst across her shoulder, burning, searing. It stole her breath away. As the image of Micah tackling the other man to the ground, where he hit his head, and Derek rolling away from them went in and out of focus, Deirdre fought.

But soon oblivion was too appealing, its greeting a sweet escape from the pain.

From somewhere far away, she heard a little boy call out, "Dee-Dee hurt."

"YOU'RE GOING TO be fine. You're going to be fine. You're going to be fine." Micah repeated the words to Deirdre like a mantra as he drove her in his pickup to the clinic outside Laramie. He said the words mostly because he didn't know if she would be okay, and he didn't know what he would do if she wasn't. Already, the blanket wrapped around her shoulder was turning redder by the minute. He was driving as fast as he could. He prayed it would be fast enough.

"Where's Derek?" she asked when her eyes popped open for a fraction of a second.

"He's okay, too. Richard's wife has him." He wasn't sure whether she heard him or not as she faded in and out of consciousness.

Several patrol cars from the sheriff's office had arrived at the ranch just as shots were fired. Micah had briefly knocked Josh Beckett unconscious, but he came to just as one of the deputies snapped handcuffs on him. He would get his trip to jail by way of a stop at the hospital so he could be examined for a concussion injury. The man deserved a lot less, in Micah's opinion, but in the United States, he was still considered innocent until proven guilty.

"Come on, Deirdre, fight." The words squeezed him from the inside out. "Fight for us."

He'd never realized until that moment just how much he wanted them to be an *us*. Would he lose her just when he'd finally realized she was the only person who could make his life and Derek's complete?

When he reached the clinic, medical personnel immediately prepped her in the small, barely adequate emergency surgery center. In the hallway, as a nurse attempted to roll her into surgery, she stopped and stared down at Micah's hand where he squeezed Deirdre's fingers in a vise grip.

"Please, Mr. Perry, you're going to have to let Deirdre go."

THE NEXT AFTERNOON Deirdre awoke in her semiprivate room at Ivinson Memorial Hospital in Laramie—truly private now, because she didn't yet have a roommate. She blinked several times as the image at the end of her bed shifted in and out of focus.

"Micah? Is that you?"

"Yeah. I'm here."

She tilted her head, studying him. "How long have you been here?"

"Other than when I had to get Derek settled at Doug and Marie's and when I had to go back to feed the animals, I've been here ever since you were transferred in."

"You need to go home, then." She adjusted herself against the pillows and winced. "You need to get some rest."

He leaped up from his chair and was at her side instantly. "Are you okay?"

"I'm fine," she assured him. "You heard the doctor. My shoulder is going to heal great. After some physical therapy, I should have full mobility. I'll even be able to go back to work."

"That's great."

"Wow. You might want to curb your enthusiasm on that one."

"I'm sorry. It's just that…"

"That what?" she asked when he didn't finish.

He drew his chair over to the side of the bed. "I don't want you to go."

She swallowed. Those were at least some of the words

she'd longed to hear from Micah, and now that he'd spoken them, she realized that they didn't make a difference.

"You don't know how much I'd love to stay."

"So *stay*."

His voice broke on the last word, and her heart fractured with it. Wanting something didn't make the impossible possible.

She pressed her lips together and then shook her head. "I can't. I have to go back to work. And even if I didn't have a job I love in another state, it would never work between us."

"Why not? I…uh…love…you."

"Love shouldn't be that hard, Micah. It should be effortless. Joyous." And him telling her he loved her should have made her feel wonderful. It only hurt—more than her shoulder, with far less promise of healing.

Instead of answering, he reached for her hand over the top of the hospital bed's bars. She knew she should pull away, but she gave herself the gift of that moment. It would be so easy to settle for so little now, but she couldn't let herself. Even she deserved more.

"Have you ever met two more wounded individuals?" she said, after the silence stretched long. "I will spend my life chasing my parents' approval when I know in my heart that I matter so little to them. I will beat myself up, trying to prove I'm worthy. Trying to prove the unprovable."

"You don't need to chase anything." He rubbed the back of her hand with his thumb.

"I know that here." She pointed to her head. "If only I could see that here." Her fingers moved to her heart.

Deirdre shifted her hand so that their fingers laced. "And you. I don't think you realize how much your father hurt you while you carried the guilt from not being able to protect him. Now you go through life waiting for people you love to be like Maeve was with him. To put themselves first and you last. I can never measure up to that test. No one can.

"But it's worse for you," she said. "You believe that allowing yourself to really love someone would make you weak."

"You're wrong."

But she could see in his eyes that he knew she was right.

"I love you, and I love Derek. So much. I wish what you're able to give me would be enough." She shook her head. "I want more."

He nodded and stood. Then he leaned over the bed bar and pressed his lips to hers. It tasted of him and tears that she had yet to cry. It tasted like goodbye.

Chapter Twenty

Deirdre sat in a straight-back chair in her DC apartment a week later doing the necessary exercises that would help her pass the physical to return to active duty. Every day the repetitive stretches to gain full range of motion became a little easier, but she cared less in equal increments about their results.

When her phone rang with the ringtone for a video call, she frowned. The cell was clear across the room. She let it go to voice mail, but thirty seconds later, the whole series started over again.

She wasn't at all surprised to see Aidan's name on the screen when she picked it up. He'd been calling that way a lot lately. She'd started looking forward to those calls, too. She touched the button, and his face appeared on the screen.

"Ever thought that a person might be busy?"

"Why? Were you busy?"

She shook her head, smiling. "Not really. Just want to know if you ever thought about it."

"I'll try to keep it in mind," he said. "How's the PT going?"

"Fine."

"And your life is?"

"Fine."

"Have you talked to him?"

"Who?" She kept her expression bland, but shivers climbed her arms, signaling she was still alive, after all.

"Are you going to call him?"

She propped the phone on the table and crossed her arms so that he could see them. "Aidan, why are you asking me all this? You're the one who gave me the lecture about how unprofessional it was to become involved with a witness."

"I stand by those words, too."

"Well, good. Glad we have that settled."

"I told you that as a US marshal. As your brother, I have to ask you if he's worth the headache."

She shook her head. "I don't know."

"Is he?"

She didn't even have to think about it. "Yeah."

"Then I guess you're busy with some things to think about, so I'm going to go now."

"You're ridiculous, little brother."

He grinned into the screen.

"And Aidan?"

He lifted a brow and waited.

"Thanks."

THOUGH DEIRDRE STARTLED at the sound of the buzzer outside her apartment building, she wasn't surprised to hear it. Aidan had called to clear the visit, since he would be in Washington for the day and wanted to stop by to see for himself how her shoulder was healing. She couldn't help feel a little jumpy, since her brother had never visited her apartment before, but it was more than that. She had a confession to make.

There was a difference between knowing that the son wasn't to blame for the favoritism their father showed him and actually admitting out loud that she blamed Aidan for it. She wanted to apologize for that and tell him about an important decision she'd made. This adulting business wasn't easy.

She hit the buzzer without speaking to him, even though he would give her a hard time for that reckless move as soon as he made it up the stairs to her apartment. Then she crossed to the door and waited for him to knock.

"I know. I know," she said a few minutes later when she opened it.

Micah stood in the hallway, his hands gripped in front of him. "Hi." He cleared his throat. "Know?"

She shook her head, her hands shaking so badly that she had to stuff the good hand in her pocket. At least the other remained hidden in its sling. "Never mind. Uh… What are you doing here?"

"I wanted to talk with you." Softly, he added. "Is that okay?"

"You came all the way here to do that? You could have called."

"You've been rejecting my calls."

He was right about that, she acknowledged with a shrug. She hadn't gone the extra step of blocking him, but she'd pushed away the hurt that came with each of his calls by tapping the "end" icon to reject. Even now, she wasn't ready to talk to him, wasn't ready to face all she'd felt when she'd walked away, but she couldn't close the door in his face. Not in a million years.

"How did you know where I live?" she managed finally.

"Aidan."

She pursed her lips. Her little brother needed to learn to stay out of matters that were none of his business. "He's been extra helpful lately, hasn't he?"

"Yeah, I know."

Deirdre narrowed her gaze, wondering what she didn't know, but he didn't offer more, and she wasn't ready to beg, so she waved him inside. He carried in a duffle bag and set it next to the door. Did he plan to stay? Did she want him to?

"Where's Derek?"

"He's at Doug and Marie's, getting spoiled."

She nodded, still having no answers. "Would you like some coffee or tea?"

"Coffee's good."

As nervous as he appeared, she was tempted to recommend against caffeine, but she led him to her sofa and went to put on a pot.

Minutes later, she carried out mugs of coffee one at a time, using her good hand. After both were in place on coasters on the coffee table, she sat at the other end of the couch. "You said you wanted to talk?"

He took a sip and set his mug aside. "I wanted to tell you that Eleanor Roosevelt misses you."

"Sorry to hear that."

"And Jane Austen and Anne Frank and Alexander Hamilton."

"Apparently, a lot of pygmy goats miss me."

"And Derek." He dampened his lips and then stared straight into her eyes. "But mostly me."

She blinked as her heart squeezed, contorted. "I've missed you, too. But you have to know it isn't—"

"Enough? I know."

Her pulse pounding in her chest, Deirdre folded her hands and waited. Would he say something that would change everything? Could anything make that much of a difference? And if he offered no more of himself than he had in Wyoming, would she still jump at the chance?

"It's just that you left your muck boots in your closet in the ranch house," he said.

Deirdre lifted a brow. "I know. I thought someone else might be able to use them."

"They're yours. I brought them for you." He paused, clearing his throat. "And I was hoping that you'd let Derek and me stay with them."

Her breath hitched. "You still don't get it. This was never about *location*. Well, not completely. It's more than that."

"I know," he said, his eyes damp.

"Then I don't understand."

He rested his elbows on his knees and positioned his chin between the V formed by his hands. "I never told anyone everything that Maeve said to me when I caught up with her."

I figured you would tell when you were ready. But what does that have to do with this? With us?"

"Everything," he said, tucking his head and shifting his shoulders. "She only said why she married Dad. Not why she killed him. But the two reasons were the same. She said, 'A lady needs things. Pretty things.'"

"So, we were right. It was about money all along."

He nodded. "You were right about me, too. And my dad. I've spent a lifetime expecting everyone to fail me. Then I keep them at arm's length, so they can't. I never leap. Not really."

"I don't understand. How does this make any—"

"But then there's you," he rushed on before she could say "difference." "After all the pain and betrayal you've faced, you still put yourself out there." He lifted his head and met her gaze. "You're still open to love. You have hope."

"Wh-what are you saying?" She thought she knew, but he was going to have to spell it out for her. And if he spelled differently, she would die.

"We can't let Maeve win." He immediately shook his head. "No, it has nothing to do with her. Not anymore."

Micah scooted closer to Deirdre on the couch and took her hands. "I was sleeping through life until you pulled that rental up the drive of the ranch and shook me awake. Now I can't imagine my life without you in the center of it. I'm in love with you. I've fallen for the agent who breaks the rules."

"But is love enough?" Her voice cracked as each word felt as if torn from her soul.

"It can be. It *has* to be. You said you love me, too." He squeezed her hands. "I'm ready to leap, Deirdre. No waiting for the other shoe to drop. No holding back a piece of me. I'm all in. I'm all *yours*."

He appeared to search her eyes. When she didn't—*couldn't*—answer, he kept talking, his words coming in a nervous rush.

"I can sell the ranch so that Derek and I can move here. You'll have the chance to get your FBI career back on track, and I'll have exactly what I want. I'll be here. With you."

For the longest time, words wouldn't come. What did a person say when everything she'd ever wanted was packaged with a bow and set right in her hands?

He finally slid his fingers away and then crossed and uncrossed his arms. "Are you going to say anything? Do you want me to leave?"

She shook her head.

"Could you at least tell me which question you're answering with that shake?"

She smiled. "I don't want you to leave."

Micah puffed up his cheeks and blew out a breath. "That's good. That's very good."

"But I don't want you to move here, either."

He sighed. "Why not?"

"When my superior at the bureau contacted me about my return date, I realized I no longer had anything to prove there. My heart wasn't in it. I fell in love with a cowboy from Wyoming and with his son and the land and the animals that are so much a part of who he is. I want to be there with him."

"Anyone I know?" he asked with a grin.

He scooted close and pulled her to him, careful not to press against her sore shoulder. His kiss, though, wasn't gentle at all, filled with both desperation and hope. Her whole body came alive under the spell of his lips. But most of all her heart.

When he finally pulled back, she pressed her forehead to his and gasped for breath.

"When do you want to make this big move?" he asked.

"Whenever you're ready."

"Oh, I'm ready." He kissed her deeply then, with a longing that was both familiar and still new. Then he smiled against her lips and set her back. "Richard's going to love this. He's always been Team Deirdre."

"Could have fooled me."

He raised his index finger. "There's one other thing—Marie said no rush or anything, but when we're ready, she'll make us our own wedding-ring quilt. She did make me promise something."

"What's that?"

"That we won't throw it on the ground." He grinned. "We'll only keep it on our bed."

"Then can you put in a special request from me?"

"Sure. What's that?"

Deirdre offered him a smile that promised they would be happily distracted for the rest of the day. And then some. "Could you ask her to get started on the quilt right away?"

THE INVESTIGATIVE TEAM had to schedule its next meeting entirely by videoconference since even an in-person plan to meet halfway between New York and Wyoming seemed a little excessive. Using her brand-new personal laptop, Deirdre joined the meeting from the downstairs office at Micah's house that she was still trying to get used to calling Micah's, Derek's and hers.

She smiled at the camera where she was one of the six tiles in the videoconference.

Sean took the lead, as he always did.

"Obviously, we are all saddened by the loss of Humphrey and more determined than ever to apprehend Maeve O'Leary," he said. "We won't let her slip through our fingers again.

"We all need to do our parts to track down any information about Maeve's other victims."

Deirdre raised her hand then.

"Yes, Deirdre," Sean said.

"Since I'm technically not in law enforcement anymore, I would be happy to resign from the team, if that's what all of you wish."

"I'm not in law enforcement," Cormac said.

"And, technically, I was on the wrong side of the law," Liam chimed in.

Sean grinned. "So all in favor of having Deirdre leave the team, raise your right hand."

No hands showed.

"And all those opposed?"

There were six votes that time.

"The noes have it," Sean said. "Now, Aidan wanted to give us an update."

Aidan waved at the camera. "Hi, everyone. I just wanted to let you know that since Maeve O'Leary remains at large, I have moved Ciara Kelly to a safe house as a precaution."

"Does Maeve have any reason to come after Ciara now that Humphrey is dead?"

Aidan raised both hands. "We don't know for sure. We have no idea whether she'll risk coming after Ciara for revenge when she has nothing to gain but satisfaction, but I would put nothing past Maeve O'Leary."

Cormac nodded. "We've all learned the hard way not to underestimate Maeve."

"Also, I can tell you that Ciara Kelly is hiding something. I feel like it's something big. And I'd know a secret anywhere."

* * * * *

COMING SOON!

We really hope you enjoyed reading this book. If you're looking for more romance be sure to head to the shops when new books are available on

Thursday 8th June

To see which titles are coming soon, please visit

millsandboon.co.uk/nextmonth

MILLS & BOON

MILLS & BOON

THE HEART OF ROMANCE

A ROMANCE FOR EVERY READER

MODERN
Prepare to be swept off your feet by sophisticated, sexy and seductive heroes, in some of the world's most glamourous and romantic locations, where power and passion collide.

HISTORICAL
Escape with historical heroes from time gone by. Whether your passion is for wicked Regency Rakes, muscled Vikings or rugged Highlanders, awaken the romance of the past.

MEDICAL
Set your pulse racing with dedicated, delectable doctors in the high-pressure world of medicine, where emotions run high and passion, comfort and love are the best medicine.

True Love
Celebrate true love with tender stories of heartfelt romance, from the rush of falling in love to the joy a new baby can bring, and a focus on the emotional heart of a relationship.

Desire
Indulge in secrets and scandal, intense drama and sizzling hot action with heroes who have it all: wealth, status, good looks…everything but the right woman.

HEROES
The excitement of a gripping thriller, with intense romance at its heart. Resourceful, true-to-life women and strong, fearless men face danger and desire - a killer combination!

To see which titles are coming soon, please visit

millsandboon.co.uk/nextmonth